AUG 1 3 2015

Taking Heart

**DISCARD
CADL**

By T. J. Kline

Rodeo Novels
Rodeo Queen
The Cowboy and the Angel
Learning the Ropes
Runaway Cowboy

A Healing Harts Novel
Heart's Desire
Taking Heart

Taking Heart

T. J. KLINE

AVON IMPULSE
An Imprint of HarperCollinsPublishers

This is a work of fiction. Names, characters, places, and incidents are products of the author's imagination or are used fictitiously and are not to be construed as real. Any resemblance to actual events, locales, organizations, or persons, living or dead, is entirely coincidental.

Excerpt from *Close to Heart* copyright © 2015 by Tina Klinesmith.

TAKING HEART. Copyright © 2015 by Tina Klinesmith. All rights reserved under International and Pan-American Copyright Conventions. By payment of the required fees, you have been granted the nonexclusive, non-transferable right to access and read the text of this e-book on screen. No part of this text may be reproduced, transmitted, decompiled, reverse-engineered, or stored in or introduced into any information storage and retrieval system, in any form or by any means, whether electronic or mechanical, now known or hereafter invented, without the express written permission of HarperCollins e-books.

EPub Edition JUNE 2015 ISBN: 9780062396549

Print Edition ISBN: 9780062396556

AM 10 9 8 7 6 5 4 3 2 1

*Baby Girl, you started this journey with me,
and it's been such a blessing to watch you spread your
wings and fly. Even through the stumbles,
bumps, and bruises along the way,
you make us so proud to be your parents.
Let your beauty shine from within and don't
let anything snuff out the light inside you.*

Chapter One

SERGEANT DYLAN GRANGER heard a series of loud *pops* as bullets hit the stone wall beside his head and rock dust crumbled into his face. He ducked farther behind the wall. Their position had been compromised again, and this time the entire unit was under attack by insurgents.

"We're not going to make it through this, Doc. We're taking too much fire," Michaels yelled at him.

"We have to make it through this. I haven't lost a man yet." Dylan ignored his partner, the junior medic of their unit, and checked the pulse of Sergeant Jefferies, the communications expert he was attending to. The soldier's blood was warm on Dylan's hands as he tried to stem the flow from the gunshot wound to Jefferies's abdomen. It was bad, but if he could get the bleeding to slow, he could save him. After seven years as a Special Forces medic, Dylan had seen more than his fair share of wounds.

"You hear me, Jefferies?" The soldier's eyes rolled back, but he tried to nod. Dylan could see the fear in his face, knew he was close to giving up.

The desert sun beat down on the three of them as bullets whizzed past, and Dylan looked back over his shoulder where the rest of the unit had managed to hunker down behind a secondary shelter. At least they were covered on all four sides. He, Michaels, and Jefferies were sitting ducks behind a solitary low wall. He had to get Jefferies to the shelter, where they would have cover and he could focus on stopping the bleeding.

He signaled to the rest of the unit for cover and noted their affirmation. "Come on, we're making a break for it," he told Michaels. "You keep pressure on the wound and I'll carry him."

Dylan slid his weapon over his shoulder and wrapped his arm under the soldier's armpits as they prepared to drag him to safety. They had to move *now*.

"Just leave me, Doc," Jefferies muttered.

Dylan could see it in Michaels's eyes. He agreed and knew their best option was to leave the injured man behind.

Not on my watch.

"Shut up, Jefferies. You have two kids to get home to. Michaels here is going to hold the compress tight, but you need to help. Press on his hands." Dylan nodded to Michaels, and they made a run for the building behind them.

The world exploded into broken rock and dust. Heat and fire surrounded them, swirling through the air. For a moment, Dylan wondered if he hadn't just found hell on earth. He lifted his head carefully, the entire world around him ringing, spinning, as he tried to regain his bearings. It took him too long to realize he was pinned to the ground under Jefferies's dead weight. The weight of a mangled corpse. Using his forearms, he dragged himself from beneath the fallen soldier and saw Michaels to his left, facedown. Dylan crawled to his side, tugging at him.

"Michaels!" He rolled him onto his back and saw the blood and dirt smeared over his face.

"My leg, Doc." Dylan looked down and saw that the man was bleeding out. He wasn't going to make it. Another explosion rocked the earth beneath them. "Grenades." Michaels's voice was barely a whisper. "Fall back while you can, Doc. Go!"

Dylan felt something hit the side of his helmet, and his vision blurred before going completely dark.

HE REACHED FOR his head and bolted upright, sweat pouring from his body, and woke from reliving the nightmare again. It had been a year since he'd left Afghanistan behind. A year since the attack on their base that had left most of his unit KIA. A year of this new kind of hell on earth.

Dylan looked at the clock and reached for the glass of water on his bedside table, hating the way his hands trembled. He balled them into fists, willing the tremors to stop, and clenched his jaw so hard he thought it would snap. He wanted the nightmares to end, wanted his life back, wanted control over this. But what the doctors diagnosed as post-traumatic stress disorder, he called the end of his world.

He'd saved hundreds of men in his service, and now he couldn't function even one day without panic attacks, pills, and doctor's visits. Nothing remained of the man he'd once been—confident and capable. He looked up and saw his brother standing in the doorway of his room.

"You okay?"

Dylan hated being such a burden on Gage, but after returning home with a bullet wound in his head and burns that ran from his neck, over his right arm, and down his chest, he knew he would never have survived without him. His brother refused to give up on him, taking him in and putting his own life on hold to help him regain some semblance of a life.

"I'm good," he lied, popping open the prescription bottle on the nightstand.

"You sure you want another one of those? I thought your doctor said to taper off."

Dylan glared at his brother. The doctor had warned him about the risks of the medication they had him on, as well as taking more than they recommended. After becoming addicted to the painkillers early in his recovery, he had to be especially careful which medications and how much of each he was taking. He didn't want to go through that battle again, but right now it was the only thing keeping him from giving up entirely. He could understand the trap so many returning soldiers fell into, finding only pills and booze could help them escape the nightmare that lived inside them, haunting them even while they were awake. The pills let him fall into a dreamless sleep, where the faces of the men he hadn't saved didn't look at him with accusation in their eyes. The pills kept him from contemplating the other option to avoid their eyes, the loaded pistol hidden under his mattress.

"Dylan, you've tried everything else. Nothing is working. Can we please just call them up and see what they think?"

This discussion again? Dylan shook his head. He didn't want a therapy dog. If the medications and therapy he was already getting from three different doctors couldn't control his PTSD, how would a dog help? He didn't even like animals.

"No. We've already been over this. If I can't take care of myself, how am I going to take care of a dog?"

"What have you got left to lose?"

Technically, Gage was right. He had already lost everything he valued in life except his brother: his job, his independence, not to mention his sanity. He owed it to Gage to at least try to have some semblance of a normal life so his brother could find one for himself again.

"What if we go and it doesn't work?" Dylan asked, voicing the concern he didn't want to admit. It was really the crux of the matter. They'd already tried everything else with little to no success. If this didn't work, he would be forced to face that he was doomed to live in this hell forever, or until he ended it.

Gage raised both hands, palms out. "Then no harm, no foul, and I won't mention it again."

Dylan untangled himself from the sheet and sat at the edge of the bed, his feet landing on the cold hardwood floor. He might as well get up since he wouldn't be able to sleep again tonight "You know I can't afford it, and the military isn't running their PTSD-canine therapy program anymore."

"I know." Gage moved into the room and reached for Dylan's empty water glass. "But I've been looking around at private trainers and other foundations to help. Or I'll pay for it."

"I can't keep surviving on your charity."

"Hey, enough." His voice was as unbending as his loyalty. "We're family. You took care of me for years when Mom got sick and Dad was drinking. You put me through college and got me to this point. Let me help you for a change, Dylan."

Dylan ran a hand over several days' worth of beard growth. He knew his brother was afraid he'd given up on life. A part of him *had*. If this last-ditch effort was what he needed to do to assuage any misplaced guilt Gage had, he'd suck it up and prove to him that a dog wasn't going to fix what was messed up about him. He was broken in ways that couldn't be fixed.

"What's the matter, Wall Street? Cat got your tongue?" Julia grinned at her sister's fiancé across the table.

Nathan had been living on Heart Fire Ranch with Julia's sister, Jessie, long enough to realize what life in the country was like. Sometimes it included the barn cats leaving half-eaten mice as a prize for those they adored. Granted, stepping on that "prize" in bare feet tended to put a damper on the rest of your day when it happened first thing in the morning. The prim and proper financial analyst still looked shocked.

Nathan shook his head, trying to keep a straight face as he reached for his coffee. "One day, I might actually get used to these things, but I will never enjoy them."

Jessie winked at her sister. "Don't let him fool you. He's already found several perks to living out here." She turned to Nathan. "Like the fact that you claim bad cell service when you want to ignore calls from clients. And what about your new addiction to fishing?"

"I see your point," Nathan said, shrugging before winking at Jessie. "I can think of a few other perks, too."

"And, that's my cue to leave," Julia said, jumping up from behind the breakfast table. The Great Dane asleep at her feet opened an eye and looked up at her. "Come on, Tango, let's go."

The dog immediately responded and moved toward the door as Julia put her mug into the dishwasher. As much as she enjoyed sharing breakfast at her sister's house, as they'd done almost daily since their parents' deaths a year ago, with Nathan there she felt a bit like a third wheel on days when her brother, Justin, and cousin, Bailey, didn't join them. She knew Jessie and Nathan were still finding their footing, and she wanted to give them the space they needed to get reacquainted after eight years apart. They didn't need a little sister tagging along.

"You coming back for lunch?" Jessie looked at Julia expectantly, and Julia could read the excitement in her sister's eyes. "We have our first group of kids coming in for a camp this week. Bailey's cleaning out the cabins for them today."

As nice as it sounded to spend time with both of them, she'd made arrangements to see some dogs at the shelter later. "Normally, I'd be happy to let you use me as an indentured servant," she teased. "But I can't today. Rain check?" The sound of Julia's ringtone had Tango's ears lifting as "Who Let the Dogs Out" rang through the kitchen.

"Ugh!" Jessie covered her ears. "Will you please change that? You have no idea how much I hate that song."

Julia smiled at her sister. "Yes, I do, but it makes me laugh, so no." She glanced at the screen, not recognizing the caller, and pressed the button. "Heart Fire Training, this is Julia."

"Hi, my name is Gage Granger. We've spoken a bit by e-mail about a PTSD dog. I'm calling for my brother."

"Yes, Mr. Granger. I remember." Julia waved to her sister, motioning that she had to take the call, and headed outside with Tango following at her heels, as if understanding an unspoken command. She opened the door of her beat-up pickup and he jumped inside, sprawling across the bench seat with his head half hanging out the lowered window. As she turned on the truck, she listened to the man on the other end explain his brother's circumstances. The more he spoke, the more she realized this was going to be like many of the other severe PTSD cases she'd dealt with, and it was going to take intense training with both the dog and new handler. She felt the butterflies flutter to life in her stomach, realizing they would have to stay at her home in order for her to train them to work together. She hadn't had any unmarried men at her facility since—

Stop! This is not Evan, this is not the past.

"When would your brother be available to come to my facility?"

"To travel?" The voice on the other end of the phone sounded surprised. "I don't know if that will be possible. Dylan doesn't…he isn't…"

"Mr. Granger, I understand that travel could cause some anxiety for your brother, but because each person has different symptoms and varying degrees of PTSD, I need to meet him to be able to match him up. His dog has to be a partner who can work with your brother's specific needs in mind. Part of that is training the dog to relate to your brother and his triggers."

"The dog's training is tailored to Dylan's needs?"

"Exactly, and I'll teach him to work with the dog. I really need him here in order to see which dog pairs up with his personality best. If you're with him a lot, it would be best if you come as well. Based on what you've told me, I have a few dogs that might work for your brother, but you'll need to plan on staying three to four weeks."

"You have accommodations for both of us?"

Julia pulled into her driveway and ran her hand over the dog at her side, trying to ignore the nervous tremor she could hear in her voice and the shake of her hand. "You're both welcome to stay in my home. That way we can work with your brother and his animal consistently. But, if you prefer, my sister has cabins on her adjacent property as well." She couldn't help but hope they would choose to stay at Heart Fire Ranch instead. "How soon can you get here?"

"We can get a flight out tomorrow. I'll make sure of it."

She didn't miss the desperation in his voice. In the past four years of focusing her training on dogs to serve people with PTSD, she'd met so many family members who wanted miracles the victim wasn't ready for. It was a recipe for disaster if everyone wasn't on board for the journey.

"Mr. Granger, as long as your brother wants this as much as you want it for him, you'll be pleased with the results. If not"—she took a deep breath, knowing that it wouldn't do any of them good to sugarcoat the truth—"you'll both be wasting your time and setting yourself up for disappointment."

There was a pregnant pause from Gage. "Ms. Hart, you're our last hope."

"Tomorrow?" Dylan stared at his brother. "Have you lost your mind? We can't leave in the morning."

"Dylan, it's already arranged. All you need to do is pack."

Dylan had hoped that letting his brother do the legwork would dissuade him from this pointless pursuit. There was nothing a dog, even a therapy dog, could do. He'd already seen the brochures and read the information about how they were supposed to help with mood swings and anxiety, but if pills and alcohol couldn't touch them, how was an animal going to do anything? He ran a hand over his beard-roughened jaw, his fingers running over the marred flesh on his neck. The burns and scars had been covered with intricately colored tribal tattoos starting behind his ear, but they didn't make the truth hurt any less. He'd been the only man from his unit to survive the attack, and he still wasn't sure why. This wasn't living.

Dylan saw the hope in Gage's eyes. He really thought a dog was going to make a difference? *Whatever.* It wasn't worth fighting over. If Gage wanted to take a few weeks off work and stay at some training facility, fine. He'd see soon enough that this wouldn't help.

"Fine." Dylan shook his head in defeat and ran a hand over his close-shaven head. "I'll have to call Dr. Miller and let him know."

"I've already called him." Gage tossed a basket of Dylan's laundry onto his bed and began to fold it. "For the record, he thinks it's a great idea."

Dylan clenched his jaw. He appreciated his brother's help, but he wasn't completely incompetent. He felt the always-present anger simmering just below the surface. "I'm not an invalid. I can still do my own laundry."

Gage looked up, eyeing him curiously. "I know you can, Dylan. I wasn't implying you couldn't."

"Then stop coddling me like I'm going to break. I'm already broken." Dylan felt the familiar curtain of rage coming down over him, but he was helpless to stop it. It didn't matter how many pills they gave him or how many behavioral exercises he tried, when an episode came on it was like a flash flood that drowned him every time. He reached out, throwing the hamper from the bed. "This is pointless."

"Dylan..."

"You know damn well I can't get on a plane, what that will do to me."

"Fine, we'll drive. It's only all the way across the country." Gage grabbed a pillow from the bed and slapped it into his brother's hands. "You want to be pissed? Go ahead. You want to throw things? Be my guest. But use this, and you clean up whatever mess you make." Gage turned on his heel and left the room.

It wasn't the reaction Dylan expected. But instead of cooling, the storm inside him built, gaining momentum until he felt it swirling in his chest. He growled in rage, throwing the pillow at the wall and looking around the room for something else to throw. It only pissed him off more that every surface was already cleared. His brother had learned that lesson after Dylan's last episode. He clenched his fists, trying to still the fury building within. Every muscle in Dylan's body seemed to tense as he fought for control, bracing his fists on each side of the door frame. He couldn't stop his fist when it rose of its own accord and slammed against the wall, putting a hole in it.

The pain radiating up his arm was enough to shake him from his fury, but self-loathing filled the vacuum left behind once his anger dissipated. He backed up until his legs hit the bed. His knees lost strength, unable to hold him as the adrenaline left him weak, and he dropped to sit on the edge of the mattress. Dylan looked at the bottle of pills on his nightstand, sweet oblivion that would make him forget, at least for a short while.

Just this once.

It was a lie. It wasn't the first time he'd made that promise to himself, and he was sure it wouldn't be the last, but he wasn't about to take the steps down that dark path again. He looked away. He wouldn't cave. Dylan buried his forehead in his hands, rubbing at his temples with his fingers, his right hand skimming the scar that ran from his temple to the back of his ear. He'd have been better off if that bullet had killed him.

Chapter Two

"Julia, you can't just let two strange men stay here." Her older brother, Justin, stood in front of her door, refusing to let her exit. His hulking frame would have been intimidating to anyone else, but she knew he was a pushover.

"It's not the first time I've let clients stay, Justin. I just sent home a very sweet mother and her son last week." She brushed past him and trotted down the porch steps, heading to the dog kennels with Tango on her heels. She didn't need Justin reminding her of things she'd already put behind her. "We grew up on a dude ranch. We've had strangers living with us all our lives."

She hoped he'd let this drop, but as he ran after her, he pressed on. "There is no way you're staying here alone. Not after what happened with Evan."

She stopped and froze midstep, not bothering to turn to face him. "Don't ever mention him again, Justin. Ever."

"Julia—"

"If you mention it again, I swear, I will find another vet for my dogs."

"You can't just keep pretending he doesn't exist." He reached for his sister's shoulders and turned her to face him. "Now that he's out of jail, do you really think a restraining order is going to do you any good?"

"I'm being careful, Justin, but I can't put my life and career on hold for one creepy guy. He's gone. I'm not taking unnecessary risks, and I'm watching my back. So are the dogs. In the meantime, I still have a life to live and people who need my help."

Justin pulled her into a protective hug. She understood that he felt responsible to watch out for her and Jessie since their parents' car accident nearly a year ago, but Jessie had already asked him to stop trying to parent them. It was annoying enough when he tried to be a protective big brother.

"I want to be here when they arrive today."

She shoved him away and threw her hands in the air. He just wasn't going to give up. "Oh my goodness, are you even listening to yourself? I don't need your protection. Stop!"

"Little sis, you're not big enough to stop me." He gave her a lopsided grin and headed for his truck, leaving her to shake her head as she walked the rest of the way to the kennels.

Julia knew Justin wasn't wrong. He sported nearly two hundred and fifty pounds of solid muscle on his six-foot-plus frame, so she was no match for him physically. Few people were, but she had spent most of her life outwitting him, and her stubborn streak knew no boundaries. Julia went into the kennel's small kitchen area and prepared breakfast for the various dogs, mentally running through the characteristics of each of the animals.

It took a special dog to be a PTSD therapy animal. From what Gage said on the phone, Dylan was a man who liked to be active and would need a dog that could keep up with him. A smaller dog would never do for him, but luckily most of her dogs were large animals. She had a few extra-large dogs, like Tango, but she was leaning toward a shepherd mix named Cruise. He was smart, sensitive, and intuitive to moods. Plus, he'd already shown a good aptitude for picking up training quickly. It was one of the trickier sides of PTSD. The dogs had to adapt quickly and learn commands based on the needs of each individual, usually while they were both at the facility.

Julia set the food in front of the dogs and went into her office at the back of the kennel, staring at the picture collage on her wall of animals she'd trained and placed in homes over the years. Her gaze was immediately drawn to the beautiful black Lab in the right corner, and her eyes misted. Misty had been a shelter rescue who had performed amazingly well, better than most of the dogs she worked with in her ten years of training. When Evan had called her looking for a dog that could help with his diabetes, alerting him to low blood sugar episodes that had become worrisome, Misty had been a perfect choice. If only she had listened to her instincts, or Misty's.

Julia turned away from the board, not wanting to think about the mistake that had been paid for with

Misty's life. Misty was the reason she'd started scent training each of her dogs since. She'd learned a lesson from Evan that she'd never forget—people lie.

Her phone vibrated on her desk, alerting her of a message. Grateful for the interruption, she opened the screen to see a message from Gage that their plane was early, and they would get a rental and arrive at Heart Fire shortly.

"Come on, Tango. We need to change the sheets before they get here." The dog lifted one brow, as if questioning her. She laughed and pointed at him. "Don't give me that look. I get enough flak from Justin. I don't need you taking his side."

The dog jumped up from the floor and moved to her right side. She reached her hand out and laid it on his massive head, rubbing behind one ear. "I think there might be some peanut butter treats in the house. What do you say?"

Tango barked once loudly and nudged the door open with his nose before looking back at her.

"I knew you'd see it my way."

DYLAN STARED OUT the window, barely paying attention to the landscape passing in a blur down the highway. The trip had been less eventful than either he or Gage expected. The only point he'd had some trouble coping was when the engines geared up for takeoff and the whine had nearly thrown him back. He'd felt himself slipping, his vision fading as his mind took him back to that day. Gage had nudged his arm, forcing him to focus on the present, and guilt overrode the flashback.

"You okay?" Gage glanced his way. Dylan hated the constant worry he could read in his brother's eyes.

He couldn't keep doing this to his brother. He'd become nothing more than a burden, the way their alcoholic father had been. Dylan had been the one who had stepped up from a young age, far too young for the responsibility of taking care of his mother and younger brother. To know that Gage might one day resent him, the way he did his father—he couldn't let that happen. As much as he didn't think a dog would help him, it might at least do enough good that he could give his brother back the freedom he'd lost when Dylan returned from Afghanistan.

He shifted in the seat of the Camaro his brother had rented. The old Dylan would have been itching to open the car on the long stretch of highway, to press his foot to the floor and let the powerful beast fly over the asphalt, like Icarus soaring toward the sun. But that man had become mortal, died the day a bullet grazed his temple and a grenade exploded beside him. He fisted his hands, trying to control the anger that rose to the surface whenever he thought of what he'd lost.

"Yeah. Where is this place? BFE? How much farther?"

Gage checked the GPS navigation. "About five miles. Just off the next exit."

Dylan's brows drooped. "Not much around here, is there?"

Gage shrugged as he turned off the highway. "Maybe that's a good thing."

"I don't like it. There's a lot of trees and ground cover. Too many hills."

He knew it might not make sense to anyone else, but the hills and wooded areas made it harder for Dylan to see anyone approaching. He might not be in combat any longer, but that didn't stop him from scanning the woods for enemies. The doctors claimed it was just part of the PTSD, but he hadn't met a soldier yet who didn't continue to watch his back, even at home.

It was the same reason he'd done Internet searches on this training facility while his brother was sleeping. He not only wanted to get a lay of the place, but he wanted to know what he should expect. He was surprised to find out it was run by a woman. He'd even watched a few of the videos posted on her website. As much as it looked like she knew what she was doing, he wasn't sure how much a dog trainer could understand about a PTSD case like his without having been in combat. The woman in the videos looked more like a cheerleader than someone who knew anything about fear, trauma, or death.

Dylan crossed his arms over his chest as they approached the entrance and a sign welcoming them to Heart Fire Training Facility. As they pulled up to the main house, Dylan saw his brother's eyes widen. The house was a sprawling two-story ranch style with a wraparound porch, but what really caught his attention was the beautiful woman seated on the steps waiting for them.

"Damn."

Dylan chuckled at his brother's response. He couldn't help but agree. She was much prettier in person than she'd been in her videos, and that was saying a lot. He turned to say something and found his brother staring at him. "What?"

"You laughed."

"Okay?"

Gage stopped the car and turned it off. "That's the first time I've heard you laugh since you came home."

Dylan clenched his jaw, reaching for the door handle. His brother was right, and it had actually felt good, until he realized that he was the only one in his unit still able to laugh. Guilt washed over him as he thought about the families who had lost loved ones because of his failure. He climbed out of the car, refusing to respond.

"Hi, I'm Julia. You must be Dylan?"

The woman moved down the stairs, a broad smile on her face as she extended her hand. Immediately a monster-sized dog bounded down the stairs and sat at her feet, staring up at Dylan. He tucked his hands into his pockets, his mouth turning down as his brows bunched in a frown. He wasn't about to put out a hand where this beast could bite. The dog cocked his head to one side, studying Dylan, then opened his mouth in what looked like a grin, his huge pink tongue lolling to the side.

She laughed. "It's okay. Tango is a big teddy bear." She seemed to catch herself. "Unless he's on alert and working."

He wondered at her hesitation and looked back at the dog, and the teeth he could see inside the sloppy grin. "Teddy bear, huh?"

His brother moved around the car and reached for her hand. "Hi, I'm Gage. We spoke on the phone. This is Dylan."

Dylan nodded at her, not moving to approach as he looked around at the facility. He assumed from the barks, yips, and howls that the solitary outbuilding was a kennel or training area. The rest of the property was open with pine trees surrounding the back of the property into the hills. She had landscaped the front with wildflowers and grasses that looked native yet too orderly to be natural.

"If you want to grab your bags, I'll show you to your rooms," she offered as she turned back to the house.

Dylan didn't miss the fact that the dog rose and followed behind her. He met his brother at the trunk of the car. "That dog is a monster," he muttered. "If you think I'm taking something like that home, you're the crazy one."

"You're not crazy and just give it a chance, will you?" Gage looked around the side of the car, making sure Julia couldn't hear the criticism. "What's the worst-case scenario? That you get to stare at her for three weeks?"

Dylan glared at his brother. The last thing he needed was any sort of romantic entanglement. He couldn't even take care of himself right now. "You go right ahead."

"You can't be serious. Are you blind?"

Dylan shrugged. He hadn't missed anything—not her curves, not her smile, not the white scar at her temple, and certainly not the way her dark brown eyes seemed to dance as she spoke. But he had nothing to offer, and he wasn't selfish enough to sentence anyone else to the hell that was his life now. It was just easier to avoid any emotion, even the good ones. Hurt followed too closely at every turn.

"Are you two coming?" she called from the doorway. Dylan shut the trunk as his brother headed toward the house.

That smile was on her lips again as she opened the door, and he felt a stab of jealousy at the opportunity he'd just passed up for his brother. He didn't fault Gage; under different circumstances, he would have taken a shot at her. Dylan had always assumed he'd be married by now, maybe with a kid or two, but now, with a different sort of future ahead of him, he was glad he'd never taken the plunge. He had enough guilt on his shoulders without a wife and kids to disappoint. Gage held open the door for him, and they followed Julia inside.

The house was tastefully furnished, more for comfort than in any particular style, but it was homey and welcoming. He thought he smelled cookies as they passed the kitchen and continued down the hall.

"I put you guys in the back of the house. There's a back door just off the hall, and these two rooms adjoin." She looked pointedly at Dylan. "If you need anything, just let me know. I'll do my best to make this an easy transition for you."

The sympathy in her dark eyes made him cringe. He didn't want this woman feeling sorry for him. He didn't want anyone pitying him. He was a special ops medic, had completed some of the most difficult military training the world had to offer, and here he was with a dog trainer assessing his ability to care for some mutt?

He inhaled deeply, stuffing the rage into the recesses of his chest. Now wasn't the time, and she wasn't whom he was really angry at. That he could recognize the fact was a step in the right direction and would make his therapist proud, but it wasn't enough for him. "Thanks, this will be fine."

Dylan went into the room and dropped his bag on the bed while Gage moved into the next room. Julia stood in his doorway and stared at him, making him wish she'd hurry up and move on. "Is there something else?"

"You don't really want to be here, do you?" Dylan didn't detect any judgment or condemnation in her voice. She was simply stating a fact.

His brother appeared at her shoulder. "He's just tired from the stress of the trip," he offered.

She glanced back at Gage then back to Dylan and arched a brow, doubtful. "Tired, huh?"

Clearly, she didn't believe Gage's excuse. She wasn't just a pretty face. This woman had a brain. Dylan didn't want to lie, so he just kept his too-honest mouth shut, setting the variety of anti-anxiety pills, sleeping aids, and pain medication on top of the dresser.

"I'll make you a deal, Dylan. You unpack and relax a bit. Feel free to use the pool in the back or wander around the property. Then, after dinner, we'll go out and you can meet some of the dogs. If you still want to head home, you can give up and fly out tomorrow. We'll just call it a minivacation."

"What's in it for you?" Dylan narrowed his eyes. In his experience, people didn't offer something for nothing. "If I don't take a dog, you don't get paid."

Gage glared at him, his eyes warning Dylan to shut up, but she laughed at him. "I offer the PTSD dogs as part of a nonprofit foundation. Anything paid for the dog goes back into the organization to rescue more dogs for training. I only take a small salary. It's enough to meet my needs."

He hadn't expected that. Nor did he expect the way her eyes softened as she continued. "It doesn't do anyone any good for you to get a dog you don't want. You won't connect, and the dog won't be able to reach you. This is a partnership between you and your animal. It can't be forced. We might even go out there and find that I don't have one to fit your needs."

Dylan hadn't thought about that. He'd assumed that any dog would work, especially since he didn't think this would do any good. The fact that she was being completely honest with him, even if that meant failure on her part, made him want to trust her, at least a bit. He stared at her intensely, trying to figure her out. He couldn't help but feel some of the weight on his shoulders lift as she smiled at him and her face lit up.

"Well?" The monster-dog plopped down at her feet, laying his head on his paws, and looked up at him. He felt his resistance caving.

"As long as it's not a horse like that one, I'll give it a shot."

"This will be great." She turned and patted Gage on the arm. "You'll see."

Chapter Three

JULIA WATCHED FROM the back patio as Dylan swam laps in the pool. He moved with fluidity, barely making a splash as he cut through the water with practiced ease, but the way he swam troubled her. He didn't act like a man getting some exercise, but a man running from something, working his body to exhaustion.

She'd tried her damnedest to get the man to crack a smile, but nothing seemed to break through his brooding reserve. Gage, on the other hand had been friendly, asking various questions while she worked on basic obedience with the three dogs she had brought back from the shelter. She liked him and wondered how similar the two brothers might have been before Dylan's diagnosis. Tango moved to her side and sat down, watching out the screen door. She absently let her hand fall to his head, reaching for his itchy ear.

Somehow she was going to need to bring up the subject of Dylan's PTSD, but so far she'd had difficulty drawing him into even the safest conversations. He was definitely a man of few words. But without discussing what requirements he was going to have for his dog, he might end up with a mismatched animal. He was already skeptical about this process; there was no sense in setting him up for failure.

She saw him swim into the shallow end of the pool, swiping the water from his shaved head. Her eyes followed the water as it trickled over his granite wall of a chest.

That man was a chiseled god. With a square jaw covered in a day's beard growth, his caramel skin was colored by a tribal tattoo that ran from just behind his ear, down his neck, and over one dark pectoral. The intricate design continued over his arm and enormous bicep onto his forearm. She noticed a scar on the side of his head and wondered if it had occurred as part of his injury. If so, this man had a story she was going to need to hear. Tango stood up, pulling her back to the present, and she turned to see who approached behind her.

She didn't miss the worry in Gage's deep brown eyes. "You really think you might be able to help him?"

Julia tipped her head to one side. "I do. But it's really going to depend on how willing he is to make this work."

"Then what are we waiting for?"

Julia jumped and spun to see Dylan standing at the screen door, wrapping a towel around his waist. He slid the door open and stepped inside. He towered over her, resolved yet intimidating. She took a step backward as he looked down at her. He was so close she could smell the chlorine and sunshine on him, and she felt her heart skip a beat before speeding up double time.

"Give me a minute to get dressed and you can show me these dogs."

"Okay," Julia agreed, trying to catch her breath as Dylan moved past her and headed down the hall. She saw Gage stare at her, a moment longer than he should have.

"Um"—she tried to compose herself again—"any idea what sort of dog your brother might be looking for? What does he like to do? Hobbies?"

"Do you mean now or before?"

"Either, I guess."

Gage shrugged one shoulder. "He used to be a pretty active, outdoorsy kind of guy. He doesn't really do anything now that he used to and, being special ops, his life was pretty much the job. There wasn't much time for hobbies when he could be deployed at a moment's notice."

"Special ops?" Neither of them had mentioned that to her.

"Bragging about me again, Gage?" Dylan sauntered into the room with a confident swagger she hadn't seen from him before. She wondered if Dylan was proud of his own accomplishments or just pleased that his brother was proud of them. He slung an arm around his brother's neck playfully. "What do you say we go look at these mongrels of hers?"

Julia held her tongue, even as she felt resentment stir. Her dogs might be shelter rescues, but that didn't make them less capable. In many cases, it gave them the best traits of more than one breed. As if sensing her displeasure, Gage glared at his brother in silent reprimand.

"Tango, watch." The dog moved to the front door and sat down, his ears lifted and on full alert. "Let's go."

"You mean to tell me that monster will guard your front door?" Dylan sounded doubtful. Both men followed her out the back door and headed toward the kennels.

She nodded. "Until I release him from the command." He looked dubious. "Would you have defied an order from your commanding officer?" She saw the flicker of resentment in his eyes at her audacity to compare him to a dog. She hadn't meant to ruffle his feathers, and attempted to smooth things over. "It's the same thing with the dogs. They see me as their leader and do what I ask because they enjoy their job and they trust me. I assume it was the same for you."

She saw Gage hide a grin as Dylan's frown deepened and he shoved his hands into the pockets of his jeans. She could tell she'd only managed to make things worse. Every muscle in his body seemed to tense and she saw his huge biceps flex, as if he was clenching his fists.

"So," Gage began, trying to break the current of tension crackling in the air, "we only have a small house in North Carolina, but it's got a pretty good-size yard."

That was the slight accent she detected.

"You won't have the dog in the yard much, unless you're with it. You'll want to keep your dog with you all day."

"How am I supposed to get a job that way?"

Julia stopped and turned to face him. "It depends on what your dog does to assist you. Service animals are protected by the Disabilities Act, and you can take him to work with you."

"I am *not* disabled," Dylan growled, the muscle in his temple moving as he clenched his jaw.

Julia stopped, frozen on her feet, and stared at Dylan for a moment before relaxing. Although he was completely capable, something in his eyes reassured Julia he wasn't going to hurt her. He was injured, physically and emotionally, but she knew bravado when she saw it.

"Yes, you are. I can either sugarcoat this for you, like I'm guessing a lot of people have"—Julia glanced at Gage—"or I can help you. It's up to you, but I'm not going to lie to you, Dylan."

She pushed open the door to the kennel and they were greeted by excited yips and barks. Julia reached for several leashes hanging near the entrance and headed down the aisle, stopping in front of a short-haired German shepherd and retrieving him from the run. She moved across the aisle and brought out a border collie and a black Lab. As she looked back at Dylan and Gage standing near the door, she could see that while Gage looked overwhelmed, Dylan was searching the eyes of the dogs. It surprised her when he'd been resistant to the idea of a dog so far.

"Dylan, why don't you walk up and down and see if there's another dog that you seem to connect with." She gave the dogs she had on leash the command to sit, and all three relaxed at her feet while Dylan frowned again.

Was this the man's only facial expression? His lips tightened into a thin line, body coiled as if ready to strike. She had yet to see him relax, even slightly.

She saw him stop for a moment at the run with a large mastiff before moving on. He squatted down on the balls of his feet, his fingers curling through the chain-link of the run at the end. "This one," he whispered, almost too quietly for her to hear.

She gave the three dogs beside her the command to stay and walked toward Dylan. She smiled when she saw he'd stopped in front of Roscoe, a beautiful golden retriever who'd been rescued after being abandoned in an empty warehouse. "Here." She put the leash into his hand. "This is Roscoe. Roscoe, meet Dylan." She reached for the dog's collar and allowed Dylan to clip the leash on him. "Now let's go play."

DYLAN WAS BEGINNING to wonder if this woman was insane. It started when she talked to the animals as if they were human, but watching her run around, leaping and jumping with them in the yard, confirmed his suspicions. All four dogs seemed to be enjoying the time with her, and, he had to admit, he couldn't help but enjoy the view it gave him of her curvy rear. But he wasn't about to make a fool out of himself the way Gage was, romping on the grass with four dogs.

Dylan sat on the stoop and leaned back on his hands, crossing his ankles in front of him, while he scanned the fenced enclosure. He was glad it was chain-link, which gave him the ability to take in the entire surroundings. He hated how he was constantly on alert for threats, even when he knew there weren't any. "I thought we were supposed to work with them."

She stopped playing and looked at him. "We are working. Part of the work you'll be doing will simply be bonding with your dog."

Roscoe moved away from the other three dogs and walked to where he reclined, climbing the steps to sit beside him. "I don't see the point in this. How is playing tag with a dog going to help me stop nightmares or relax when I feel a panic attack?" Dylan sighed, frustrated. "This is just one more thing that isn't going to work."

The dog lay down with his head over Dylan's thigh and looked up. Without warning, Roscoe nudged him in the belly. Dylan ignored him. "I'm tired of the medications, the therapy visits and—" Dylan sat up, putting a hand on the dog's back. "What's he doing?"

Julia smiled and walked toward him, leaving the other dogs in the yard. "His job. Technically speaking, he's redirecting you, making you focus on him and drawing you out of your head. Congratulations, Dylan, I think you have your dog."

"What? I don't actually..." He looked down at the dog's head, still lying in his lap, staring up at him with deep brown eyes filled with understanding. It was strange, but he really felt as if this dog had seen just as many trials in his life as Dylan had. "Abandoned, huh?"

"Yes. But he's been a very quick learner." Julia sat down on the grass near Dylan's feet as Gage walked toward them from across the yard. She drew her knees toward her chest and wrapped her arms around them, smiling at him. "You should spend the rest of today getting to know him."

He looked away from the dog to see her smiling at him again. Damn, if this woman didn't have the prettiest smile. He arched a brow at her suggestion. "Like what, a date?"

"It's a little like that," she said, laughing.

"This is our new roommate?" Gage crossed his arms and looked down at him. "Roscoe, huh?" The dog flicked his eyes toward Gage when he heard his name, but otherwise he remained focused on Dylan.

"I'll just go put the other three away while you guys hang out back here. I'll be right back." Julia clipped the leashes on the other dogs and led them back inside.

Gage laughed as she went inside. "Did you have to pick the one with the most hair?"

Dylan glared at his brother. "I don't think I actually picked him," he pointed out. "He chose me. Now that we have him, how long before we can leave?"

"Why would you want to? You've got everything here you could possibly want, including a beautiful woman who is completely focused on you."

"That is the last thing I need, right after a damn dog." Dylan didn't know how to explain it to his brother, who didn't seem to see him as a burden. He needed to get back on his own two feet. "I don't understand why you aren't in more of a hurry to get home. You have a business to run."

"You and I both know I can work wherever I have an Internet connection. Julia already assured me over the phone that I can use her Wi-Fi as long as I need it. Face it, we're here for the duration."

"I don't want to *be* here." Dylan jumped to his feet, knocking the dog from his leg.

"Tough shit," Gage countered. "Julia was right about one thing. You're getting used to people lying to you. You're not getting any better sitting at home, hiding in your room. It's time you learn how to keep living, in spite of this."

The dog pawed at Dylan's leg, but he ignored it as the pent-up fury bubbled over, like lava from a volcano. "You have no idea what you're even talking about." He shoved his hands into the middle of Gage's chest, knocking his brother backward a few steps.

Roscoe began barking, moving between the brothers. "The hell I don't." Gage took a step closer to his brother. "You want to take a swing at me? If it makes you feel better, then go ahead. It's not going to change anything."

Roscoe jumped up on Dylan and grabbed a mouthful of denim at the knee of his jeans, growling as he tugged backward, knocking Dylan off balance. He stumbled and caught himself as the dog let go. It was enough to jolt him from behind the curtain of rage that dropped when he lost his temper. He stared down at the dog, who was watching him intensely, waiting to see what he would do.

"Gage, I…"

"Don't," he warned, waving a hand, dismissing Dylan's need to apologize. "If that doesn't prove that you need to be here, I don't know what will."

JULIA HEARD ROSCOE barking and locked the kennels quickly. Running back out to the yard, she recognized the dog's anxiety and made it to the door in time to see Gage storm off as Dylan dropped his head into his hands.

"Roscoe, down." The dog immediately followed her command and lay at Dylan's feet, staring up at him. "Are you okay?"

"No." He looked torn, as if he wanted to follow his brother. Or run in the opposite direction.

"Do you want me to go after him?" She wanted to help but wasn't sure what to do. With the dogs, she followed her instincts, but with Dylan, she had no point of reference.

"No."

She took a step toward him, and he looked up at her from hooded eyes. "Dylan, you're going to have to open up to me. I know you want to keep it all bottled inside, but when you do, it's going to be a poison in there."

He laughed but it was a painfully bitter sound. "Trust me, you don't want to know what's inside. It's like an atom bomb. If I took the lid off..." He looked down at the dog. "What am I supposed to do with him now?"

"Why don't we go back to the house and we can talk about it. Let's find you somewhere you can sit and relax."

"Relax? I don't even think I know what that means anymore."

"Come on. I'll get dinner started and we'll talk while we wait."

JULIA SAT ON the couch with her feet up on the coffee table as Tango sprawled out on the floor. Dylan sat across from her in the recliner, but his back was ramrod straight.

Roscoe sat at his feet, staring up at him as if he couldn't relax until his master did.

"Would it make you feel better to inspect the house?"

He looked surprised by her offer. "Actually, it would, but I don't want to impose."

"Go ahead. There's nothing to hide here. Take Roscoe with you."

Dylan looked skeptical. "You're sure you're fine with me doing this?"

She shrugged. She didn't really want him snooping around her house, but she knew it would set him at ease, at least as much as anything would at this point. Dylan rose and began to move around the house, slowly checking each room before returning to the living room and slumping into the recliner again. She saw the change in him as his shoulders lost their rigid inflexibility. He leaned back into the chair, and his hands lay open on the arms.

"I'm sorry, I just—"

Julia held up a hand. "No apology necessary. I get it."

She heard him take a deep breath and sigh loudly as he sank farther into the chair. Roscoe relaxed and lay down at his feet. It was the first time she'd seen him let his guard down, and she remembered how exhausting it was to be on high alert nonstop with no real danger except what your mind conjured. He closed his eyes, and she took the opportunity to assess him. There was his quick temper, but she knew a large part of that was likely coming from frustration. He had an air of confidence about him, like a man who knew who he was and got what he wanted, yet she could sense doubt in him.

"How many years apart are you and Gage?" She hoped family would be a safe subject, something that wouldn't stir any demons to the surface.

He turned his gaze in her direction. "I'm older by two years. He's a great guy, and I don't know what I'd do without him. Since I got back—"

She shook her head and held up a hand to stall him. "Let's talk about other things for now. What about your parents?"

A shadow covered his deep brown eyes. "Divorced. Dad was an alcoholic and Mom finally had enough. After their divorce, he pretty much ran out. Not that he was around much before anyway. He practically lived in the bar down the street."

"Are you still close to your mom?"

Pain clouded his eyes. "She died a few years ago. Cancer."

Julia wasn't doing too well on conversation. She might rethink the entire idea. She took a breath, wondering what subject might prove safe to discuss. She didn't want to discuss his time in the military, at least not yet, and family seemed to be a sore subject. Gage had already told her he didn't really have any hobbies since returning. She wasn't sure where to go from here.

"How'd you get started doing this, Julia?" It was the first time he'd initiated any conversation with her, and his brown eyes were intense, almost as if he could see into her soul.

"Training dogs? I don't really know. I sort of fell into it." As if he knew she was talking about him, Tango sat up and looked at her. She patted the couch beside her and he hopped up, laying his head in her lap. "As a kid, I always seemed to be the one who found strays or took them home. I never understood people who didn't have at least three dogs." She laughed. "My parents always joked that they'd stolen me from a wolf pack."

He gave her a half smile, and she found it transformed his face. While brooding and serious, he seemed mysterious and dangerous. His sheer size alone was intimidating. But when he smiled, he was devastating. His sharp features softened and his eyes took on an amusement that made him sexy. Which, in her book, was just as dangerous. Her heart did a quick skip before she reminded herself that he was a client. A client in dire need of her help.

"How did dog training turn into fixing crazy people?"

"I don't fix anyone." She tipped her chin down and gave him a disparaging scowl. "And you're not crazy."

"Tell that to Uncle Sam," he muttered.

She let his comment slide. "About four years ago, a dog I was training for a search and rescue team went out to find a boy who'd gotten lost. He was autistic, so he hid. The men had been looking for two days, but the dog found him within fifteen minutes. Then he wouldn't leave the boy's side." She ran her hand over Tango's head, staring down at the dog to keep from meeting Dylan's piercing gaze. "The boy connected with him and showed improvements his parents hadn't seen in him before, socially and emotionally. The two of them have been together ever since, and now he's able to attend school."

She looked up at him, wanting him to understand that Roscoe could help him as well. "If you give him a chance, Roscoe *will* turn this around for you."

"You sound so sure." Dylan shook his head and looked at the dog. "I want to believe you. I really do. But I just don't have any hope left in me."

Chapter Four

Dylan was sitting on the couch when Gage finally returned. "Where were you?"

"Took a ride into town. Why?"

Gage still looked pissed, as if the time in town hadn't cooled his temper any. Dylan couldn't blame him. He didn't deserve to be strapped down to a brother who couldn't even make it through a night without a prescription, who lost his temper over nothing and thought people walking by were trying to kill him.

"Look, Dylan, I think you need to stay here."

"I thought we'd already established that." Dylan noticed that Roscoe had moved into a sitting position, his eyes focused on his face. He took a deep breath and reached a hand out to the dog's head, patting him absently. "After you left, Julia and I talked a bit."

"Good. But I think this needs to be more than that." He shifted nervously, shaking the keys he still held in his hand. "I rented a room in town."

Dylan's hand stilled on Roscoe's head. "What?" The thought of his brother staying a few miles up the road shouldn't have made him as anxious as it did. They'd lived apart for years, but Dylan knew he'd come to rely on his brother too much since he'd been home. His reaction proved it. "I thought this was going to be a vacation for you. What about all that 'staring at a pretty face' crap?"

"Keep your voice down." He looked toward the hallway. "This isn't a vacation, and you know it. You need time to learn to work with this dog without me around. I'll be here when Julia says I need to be, but other than that..." Roscoe jumped onto the couch and laid his head in Dylan's lap, nudging his hand again. "You need to get back on your own two feet, and I've been keeping you from doing that."

"So, you're turning your back on me the way Dad did?" Dylan wasn't sure why his mouth kept going. He knew it wasn't how his brother felt. Gage wouldn't abandon him, but it was as if the anger had a voice of its own. "You're going to drop me off here and just leave?"

Dylan felt the rage bubbling up again. He was so tired of being angry and resentful, which only made the guilt worse. But, so far, nothing had been able to still the anger. He couldn't control when it rose to the surface, drowning him in waves of fury until it finally receded on its own, usually leaving a mess of hurt behind. He took a deep breath, letting it out slowly, trying to still the tide that threatened to overtake him. It wasn't working. He needed to get away—from his brother, this situation, this life that had become a living nightmare.

Roscoe bumped his nose against Dylan's chin, hard enough to knock his head backward a bit. "What the *hell*?"

Dylan pushed the dog from his face, but Roscoe wasn't going to be deterred. He rose to his feet, but the dog just sat up on the couch, pawing at his leg. He looked up at Gage and saw the shock on his face. "What?"

"You were gone, Dylan, the way you get when you fall into an episode. You were pissed and ready to lose it like you do. He pulled you out." Dylan looked down at Roscoe, who simply cocked his head to one side, staring up at him with those deep brown eyes. "This is the right thing, Dylan. It's not going to be easy, but it's *right* and I think you see it."

Gage turned and made his way down the hall for his room. Dylan followed with Roscoe right behind him. He watched from the door as his brother stuffed his clothing into his duffel and went into the bathroom to retrieve his toiletries.

"Are you even going to let Julia know you're leaving?" He knew he sounded slightly panicked, but his brother had become something of a lifeline for him over the past year. His was the first face Dylan saw after coming out of his induced coma from the gunshot wound to his head, and he was the only reliable reality in his life since.

"You can tell her in the morning. I'm staying at the Crazy 8 Motel about five miles up the highway. You both have my cell." He shot Dylan an impish grin. "Though if I was stuck in this house with her alone, I wouldn't bother calling you."

"Shut up." Dylan shoved his hands into his pockets.

Gage laughed as he swung his duffel over his shoulder and headed for his car. "I'll come by tomorrow and see how you're doing. This is going to work, Dylan. I know it is."

Dylan stood on the porch with Roscoe at his side as he watched his brother drive away. It was the first time in a year he'd been alone. The freedom was exciting. More than that, it was terrifying. But Dylan Granger had never been a man to give in to terror. He'd embraced it all his life. He looked down at the dog, who met his gaze, his tongue lolling out to the side.

"Okay, Roscoe, so what comes next? Because now we're on the front lines with only each other for backup."

JULIA ROSE THE next morning to a quiet house. Dylan's door was shut and Gage's room was empty. Not just unslept in but void of all his clothing, and it worried her. She'd seen how troubled Dylan had been after the fight with his brother. Something like this could set him back, which would make training nearly impossible.

Tango padded over the hardwood floors behind her, looking for his breakfast. She poured his food into his bowl and refilled the water dish before slipping her phone into her pocket, heading to feed the other dogs. She needed to do some basic obedience training with the new dogs before she and Dylan started working today. As she opened the door to the kitchen, her phone buzzed with a notification. She withdrew it from her pocket, assuming it was her sister chastising her about being late for breakfast, and looked at the message on the screen. Her heart dropped into her belly and a cold dread slid down her spine when she saw the text.

Watching you, my love. Is he your new boyfriend? Not for long.

Julia looked behind her, as if the text would conjure Evan. It had been so long since she'd last heard from him that she'd assumed he'd given up on tormenting her. Apparently, he'd only been biding his time. It didn't seem as if the restraining order deterred him at all. She needed to figure out her next move. Calling the police wouldn't do much good unless he actually threatened her or had been seen too close by. Since he hadn't, there was no violation of the court order. Maybe Evan was just trying to get under her skin again. If so, it had worked. Telling her brother would simply make him overreact and he'd try to put her into lockdown. She needed to warn Dylan and Gage, at least make them aware of the situation, but she worried what it might do for Dylan's frame of mind. She had to let Dylan know about her ex, but for today, as he started his training, maybe silence was the best option.

Her heart began to slow its racing as she dished up breakfast for the dogs, praying she was making the right call. Evan hadn't been like this when he'd first come to stay at the ranch. They had trained Misty not only to recognize the signs before his blood sugar dropped, but also to retrieve his medications. Evan had needed her and, she found, it felt good to be needed. She hadn't planned it, but she couldn't help falling for him. When the end of his time at her facility became imminent, he changed overnight. He started pressuring Julia to let him stay. Misty began to shy away from him, refusing to work with him and positioning herself between him and Julia more often. Julia shook her head, not wanting to think about the final day he'd been on the ranch or what had happened to Misty.

She pushed back the painful memories and took a deep breath. She'd moved beyond what happened. The past was behind her, and she would make sure Evan stayed there as well. She would never trust anyone over her dogs again.

DYLAN ROLLED OVER and jumped backward as his hand was met with soft fur instead of sheets. "Damn it, Roscoe. You're not supposed to be on the bed."

The dog didn't look even slightly apologetic as he stood and licked the side of Dylan's face before jumping to the floor. Dylan swiped his hand over his face, the rasp of his beard loud in the silence.

"Ugh! That was disgusting. Don't do that again!" He must be losing his mind if he was talking to this dog as if he could understand him. But he had to wonder when Roscoe dropped his head to his paws and looked up at him sheepishly.

He pulled a T-shirt over his head and slid on the same jeans he'd tossed at the foot of the bed last night after Gage left. What should have been a sleepless night filled with nightmares had oddly enough been incredibly restful. He glanced at the dog, who noticed and wagged his tail enthusiastically. Hell, if letting the dog sleep on the bed meant a dreamless night, he'd tuck the damn animal under the covers.

He heard the sound of tires on the gravel driveway and walked to the front porch, assuming Gage was back for breakfast. He didn't see Julia, but from the barking he could hear in the kennel, she must be out with the dogs. He saw a truck moving slowly down the driveway. Seeing it wasn't Gage, he wondered if he shouldn't go find Julia and let her know she had company, but the driver waved at him through the lowered window and parked in the circular driveway.

"Hey, is Julia still feeding?"

Dylan arched a brow and crossed his arms, waiting at the top of the porch as the driver climbed out of the truck and approached, holding a hand out. "Hey, how ya doing? I'm Evan, a friend of Julia's."

The small hairs on the back of Dylan's neck rose, something that hadn't happened since returning home. His instincts were on high alert, but he had no reason for them to be going haywire. Years of experience had taught him to listen to his intuition, but the past twelve months had showed him he couldn't trust his mind's version of reality any longer.

"You always show up before breakfast?" He leaned against one of the posts and looked down at the man in front of him. He looked like a lawyer in his slacks and polo shirt. Everything about the man looked average, from his height and wiry build to his mousy brown curls and brown eyes.

"I was just in the neighborhood and decided to surprise her. It's been a while since I talked to her." He took a step closer, and Roscoe let a low growl slip from his throat. Evan immediately backed up a step, his eyes flicking toward Roscoe nervously. "Nice dog. Is it one of Julia's?"

"He's mine." Dylan glanced at Roscoe, who had moved to stand at his side, the hair on the scruff of his neck rising as he continued to growl quietly. He pushed himself away from the post. "Julia is busy right now, but I can tell her you came by."

The stranger narrowed his eyes, and Dylan recognized the madness in them. He'd seen it in his years as a medic. It was the same look he'd seen during a mission where they'd been clearing a town and had been approached by a suicide bomber. That man had the same glazed look of delirium Dylan saw in Evan's eyes. He moved down the steps quickly, taking advantage of Evan's surprise to put him into a headlock. He pressed him against the truck, patting down the front of his shirt for a weapon. A haze of dust clouded his vision as he lost himself in memories.

"Hey, are you nuts? Let go of me!" Evan struggled against him, but he was no match for Dylan's strength or skill. Roscoe began barking, trying to force his way between the two men.

Confusion settled in Dylan's gut. This man was unarmed and harmless. What was wrong with him?

Dylan pushed himself away, and Roscoe immediately backed off but remained watchful, standing in front of Dylan and watching the stranger.

"You're insane. Just tell her I'll come by another time." Evan jumped into his truck, but Dylan saw the man's hands shaking as he started the vehicle. "You'll be hearing from my lawyer." He gunned the truck and headed down the driveway, spewing gravel behind him as he went.

"Crap." Dylan ran his hands over his head. What the hell was he doing? He couldn't cause this kind of trouble for Julia. He looked down at the dog. "I thought you were supposed to stop this from happening," he accused, realizing how ridiculous it sounded for him to blame the dog.

How in the world was he going to explain to Julia what he'd just done?

JULIA HEADED BACK to the house, feeling more optimistic about her decision to keep quiet about Evan today. He hadn't texted her again, so he was probably just trying to scare her a bit. She wasn't going to give him the satisfaction of letting him know she'd altered any part of her life for him. Tango ran ahead and leapt onto the patio, wagging his tail furiously.

She followed him to find Dylan sitting on the porch swing with Roscoe at his feet. "Good morning." Tango nosed the other dog, ready to play.

He held a cup of coffee out to her. "Morning. I wasn't sure how you took your coffee, but I found cream in the refrigerator so I made an assumption."

"Good guess." She took the steaming mug and leaned against the post, watching him. "Where's Gage? All of his things were gone this morning. Is everything all right?"

"He's decided to stay in town."

"Did I...I mean, I hope that I—"

Dylan shook his head. "It wasn't you. It was me. He thinks that I'll do better without him here."

She could see the hesitation in his eyes. "But you disagree?"

"Not really. He's probably right. He usually is." He sipped his coffee. "It just feels strange." He seemed indecisive and, from what little she knew about him, it was out of character. He might be a man of few words, but those words were deliberate. Finally, he sighed. "Who's Evan?"

The breath was sucked from her lungs, and she felt her knees weaken. Dylan jumped from the swing, his coffee mug falling to the ground and spilling liquid on the porch as he reached out to catch her.

"Whoa, take it easy, there." He wound one arm under hers and another around her waist, lifting her easily and setting her on the swing. "What was that?"

She ran shaky fingers at the edge of her bangs and brushed them away from her eyes. "I...I guess I got light-headed."

He arched a brow and she knew he didn't believe her. "Julia, just sit for a minute."

"I'm fine. How..." She gave him a sideways glance. "How do you know about Evan?"

"Look up and follow my finger." He bent over and looked into her eyes, his gaze straying over the scar at her temple. He tipped her chin up with a finger, assessing her. "He was here this morning, and I'm afraid I may have caused you some trouble." He squatted down at her knees and reached for her wrist, his fingers checking her pulse.

Julia felt her skin ignite wherever his hands touched. Shivers of heat traveled over her flesh, warming her. She was certain he would think she was ill because her heart felt as if it was going to race right out of her chest. His thumb brushed her wrist, and she found herself wanting to lean into him, to lay her head against his massive chest and just shut out the world for a moment.

"I think you're going to live." Dylan's voice was husky as he looked at her, his deep chocolate eyes even darker than usual. "But you still look pale. Does this have anything to do with this Evan guy?"

She moved her hand away from his fingers. Her decision to keep quiet didn't matter now, especially if Evan had been audacious enough to ignore the court order and show up on her doorstep. "He isn't supposed to be here. I have a restraining order against him." She tipped her head to the side and brushed her hair back from her face. "You said you caused trouble? What happened?"

Dylan slapped his hands against his thighs and stood up. "I might have put him into a headlock." She looked up at him in awe. "And slammed him into his truck. He said something about an attorney." Her mouth fell open as he wiped a hand over his mouth. "I don't know what happened. I just…I snapped."

"What about Roscoe? He's supposed to…" She couldn't blame the dog. He and Dylan had only begun bonding and, until then, he couldn't be expected to react to Dylan's triggers as he eventually would. "Are you okay?"

"Me?" A snort of laughter burst from him. "I tell you this guy is threatening to sue you because I couldn't control my temper, and you want to know if I'm okay?"

"Evan Reece won't do anything." She prayed she was right, but Evan knew what he was doing. She couldn't prove he'd been there. "He just got out of jail, and showing up here is a violation of his probation. He's not going to say a word to anyone." She was surprised her voice remained calm, but, looking at her hands, it was apparent she couldn't keep the tremors of fear from rippling through her body. She pulled her knees to her chest and wrapped her arms around them in an attempt to hide the reaction from Dylan. "I'm sorry. I should have told you about him, but I haven't heard from him since he went to jail. Until today."

"Who is this guy?"

She sighed, wondering how much she should tell him. She didn't want to risk his welfare and recovery. She hadn't expected Evan to ever show up again. She rested her chin on her knees and considered telling him it was best if he left, but even the thought flooded her with disappointment she didn't want to acknowledge.

"He was a client who stayed here while we trained a dog for him. When he was supposed to leave, he started acting strangely." She tried to stop the shiver of fear that crept over her, and she wanted to hide from what had happened. It might have been four years ago, but retelling it brought it back as if it was yesterday. "His dog, Misty, started sticking closer to me, trying to protect me, ignoring her training. I think she was trying to tell me something. When I insisted he leave, he attacked me."

"Attacked? He hurt you?" She saw the fury rise in his eyes.

Tango positioned himself between her and Dylan, sitting up and putting his head on her arm as if reminding her of his comforting presence. "It wasn't long after I was out of the hospital that I got Tango."

Dylan took a deep breath, squatted down in front of her again, and reached for her hands. His fingers twined with hers. His hands were warm and gentle, but she felt a current of warmth flood through her palms and up her arms. She tried to focus on anything other than the heat spreading through her limbs.

"A client?"

She looked away, unwilling to admit the feelings she'd had for Evan. It had been a whirlwind romance, and she'd believed everything he told her about himself. It wasn't until he started pressuring her, saying strange things about always being with her, of owning her, that she started to question the relationship. When she woke and found him staring at her while she slept, she should have listened to the alarm in her head warning her that love wasn't supposed to be obsessive like this. How could she explain away her naiveté? Dylan didn't press her for more.

"Now he's out and looking for you?"

Dylan's question jerked her back to her present predicament. Evan *was* back. "I guess so. He texted me this morning, but I thought he was just trying to mess with my head. I never meant for you to get involved in this. You have enough to deal with right now, and this is just making things worse."

Dylan's lips curved in a lopsided grin, and he shook his head. "Are you for real? You find out some maniac is stalking you and you're worried about me?" Tango pressed his nose into Dylan's ear, and he couldn't help but laugh as he pushed him away. "I think he's telling me to keep my distance."

"If he was doing that, you'd see teeth." She returned Dylan's smile as she reached out to pet the dog's velvety head. "What do you think about grabbing a quick breakfast and getting started on training early?"

"Training," he repeated. His eyes focused on her mouth, and she felt her heart take another leap. She had to get control of this. He was a client, and she didn't fall for them now—ever. She'd learned that lesson the hard way. "How about if you fix breakfast and I'll clean up this coffee?"

She'd forgotten about the mess on the porch. "Sure. And depending on how the two of you do, I have an idea for this afternoon." She rose from the seat, and Tango jumped to his feet as she headed for the front door. She forced herself to focus on putting some distance between them.

"I hope it includes calling the police." His voice was somber, not allowing for any argument. When she didn't answer, his brows pinched together. "If you don't, I will."

His expression was dark and she could see the dangerous soldier he'd once been, but he didn't frighten her and she wasn't about to be bullied into anything. It didn't work when her brother tried it, and it wouldn't work for Dylan either.

"Go ahead, and be sure to let them know how you assaulted him as well." She let the door slap shut behind her before he could reply.

Chapter Five

TRAINING ROSCOE WASN'T what Dylan expected. Maybe it was because his mind equated *training* with his military service. Julia's version was relaxing and, dare he admit it, fun. As he and Roscoe walked around an obstacle course, as he directed the dog through various maneuvers the way Julia instructed, Dylan found himself enjoying each successful maneuver Roscoe completed. Until today, he'd almost forgotten what it was like to enjoy himself. Even smiling felt awkward, although it was surprising how quickly he was getting used to doing it again since arriving. Being with Julia was easy. She might be brutally honest, but she didn't push him for things he couldn't give. She still hadn't asked about his injuries or pressured him to talk about what happened to get him here. Being with her made him think he might be able to let go of the nightmare that seemed to haunt his waking moments.

"That's exactly right," she said as he navigated Roscoe through a tunnel. "See how he's looking at you when he finishes? Don't forget to praise him."

Dylan didn't need to be reminded. The dog was quickly breaking down the arguments he'd used against getting a service dog. In the two days he'd been at the facility, he'd already spent more time focused on something other than his PTSD than he had since returning from overseas. There was no amount of praise he could give Roscoe that would show how appreciative he was for that small accomplishment. Dylan reached down and rubbed the dog's golden head as Julia approached with a broad smile on her lips.

Just a glimmer of that smile made him want to return it. Gage was wrong. She wasn't beautiful. She was angelic. Her long, dark blonde waves swung over her shoulders, and her bangs fell into her brown eyes again. Dylan stuffed his hands into his pockets to keep from running his hands through those silken tresses. It had been a long time since he'd noticed a woman, let alone wanted to touch one, but, like the dog, Julia was quickly, almost magically, chipping away at the wall his accident had erected around him.

Chipping? She was breaking it down so quickly, she might as well be using a sledgehammer. He had to do something, anything, that kept him from thinking about that smile that was making his pulse pound against his ribs.

"What now?"

She laughed at him. "I think we need to give Roscoe a break. You two have been at it for almost two hours."

Dylan glanced at his watch. He'd been enjoying himself so much that he hadn't realized so much time had passed. He wondered when Gage was coming and hoped it wasn't soon. The feeling surprised him. Not only because his brother had been the one constant in his life, but because he knew he didn't want to compete for Julia's attention. As much as he knew it was wrong of him, he wanted to get to know her better.

"Come on, I have an idea."

She led the way back to the house and dropped the tailgate of her truck before calling Tango to her side. The dog came bounding through the dog door at the back of the house and skidded to a halt at her legs. She patted the back of the truck and he leapt inside.

"Are we going somewhere?"

"You'll see." She let Roscoe in the cab of the truck and slid behind the driver's seat. Dylan paused with a hand on the door, curious about what she had planned but hesitant to put himself into a situation that might trigger an episode. "You coming?"

He climbed into the truck and looked around curiously as she drove to a gate partway down the driveway. He hadn't noticed it when he'd arrived, but he hadn't been paying much attention to anything but his desire to go home. She drove over well-worn ruts in the open field as he watched her. She was a bit of an enigma.

She was quick to smile, stubborn, but confident enough to stand up to him. There was a softness about her, a tenderness he'd rarely seen in the people who surrounded him. She was optimistic yet, by her own account, she'd seen the worst the world had to offer. He was drawn to her, like a magnet.

"Have you ever ridden a horse?" She turned her face toward him, and he could see the playful gleam in her eyes.

"Do I look like the kind of guy to ride a horse?" His hand settled on the back of Roscoe's head, scratching his neck absently.

"You never had a pony ride as a kid?"

"I didn't exactly have a model childhood," he reminded her.

"Then it's about time. My sister has some great horses. She runs a horse rescue, but a lot of her horses end up being used for therapy."

His lips quirked to one side. "You've already convinced me to take a dog home. Now you want to talk me into a horse?"

She laughed and the sweet sound fell around him like music. He found himself joining her, and it stunned him. Roscoe looked up at each of them before laying his head back into Dylan's lap.

"No, I just thought it might be relaxing for you to go for a ride and for Roscoe to get out and run."

"And so that he'll know how to react when I get injured?" Her head swiveled toward him, ready to deny the assumption until she saw the grin on his face. It felt good to laugh and joke with someone, to have someone treat him as if he was normal. As much as Gage had given him since his return, normalcy hadn't been a part of that life. He could see the shadows in Gage's eyes when he looked at Dylan, waiting for him to snap or to fall apart.

With Julia, he was just a man—competent and confident—without pressure to be more than he could be.

"I might have to make you pay for that," she warned as she pulled the truck to a stop in front of a barn. She got out and let Tango jump from the back of the truck.

In a nearby pen, he saw a woman working with a horse, but his eyes focused on the man who came out of the house. "Julia!"

He trotted down the porch steps and met them at the barn, enveloping her in a bear hug.

"Dylan, meet my future brother-in-law, Nathan Kerrington."

Dylan stuck out his hand and gave the man a firm shake.

"In the corral over there is my sister, Jessie."

"What brings you this way? I assumed you'd be too busy to come visit this week." Dylan didn't miss the way Nathan eyed him, as if he was sizing him up.

"These two are doing so well, I thought we'd take a ride to The Ridge."

Nathan's brows shot up on his forehead. "Are you sure about that?"

She ran a hand over his arm. "I am. Why don't you two talk while I saddle up Grady and Bella?"

Dylan watched as Julia disappeared into the barn with Tango on her heels. At her departure, he felt suddenly cold, as if the sun had disappeared behind a cloud. She brought vibrancy and life wherever she went.

"Just so we're on the same page, Julia's like a little sister to me and I will protect her like family."

Dylan met Nathan's eyes and saw the honest threat there. The man had no idea what Dylan had done for a living, but he wasn't even hesitating. From the looks of him, he was fit but he was no match for Dylan's size.

"I completely understand." He arched a brow at the man but gave him a curt nod of acknowledgement.

Nathan let a slow smile spread to his lips, as if he knew something Dylan didn't. "Keep in mind, I wouldn't need to raise a hand. Her older brother is six-four and wrestles with steers for a living."

Dylan cocked his head to the side, finding himself gaining a little more respect for the man. "Duly noted."

Nathan laughed and reached down to pet the dog. "So, you're going to end up with Roscoe, huh?"

"Looks that way." The dog looked up at him longingly, so he reached down and petted him.

"You won't be sorry. Julia knows what she's doing." He looked toward the barn. "And she understands how the dogs help with trauma."

"She told you about my case?" Dylan was surprised she would say anything.

Nathan's eyes shot back to Dylan. "No. I meant her."

"So you grew up here?"

Julia followed Dylan's gaze as he looked off The Ridge at the river below. The water would be fairly low until the fall rains came but it was still swiftly coursing over the rocks and brush, enough to make a quaint picture. "Yep, until I went to college and built the house at the other end of the property."

She moved back from the edge of the cliff and sat on one of the logs near the fire pit. Her parents had set them up for campers when the ranch had taken in guests. These days, the only time it saw any use was when her sister held retreats for troubled teens.

Dylan turned his back to the view and walked toward her, scanning the trees around them. Roscoe nudged his arm and he rubbed a hand over the dog's head, but remained focused on her. Pride swelled in her a bit more than she wanted to admit. She was pleased with the way the two of them were bonding so far. Roscoe was hard not to love, but she was surprised Dylan had opened himself up to the dog so quickly after denying he wanted or needed one yesterday.

"How'd your sister end up with the property?" He moved closer to her but remained standing, his hands in his pockets again.

"My brother, Justin, and I both went to college, but Jessie stayed at home with Mom and Dad to help run the dude ranch. When we finished, our parents gave Justin and me part of the property to build our businesses. After they were killed in a car accident last year, it made sense for her to stay."

"I'm sorry. I didn't know."

"I appreciate that. It's been tough the last two years between the trial and then losing Mom and Dad." Tango looked up, ready to comfort her.

She could see the curiosity in Dylan's eyes. He wanted to know what had happened but wasn't sure whether he should ask. It wasn't something she liked to talk about, but she knew that sharing some of it with Dylan would make it more likely for him to do the same. And he needed to talk about what happened. If for no other reason than to see how Roscoe could ground him during an episode.

"You don't have to talk about it, Julia." He stopped her as she opened her mouth to speak. "Some things don't have to be spoken to be shared."

Dylan sat down beside her on the log, opposite the dog, and reached for her hand. His large palm engulfed hers as he wound his fingers through hers. It was sweet and comforting. She knew it wasn't meant to send a bolt of longing to her heart, but it did. It had been so long since she'd had anyone other than her family care about her welfare.

After Evan, she'd hidden away with her dogs, letting others see only the cheerful window dressing she put on to hide the fear. She couldn't let herself go again, couldn't let herself get close to anyone, because falling meant getting hurt. Jessie knew the truth, as did her brother and cousin, Bailey. They had seen the physical scars she bore from Evan's brutal attack, but no one realized what Evan had truly done to her. They didn't see the scars inside, the wounds that still festered because she hadn't seen the truth before Misty had been killed. Now she second-guessed herself, always doubting her instinct to believe in others. She'd fallen for a client, and he'd forever tarnished her ability to trust, to love.

They sat for what felt like an eternity in silence, holding hands. His thumb caressed the pad of hers. Roscoe had lain down at his feet and gone to sleep as they watched the trees rustling in the breeze. Only the occasional twitter of birds and chatter of squirrels could be heard. Dylan sighed and she turned to look at him.

"This place is amazing. Normally, I'd be worried about the trees, but right now I'm not." He sounded awed but relaxed.

"How long has it been since you got home?"

"A little over a year." He touched the side of his temple, and she could see the scar, just above where his tattoo began. "This is what actually sent me home. I took a bullet to the head while trying to carry another soldier to safety. It glanced off and just left me this awesome scar."

She gave him a shy smile. "Chicks dig scars, right?"

Dylan's brows dropped into a frown, and she immediately regretted her words, until he chuckled quietly. "I guess there's always a silver lining, right?"

"What made you want to join up in the first place?" She knew she was pushing her luck trying to get him to talk about his past, but as long as he was providing answers and seemed comfortable with the conversation, she'd listen.

His thumb traced a pattern over her wrist, sending tingles of pleasure shooting up her arm. Her chest constricted and she knew she should pull away, but she couldn't force her body to cooperate with her brain. He looked at her for a moment, then down at Roscoe.

"It was the only way I could support my mom and brother. After my dad ran off, it was up to me. In high school, I held odd jobs whenever I could manage them while Mom worked three of her own. As soon as I graduated, I knew there was no way I could support them and afford to go to college. So I enlisted and scored really high. Before I knew it, I was training for special ops and working as a medic."

"Why a medic?" His reaction to her on the porch made sense now. He'd immediately fallen back on his training.

"I like saving people, reading their needs. I was good at it." He met her gaze and his eyes were soft, almost liquid. "Like you."

"Me?" she squeaked.

Dylan laughed and released her hand. She couldn't help the disappointment that slammed into her chest at the loss of his touch, shocking her with the intensity. He was dangerous to her senses and her heart, and she vowed to keep more distance between them.

Until his fingers brushed her bangs back from her eyes and settled at the curve of her jaw. Her heart pounded against her ribs, ready to burst from her chest.

"Yes, you."

Heat crept into his eyes, and she wanted to look away from the scalding hunger she saw there. She knew it had to be reflected in her own. Every cell in her body was begging her to lean forward, to press her lips to his, but her fear was louder and more fervent than her yearning. His fingers trailed over the side of her neck, and sparks flared in parts of her body she'd long ignored.

"Julia, I—"

A wet, slobbery tongue covered the space between the two of them as Tango licked Dylan from his chin to the top of his forehead. He jumped up from the log and swiped a hand over his face, grimacing. Roscoe jumped up from his position on the ground, instantly alert.

"That was disgusting. I swear he's warning me to stay away from you."

Julia couldn't help the giggles that bubbled from within her chest as she tried to hold back her laugher. She knew Tango licked only people he liked, and he seemed to have taken an uncommon liking to Dylan, whether he wanted him to or not. "Tango, down." The dog sat and lowered his head, sheepishly, but still managed to look up at Dylan. "See, he's sorry."

"Yeah, well, I hope you don't mind if I keep my distance and stay over here." He sat at the other end of the log, but she could see the corner of his mouth turn up as he tried to hide his grin.

She wasn't going to admit that the log felt empty without him seated beside her. Any more than she was going to admit how much she'd wanted to feel his lips on hers, or to feel his hands on her skin again. She had to find something to distract herself from these thoughts that were bound to lead to the ache of loneliness.

"So, tell me about your brother."

DYLAN CURSED THE stab of jealousy that pounded in his chest when Julia asked about Gage. If it hadn't been for that damn dog, he'd be kissing her right now, letting his fingers brush over her cheek, tasting her—

What in the hell was he thinking? He should be grateful Tango saved him the rejection. If she was asking about Gage, she obviously hadn't wanted to be kissed by him. It had been so long since he'd been with a woman, he couldn't even read the signals he thought she was giving.

"What about him?" He heard the clipped tone of his voice and forced himself to take it easy. She could be just making conversation, inquiring about his family the way he had hers. He might be reading far more into her question than she meant.

She looked at him oddly, narrowing her eyes, as if she could read his thoughts. "I don't know. What does he do for a living? Did he join the military, too?"

Maybe not. "No." Dylan tried to keep the bitterness from his voice. "He actually owns his own IT company. He started it with some friends from college and then bought them out about four years ago."

She gave him a sideways glance as if trying to read his expression as Roscoe sat up and looked at him. "A regular genius, huh?"

"The golden child of the family, that's for sure." At least, that was the way his mother had always introduced them. He didn't tell Julia that, though. Or how he'd been the one to put his brother through college. Or paid for their mother's cancer treatments.

He didn't begrudge his brother's success and was glad to have been a part of helping him attain it. It didn't matter to him that he'd never really had a childhood or the high school experiences his friends had playing sports and dating. He'd never had the money for either, nor had he had the time. Instead, he'd learned from a young age the value of hard work, responsibility, and loyalty. It had shaped him into the man who'd saved lives on the battlefield, the man he was today.

The man you used to be, his brain reminded him. *That man is gone.*

"We should head back." Dylan rose and moved toward the horses, leaving Julia no choice but to follow him.

Chapter Six

Dylan and Gage sat at the kitchen table, watching carefully as Julia instructed Dylan on how to cook with Roscoe in the kitchen. Food was always a distraction for the dogs, so he would need to be vigilant to make sure Roscoe was concentrating on him rather than a treat.

"So, which of you does most of the cooking?" She looked back at the pair as she cut up the carrots and tossed them into the pot. The evening air held a chill, and beef stew would be a good choice to fill up these two.

"I do," Gage said. He jumped up from the table and walked to the counter, grabbing a piece of the chopped carrot. "But I avoid it when I can and order out." He shot her a disarming grin and winked. "I like to do my part to keep the local take-out places in business."

"And I'm sure they appreciate it." Julia returned his quick smile, marveling at how two men could look so similar yet be so different. She wondered again if their personalities had been more alike before Dylan's injury, and if it had caused his broody disposition. "Dylan, I'm sure you'll be cooking once you have your own place again, so why don't you come chop the celery so Roscoe gets used to it?"

"You're making a pretty big assumption." He frowned but rose from the table and came to stand beside her. Roscoe followed and sat down at Dylan's feet.

Julia's gaze jumped to Gage's, and she wondered if she'd said something wrong. Gage shrugged a shoulder slightly and shook his head. Dylan had seemed even more moody than usual since they left The Ridge and hadn't quite snapped out of it, even after Gage arrived. She looked up at Dylan and wondered if they should just call it a night. He and Roscoe were doing well. There was no need to rush either of them.

"You know what?" She smiled up at Dylan and set the knife down. "Why don't the two of you finish chopping up the celery and drop it into the pot with everything else? We'll let this simmer, but I'm in the mood for pizza and a movie. I'll call it in while I go feed the dogs. What do you guys say?"

"I'm game." Gage sounded overly enthusiastic, and she wondered at the reaction.

"Whatever." Dylan shrugged, looking somber.

Julia arched a brow at him and shook her head. "Don't sound so excited, Dylan."

"I'll probably just go to bed early."

Gage glared at his brother, but Julia wasn't going to be deterred by his foul mood. "Suit yourself. That just means more for us." She winked at Gage and watched fury fill Dylan's eyes as she exited the kitchen.

"WHAT'S YOUR PROBLEM?" Gage spun on him as soon as Julia was out the back door.

Dylan knew Gage wasn't about to let him off easy. "Nothing, leave me alone." Roscoe pawed at his leg but he ignored him.

"So, you're just planning on being an ass tonight? Because if so, I should warn Julia."

"Shut up, Gage." Dylan grabbed the knife and began chopping the celery as his brother leaned a hip against the counter.

"You know, you're adorable when you get all domestic."

Dylan set the knife down and pounded the side of his fist against the cutting board. Instead of looking intimidated, Gage winked and blew him a kiss, quickly moving out of arm's reach. Roscoe jumped up at the commotion and moved between the brothers. "Is everything a game to you?"

"Okay, I'll stop, but only if you tell me what's going on. Did something happen today while you guys were on your ride?"

Dylan glared at his brother before swiping the celery into the pot. "No. Yes. Crap, I don't know." He ran a hand over his shaved head before wiping it over his mouth.

"You don't have long before she gets back in here, so spill it."

"I almost kissed her," he blurted.

Gage froze in place for a moment before frowning. Dylan knew this would be his reaction. Gage had already expressed his interest in Julia. Suddenly, a smile spread over his lips and Gage actually laughed out loud. "You should have. What stopped you?"

"What do you mean, what stopped me?" Was his brother insane? There were at least one hundred reasons for him not to kiss her. He slid the cutting board into the dishwasher and put the produce back in the refrigerator. "I can't kiss her."

"Why not? It's a kiss, not a marriage proposal."

"She doesn't want to kiss *me*." Dylan loaded the dishes into the dishwasher and looked pointedly at his brother. "She's interested in someone else." Gage waited for him to say more. Did he have to spell it out to him? "You, Gage. She's interested in you."

Gage burst out with a loud guffaw, which only pissed Dylan off even more. This wasn't funny. He didn't like feeling envious of his brother. In all their years, he'd never once coveted anything his brother had. Dylan was proud of what he'd accomplished on his own. But this was different. He didn't want to want Julia. It wasn't right, and doing what was right was the only constant in his life, the only thing he could hold on to from the man he'd once been. Too bad knowing it was wrong didn't seem to lessen the wanting.

"Don't make me beat the crap out of you."

Gage waved his hand at him, barely controlling his laughter. "No, it's just...I can't believe you."

Dylan clenched his jaw, refusing to be drawn into his brother's antics "Screw you, Gage."

"Wait! I'm sorry."

"Dylan, she isn't interested in me. I have no clue why you'd think she was, but Julia's made it pretty obvious from the start that I don't even register on her radar."

"She asked about you."

"Heaven forbid she make polite conversation and get to know about your family. What's her sister's name? What does she do for a living?"

Dylan looked at his brother, confused. "Jessie said she rescues abused horses."

"What about her brother?"

"Justin. He's a veterinarian in town."

"And you know that because you've gotten intel on her? Or because you asked her about her family?" Gage threw his hands in the air. "Geez, chill out. If you want to kiss her, kiss her. If she doesn't want you to, she'll let you know."

Maybe Gage was right and he was just overthinking this. It was only a kiss. People did it all the time, and he'd kissed more than his fair share of women, even if he didn't date often.

That was before.

And therein was where his problem lay. His life was split into two parts—life before his injury and life after. Life before hadn't been easy, but he'd enjoyed it, lived it as capably as possible. But life after was a different story. Life after was haunted by memories and regrets, of loss and never-agains. He wasn't a man, he was the shell of one.

He had nothing to offer a woman now, and it wasn't fair to start something he couldn't see through.

"You don't get it."

"I *do* get it, but this entire trip is about you making changes for the better. I'm going to help you make this one."

"What are you talking about?"

Julia appeared at the back door and stamped her feet before opening the door, greeting them both with a bright smile. Dylan felt his heart skip whenever he saw her smile, and it didn't disappoint now.

"Okay, the pizza is on its way. I just ordered pepperoni since I forgot to ask what kind you both preferred."

Gage shot Dylan a quick glance before he rose. "I'm so sorry, Julia, but I can't stay. I just got a call from work and there's some sort of issue with our biggest client. I have to head back to town and work tonight."

"Oh, okay." Julia didn't seem overly disappointed by his brother's sudden departure. "No biggie. We'll do it another night. I hope it's nothing serious."

Gage gave him a pointed scowl. "I think if a few people can get their act together, it will all work out beautifully." Dylan clenched his fists at his sides and glared back at his brother. Roscoe began pawing at his leg.

"Are you all right?" Julia looked up at him and back down at the dog.

Dylan followed her glance and realized the dog was alerting her to his state of mind and the frustration that swirled in him like a whirlpool. "I'm fine. Come on, Gage. I'll walk you out."

As soon as they were outside, he shoved his brother's shoulder. "What the hell was that? You're leaving?"

"I'm doing you a favor, and for crying out loud, if the opportunity presents itself tonight, kiss her. If only for the sake of climbing back onto that horse. You were injured. You're not dead." Gage shook his head as he slid behind the wheel of the Camaro. Dylan was tired of feeling as if he was nothing more than a disappointment. "Will you, please, just start living again?"

If only he remembered how.

Julia let Dylan pick out the movie as she set the pizza on the coffee table, ignoring the pathetic, mournful glances both dogs cast at the food. She watched as he squatted down in front of the television with an easy grace, confident in his own skin, yet oblivious to his sex appeal. She took a deep breath, trying to calm her suddenly overactive libido.

It made no sense that, after nearly four years of having no attraction to any men, this dark, brooding male was the one to wake her body. It was true that Dylan practically oozed sexuality, but he hadn't given her any indication that he saw her as more than his dog's trainer. She couldn't count the moment they shared on the log, since she'd been vulnerable at the time and he'd simply been offering a shoulder to cry on. She needed to regain control of herself and shake off whatever hormonal overload she was suffering from.

He walked back and sat beside her, leaning forward to slide a slice of pizza onto a paper plate. "Jim Carrey okay?"

"Sure." She was a bit surprised by his choice of movie since he didn't seem like the comedy type, but she also wondered if he just felt the need to laugh. She was more shocked that he'd chosen to sit so close when there were recliners on each side of the couch, but she wasn't about to complain, even as her pulse leapt into hyperdrive. Any thoughts of eating went right out the window as her stomach did a nervous flip.

Julia picked at her pizza, finally setting what was left of the slice on top of the box and turning her attention to the movie, instead of the man beside her. She forced herself to relax, curling her legs under her and letting her head rest against her palm. Dylan was reclined in the corner of the couch, his eyes focused on the television with a ghost of a smile on his lips. She let her eyes stray over him.

He was incredibly handsome, the way only movie stars and sports figures were. Muscular, tanned, and rugged. Real people weren't supposed to look the way he did. But there was a sadness that seemed to cling to him, even when he laughed, as if he couldn't let himself go completely. She remembered how it felt to hold a part of herself hidden from life. She still did it at times, although not as often as she had at first after being released from the hospital. There was always a fear that lingered, something that couldn't quite be buried. She saw that same pain in Dylan's dark eyes.

She laid her head on her arm, blinking slowly. The last thing she heard was Dylan's warm laughter, and she knew she couldn't help but fall in love with the rich sound of it.

Dylan heard the rattle outside the back door at the same time as the dogs jumped up. Tango gave a low growl in his throat while Roscoe edged closer to the kitchen before looking back at him. He glanced at Julia, who'd fallen asleep on the couch. He didn't want to wake her, so he eased himself from the cushion and made his way toward the sound.

He signaled at Roscoe to heel and noticed that Tango had moved to stand between him and Julia. It was right where he wanted him to be, and he was surprised by the dog's protective instincts, although he knew he probably shouldn't have been. He heard another noise in the backyard, but this time it sounded like footsteps. He pressed his body against the wall, sliding through the doorway into the dark kitchen. Squatting low, Dylan moved into the shadows, creeping forward on the balls of his feet, and edged closer to the back door, listening for any other sounds. A dog barked in the kennel once but fell quiet. He heard a whisper of sound, like the wind through the shrubbery—or a person snapping a branch. The dog in the kennel began barking again, letting out a howl before the entire group joined in, creating a cacophony of canine singing. He heard distinctive footsteps this time and the slam of the back gate.

Moving quickly, he ran into the backyard, remaining low so he wasn't seen. Pushing open the gate, he could see a shadow disappearing behind the kennel, too far away to make out. The intruder might be gone now, but Dylan had his suspicions as to the identity of the shadow. This time, he didn't care how much Julia argued. He would insist she call the police.

Roscoe scratched at the door, jumping up to see Dylan through the window as he made his way back through the gate, making a mental note to get a lock on it tomorrow. He went back inside and found Tango still standing, watching for any threat to his mistress while she slept on the couch, oblivious to the danger.

"Good boys," he praised the dogs, reaching one hand to Roscoe's head and noticing how it shook.

He slid back onto the couch, marveling at the fact that he'd been able to remember his training, use it, and yet not slip into the darkness that was usually triggered when something reminded him of his time in the service. It had been the first time since returning from overseas that a stressful situation hadn't triggered an episode. As grateful as he was for the success, he wondered why.

It could have been Roscoe, or that his mind wouldn't let him slip with Julia in danger. Whatever the reason, Julia wasn't out of danger yet. He had to make her understand that this situation wasn't something she could ignore. It wasn't going to simply disappear. If it had been Evan outside her house tonight, as Dylan suspected, he was getting more brazen and was bound to make a move soon.

He looked at Julia, still sleeping soundly. In a very short time, she'd managed to open him up to the possibility that he could change, that there might be a way to function again after this injury, and that she might hold the answers. He brushed back the hair that had fallen across her cheek. Her skin was so soft and warm. It seemed impossible that he'd known her only a few days. There was a connection between them he couldn't explain, but he'd felt it from the moment he'd seen her waiting for them on the porch.

It wasn't just an attraction to her physical beauty but to her compassion, her tenderness, to the gentle spirit that seemed to radiate from within her. Julia had reached inside him and awoken a desire he'd thought had died. She made him long for more, to seek out what he'd once had and to restore the man he'd been. She made him want to hope again.

Dylan let the tip of his finger brush the shell over her ear, and she sighed quietly in her sleep. Tango looked up, lifting his head from the floor, but lay right back down. Dylan was finding it more difficult to remember why he shouldn't just kiss her with each passing second, why he couldn't take this step toward normalcy, especially with someone as special as Julia. The music from the end credits of the movie played. This was what he'd always wanted—someone to sit and eat pizza with, who was content just to hang out and watch a movie on the couch.

Julia's eyes opened slowly, still hazy with sleep, and she looked up at him innocently. She rubbed her eyes, and that sweet smile was instantly on her lips. "Did I fall asleep?" She stifled a yawn. "I'm sorry, I—"

Dylan didn't give her a chance to say anything else. He tipped her chin up and leaned forward, brushing his lips against hers gently.

Chapter Seven

JULIA GASPED AS Dylan's lips touched hers. She'd been thinking about this all night, even dreamed about it, but never thought she'd wake to find his hands stroking the edge of her jaw. His thumb traced the hollow of her cheek and she leaned into him, wanting more but afraid to ask for it. She felt Dylan tense as her hand lifted to his face, the rasp of his unshaved cheek sending fire through her veins and coiling in her chest. Tango moved at her feet, and she gave him a hand command to stay. There was no way she was allowing the dog to interrupt this again.

Dylan's lips were soft and gently insistent, but his arms were confident as they moved around her back, pulling her closer as he deepened the kiss like a man drowning. She clung to him, winding her arms around his neck, letting him lead the way. It had been so long since she'd felt any sort of yearning that she wasn't sure whether to pull back or give more. She let Dylan guide her as he nipped at her lips, plucking them between his, stealing her breath and her ability to think. She was dizzy when he drew back only far enough to lean his forehead against hers. The sigh that escaped him was warm on her face.

She could see the turmoil in his eyes. She wasn't sure whether it was regret or doubt, but she didn't want to hear him try to apologize. "Dylan, it's okay."

His eyes were hot when they met hers. She saw the doubt in them but she also saw desire, and he didn't try to hide it. "What is?"

"It's just a kiss." She was ignoring the fact that her heart was still racing, pounding against her ribs as her pulse burned through her veins.

He laughed but there was nothing pleasant about it. The sound was hollow and sad. "Is it? Is it *just* a kiss?" He tipped her chin up so she was forced to meet his gaze. She felt scorched by the heat she saw there. She'd wanted him to open up, to allow her a glimpse of his vulnerability. Now that he did, it frightened her. "Because that wasn't just some kiss."

"I know." She hadn't meant to whisper the words, but they fell from her lips without her bidding. "But…"

Dylan didn't let her finish what she'd been about to say. His lips sought hers again, asking more of her without demanding, seeking what she wanted to give him freely.

Dylan leaned toward her, his hand at the base of her neck, his lips finding the hollow behind her ear, and she arched against him. He groaned deep in his chest, and she trembled in response, her body on fire from the simple touch. She'd never felt this way with any man before, but Dylan wasn't like any man she'd ever known. Her fingers trailed over the side of his neck, and she felt his scar under her fingertips.

Dylan froze, every muscle in his torso tensed, as if ready to bolt. She could read his expression as if she were hearing the thoughts running through his head. "Dylan, don't."

He clenched his jaw under her hand. "Don't what?"

"Don't shut me out." She heard the pleading note in her voice. "Please?"

"Julia," he whispered, his voice strained almost to the point of being hoarse. "I'm broken."

She wasn't sure how deep his scars went beyond those he'd covered with the tattoos, or what other injuries he'd sustained, but it didn't matter to her. She was beyond the point of thinking with her head. It might be another mistake, but Dylan made her want to trust herself again.

Julia let her fingertips trace the tattoo on his neck and to his collarbone where it disappeared beneath his shirt. "This doesn't define you unless you let it." She laid her open palm against his chest, over his heart. "This defines who you are, and this"—she ran her fingers over his head—"decides who you'll become. We're all broken, Dylan. Don't let one bad experience outweigh the good ones."

Before he could push her away, she leaned toward him. But instead of kissing him, she let her lips fall on the scarred flesh. She knew she didn't see him the way he saw himself. His vision was skewed, the way hers had been after the attack that landed her in the hospital with 141 stitches and three broken bones. Dylan had covered the scars he could see, but he had never tended to the ones inside.

Dylan bent his head forward, his hand tipping her chin up so she looked into his eyes. "I'm not sure what miracle brought me here, but right now I'm not going to refuse the gift."

He pressed a soft kiss to her lips, and she tucked her head into the curve of his neck, content to feel his breath warming her cheek, to feel his strong heartbeat under her hand. The muscles of his chest twitched, and he wound his arms around her, drawing her closer. Tingles of pleasure spiraled through her chest and centered in her belly, pooling in places that left her wanting more. Julia's hand slid to his stomach and rested over the hard muscles beneath. She felt him sigh.

"Woman, are you trying to test my self-control?" The husky rasp of his voice was dangerous, but she could feel him smile against the top of her head.

She couldn't help but feel intoxicated by the admission because she was barely holding back from throwing herself at him. It went against everything she believed, or at least what she'd thought she held true. She might not subscribe to fairy tales, but she couldn't explain the connection between them or understand the way the air seemed to sizzle when he was in the room. It was the best way she could describe his presence—electrifying—and she found herself wanting to be shocked.

"I can't imagine you ever losing control, Dylan," she whispered against his skin and felt the goosebumps break out over his forearm.

He groaned quietly. "There's a first time for everything." He ran his hand down her arm, and she shivered against him. "I have a feeling this is something neither of us expected, so we should probably take it slow."

She tipped her head back to look up at him. "Well, that's not something you hear every day."

He pinched her chin between his thumb and finger, his eyes growing somber. "I don't want to hurt you."

"You won't, Dylan," she assured him. It wasn't in him. He might not see it, but he was a good man, ready to shoulder responsibilities, even those that weren't his to own. He was too filled with self-deprecation to see his true worth, and words, no matter how honest, wouldn't change his view. But maybe, she could help him see who he really was again.

JULIA WOKE ON the couch with a throw blanket wrapped around her. She stretched her stiff muscles to work out the kinks from sleeping in an odd position, and tried to remember why she was on the sofa. She saw Tango lying between the living room and the kitchen, listening to the sound of pots and pans clanging in the kitchen, his head cocked to the side. Memories of last night flooded back—the touch of Dylan's hands on her skin, the yearning that flooded her veins, the way she fell into a deep sleep against his chest, safe and content with his arms wrapped around her and his heart beating in her ear.

She rose and made her way to the kitchen, seeing him searching the pantry. "Looking for something?"

He stood and her mouth went dry as she stared at his broad, bare chest. She tried to swallow, but it caught in her throat. The man was an Adonis. Hell, he'd make Adonis wish he was Dylan. Muscles rippled as the light filtering in through the windows highlighted every taut crevice and hollow of his body. Her eyes fell to the tattoo that she could now see swirled over one pectoral and the ribs below. He stalked toward her like a panther that'd spotted its prey but a grin curved his lips.

"Good morning, sleepyhead." His hand found her chin, and he tipped her face up to drop a quick kiss on her nose.

It was *not* where she wanted him to kiss her, but she couldn't find her voice to say so. She was barely able to breathe.

"I'm trying to fix pancakes, but I ended up with batter on my T-shirt and now I can't find the syrup." He turned to move back to the pantry.

Julia reached out her hand, grasping his, and pulled him back toward her. She hit the wall of his chest and wound her hands around his neck. Standing on tiptoe, not giving him a chance to escape, she pressed her lips against his. His skin was hot against her, burning through her T-shirt and scorching her. When he slid his tongue against hers, she wanted to melt into a pool of molten desire at his feet.

She wasn't supposed to feel this way, had thought she would remain the single "dog lady" forever, and then he'd waltzed in and sent her entire world into a chaotic tailspin. It excited her; it scared her. But, even if she'd wanted to run, his hands buried into her hair, cupping the back of her head, wouldn't let her. She ran her hands over his shoulders and down his chest to rest at his waist, needing to touch him, to feel his skin under her fingers. His hands slid down her spine to her lower back, slipping under her T-shirt to send electric pleasure over every nerve ending.

Dylan pulled her body closer even as his lips released hers and he fought to catch his breath. She laid her head against his chest, pressing soft kisses to his skin. "So much for taking it slow," he murmured against her hair. "You're dangerous."

She smiled against him. He had no idea the fantasies that were wreaking havoc in her mind. How she wanted to tear her shirt off, to find out what sort of fun they could have with the syrup—things she had never imagined before, she wanted to try with Dylan. That made him far more dangerous to her well-being. She wanted to lose herself in him, and she'd made that mistake with only one other man.

But Evan had never made her feel the way Dylan did. With him, there had been danger—but because he exuded unpredictability. She'd once thought his spontaneity charming, until he turned on her. And Misty.

Dylan must have felt the shift in her thoughts, and he ran a hand over her back. "You okay?"

"I'm sorry." She tried to extract herself from his embrace, but he wouldn't let her. "I don't know what came over me."

Dylan looked at her, his eyes dark with longing but tinged with worry. "Don't be sorry. I'm not."

"I'm not usually like this."

"I know, Julia."

"I mean, I don't usually throw myself..." She didn't finish her sentence. She didn't want to voice the words he must be thinking.

"I know you don't," he interrupted.

She managed to move away from him and retrieved the syrup from the pantry. "How would you know? I could be the world's biggest slut. We only just met a few days ago."

"Sure." Dylan let his brows shift skyward. "And I could be a criminal mastermind. Or a superhero. Or—"

"A psycho who's going to turn on me when it's time to leave," she blurted.

"What?"

She could see she'd shocked him, and now that she'd opened Pandora's box, she was going to have to tell him the entire story. She didn't want to talk about it. What in the world had ever possessed her to say anything?

Fear.

The one word rang through her mind. She was so afraid of falling in love and being wrong again that she would rather sabotage any chance of a relationship before it happened. She was so afraid that pain would follow, she would rather avoid it at all costs.

Dylan wasn't Evan. Rationally, she knew that. But her fear wouldn't retract its claws. As he took a step toward her, she backed up.

"Julia, come here." He reached for her hand, and this time she let him take it, feeling that now-familiar heat settle in her stomach. Dylan pulled out a chair and took the one across from her. Tango came to her side and laid his head into her lap.

"I'm not going to ask you what happened, but I'll listen if you ever want to talk about it." He shook his head and looked down at their hands, running his thumb over the back of hers. "I told you last night, I don't want to hurt you. I will do anything to avoid that." He looked up, his dark eyes showing the agony she could hear in his voice. "Even if that means leaving now." Julia felt her heart stop and plummet.

"I don't know what this is or where it's going, but I know this isn't…" He paused, searching for the best way to convey what he felt. "Julia, I've never felt like this, not this quickly. It's like there is something that bonds us. But, I don't know how much I have to offer you."

His vulnerability surprised her. She hadn't expected him to open up, to be as honest as he was. She understood his confusion. She felt as if she'd known him for years instead of days. The thought of him leaving now, without exploring whatever this was between them, made her ache, and that ache was more painful than the fear. She laid her hand against his cheek, the morning beard growth scraping her palm as the scent of him, all male and musky, filled her nostrils. She leaned forward and kissed him gently, barely brushing her lips over his. Tango protested his head being stuck between them and pulled backward.

She smiled. "We should do something fun today for your training."

He smiled against her lips. "From the looks of your refrigerator and pantry, you need to do some grocery shopping."

She frowned. "I hate shopping," she complained.

"That settles it, shopping it is."

He wasn't wrong, and she needed to get it done. Maybe they could take Roscoe and work on his training at the store. It was something he and Dylan would need to learn to do together. She wasn't sure either of them was quite ready for it but didn't know how well that warning would go over. "Dylan, are you sure you're ready to take Roscoe out?"

"Julia, for the first time in a very long time, I feel normal. Better than normal." He rose from the chair and warmed up several pancakes in the microwave. "And it's all thanks to you and Roscoe."

She felt warmth flood her cheeks as she blushed. "But you might be taking on too much too fast."

He winked at her. "I'll have Roscoe by my side, and so far, he's been incredible at helping control my episodes. And you'll be with us. I don't think it can get any better than that."

"Are you sure you want to do this?" Julia cast a sideways glance at him from the other side of the truck. "You realize this is going to be new to him, right? Working with you in this environment?"

"It will be fine. We're going to get groceries. If it gets to be too much for either of us, we'll just come back and wait in the truck."

He didn't want her to see how nervous he was about being in a crowded store. Unfortunately, he wasn't hiding it from her well enough. Just because he and Roscoe were doing fine at Julia's, where there weren't distractions, didn't mean things would go well here. He knew she was worried about something triggering an episode, but he hadn't had one since he'd arrived. In fact, he hadn't felt this good, this productive, since before he'd been shot. Even in Afghanistan, he'd always been on high alert, waiting for an attack at any moment. Here, he'd been able to shut off the hypervigilance enough to get a full night's sleep for a second night in a row. He'd even forgotten to take his sleeping pills last night.

"I'll make you a deal," he offered, wanting to see the worry disappear from her eyes. "If all goes well here, I'll take you out to dinner tomorrow."

She pulled into the parking lot of the local Sak 'N Save and turned off her truck. Roscoe sat up between them, and she gave Dylan a half smile. "Are you asking me out on a real date?"

He opened the door and clipped Roscoe's leash on his collar. "You better believe it."

Dylan didn't miss the way her cheeks flushed with color. It was worth it to ignore the twist of guilt in his gut. He shouldn't be flirting with her, shouldn't even be attempting to pursue this. He wasn't being honest with her, not completely. And until he was, it wasn't right. But if that were the case, why didn't it feel more wrong?

She tucked her keys into her pocket and slid her purse over her arm. "You ready?"

Dylan clicked the last snap on Roscoe's vest proclaiming him as a service dog in training. "You sure the store manager won't have a problem with this?"

"I've known Rick for years and bring all of my dogs in here for training. He won't mind at all. You just need to decide what you want to eat for the next week."

Together, the three of them walked into the grocery store, and Julia grabbed a cart from the rack. Roscoe didn't even flinch at the metallic clang, instead staring up at Dylan, taking his direction.

"Be sure to talk to him," she reminded Dylan.

They made their way to the produce, and Dylan watched as she moved through each aisle. It was the first time he'd been in a store to do more than walk in and right back out. He could feel the tension in his shoulders, tightening his spine, but he fought it, wanting to prove to Julia, and himself, that he could be normal again. He and Roscoe followed a few steps behind her as she plucked celery from the shelf and dropped it into the cart. She eyed him and he could see the worry creasing the space between her eyes. He forced a lopsided grin to his lips, but it felt more like a grimace of pain.

"Are you sticking with the rabbit-food theme this week? Or just trying to starve me?"

She gave him a quiet laugh, but he could tell she was reading far more of his tenuous emotional state than he wanted her to see. "We'll get to the rest of it in good time."

After selecting bell peppers, two onions, and several prepackaged bags of salad, she moved to the dairy aisle, grabbing eggs, butter, and cheese. "Omelets for breakfast tomorrow?"

He nodded, barely listening as he scanned the aisles, noting two people at the end and one mother with her child turning into the space behind them. Roscoe whimpered and looked up at him with his golden brown eyes.

Dylan looked to Julia for instruction, but she stared at him, not the dog.

"Is Roscoe okay?"

"Are you?" she countered and he realized Roscoe was simply conveying his own reaction to the situation. He took a deep breath and let it out slowly.

I am in a grocery store. There is no threat here.

He'd been using the tactic whenever he left the house, trying to convince his body to accept what his brain was telling him. "I'm good," he assured her, knowing he was lying but unwilling to admit it.

They turned down the next aisle, and he instantly realized it was a mistake. Two women, both with young children in the carts, stood at the end of the aisle, trying to select cereal for their kids. Both sides of the aisle were stacked several shelves high with boxes. Boxes he couldn't see past. One of the kids began to wail, refusing his mother's choice of cereal. It turned into a keening cry and a high-pitched scream. Dylan froze.

In an instant, he was transported back in time. He could feel the heat of the desert wind on his skin as the sand blasted his face. He no longer saw cereal but caves cut out of the mountains as he hid within them. The cries of the child were no longer those of a two-year-old having a temper tantrum but those of the women and children they'd been sent in to evacuate when insurgents attacked an unprotected village. He could hear the bullets as they whizzed by his head and off the rocks. The dull thud as they ricocheted and met flesh.

His hand felt wet, as it had when blood had trickled into it from a bullet that grazed his elbow. A sharp pain sliced down his thigh, and he reached for his leg, wondering if he'd been shot. And then he felt the scratch again. Looking down, he saw Roscoe. But that didn't make sense, because he didn't have Roscoe in the desert.

His brain, unable to rectify the presence of the dog in his flashback, snapped back to reality. He stood in the middle of the cereal aisle, bent over, grasping his thigh as Roscoe nosed his face, flipping Dylan in the chin, adamantly licking at him. His hands were shaking and his breathing was ragged. Every muscle in his body was weak, and he wanted to slide to the floor. His flashbacks always left him feeling as if he'd just finished a marathon. The doctor explained that his body released exorbitant amounts of adrenaline during them, in response to the threat it perceived. All he knew was the two women were hurrying out of the aisle.

Dylan tried to stand, reaching for the cart to steady himself. He was left to face Julia and her disappointment in him.

"Is it finished?" Her voice was quietly reassuring, and relief flooded through him. She covered his hand with her own tentatively, as if afraid to touch him.

"Yes." His voice was a raspy whisper and his throat hurt. "Roscoe..."

He wasn't sure how to explain what had happened. How he'd followed the dog back to reality. One hand gripped the front of the cart while the other clutched the leash as if it were a lifeline. It took every bit of strength he had to keep from falling to his knees. He looked up to see one of the store clerks at the end of the aisle, looking to Julia for reassurance. She waved the clerk off as his stomach did a somersault and he was barely able to keep himself from heaving his breakfast.

She put her hand against his cheek, forcing him to look into her eyes. God, he'd never been so grateful to see a pair of sweet, brown eyes. "Let's get you out of here and back to the truck."

Julia ducked under his arm and left the groceries in the aisle, walking him out the electric doors and straight to the truck in the parking lot. She opened the passenger door, pushing him toward the seat as Roscoe sat at his feet, staring up at him anxiously. He could feel the sweat, clammy on his skin as it cooled.

"Better?"

Dylan shook his head and buried his forehead in his hands. "I don't know what...I thought I was doing better."

She ducked her head so he was forced to look at her. "You *are* doing better, Dylan. How many episodes do you usually have?"

He didn't want to admit the severity of his dysfunction to her. Wasn't it enough that it kept him from feeling like a man? Did he have to confess it to her as well? "At least one or two a day," he muttered, avoiding her eyes.

"And how long do they usually last?"

He clenched his jaw, trying to hold his temper. "I don't know. Fifteen, twenty minutes."

"Dylan, this was the first flashback you've had in at least two days, right? And it lasted less than five minutes. Roscoe recognized it as soon as you were gone and brought you right back out of it." She sounded excited, but the only emotion he could muster was frustration.

"I can't even get through a grocery store, Julia." Dylan couldn't hide the bitterness from his voice. He didn't want to take it out on her, but she sounded so damn pleased.

She stood and squared her shoulders, crossing her arms as if preparing to do verbal battle with him. "Don't you dare minimize this. That was a huge step in the right direction. Roscoe picked up on your trigger and brought you right back to the present. That may not have been a fun training exercise for you, but it was a necessary one for him. He's already connecting to you in a way I can't teach him. And you've connected to him. It's all part of the process, Dylan. Roscoe won't make the past disappear, but he will make the future promising again."

He looked down at the dog. Roscoe jumped up with his paws in Dylan's lap and laid his head over his thigh. He slid a hand to Roscoe's head.

"Don't be so damn stubborn about pouting over what went wrong that you forget to praise him for what he did right."

Chapter Eight

JULIA WAS BEGINNING to worry that the store had been a huge mistake. Dylan had remained silent since his episode in the store and when she'd come back out with the groceries. He'd unloaded the cart but had yet to speak a word. The entire ride home was in silence, and she let him brood. It frustrated her that he couldn't recognize the progress both he and Roscoe made today. Dylan having a flashback had been her worst fear realized, but Roscoe had performed his duties better than she could have ever hoped he would.

When they arrived at the house, Dylan disappeared into his room, locking the door behind him. She would have worried more if he hadn't taken Roscoe inside with him. As long as the dog was with him, she could allow him the space to process what had happened on his own, knowing Roscoe would alert her to trouble and protect Dylan from himself if the need arose. Dylan didn't need her judgment. He needed her trust.

Julia unloaded the groceries and cleaned up the kitchen before deciding he'd had enough time. She headed down the hall and knocked softly on his door. "Dylan, I'm heating up the stew. Did you want to see if Gage is coming for dinner tonight?"

She heard rustling from within the room just before he opened the door and leaned against the frame. He didn't come out, nor did he welcome her in, and his cold treatment stung. "I already called him. He said he's just going to stay and work again."

She arched a brow, wondering at Gage's obvious ploy to force them to spend time alone. She didn't want to push Dylan, but she didn't want to chance him regressing either. They certainly didn't know one another well enough for her to barge in and demand he talk to her, especially when he was already shutting her out. Literally. Julia wasn't sure how to help.

"Um, okay." She paused, hoping he'd say something. When he didn't, she tried to hide her disappointment. "If you need me, I'm going to go work the other dogs for a little while and feed them before dinner is ready."

"Okay." With that, he turned away and shut the door again with a soft click.

Julia brushed her bangs from her face and blinked back the burning in her eyes, willing herself not to cry just because Dylan wanted to be a stubborn ass.

She scolded herself. It had been a hard road for her when she'd first come home from the hospital, too. She needed to remember that and give him time and space without expecting miracles. What she really needed to do was to lose herself in her dogs for a few hours.

Two hours and several hundred commands later, Julia decided she had cuddled with each of the dogs and stalled going back into the house to face Dylan long enough. After feeding them, she decided that it was best to be completely honest with him. Maybe if he knew the truth about what she'd endured with Evan, he'd realize they shared a common ground and he'd be more likely to open up.

After a quick shower, she wound a towel around her head and slipped into a pair of yoga pants and a T-shirt. It was cool outside tonight, but the moon was high and full, and there was no reason not to enjoy dinner on her back patio. She quickly ran a comb through her wet hair and went into the kitchen, casting a glance at Dylan's room, disappointed to see the door still shut. She debated walking past without saying anything in case he wanted his privacy, but she also remembered how important it had been to her to feel connected to her siblings when she arrived home, to know she wasn't forgotten.

She tapped the door lightly with her knuckles.

"Yeah?"

As much as it hurt to have him avoid her, she felt a measure of relief when she heard his voice. "Dinner is ready whenever you are."

She wanted to invite him to join her on the patio, especially considering this would have been their date, but her pride wouldn't allow it. She laid her forehead against the door, waiting for him to answer a moment longer.

"Thanks," he called. "I'll be out in a few minutes."

Her heart sank as she headed into the kitchen and dished up her food, setting out a bowl for Dylan in case he actually surfaced. Tango followed her, sitting to watch the doorway behind her. She had no more ladled the stew into her own bowl when she felt his arms circle her waist and his lips at her neck. Electric desire warmed her core, melting her to her spot at the sink. She couldn't have moved if she wanted to. Why hadn't Tango alerted her to Dylan's presence?

"I'm sorry," he whispered against her skin, sending shivers of heat to pool between her thighs. "I just needed some time to think, to reevaluate what it was that I want." His big hands at her waist turned her to face him.

Julia couldn't meet his eyes. She was afraid of the rejection she might see there, in spite of his touch. She stared at the hollow at the base of his throat. "Julia," he whispered, tipping her chin up with a finger. "I don't want to shut you out. Especially when you've already done so much for me."

She felt her eyes mist over as she tried to swallow the lump lodged in her throat. "Dylan, I don't expect—"

He didn't let her finish as he dipped his head, taking her mouth hostage. It was a slow assault on her senses as his lips caressed hers and he sucked at her lower lip. His tongue snuck out, tasting her, teasing her, taunting her to follow. He was tender, apologetic, and so incredibly sensual that she melted against his chest, holding herself up with her hands on his shoulders. She was surrounded by the heated scent of soap and male. Dylan's arms circled her waist and wrapped around her back, lifting her into him so she felt him fully against the front of her. Every part of him was rock hard, like an impenetrable granite wall. Her entire body went liquid, need lapping at her and heating her until she thought she would explode from within.

She whimpered quietly, wanting more of him but unable to ask for it when she couldn't even form a coherent thought. She wanted to touch him, to taste him, to breathe him in, but the only sound that came from her lips was a squeak. Dylan loosened his hold on her, and she dug her fingers into his shoulders in protest, wishing he could read her mind. He slid his hand over her arm, his fingers moving into her hair, and gave her a faint, lopsided grin.

"That wasn't the way my apology was supposed to go but…" She could hear that he was still trying to catch his breath as well. "Julia, say something." He brushed his thumb over the pulse at the side of her throat.

Words, breathing—hell—any sort of brain function was beyond her as she tried to settle both feet back on the ground after his earth-shattering kiss. She could only stare up at him and wonder how to make him understand how much she wanted him.

He growled deep in his throat and closed his eyes slowly as they darkened with desire. "Julia, if you keep looking at me that way…"

He let the insinuation hang heavily in the air, and she felt it settle on her with an anticipatory hunger. "Who Let the Dogs Out" rang out through the kitchen, ruining the moment as thoroughly as if cold water had been thrown in her face. She slid the phone out of her pocket, feeling as if she was coming out of a trance, and saw her brother's picture on the screen. She glanced at Dylan, shrugging apologetically as she pushed the button on the phone.

"Julia, I'm starving. Jessie and Nathan are going out for a date tonight, and I'm just leaving the clinic. Please tell me you have food and I can stop by." She could hear the plaintive complaint in his tone. As much as he thought he watched out for them, Julia and Jessie had both spoiled their bachelor brother.

"Yes, I have some stew already heated up, you big baby. Come on over." She disconnected the call and glanced at Dylan. "Looks like we're going to have company after all. I should probably warn you about my brother."

Dylan's eyes were hot and intense, but he almost looked relieved as he turned toward the sink and dished himself a bowl of stew. "I can handle a brother far better than I can being alone with you right now."

"You only say that because you haven't met Justin yet."

DYLAN WONDERED IF he'd been too quick to assume he was ready to deal with Julia's brother. As soon as the man walked into the room, Dylan felt his judgment. He wasn't accustomed to meeting people his own size, let alone someone who probably outweighed him by thirty pounds. Justin Hart was a monster of a man whose eyes followed every move Dylan made around Julia. It was obvious that Justin adored his youngest sister, and he didn't bother to hide the fact. Nor did she, despite her many complaints about his overbearing nature.

Dylan was careful to keep his distance from her, knowing that as soon as he touched Julia, her brother would launch a full-scale attack that would make his special ops unit look like kids playing capture the flag.

Julia was uncomfortable. Her eyes shifted from one man to the other, but it was Tango who gave her away. Unable to settle at her feet, he stared up at his mistress, his eyes concerned as he laid his head on her lap.

"I'm going to get a glass of wine. Does anyone else want anything?"

"I'll take a beer if you have one," Justin answered, raising a brow at Dylan. "You?"

Dylan met his gaze and held it, weighing the ramifications of either choice. "Sure. Let me help you." He rose and followed Julia through the door into the kitchen with both dogs padding behind them.

Julia took a deep breath and released it slowly as soon as she was away from her brother. Dylan understood her discomfort, but he didn't blame her brother for being protective. She reached for a bottle of red wine in the pantry before digging in a drawer and retrieving a corkscrew.

"Beer is in the refrigerator." She gave him an apologetic smile. "I'm sorry, Dylan. I don't know why he's acting so antagonistic."

Dylan reached for two bottles of beer from the refrigerator. "You're his baby sister and he doesn't know me. I get it. I'd probably act the same way under the circumstances."

"But it's so annoying." She frowned and dug the corkscrew into the top of the bottle as he twisted the caps from the beers he held.

He leaned forward and kissed the top of her head. "A little, but he doesn't scare me."

Dylan didn't want Julia to feel awkward. They already had enough strikes against them with his issues without adding an overprotective brother to the mix, so he decided to head back out and have a chat with Justin. If nothing else, he'd let him know he was making Julia uncomfortable. Dylan held the bottle out to Justin as he walked past him and sat in the only chair that faced him, letting his own beer hang from his fingers between his knees.

"You don't like me, I get that. I can even respect that, but could you at least show your sister some gratitude for her hospitality and stop making her feel like her every move is being scrutinized?"

Justin took a long draw from the bottle and met Dylan's gaze, his brows climbing high on his forehead. "Not a man to mince words, huh?"

"I just wanted to get that off my chest before your sister came back out."

Justin nodded but didn't appear any friendlier. "Then let me get something off my chest. I don't like you staying here. I didn't like it when I heard there were two of you staying, and I really don't like it now that you're with her here alone." Justin's blue eyes gleamed with ferocity. "If anything happens to her, if you hurt her in any way, I *will* kill you."

Dylan didn't take his threat lightly, but he wasn't scared by it either. "I wouldn't blame you."

BY THE TIME she had composed herself and poured a glass of wine, Julia was ready to go back outside and give her brother a piece of her mind. He had no right in being such a jerk, in her house, to her *client*, when she was the one feeding his pathetic butt. The rumble of male laughter floated into the kitchen, and she leaned closer to the door to hear what was going on out there. Tango cocked his head as if he was trying to listen, too.

"She only *seems* sweet and innocent. I'm warning you, Dylan, don't piss her off. She's like a rabid possum that's been cornered when she doesn't get her way."

"No way." She heard the doubt in Dylan's voice. "Julia?"

"She's mellowed out since…well, since she got Tango." Justin paused for a moment as if losing his train of thought. "But, when she was little, man, she and Jessie made my life hell. There was this one time—"

"Okay, I think that's enough bonding time for the two of you." She pushed open the door and broke up the gossip session.

"I was just going to tell him about the time you and Jessie shaved my eyebrows for being mean to your prom dates." Justin tried to look innocent, his blue eyes wide, but the smirk on his face belied the attempt.

"Yeah, and that story always leads back to what you did in retaliation."

He laughed and tipped his bottle toward her. "You deserved to have those baby pictures plastered all over the lockers."

Her mouth opened in outrage. "Those weren't baby pictures, you jerk. I was seven and going through an awkward phase."

"Yeah, you were." Justin tipped his bottle and polished off the beer, grinning like an idiot. Dylan couldn't help but laugh at the banter between the two of them.

Julia glared at Justin. "I think it's time for you to go."

Justin looked at his watch. "You're right. Come shut the gate behind me?"

"Fine," she said dramatically, and sighed. Dylan raised his brows and looked at the beer, still in Justin's hands. "Justin is on the other side of my part of the property. He and Jessie have me pretty well sandwiched between them where they can keep an eye on me." She rolled her eyes. "I'll be right back."

Dylan rose and shook Justin's hand. It's wasn't exactly a friendly handshake, but there was far less animosity than had been there during dinner. Julia made a mental note to ask Dylan about it later.

She held open the gate as her brother drove through, braking as he came up beside her and rolling down the window. "I like him, Julia. He seems like a good guy."

She hooked one arm over the edge of the gate. "Why? Because he wasn't afraid of you?"

Justin shrugged but his eyes were grave. "I'm not sure. I guess because I get the feeling he could protect you even better than I can."

She wanted to tell her brother she didn't need anyone's protection, especially with Tango around, but she knew it was a lie. She hadn't told Justin yet about Evan's reappearance, and he was going to hit the roof when he found out she'd kept it a secret. He'd been like a warden during the trial. If he knew Evan was out and had come by the property, he'd camp out on her porch. All the more reason to keep quiet a bit longer.

"I don't suppose you'll be fixing breakfast tomorrow?"

Julia rolled her eyes and shook her head, laughing. "Typical Justin, always thinking with your stomach. Yes, you can come by in the morning."

"Love you, sis." She watched the taillights of his truck as they faded in the distance over the worn dirt trail between their houses. Making the road between the three houses had been Justin's idea, and she still thought it was one of his best.

She looked down at Tango, sitting at her side. "What do you think, big boy? Think it's time to finally tell Dylan what happened? Or you think that will make it worse?"

"You're not giving Dylan much credit."

She jumped and spun to find him walking toward her with Roscoe at his side. "Tango, you are supposed to alert me," she scolded. At least the dog had the good sense to look shamed, although it didn't last long. His big tail thumped against her leg as Dylan came closer.

"He likes me." Dylan reached out and slipped his hand around hers. "Let's go back to the house and you can decide whether or not to tell me."

"Dylan, it's not that I don't want to tell you," she tried to explain.

"You just don't know if it would make it worse?" She could hear the hurt in his voice, but he was misunderstanding, and she wasn't sure how best to explain it.

She didn't talk about Evan. In fact, until his text, she did everything possible to avoid thinking about him altogether. It had taken years of working through the mental anguish he'd caused, as well as the fear that dogged her. The last thing she wanted was to relive that agony, even in the retelling. But, more than anything else, she didn't want to dredge up Dylan's memories. She didn't want him to feel obligated to tell her about the nightmare that had led him to her doorstep. When—*if*—he opened up to her, she wanted him to do it without reservations.

Her ringtone suddenly sounded in the near darkness, and she tugged the phone from her pocket. *Unknown*. She sent the call to voice mail and silence surrounded them again. She was just about to put her phone back in her pocket when it rang again. She frowned and glanced at Dylan as she answered it.

"Hello, Heart Fire Training."

The sound of a ragged breath rattled over the cell phone line. Her heart immediately began to race. "Hello?"

"You're still mine, Julia. And he won't stop me from having you."

She dropped the phone as the line disconnected.

Chapter Nine

"Get low and get inside. Take Tango and wait for me in the living room." He picked up the phone and pressed it into her hand. Dylan slid his own from his pocket and dialed her number. "Stay on the line with me. I'll be right there," Dylan urged her, guiding her through the front door. "Stay low."

"Dylan," she whispered, her voice catching. "Where are you going?"

"Just to the kennel to check on the dogs. They're too quiet. If he's close enough to see us, and it sounds like he is, they should be barking." He saw understanding light in her eyes. "I'll be right back, and I'll be on the phone."

"Fine, but take Roscoe."

Dylan looked at the dog. He wasn't sure he wouldn't give his position away, but he was more worried about slipping into an episode that would render him useless when Julia needed him most. "Okay," he agreed.

She nodded and went inside. He heard the soft click of the lock behind her. He slid the phone to his ear. "Good. Now, go lock the other doors. Keep Tango with you."

"Like he'd leave my side. Tango, watch," he heard her command.

"If he acts like anything is wrong, you get out." He moved into the shadows on the side of the house, blending in with them completely and moving to the back patio. His eyes scanned the backyard. He saw her move the blinds at the back door as she locked it. "Okay, the backyard is clear. Go back to the living room and wait for me to knock on the front door. Stay quiet unless something happens."

"Be careful." There was a slight tremor in her voice, but Dylan could hear the stubborn strength he knew she possessed.

He ran through the trees at the back of the property, grateful for the training he'd already done with Roscoe, who remained glued to his side unless told to wait. Dylan crept along the edge of the kennel and heard one of the dogs start barking before several more joined in the chorus. He moved inside the door, and the dogs hurried to the front of their runs, expectantly. He scanned each dog and run, looking for any signs of someone present or distress in the animals. Not that he could read them well, but he assumed they wouldn't be barking at the entrance as if they wanted to play if something were amiss. He made his way into the kitchen and flipped on the light. The entire kennel was clear.

Dylan lifted the phone to his ear. "Julia, you there?"

"Yes. Are the dogs okay?"

He flipped off the light and signaled Roscoe to heel as he headed back for the house. "Everything is fine. It could have been a lucky guess. It doesn't look like anyone was in here."

"Good." He heard her breathe a sigh of relief into the phone, even as he heard a low growl in the background. "Tango, hush. I thought you said you were coming in the front door?"

"What?" Cold fear choked the breath from him as he waited for her response.

"Why are you at the back door?"

Dylan shoved the phone into his pocket and bolted into a dead run for the backyard, launching himself at the fence and over the top without even thinking. Roscoe was right behind him, at a full run, barking the entire way. The gate at the other end of the yard clamped shut and he heard the sound of gravel crunching under feet as someone crashed through the shrubs and down the driveway. As much as he wanted to continue to chase the intruder, he didn't want to leave Julia alone at the house, so he slowed. Roscoe, however, had other ideas and continued running past Dylan after the prowler.

"Roscoe, come," he called. There was the roar of an engine and a growl before he heard a quick, pained yip. The buzz of a motorcycle engine grew distant and Roscoe returned, limping but with a scrap of bloody denim between his teeth. Dylan squatted down to catch his breath and took the material from the dog's mouth. "Good boy." He rubbed the dog's head as he panted. "Come on, let's get back to the house."

"Julia?" He looked at the phone screen to make sure they hadn't been disconnected. "Julia?"

She came running through the front door and down the porch steps, throwing herself against his chest. She slapped at his arm. "What the hell were you thinking, you maniac? You could have been killed!"

Dylan reached for her wrists to stop the assault and saw the tears reflected in the moonlight. "Julia, I'm fine."

"But he could have killed you," she repeated, amid barks and yips from both dogs as they tried to press between the couple.

Dylan pulled her into his arms, his confidence returned. "I've had far more skilled killers try, and they didn't succeed."

"Ugh!" She shoved at his chest then turned her back on him, heading toward the house. She spun on him again. "Do you have any idea how scared I was when you took off after him?"

Dylan clenched his jaw. "He was trying to get into the house. Did you think I was going to let him hurt you? I'd kill him first." He pulled her toward him, enveloping her. "And, trust me, I know hundreds of ways to make it as painful as possible."

He heard the murderous tone of his voice and tried to control it. The last thing he wanted was to scare her. "Julia, I promised not to hurt you, remember?" He brushed back the bangs that fell into her eyes. "That includes not letting anyone else hurt you *because* of me."

She collapsed against him, laying her head against his chest in complete trust. "Dylan," she whispered as she wrapped her arms around his waist, letting her tears soak through his shirt.

He knew it was the effect of the adrenaline on her. Now that the fear had run its course, she would feel completely drained. He could already feel it happening to him. However, he wasn't about to let her see that.

"Come on. Let's get you inside." Dylan bent and scooped her up as if she didn't weigh any more than Roscoe. But Roscoe wouldn't wind smooth arms around his neck or curl against him. Julia sent heat invading parts of his body that needed to remain unaffected right now. Unfortunately, he couldn't stop the emotions winding themselves around his heart. She made him want to protect her, even at the risk of his own sanity, which, oddly enough, seemed to remain intact only when she was present.

DYLAN LAID HER down on top of her comforter in her room and started to leave. "No," she pleaded, reaching for his hand. "Stay for just a little while."

Julia didn't remember ever being as scared for someone's safety as she had been when she saw Dylan running down her driveway. Anything could have happened to him. She knew better than to underestimate Evan. She'd made that mistake once, with dire consequences. She had to tell Dylan the truth. Now that Evan had set his sights on Dylan, he deserved to know what he was up against.

Tango jumped onto the bed and curled up at her feet, commandeering the bottom corner of the bed. Dylan locked her bedroom door and kicked off his shoes, letting them fall to the floor. Without hesitating, he curled himself around the back of her and wrapped her in his arms, pressing his lips to her temple.

"Roscoe, watch," he commanded, and she was awed at how well he'd picked up on her training techniques. Roscoe sat at the end of the bed, facing the door. "Okay, it's time for you to sleep."

"I can't." She was exhausted but her mind wouldn't settle. There was too much she had to explain to him, too much to warn him about. "Dylan, I—"

"Shh, tell me in the morning."

She rolled over and faced him, her fingers reaching up to touch his face. The tips grazed the edge of his scar and she cringed, knowing she didn't want to cause him any more pain. She needed every bit of reassurance that he was safe. "I need to tell you now."

Dylan lowered his head and pressed a feather-light kiss to each of her eyes before brushing his lips over her forehead. "No, you don't."

"I do," she insisted, and started to press herself into a seated position on the bed. Tango raised his head to look at them.

"Okay, settle down." He brought her back down under him, brushing her hair back from her cheek, his knuckles barely caressing her skin, yet sending a shiver of longing into her belly. Her hands pressed against the pectoral muscles of his chest, and she yearned to let her fingers caress him. But desire had to wait until he knew it all.

"Evan is dangerous. More than you realize." She looked up at him, making sure he was giving her his full attention. "Dylan, I don't want you to risk your recovery because of him."

His fingers caressed her arms from the tip of her shoulder to her elbow. "Julia, the man is stalking you and you refuse to call the police. If you're this worried about my safety and my sanity, why would you risk your own?"

He was right. She was trying to convince him of the danger without admitting the danger Evan was to her. There was nothing they could do if she couldn't prove the intruder had been Evan, but if it would put Dylan's mind at ease, she'd do it. "I'll call them in the morning, I promise."

She felt the muscles of his arms relax and he lay back, stretched out, tucking her into the curve of his shoulder. "Tell me what happened."

Julia took a deep breath and stared at the center of his chest. She plucked at his T-shirt, stalling to find a way to make the story easier to tell. "I told you about how Evan came here to get a dog to help with his diabetes, and how about two weeks into training, he started acting strange."

Dylan didn't say anything, but his hands traced patterns on her back, along her spine, and over her arm. It would have been relaxing under any other circumstances. She worried at his lack of participation in the conversation already.

"I didn't tell you that we dated briefly." She felt him stiffen under her hands. "It wasn't serious and it was short-lived, only three dates, when he started trying to force me to…" Julia took a deep breath and dug her nails into her palms, forcing herself to stay in the moment. "He wanted more than I would give. When I said no, he started acting out. Misty, his dog, began growling at him and refusing to work with him. One night he was standing in my room over my bed while I was sleeping. I ordered him to leave the property. He refused, apologized, and blamed it on his medical issues."

"You believed him?" It was the first words he'd spoken since she began. She looked up at him, and relief coursed through her when she saw the compassion in his eyes.

"Yes. I guess I just didn't want to believe that anyone would deliberately do something so creepy." She closed her eyes, pressing her face against the hard wall of his chest, drawing from the steady heartbeat she could hear within him. "Two days later, we took Misty out to do some work in the woods, and he grabbed me and pushed me against a tree."

She felt him tense under her hands, matching the tension she could feel in her own body. But she had to get this out, to purge the poison from her mind again. "I hit my head and everything went blurry. He tried to force himself on me again, but Misty...she turned on him. First, she bit into his leg and he kicked her."

The memories came flooding back. The pain radiating through her head, her vision too blurred to get away, the nausea, the yelp of pain when his foot connected with Misty's ribs as she tried to protect Julia. She had no idea how she managed to remain conscious long enough to run back to the house while Misty held him off, or where she found her cell phone. But she clearly remembered Evan's attack when he followed her inside and found out she'd called the police.

"I told him I called the cops. I thought that would scare him away. Instead, it made him more violent." She couldn't meet his gaze, even knowing he wasn't likely to judge her. "It was stupid. I should have locked the bedroom door and hidden." She closed her eyes, trying to steel herself against falling into the memories. "I didn't see it coming when he swung at me. Then Misty came in through the dog door in the back."

"He hit you?" His voice rumbled low in his chest, almost a ferocious growl.

Julia nodded. "Several times. When he threw me onto the bed, Misty stood over me, trying to protect me. She attacked him and must have been able to stop him. The police found him bleeding at the end of the hall with Misty lying in front of my bedroom doorway." She could barely bring herself to say the next words. "Justin couldn't save her."

Dylan held her to his chest, a hand brushing over her hair. She could feel his body trembling beneath her, and she looked up at him. She could see fury in his eyes, but it wasn't directed at her. His lips were pinched into a thin line. "What happened when the police arrived?"

"I don't know. I woke in the hospital a few days later. They kept me out for a few days because there had been a lot of swelling on my brain. Apparently, Justin said it was touch-and-go the first few days."

Dylan ran a finger over the scar at her hairline. "That's how you got this?" Julia nodded. "Did he…"

She shook her head. "They checked at the hospital and said no. I think Misty chased him out and wouldn't let him back inside." Her tears fell against his chest, wetting his T-shirt. "She died protecting me."

Her breath caught in her throat and the sobs came. She couldn't have said more if she'd wanted to, but it wasn't necessary. Dylan seemed to understand that what she needed most was to be held, to release the pain and sorrow and regret. He pressed his lips over her forehead, touching them to her scar before looking into her eyes.

"I promise you are safe tonight. Nothing is going to touch you while I'm here."

Julia clung to him, her arms around his waist as her tears continued to fall. She wasn't sure when they stopped. She was only aware of the strong foundation she lay against, the steady heartbeat in her ear, as she floated into the sweet oblivion of sleep.

I WILL KILL *the man.*

Dylan had saved lives. It was his job to rescue fallen soldiers, to protect the sanctity of life. But if he ever saw Evan again, if he got the chance to be close enough to get his hands on him, the only thing on Dylan's mind would be which painful method he would choose to murder the man. That monster made what he'd faced in Afghanistan seem easy. At least there, Dylan had been prepared for the evil he faced. He'd known he was in enemy territory, and that danger was as much a part of living as breathing. But Evan had been welcomed into Julia's home; she'd tried to help him. All the while, her enemy had been lurking beneath the friendly surface.

He ducked his chin to look at her. She'd cried herself to sleep, but her tears still burned against his skin, burned his heart. With what had already happened, why hadn't she called the police as soon as Evan texted her? She had to have assumed the man would only escalate his attempts to get close to her again. He'd nearly killed her the last time. Would have, if it hadn't been for the dog.

Dylan glanced down at Roscoe, sleeping on his side of the bed. He knew if he were to reach out his hand, the dog would immediately be under his fingers. As if knowing Dylan's attention was on him, Roscoe opened an eye and met his gaze. Dylan gave him the hand cue to stay. In only a few days, he and the dog had connected more than he'd thought possible. How bad must things have been for Evan's dog, who was likely just as connected to him as Roscoe was to Dylan, to turn on him and die protecting Julia?

Julia stirred against him, and he realized his fingers were digging into her waist. He relaxed his grip and tried to focus, reminding himself that until he got his hands on this man, he had to control the rage that pulsed through his veins. Tango whined at the end of the bed and moved his head to lie over Julia's feet, looking right into Dylan's eyes with his whiskey-colored gaze, as if he understood and agreed that, together, they would protect her to the death.

Chapter Ten

JULIA TRIED TO blink, but her eyes felt swollen and caked with sand. She groaned as she forced them open, and her hand slid over the soft cotton by her head. Her fingers touched solid muscle and warm flesh.

This isn't my pillow.

She started to sit up, but she was held in place by strong arms. A moment of panic started to take root until the memories of last night came flooding back to her. She lifted her eyes slowly, not sure what to expect from Dylan but hoping he was sleeping and she could sneak away.

"Good morning, beautiful." He brushed her bangs back and stared down into her eyes. "I probably should have woken you a few hours ago, but you looked so content, I wasn't about to ruin that peace for you."

"What time is it?"

She curled her fingers in front of her mouth, feeling incredibly self-conscious. Had she snored? Did her breath stink? Had she really soaked his shirt crying last night? Her father's voice echoed in her head—*Cowgirl up*.

She and her sister had heard the phrase their entire lives. Her father, Colton Hart, had taught his daughters that they were just as strong as any cowboy. He had instilled in them the ability to buck up under whatever circumstances life threw at them and move on with their heads held high, even though at times it had made him seem callous.

"Time to make a call to the police station."

"Dylan," she began, but the look on his face stopped her.

He couldn't understand her desire to not start the entire fiasco again. She hadn't told him about the drama that ensued when people found out about the attack, the media circus that had surrounded her family. Most of the people who'd grown up knowing the Harts stood by her, but those who hadn't, mostly outsiders, insinuated it was her fault, that she was stupid and naive to have allowed a male client to stay at her home. She hadn't wanted to admit that they were likely right, but there wasn't really another way to work with her clients. She'd been publicly crucified, even before the trial.

She was afraid of Evan, afraid of how easily he'd fooled her, afraid of what he could do again, especially now that he was out for retaliation and declaring ownership of her. He had nothing left to lose, and that, in combination with his deranged mental state, was a dangerous combination. She pushed herself up and swung her legs over Tango and off the side of the bed.

Dylan sat up and reached for his phone. "Don't tell me you're not going to call. If you don't, I will."

His voice didn't allow for argument, but that didn't mean she was going to acquiesce easily. He had to realize what calling would entail.

"Are you ready to leave so soon? Because if I call them, that's what will have to happen. You'll have to go stay in town with your brother. I can't have that circus again, Dylan. You have no idea how horrible it was once the media got wind that there was a story."

She could see understanding dawn on him. His eyes grew fierce, the way they had when she told him about Evan's attack last night. "It wasn't the locals, it was everyone else," she said. "If they find out that you're staying here, alone... You can imagine what people will say, even if it's all untrue."

She ran her hands through her blonde hair and pulled it back into a messy ponytail, reaching for a hair tie on the nightstand, and stood up. Tango jumped off the bed, and she brushed at her T-shirt.

"Then Gage can come back."

She shook her head, a caustic laugh breaking over her lips. "Yeah, because staying with *two* men would look so much better."

"There has to be some sort of answer, Julia. You can't *not* call the police. You said the locals weren't—"

"All we have in town is a small sheriff's way station. They'll send one of the deputies out and then call the main office, which puts me right back where I started. It won't make a difference anyway. I know it was Evan, but I can't prove it. He's dangerous, but he's not stupid. He knows I can't prove he violated the restraining order. The most the police can do is watch him."

"If they're watching him, he can't hurt you," Dylan pointed out. "Where did you stay after the last attack? I know your brother wouldn't have let you stay here alone."

Julia shook her head. "No, he came and stayed here for a few weeks. But I can't ask him—"

"Fine," Dylan interrupted. "I'll tell him that Evan texted you the other day and you chose not to tell anyone about it. I'm sure that will go over with him like a lead balloon."

He'd met her brother only last night, but she knew they'd gotten along, at least as well as her brother would with any man who might have kissed one of his sisters. She glared at him, knowing he wouldn't think twice about ratting her out to Justin. "I knew better than to introduce the two of you. You're two peas in a pod."

Dylan moved around the bed and pulled her back into his embrace. His lips brushed against hers in a breath of a kiss. It was all she could do to keep from twining her arms around his neck and pulling him down to her, losing herself in the warm tremors that broke out over her flesh when he touched her. "Because we both want to protect you? Because neither of us wants to see you hurt?"

"No," she said on a breath against his lips as she smiled. "You're both pains in the ass."

"What's going on?" Justin eyed the two of them, and Julia cursed the fact that he knew her well enough to see her anxiety.

"More pancakes?" She slid the syrup his direction.

"Stop stalling and tell me what's going on." He arched a brow and looked at Dylan. "I swear if you—"

"It's Evan," she interrupted, and watched her brother's face go pale. She hated that worry had creased his brows and that she was the reason for it.

"What about him?"

"He's contacted Julia." Dylan spoke before she could break the news to her brother. She glared at him, but Justin jumped up from the table, knocking the chair over as he reached for his phone in his pocket.

"Stop, Justin." She reached for his arm, but he jerked it from her grasp. Roscoe and Tango both jumped to a standing position. "You can't call anyone."

"I'm calling the police." Justin glared at Dylan. "Why haven't you called them?"

"Because your sister refuses to call and go through that media frenzy again." Dylan shook his head and slipped the phone from between Justin's fingers, standing to face him down. "And she's right. If she can't prove it was Evan, they can't do anything."

"This isn't something you can shove under the rug, Julia. That guy is dangerous." Justin worked his jaw, barely containing his self-control. "Give me my phone."

"Not until you sit down and listen to what she has to say."

"Who the hell are you to tell me what is best for my sister? You probably don't even know the entire story." Justin shoved his hands against Dylan's shoulders, but she was surprised he didn't even budge. The two of them stared at one another like dogs preparing for a fight.

"Stop, both of you." She slipped between them but faced her brother. "I need a favor."

"For me to call the police? Sure thing." He held out his hand, waiting for his phone.

Julia sighed at her brother. As much as she adored him, at times he was nothing more than an overbearing child. "I will call the sheriff, but only if you come stay here. Gage will come back as well. I'm also thinking of asking Bailey to come stay." She shook her head, still convinced this was a bad idea. "I'm just worried about putting everyone in danger."

Justin reached for her shoulders, but his touch was warm as he pulled her into a hug. "Julia, you don't even need to ask." He leaned toward her ear and whispered, "I'd already planned on moving in until Dylan's gone. We've been down this road once; that was enough."

Disappointment flooded her. He didn't trust her. He thought she was going to make the same mistake with Dylan that she'd made with Evan, and he wanted to keep a close eye on her. He wasn't wrong. She was falling for a client, hard, but Dylan wasn't like Evan.

Justin pulled away from her and looked at Dylan behind her. She couldn't see his face, but she could practically feel the tension radiating from both of them and wondered if Dylan hadn't heard what Justin had whispered. "Don't worry, sis, with all of us here, only a fool would try anything."

She wasn't sure if Justin was talking about Evan, or trying to warn Dylan to keep his distance.

DYLAN'S GAZE DIDN'T waver as he glared at Justin over Julia's head. The double meaning of Justin's statement wasn't lost on him. He'd heard Justin's comment to Julia, and his fist clenched at his side to keep from punching the man square in the mouth. How dare he make Julia feel as if their relationship might be a mistake? To insinuate that he wasn't any better than Evan?

"I'm going to call Gage and tell him to come back."

He wanted to reach out to her, to pull Julia into his embrace and carry her back to the bedroom, where they could hide from the world, from crazy exes and overprotective, judgmental siblings, but this was real life. And real life didn't allow time for fantasies now.

Or later.

He ignored the thought, pushed it away forcefully, and pulled his cell phone from his pocket, dialing his brother. Gage picked up on the second ring.

"Hey, what's up?"

"I need you to come back here and stay."

"Miss me already?" his brother teased. When Dylan didn't answer, worry tinged Gage's voice. "What happened? Is everything okay?"

It bothered him that his brother immediately assumed something had gone wrong, most likely that it was Dylan's doing. Or maybe he was just reading too much into the comment.

"It's a long story, but Julia needs our help. She's got a stalker ex, and he's back on the prowl. I'll explain it when you get here. Hopefully, you beat the police."

He heard the phone shift and shuffling of papers before a laptop snapped shut. "I'm on my way."

"Okay. And Gage," he added, "thanks for the push, man."

"Anytime."

JULIA SAT AT the kitchen table while Deputy Chase McKee jotted down his notes. She'd been thrilled when she saw Chase exit the patrol car. He'd grown up in town and worked as a deputy under his father's supervision. His nonjudgmental questions helped to lighten the overwhelming desire Julia had to hide from everyone. Tango laid his head on her thigh, and she rested her hand behind his ear.

"Are you sure it was him, Julia?"

"Last night? No," she confessed. "I didn't see him or the vehicle he had, but there was someone here and they tried to get into the house. And Evan did text and call me."

"And you're completely sure it was him on the phone?"

She met his curious green eyes. "I'll never forget his voice, Chase. That was him."

Chase closed his report folder and stood up. "I'll get this report filled out and I'll try to keep a lid on things for you." His eyes turned sympathetic. "Dad told me it got pretty bad during the trial. I'm sorry I wasn't here to help you more, but right now, we're the only two who know."

"Thanks, Chase." She looked down at the dog still lying over her lap. Chase reached over and patted Tango.

"Everything else is okay? Justin is staying, too, right?" She nodded. "I'll have to dust the door. Hopefully I can get a clean print." He looked out the window where Dylan, Gage, and Justin all waited on the front porch, giving them privacy to talk. "No Bailey today?"

"She's coming over after she's finished helping her dad at the car dealership." She might be preoccupied with her own worries, but she didn't miss the way Chase perked up when he asked about her cousin. "You want to stay for dinner? She should be here by then."

He looked thoughtful before tucking the metal clipboard under his arm. "Naw, I gotta head back to the station. I promised Dad he could spend the evening with my mom for her birthday." He walked toward the front door. "Have you checked up on this new guy yet?"

She cocked her head at him. "I already have one brother breathing down my neck. Now you, too?"

"You can't be too careful, Julia. I'll run a background check on him and his brother. I'm sure they're fine. Don't be too hard on Justin. You three girls are all he has left." She followed him out to his car, where he retrieved his gear from the trunk. "Thanks for letting us talk privately, guys." He waved to the three men on her porch, and they headed back inside. Dylan stood at the door and waited for her with Roscoe at his side. Chase laughed quietly. "Yeah, he's probably fine. Looks like he's giving Justin a run for his money on who's more overprotective."

She looked at Dylan and smiled. "Dylan wins, hands down."

DYLAN LEANED BACK into one of the patio chairs watching Julia play with the dogs while his brother sat across from him, his gaze intent. "Well, that was fast."

"What was?" Dylan didn't let his gaze stray from the woman jumping and prancing on the lawn like a woodland imp.

"You, falling for her."

Dylan sucked in a deep breath, preparing to deny what even he knew was the truth, wondering why he was even bothering to try to hide it. Did he really think he was fooling anyone? He blew out the breath in a heavy sigh. "Yeah, I know."

Gage leaned back in the chair with his eyes wide. "Whoa! Wait, no rebuttal, no argument? No denial?"

"Why bother?" Dylan shrugged and met his brother's gaze, letting the weight of defeat settle over him. "It doesn't matter. In two weeks, we'll be gone. It'll be better that way. I can't strap her down to this crap I'm dealing with. She's already moved past hers."

Gage narrowed his eyes. "Her what?"

"She had PTSD, or *has* it. I guess you never really get rid of it. This guy attacked her."

"The stalker ex?"

"Yeah." Dylan shook his head and ran a hand over the top, his short hair rasping in the quiet of the evening. "She has enough to deal with on her own."

"So, you're going to play hero for her and then, what, abandon her?" Gage crossed his arms and put his feet up on the wicker ottoman. "You're a real knight in shining armor, aren't you?"

"It's not like that, Gage."

"Then, please, explain it to me, because it looks like she's falling for you and you've already fallen for her—hard—but you're too guilt-ridden to even take a chance that she might *want* someone like you. Did you ever stop to think that maybe she's looking for someone who can understand how she feels? Someone who understands the fear and trials and complications that come with PTSD?"

"Gage," he began to argue.

"Don't argue, Dylan, because, let's face it, you really can't. You haven't even given her a chance to let you know what she wants. You've barely been here a few days, and you have no idea how much better you seem. You said yourself, you didn't even have an episode last night. You've had one—*one*—episode in three days, and you haven't needed one sleeping pill. No one else has been able to do that for you in the past year."

Gage rose from the chair and laughed as he looked toward Julia, who stood with the dogs, watching their exchange, her brow creased as if she was concerned for Dylan. "The dog might have helped, but I think it's the other blonde over there who has you improving. Quit wasting the opportunity right in front of you, and be happy."

Chapter Eleven

JULIA LAY IN her bed, wrapping her arms around her pillow, but it just wasn't the same. She missed Dylan. Telling him about her relationship and the extent of the attack had been emotionally draining, more than any night since she'd rescued Tango from the shelter and brought the mangy beast home, but even cuddling with him didn't compare to being held by Dylan. The heat of his body beneath her cheek, the way his arms broke out in goosebumps when her palms ran over his skin, the way his kiss ignited a fire that started from her cheeks and pooled in every crevice all the way to her toes.

After spending so much time alone, three additional people in the house this evening made for a crowd rather than company. They worked Roscoe in the obstacle course and she'd begun teaching Dylan a few new commands he would need after returning home, but the additional eyes made her nervous. The mere thought of Dylan leaving was enough to freeze the breath in her lungs. She didn't want him to go, but she couldn't ask him to stay. They barely knew each other, yet they seemed to know everything they needed to. He understood her like no one else. Not even her therapist had been able to read her moods the way Dylan did.

Tango nudged her hand for attention and she smiled. Dylan was a lot like the animal she adored—athletic and brutish at times, but tender and protective with her. They had connected on an instinctive level, and while she couldn't explain it, she couldn't ignore the pull. She punched a fist into the pillow and flopped to her other side, staring at the door, willing him to knock, to come inside...something. But the house remained quiet.

Dylan and Gage had checked all the doors, windows, and locks before everyone headed to the spare rooms she usually kept for guests. She kicked one foot free of the blankets, trying to get comfortable. Tango sighed and shot her an annoyed glance, one doggy brow lifting.

"What?" she asked the Great Dane. He simply sighed in response. "Oh, fine. I'm sorry I'm disturbing you."

Julia tossed the blankets back. She might as well get a book or something since she wouldn't be sleeping tonight. She adjusted the waistband of her light flannel pajama bottoms and shook her finger at the dog. "You just remember that the next time I stay up with you when you get a bellyache from sneaking a whole jar of peanut butter."

Tango sighed again but climbed off the bed, ready to follow her into the living room. Julia opened the door and stopped short as a massive, dark chest blocked her path. She yelped and her gaze locked on pectorals that would make a fitness model jealous and caused her mouth to water. She could see the dark shadows playing over the ridges of his abs and wanted to let her fingers follow her gaze. Instead, she lifted her chin, slowly, enjoying every second, every inch, as she looked him over.

"Julia, did I wake you?"

It was as if her mind had conjured his presence. The sleepy rasp of his voice did her in. She couldn't stop herself if she had wanted to, which she had absolutely no inclination to do. Her hands slid over his shoulders, and she wound her fingers over the back of his head, dragging him down to her. She molded her lips against his. It wasn't the sweet, seductive caresses they had shared up to this point. This kiss was filled with need, hunger, and a desire restrained too long. Dylan's arms circled her waist, lifting her from the floor and carrying her back into her room.

Julia pushed the door shut with her foot just as Roscoe scooted into the room. She let Dylan move her backward toward the bed. It was exactly what she intended, and she was grateful he could read her mind without needing to speak a word. He set her on the bed and reached for her, his massive hands cupped her cheeks gently, and he took a step away from her. She gasped for breath as he withdrew, her fingers clinging to his muscular forearms.

"Dylan?"

He shook his head and avoided looking at her. "This wasn't what I intended, Julia. I was just checking on you."

She gave him a wicked smile. "You might want to keep checking then."

He groaned under his breath and slid his hands to her upper arms, putting her a few inches farther from him. "You're killing me." He stared at the floor.

"Dylan, look at me."

All jokes were forgotten when he glanced up at her through his thick, dark lashes. His gaze wasn't his usual tender caress, rich and warm. It was hot, hungry, and erotically aroused. A jolt of desire shot to her core, heating her with electric need. She wanted this man, and she wanted him to want her.

Not love. She knew she wasn't ready for that any more than he was. They were both too broken for love. But the need—to touch, to taste, to be filled with something besides the lonely emptiness. She needed to know someone understood.

"I need to go." Dylan let go of her arms and turned to leave the room.

"Dylan." She grasped his wrist. She had no idea what she'd been about to say, but it didn't matter. The only thing that mattered was that the sudden loneliness she saw in his eyes faded. When he turned back to her, it was replaced by yearning. "Don't go," she whispered.

"If I don't—" She could hear the agonized restraint in his voice.

"I know." She moved between him and the door. Her hand slid over his chest to his neck. "I want you to stay."

"I can't stay." She could hear the tortured anguish and felt rejection rip into her.

DEAR GOD, DID she realize what she was doing to him? Every inch of his body seemed engulfed in flames. He clenched his fists at his sides, even as she held his wrist lightly in her fingers. It was taking every bit of self-restraint he had not to throw her onto the bed and ravish her. He'd been fantasizing about this moment since they'd driven up to see her waiting on the porch. But that had been purely physical.

Since then, Julia had reached into his chest and taken hold of his heart. He wanted to protect her, to make her smile, to be the one to show her how a real man loved and not just physically. But, if he let himself open up to her, she was bound to be hurt. He couldn't hold himself together. His episodes would return, and he was bound to fail her the way he had his brothers in Afghanistan. He'd promised her that he wouldn't hurt her, and he meant to keep that promise.

"I can't stay," he repeated, this time with more resolve behind the words. He wanted to kiss her again but knew if he did, he was lost. "I made you a promise, and the only way for me to keep it is to leave. Now." He headed for the door. He had to get out as quickly as he could.

He wasn't sure what had even possessed him to go to her door. He'd been lying in bed, unable to sleep because the thoughts of her down the hall had kept him tossing and turning. When he convinced himself he'd heard a noise, he used it as an excuse to walk by her room, listening for any sound to indicate she was awake inside. He'd been about to return to his room when she'd opened the door and run into him.

"You *are* hurting me, Dylan. Can't you see that?" He froze midstep, unable to face her. He heard the catch in her voice and knew if he saw the emotion in her face, he'd be finished. He couldn't tell her no again. He needed her too much. "Every time you pull me close then push me away again hurts. I can't keep doing this. I'm broken enough; I don't need you to crush the shards that are left."

The torment he heard pricked his conscience. He wanted to be the honorable man he used to be, he wanted to be the impenetrable man he'd once been, but her words sliced into him, cutting him to the core. She was like a drug: from that first kiss, he was addicted. He couldn't get enough of her, and there was no way to work her out of his system.

Dylan turned, burying his hand into her hair, and his lips found hers. "You're not broken. You're perfect and beautiful and flawless." He thrust his tongue into her mouth, tasting, dancing, teasing, and torturing. She mewled in her throat, clutching at his shoulders, her fingers kneading into the sinewy muscles of his arms.

She tore her mouth from his and reached for the hem of her shirt, but his hands beat her to it, pulling it over her head, her hair falling back over his face like silk as his lips found the curve of her neck. Whether right or wrong, there was no way he could stop himself now, not even if he wanted to. Not from kissing her, not from running his hands over the bared skin of her back, and not from marveling at the way making love to her would feel like summer, and sunshine, and all things good he'd long forgotten. This is what heaven would be like.

Her breasts were crushed against his chest, and her pulse raced against his lips at her throat when his thumb came around to caress the soft curve of one. She sighed at his touch and dropped her head backward, giving him access to every glorious inch of skin.

Walking her toward the bed, Dylan stopped just short of it. "Off," he commanded Tango. The dog simply stared at him, as if daring him to repeat the command. Dylan looked down at Julia and gave her a lopsided grin. "I have to draw the line at making love to you while the dog watches. At least Roscoe stays on the floor." He saw Roscoe lift his head at hearing his name before settling again. "A little help?"

"You need to let him know you're in charge. Do it again, but this time make him see you mean business."

How was he supposed to focus on training the dog when his hands were full with her luscious curves, which had tempted him for what felt like forever? "Get off the bed," he ordered, his voice conveying every bit of the frustration he felt.

Tango slid off the bed, and Julia smirked at Dylan as he flipped the blanket over the end of the bed. "See? I told you." She took a step closer to him, closing the distance between them again, and slid her hands around his waist, peering up at him through her lashes innocently. "Where were we?"

Dylan slid his hands up her ribs, barely skimming the curve of her breasts. "I was just admiring."

His fingertips moved over her collarbone, and he could feel the electric jolt of pleasure shoot through him like white-hot lightning. Her breath caught and came in short puffs against his bare skin, her eyes melting into pools of desire. He dipped his head, his lips nipping at her jaw, the hollow below her ear, the curve of her neck as she arched and whispered his name. His thumb brushed over the taut peak of her breast, and she cried out softly at the pleasurable pain. He felt it with her, and it shocked his senses.

Laying her back on the bed, he leaned over her, staring down into her innocent face. She was so beautiful, so tender, he couldn't imagine a woman like her would ever want a man as ruined, physically and emotionally, as he was. He lay down beside her, content to look at her body, to trace the curves with his fingers. His hands cupped her breasts, and her eyes fell closed as her body arched into his hands. Dylan reveled in the knowledge that she longed for his touch as much as he wanted hers.

His fingers trailed over the flat plane of her belly to her hip and the waistband of her bottoms. His eyes flitted back up to hers. "Are you sure this is what you want?" He prayed she'd say yes, because trying to stop now might kill him.

She traced his jaw with her finger and raised herself up to kiss him. "Yes, Dylan. I want you." He heard the tentative tremor in her voice belying the bold statement.

Dylan rose and slid her pants from her legs, taking the soft cotton underwear with them. He hovered over her, tracing his finger over the curve of her belly to the seam of her hip and pelvis, pressing a kiss at her waist and making her jump in anticipation. He wound his arms around her waist, drawing her to him, and inhaled the sweet scent of her, sliding up her body, feeling her shiver against him as the scruff on his jaw scraped her skin.

"I should have shaved," he murmured against her skin.

"Hmm, don't you dare," she argued, her voice barely a whisper of sound.

Dylan's lips found the curve of her breast as his hand circled the other, fondling, teasing. When his mouth found the peak, she gasped, arching into him and biting her lower lip. It was almost his undoing. But when his hand moved lower, finding the center of her pleasure, stroking her, he was shocked at how she gave in to the ecstasy.

Her hands roamed his body, her lips kissing the scars under the covering of his tattoos and chipping at his heart. This woman drove him mad with desire, making him hungry for a life that should have been, that he could never offer her.

If only...He quickly halted that train of thought. There were no "if onlys" in life. He'd made choices, saved lives, and he wouldn't change that. He hadn't known Julia then—their paths would have never crossed—so there was no "if only" for them.

Dylan couldn't wait any longer. Her touch was driving him wild with want, and he needed to make this special, something pleasurable, not a race to maintain self-control. He slid his sweats off, and she reached for him.

"Wait, Julia. Not quite yet." He pressed soft kisses against her belly, moving back up her body. "If you touch me, I'm a goner," he warned.

She smiled and he could see the pleasure in her eyes. He wanted her to know how she affected him, how much he yearned for her. He wanted her to realize how much she had come to mean to him, how special she was. He wanted her to know he loved her.

The realization surprised him at its intensity.

There was no logical, reasonable way for him to fall in love with her so quickly, but there was also no doubt in his mind. He loved Julia. Loved her gentle spirit, her tender heart, the way she opened up to him in spite of the pain she was feeling. He loved her smile that was so quick to surface, and the way she pushed him to gain control of his life again.

"But I *want* to touch you." Her voice was a soft purr of seduction without her even trying, and his entire body throbbed in response.

"And you can. Later." Dylan pressed a kiss against her lips, nipping at the corner of her mouth. "Do you have something?"

Her face fell and she bit her lower lip. "I...you don't?"

Dylan dropped his forehead to her chest and groaned. He hadn't planned on this and hadn't been with a woman since he'd last been deployed. He'd assumed she would have some sort of protection in the house. He was certain Gage would have something, but he wouldn't tarnish Julia's reputation that way. "No."

JULIA HEARD THE disappointment in his voice, felt her heart crash to her toes. This couldn't be happening. Since Evan, she'd closed herself off, unwilling to trust herself to get close to anyone. She'd given up on finding anyone who could face the broken mess she was inside. And then Dylan showed up. Just as broken and messy as she was, but he needed her, allowed her to touch his wounded soul. They were able to give where the other was lacking.

This was the first time she'd wanted to give herself to a man since Evan's attack, and to be stopped by something as stupid as not having protection seemed too far-fetched to be believable. She sighed in disappointment and ran her fingers over his back as he dropped his forehead against her chest. She knew Justin would have something in his wallet, but she didn't dare sneak in to find out. His relationship with Dylan was tenuous at best right now.

She felt Dylan smile against her breast. "It's okay. Just knowing you're that disappointed…" His lips circled her nipple, and fire seared through her again. "There are other ways."

Dylan's fingers ran over the side of her hip and feathered over her inner thigh. When his fingers found her again, wet and aching, she sucked in a shaky breath, unable to do anything but feel. His body pressed against hers, pinning her down, but without the fear she'd worried she would feel with a man after Evan. Dylan's lips moved over her skin, ravishing her with the rasp of the stubble over his jaw as he headed lower. When his mouth touched her, she bucked against him, the onslaught of pleasure lifting her from the bed.

Dylan caressed her, tasted her, tormented her, and made love to her with his mouth. He explored her body with his hands and lips, as if trying to memorize every dip and arch. When she finally cried out in release, he rolled over, holding her close, as if he couldn't bear to let her go.

"Dylan?" she whispered against his smooth chest as her finger traced the whirls of his tattoo design. "I have an idea."

He ran his hand over her hair and smiled down at her. "Yeah?"

"Hand me my phone?"

He arched a brow in question but reached for her cell on the nightstand. She quickly sent a text message to Bailey and smiled at the reply, handing the phone back. "Bailey to the rescue."

"What?"

She didn't bother to enlighten him but rose from the bed and moved to stand at the door. Tango lifted his head to watch her but laid it back down just as quickly when he realized she wasn't leaving. The soft pad of feet sounded in the hallway, and she saw the slip of foil shoot under the door. Holding up her prize between her fingers, she smiled as she walked back toward Dylan still on the bed.

Dylan chuckled, sounding more lighthearted than she'd ever heard him. "Did you seriously text your cousin to bring you a condom?"

"Would you rather I texted my brother?"

She couldn't help but feel slightly self-conscious as she made her way back to where he lay, propped up against one of her pillows and looking oddly delicious on her bed, wearing nothing but a hungry, slightly cocky grin as his eyes slid over every part of her, heating her insides to molten quicksilver.

He plucked the condom from her fingers and pulled her down on top of him. "You surprise me, Julia."

Her fingers splayed over the massive wall of his chest. She wanted to come up with a witty retort to his comment, something to lighten the mood, but her brain was barely functioning at this point. With his body hard and heated against her, she couldn't do anything but feel—the tingles that tripped down her spine as his hands curled around the cheeks of her butt, the shallow breaths that kept her balanced on the precipice of dizziness, and the exquisite ache between her thighs as she waited for him.

She slid her fingers over the planes of his stomach, over his thighs, and—reaching between them—let her hands find the one place she knew he ached as much as she did. Dylan growled as she touched him, but she wanted him to know the same agonizing pleasure she had. Her lips moved over his chest as she stroked him. He shifted, rolling over and pinning her beneath him. It was mere seconds before he brushed her hands away and tore open the package, sheathing himself and pressing against her.

"Julia?"

She could hear the hesitation in his voice, giving her one last chance to change her mind. And she loved him for it, even if she couldn't admit it aloud. Dylan was again putting her needs above his own desires, her honor above his wants and thinking of her future instead of his own.

"After all we've gone through to get here, don't you dare think of stopping now." She slid one hand around the back of his head, drawing his mouth to hers and the other to his lower back. Dylan slid into her with painstaking slowness, and they groaned in unison as their bodies joined.

She felt him shake, his hands trembling as he withdrew and repeated the languid ravishment of her body. She clung to his strength as his confident strokes grew more urgent, taking her to the edge of bliss. She couldn't deny herself any longer when he thrust into her, trying to hold back his own release. She cried out and he took her mouth hostage, their tongues dancing, their bodies one as the world shattered around them.

Dylan held his weight over her, balancing himself on an elbow at each side of her head, staring down at her, and he brushed her bangs away from her eyes. "I'll say it again, Julia. You surprise me."

She returned the smile as her body relaxed beneath him, still recovering from her orgasm. "And you far exceeded my hopes," she teased. Dylan bent to kiss her lips gently, lingering on the touch. She felt her heart skip with abandon. Maybe their broken places could be meshed together to form one perfect whole.

Chapter Twelve

DYLAN TRIED TO stretch out his legs without waking fully, but there was something at his feet that prevented any movement. He pushed against it and chuckled, realizing Tango had climbed onto the bed while they slept with Dylan curled around Julia's back. Not to be outdone, the dog had edged between them and lay sprawled on his back at the foot of the bed, sound asleep. He pushed against the dog slightly and Tango sighed, flapping his big lips and rolling over, curling into a ball closer to Julia's feet.

"His sleeping act didn't fool you, huh?" she whispered and rolled over, curling into his chest like a purring kitten.

"Nope, but I didn't mean to wake you." His knuckles grazed over the line of her jaw. "I should probably get back to my room before anyone else gets up."

She twisted her lips to the side. "You don't have to go, Dylan. I'm a big girl." She looked up at him, innocently.

Contrary to what she claimed, with her long lashes and trusting, dark eyes, she looked young and naive. She had no idea what sort of disaster he brought with him. He traced the line of her cheek, wishing he could make love to her again. Once hadn't been near enough to slake his thirst for her.

"Your brother doesn't particularly trust me already. I don't even want to think what he'd do if he found me in here."

She grinned at him, and he caught a glimpse of the spitfire in her. "Do you think I care what my brother says?"

He laughed and rolled onto his back, pulling her into the crook of his shoulder. "I'll stay for a few more minutes. But only because it's early and I don't want that dog to think he won."

She laughed, her breath warming his chest, and he felt himself stir to life. This was going to be a long day if he couldn't get his body under control. He tried to think of anything that might still the reaction—baseball, football, hockey, cleaning the kennel with her as he promised to do today—but with her finger tracing the pattern of his tattoo over his chest, he couldn't think of anything but how those hands had touched him last night.

His laid his hand over hers. "Unless you have another foil packet hidden somewhere in here, I should go."

Dylan didn't miss the disappointment that flickered in her eyes, and he hated being the reason it was there. Then she smiled at him, and he felt his stomach tighten in knots.

She shrugged and sighed. "Okay, I was just getting up to take a shower anyway." She flipped back the sheet and walked into her bathroom.

He watched her walk away, appreciating the sight of her backside, certain she was putting a little extra sway in her hips for his benefit. She knew damn well how difficult she was making it for him to leave. He hadn't missed the overconfident smirk on her lips as she headed into the bathroom. He heard the water come on and swung his legs over the side of the bed. Roscoe opened one eye and raised a doggy brow at him.

"What am I supposed to do now?" The dog sighed and shifted position to lie on his side. Dylan nodded at the dog on the floor. "Yeah, no way I'm leaving now."

He rose from the bed and made his way to the shower, watching her through the clear glass as water rained down over her head, slicking her hair down her back. Steam rose in the stall as he opened the door silently and moved behind her, wrapping his arms around her and cupping her breasts. The water warmed her skin, but he felt feverish hot already.

She jumped in surprise but immediately leaned backward against him, letting his hands move over her body with complete trust, surrendering herself to the whirlwind of emotions that seemed to rise between them. His lips found her neck as the water soaked them, wetting her skin as his hands roamed down her stomach, between her thighs. She gasped, then sputtered as water filled her mouth.

Dylan bit the shell of her ear playfully. "It might be a bit dangerous in here for you. I wouldn't want you to drown yourself." He pushed open the door, and she turned in his arms as they stumble-walked back into the bedroom, nearly slipping on the tile floor where water pooled under their feet.

"Towels," she pointed out, reaching for the cabinet.

"Do we need them?" His hands slid over her slick, wet body, and he licked the moisture from her shoulder as he stopped in the doorway leading to her room. "Julia, I'll go to the store today, but for right now, we should probably wait."

She spun them so the back of his knees bumped against the bed and shot him the same feline smile, filled with confident seduction. "Like you said, there are other ways." She pushed him lightly so he sat on the bed and stepped between his knees. "Turnabout is only fair."

"Morning, Bailey." Julia had just started the coffee when Bailey came strolling into the kitchen and reached for a mug.

A gloating smirk spread on Bailey's lips, and her blue eyes twinkled mischievously. "You're awfully chipper this morning. I thought you'd be tired after staying up so late."

"I thought you went to bed before I did." Justin cocked a brow at his sister, confused. Julia glared at Bailey before turning toward Justin. She told Dylan she didn't care what Justin said, but she wasn't about to instigate an argument where there didn't need to be one.

"I did, but I couldn't sleep."

Bailey snorted into her coffee mug as she took a sip, and Julia shot her another shut-up glance. It probably would have worked if it had been anyone but Bailey. As much as she adored her smart-aleck, rocker-glam cousin, Bailey had a way of saying too much at the wrong time.

"Where're your infamous guests? I didn't get to meet them last night."

There she goes again. "I think Gage is still sleeping. I heard Dylan up a little while ago."

Bailey's grin spread even wider, if that was possible. "I'm not surprised."

Julia sighed, giving up trying to verbally outwit Bailey. Stuffing her with food was the only hope Julia had to shut her cousin's mouth. "Breakfast, Bailey? I've got eggs, toast, and bacon."

"Get it to go if you're riding to the clinic with me. I'm heading out in five," Justin informed her.

Bailey rolled her eyes and shrugged, finishing the last of her coffee. "I guess I was lucky to even get this." She slid the mug into the dishwasher. "You heard the boss man. Can we wrap it up?"

"You bet."

Justin eyed the two women before heading out to his truck.

Julia turned to her cousin. "Thank you."

Bailey laughed out loud. "For which part, the loan or keeping quiet?"

"If that was you keeping quiet, I'd hate to see you when you tell all!" Julia shoved her cousin toward the door. "Now go, before your *boss* gets all pissy and comes back looking for you."

Julia was standing at the sink when Dylan and Gage finally came into the kitchen. "Morning, guys." Her eyes skimmed over Gage and settled on Dylan. She couldn't help but admire how incredible he looked in his rust-colored T-shirt and jeans. Good enough to eat. She licked her lips and pressed them together, barely able to tear her eyes away from him as Roscoe trotted into the kitchen.

"Good morning, Roscoe. Ready for breakfast?" The dog answered with a quick, cheerful bark before sitting at Dylan's feet. She held the bowl out to Dylan. "I dished up his food, and Tango's already eaten." Julia poured two cups of coffee as the dog was fed. Gage rose to take them. "Sit and eat," she ordered.

Gage laughed. "You give me commands like I'm one of the dogs."

She stopped short, frowning. "I'm sorry, I just—"

"I'm kidding. You made breakfast and you're serving me coffee. You could tell me to go wash your truck and I would." She smiled and lifted both brows in doubt. "Okay, maybe not that far. Your truck's pretty dirty."

"Your brother and cousin already left?" Dylan asked, looking back down the hallway.

"Yes, why?" She knew exactly why but wasn't about to miss the opportunity to tease him.

"Gage wanted to meet Bailey."

"Really?" She flicked her eyes toward his brother, surprised to see him nod and shrug.

"You'd be a hard act to follow, Julia, but if she's anything like you...well, I *am* a single guy."

"Thanks, I think." She scraped Justin's dish and loaded it into the dishwasher and wondered if she'd ever teach him to use one. She rinsed out his mug and turned to face the brothers.

"So," Gage began tentatively, "I was hoping we could take a trip into town. What do you think, Julia?"

She turned, glancing at Dylan. He'd mentioned going into town, but she'd assumed he was kidding, especially considering the way their last trip had ended. She leaned one hip against the counter. "Where did you want to go?"

Gage shrugged and looked at Dylan for support. "I guess it's really your decision, Dylan. Do you feel ready to try again?"

"You think Roscoe is ready?"

"Roscoe did fine," she reminded him, quietly. She hoped he realized she understood if he wasn't ready to go through another episode. She didn't want to push him too quickly, but she didn't want to hold him back either.

Dylan held her gaze for a moment before giving her a wink. "I think it's a good idea. There was something I didn't think to pick up the last time we were there."

GAGE FOLLOWED THEM in the Camaro, and Dylan couldn't have been more grateful for the privacy. At least this trip to town gave him a chance to talk with her a bit about last night, and where they could go moving forward.

"Was this trip your idea?" Her voice broke into his thoughts, and he glanced over at her. It had taken a while, but he'd been able to convince her to let him drive, and it felt amazing to be behind the wheel again. He might still have his regular prescriptions, but now that he hadn't been taking medication to sleep at night, he was amazed how alert he felt. Maybe it was just the full nights of uninterrupted sleep, more than he'd had in the past year.

He grinned sheepishly and watched her cheeks flush with color. Dylan reached over Roscoe and twined his fingers with hers. "You're beautiful when you blush."

The dog looked from one human to the other from his spot curled up between them before giving up on getting attention and dropping his head back onto his front paws. "I think you should try a quick trip in and out first," she suggested quietly.

"You think I'll have another episode?"

She shrugged. "It's a possibility you should be prepared for."

"I haven't had any since that last one, not even with what happened the other night," he pointed out.

"It really just depends on what triggers them. Now we know chasing down crazy ex-boyfriends isn't one of your triggers."

Dylan shook his head, growing serious. "Don't joke, Julia. I talked to Chase this morning, and they haven't seen that motorcycle yet. Until they know where he is, I don't want you going anywhere alone."

She sighed and turned to look out the window, seeing Gage in the rearview mirror. "Then it's probably a good thing you need me to help you with Roscoe. I'll have you with me all the time."

The ride was short but pleasant, and he couldn't help but think how he wanted this life beyond the next two weeks. He wanted more time, but he wouldn't force himself on

Julia. The past few days were a great start to his healing and a foundation for a relationship, but he had to do better than this. He had to know he could offer her more than a broken mind and a helpless has-been of a man. If he could prove to his therapist he was getting better, he could lower his medications. Or get off them entirely.

He rubbed his thumb over her hand, feeling the desire burst bright in his chest again just as the Sak 'N Save pulled into view. He parked the truck while his brother pulled in next to them.

Gage pointed at the mail center across the street. "I need to go to the office supply to get this contract notarized. Why don't we meet at the coffee shop in twenty minutes. Is that enough time?" He looked from Dylan to Julia.

"It should be fine. I just have a couple things to get." Dylan clipped the leash on Roscoe as he jumped down from the seat. "Man, it felt good to drive again."

"Then hold on to the keys and you can drive back," Julia said.

Dylan ignored the warning look Gage shot him. He knew the risk, but Julia's confidence in him would be enough to get him through this.

WITH EVERY MINUTE they spent in the store, the pride she felt in both Dylan and Roscoe grew. Both had learned to trust one another quickly, more quickly than she'd even hoped they would. When Roscoe hesitated, Dylan immediately focused on the dog, waiting to see if it was a trigger or simply some reaction the dog was reading from him. They were able to make their purchases and exit the store without any trouble and with five minutes to spare before heading to meet with Gage.

"Crap!"

"What?" Dylan turned to see what happened.

"I forgot I needed butter." She knew it wasn't dire, but there was no sense driving all the way back another day when they were still here. "Why don't you just wait at the truck, and I'll just run back in." She didn't want to push their luck. She could see the pride in Dylan's eyes at how well the two of them had done. She didn't want him to be disappointed if he had another episode.

"I'll go with you."

She bit her lip, nervously, making the decision to keep her concerns to herself and protect him for a change. "I don't want to overload Roscoe, and if we're still going to the coffee shop, that's a lot of new circumstances to throw at him in a given day."

Dylan arched a dubious brow and looked at the dog. "Are you sure you aren't just worried about me having another episode?"

She took a step closer to him, laying her hands at his waist. "I'm just going to run in and out. You two would slow me down." She stood on her toes and pressed a quick kiss to his lips, shocked that even that small token was enough to make her heart flutter wildly. His hands found her waist and squeezed for just a moment.

"I'll wait for you. Just hurry."

She turned to leave and he pulled her back, winding his arm around her waist and kissing her fully. She could feel every part of her body awaken, yearning swirling through her as she melted into him. Breaking the kiss, she sighed as he kissed her forehead.

She smiled, loving that he didn't want to release her any more than she wanted to be released. If she had her way, they would forget the coffee shop altogether, head back home, and disappear into her room for the rest of the night with one of his purchases. "I can't hurry back unless you let me go first."

He growled playfully. "Fine." He released her slowly, as if it pained him, and she tried to convince the butterflies doing a quick two-step in her belly to settle.

She hurried through the electric doors and to the back of the aisle where the butter, eggs, and cheese were stacked. Julia plucked a package of butter from the shelf and spun to hurry to the checkout.

"Well, hello. Fancy seeing you here."

The icy voice froze the blood in her veins. Julia saw Evan standing no more than three feet away. If he hadn't spoken, she almost wouldn't have recognized him. He was more muscular than he'd been years ago, but thinner, more haggard. She scanned the aisle around her, praying that someone was nearby, but the store was painfully deserted this early. A lump lodged in her throat, and she couldn't break it up to speak. Evan took a step toward her, and she immediately backed up, almost falling into the open refrigerated shelves. He laughed bitterly.

"What's the matter, baby? Don't you remember me?" His eyes glittered with evil malice. "We had some good times." He glanced down the aisle before closing the distance between them. "Where's your new boyfriend? I'd love to have another chat with him. It was cut short the last time."

When she didn't react, he looked disappointed. "You already knew?" he asked with all the wide-eyed innocence of the snake in the Garden of Eden. "That's too bad, I wanted to be the one to surprise you with that news. I guess a whore like you probably always keeps at least one man around. And now I see you have a house full. Is that on my account?"

"You've been watching my house."

Evan laughed. "I've been watching you since I got out, sweetheart. You should know I'm never too far away."

"I'm calling the police as soon as I leave here," she warned, hating that her voice wavered, knowing he heard it.

A wide smile broke out over his lips. "If you do, I'll make sure that boyfriend of yours ends up the same as that mutt who bit me."

Julia felt her knees start to buckle. Evan grasped her face roughly in his hand. He wasn't big, but he was strong and she felt helpless. "Give me a reason to kill him. I'd take so much pleasure in watching him die trying to save you."

The thought of him hurting Dylan, or anyone else she loved, was enough to snap her from the hypnotic spell he'd cast over her. She shoved against his chest as hard as she could and ran out the doors, her stomach roiling as she fought to breathe. She saw Dylan still waiting at the truck and ran toward him.

"Julia, what's—"

"We have to leave!" She looked back over her shoulder, expecting Evan to follow, but saw no one. "We have to leave now."

Evan wouldn't just disappear. She knew he wasn't far behind.

Chapter Thirteen

Dylan could see the panic in her face and ran to her, meeting her partway across the parking lot. Julia dragged him back toward the truck. "Come on, we have to go. Get in." She tried to take the keys from him.

Dropping the leash at his feet, Dylan reached for her face, forcing her to stop and meet his gaze, pinning her body between him and car. "Julia, look at me. Look at me," he ordered. Her eyes flicked toward him then back toward the store. "Hey, what happened in there? Talk to me."

Roscoe pawed at her leg, recognizing her anxiety and reacting instinctively. Dylan knew, had Tango been with them, he'd have been doing the same. Her breathing was shallow, and her entire body shook with fear. Dylan had seen her upset, but this went far beyond that. This was sheer terror. There was only one thing he knew that would cause this sort of reaction in Julia.

Dylan enveloped her in his arms, holding her tightly as she buried her head in his chest and clutched at his shirt. He let his eyes scan the front of the store. He couldn't leave her here to go inside and find him, but he was sure Evan was in the vicinity. It was highly likely he would sneak out one of the back delivery doors. Controlled rage slid through his veins like a drug. If he could get back there...

"Julia, we have to call the police," he murmured quietly. "They can catch him here, and it will be over."

"No! We can't!" If she was panicked when she first ran out of the store, his suggestion sent her into a full frenzy. "Promise me."

"Shh, okay, we won't call them." He didn't like lying to her, but he had to calm her down. "I'm going to let Gage know we are heading home, all right? Let's get you into the car with Roscoe."

She nodded, still trembling as she took the dog's leash and slid into the truck. Dylan shut the door behind her and dialed Chase's direct line as he walked around the truck to the driver's side.

"This is Chase."

"We're heading back to the house." Dylan paused, knowing Julia could hear his side of the conversation. He tried his best to make his conversation sound as if he was talking to his brother while getting Chase the information he needed. "Something happened in the Sak 'N Save, but Julia doesn't want to talk about it right now."

"Dylan, is this about Evan?"

"Yeah. We'll meet you there instead of the coffee shop, okay?"

"I'm on my way to the grocery store now. Take care of her."

"Thanks, Gage. You go ahead and get your work done, and I'll take her home. We'll be fine. I'm going to let her rest."

"Gotcha." Dylan liked Chase. The man was intelligent and reminded him of Michaels, his junior medic, before he'd lost his life during their final mission. "I'll come out to the house later tonight."

"Sounds good." Dylan hung up the phone and, before opening the driver's side door, quickly texted Gage that they were heading home and to meet them there.

Julia's eyes hadn't left the front of the store, and her left hand shook as she absently petted Roscoe, who sat on the seat with his chin on her shoulder. Dylan tossed his phone onto the seat and started the truck. He had to get her away from here, away from whatever had triggered this panic attack.

The ride home was silent but for the occasional whine from Roscoe as he sought Julia's attention. She simply stared out the window, trance-like. It had Dylan worried. Even telling him about Evan's attack hadn't caused this sort of reaction from her, and he wasn't sure how to bring her back from the depths her mind had hidden.

"Julia, we're almost home, babe," he murmured in the stillness of the cab, more to himself than her.

She turned toward him as he pulled into the driveway, her eyes still frightened but coherent and present again. "Dylan, you need to pack your things and leave."

HE'D BARELY DROPPED the truck into Park before she had the door open and bolted for the front door with Roscoe. "Wait, what?" He jumped from the truck and slammed the door. "I'm not going anywhere."

Dylan stomped up the porch and stood in front of her, refusing to unlock the door until she explained. Tango came running from the backyard but skidded to a halt as soon as he saw Julia. He immediately whimpered and laid his head on her feet. "See, even this dog knows there is something wrong." He reached for her arm, but she moved away quickly. "Talk to me. What is going on?"

"Open the door, Dylan. We can talk inside." Her voice, usually sweet and melodious, held no emotion at all. That scared him more than her panic attack. At least with that, he could *do* something. This deadness? He had no idea how to break through it.

Dylan clenched his jaw and unlocked the door, swinging it open for her and the dogs to move inside. He locked it behind him, knowing Gage would still be a while, and jammed his fists into his pockets, ignoring the painful stab of the keys against his hip. "Damn it, Julia, quit walking away from me."

She spun on him. "I'm not walking away. I'm saving your life."

"What happened?" His voice rose and he saw her flinch at his tone. He hadn't meant to yell, but he couldn't handle not knowing any longer. He couldn't help her if she kept him in the dark.

"He was waiting for me when I went back inside. He's been watching us all along. He knows everything,

Dylan." She looked lost. Hurt, anger, and desperation all flitted through her eyes simultaneously. "He's probably watching the house right now."

"First, no one else left that parking lot before we did. Second, Chase is checking it out, and third, Gage is on his way."

"You called Chase?" He saw the panic rising in her again.

"Yes." Did she really think he wouldn't? If Evan surprised her in the store, he was damn sure going to let the cops know so that they could find him before he disappeared again.

"Get out! Get your stuff and get out." She shoved him toward his room. "Take Roscoe and go home."

She began ransacking the bedroom for his duffel bag, tossing his clothes onto the bed. Dylan reached for her hands, stilling her momentum, and drew her to him, pulling her on his lap as he sat on the edge of the bed. "Come here. What is going on?" She shook her head, refusing to speak. "Let's get one thing straight right now, Julia. I'm *not* leaving until he's found. Unless you have Chase physically remove me, you're stuck with all of us here at the house."

"He knows you're staying here," she whispered. "He knows everyone is."

"Good." He brushed her hair back from her face. "That will make him less likely to come back. Between your brother, me, Gage, and Chase—"

"Dylan," she interrupted, "he threatened to kill you if we called the police. I told you not to." Her voice shook and now he understood her fear. She was afraid for herself, but she was also trying to protect him.

Dylan smiled down at her, trying to keep it from looking patronizing. Did she realize the absurdity of her fear? She thought that *he* was the one in danger? "Julia, I've been special ops for seven years. I think I've managed to pick up a thing or two about protecting myself. He isn't going to touch me." He leaned forward so that his nose touched hers. "I won't let him touch either of us. I will protect you."

She buried her face in the crook of his neck as his hands ran over her back, trying to soothe the fear that threatened to overtake her. His words were a ferocious promise and reminded him of the man he once was. He knew he shouldn't make the promise, not after what had happened on his last mission, but he couldn't stop the instinct that took over when he was with her. He would protect her or die trying.

JULIA LAY AGAINST Dylan's chest, hating herself for falling apart today. The shock of seeing Evan shattered whatever coping skills she'd developed over the years. She probably could have dealt with hearing him threaten her. She'd expected it. But to know he was coming after Dylan was more than she could bear. She knew Dylan thought it was ridiculous for her to worry about his safety. Maybe he was right, considering all he'd been through and his training, but, in the face of what he was currently dealing with, Evan's threats weren't something she would take lightly.

Dylan's hands stroked her back, massaging the tension away. She wanted to hide with his arms around her, to fall asleep knowing he would envelop her. She couldn't deny it felt good that he wanted to protect her. A part of her soared at his refusal to leave. Until she remembered what happened to Misty, who had also tried to protect her from Evan.

Julia looked toward the hall, wondering when Gage and Chase would arrive, and saw Tango and Roscoe sitting in the doorway watching the two of them intently. How could she have ignored the dogs? She was surprised either of them allowed it. Their usual response to tears was to put themselves front and center, demanding attention and drawing it away from the circumstances causing them. Instead, they watched as Dylan soothed her, comforted her, and lifted her from the panic that had set in when she'd first entered the house.

"I'm sorry Dylan." She pressed a kiss against his neck. "Today was supposed to be fun, and I ruined it. You and Roscoe did so well. We should be celebrating instead of...this."

He looked down at her, his thumb caressing her jaw gently. "You didn't ruin anything." He brushed his lips against hers, as lightly as a breeze in summer. "I wasn't with you when you needed me." She saw his eyes darken with regret. "I won't let you down again."

"You didn't let me down," she assured him, but he shook his head in denial.

Dylan closed his eyes and took a deep breath. "I just want to be the man I was again."

Julia slid her hand over his cheek. "I didn't know him, but who you are is more than man enough, Dylan. You are good and kind and brave." She gave him a flirtatious smile. "You're a teddy bear even if you look like a tough guy."

"I *was* that tough guy once."

"You still are." She laid her hand against the side of his neck, covering his scars with her fingers. "Tell me?"

Dylan shrugged. "It's ugly. Are you sure you want to know?"

"No matter what you tell me, it won't change how I see you," she assured him. How she could honestly say it after knowing him for only a few days, she wasn't sure, but she meant it with her entire being. She'd seen movies about soldiers and what they endured, had plenty of training from psychologists on the aftermath of PTSD, and had faced her own demons. There was nothing he could tell her that would change her opinion of him.

Dylan ran a hand over his head. "Okay." He took a deep breath when they heard the knock at the front door. The doorbell clamored, jarring them to reality. Her eyes shot to his, worried that Evan had followed them to the house again.

"Really, you two?" Gage's voice carried from the front porch. "You tell me to hurry back, and then you lock me out?"

Dylan ran a hand over her cheek. "Later, I promise." He kissed her nose and rose to let his brother inside. Julia followed him with both dogs trailing behind.

"Here you go," Gage announced as he swept into the front room holding a cardboard tray with three coffee cups. "I was already paying when you texted me, so let's go drink these out back while you tell me what interrupted our outing." He headed for the backyard with Dylan, Julia, and the dogs following behind.

Dylan automatically scanned the backyard and the trees behind it for safety. Seeing nothing amiss, he looked at Julia for permission to tell Gage what happened. She nodded, reaching for the coffee Gage held out to her, and listened as Dylan briefly explained her history with Evan, and her panicked state when she came out of the store.

She held up a hand and sipped the strong brew. "Wait." Julia hadn't realized how disjointed the day's events were from Dylan's point of view. "You weren't sure what happened, were you?"

"Not exactly, but I didn't want to push you," he confessed.

"And yet, you still made sure to get me out of there." She shook her head, awed at the instinct of the man who was stealing her heart more with each day.

"Why don't we wait for the sheriff?" Gage asked. "I get the feeling this isn't a story you're really going to want to repeat more than once."

DYLAN LISTENED WITH growing fury as Julia recounted the confrontation with Evan to Chase. His hands clenched the edge of the chair, his coffee forgotten on the table. When she mentioned how Evan grabbed her, he couldn't hold his tongue any longer and jumped up.

"That son of a bitch touched you?" He began pacing, his mind beginning to conjure images of what he would do when he found Evan. He only prayed he found him before Chase did so he could satisfy his thirst for vengeance. "What good is a restraining order if he's going to do whatever he wants anyway?"

"Dylan, sit down." Gage reached for his brother's arm, but Roscoe moved between them, edging Dylan back toward his chair. "You're not helping."

The dog pawed at his leg, and he looked down. He sat and Roscoe put his front paws into Dylan's lap. He took a deep breath. It didn't calm him, but it was enough to bring his mind back to the present and focus on the task at hand—Julia's emotional state, rather than his own.

"He said he'd kill Dylan if we called the police, Chase. He can't find out you're here."

"I have my own car today since I'm technically off duty, but if he's watching the house, or," he corrected, "having someone else watch it, he's going to find out."

Dylan reached over and took Julia's shaking fingers into his hand. "I told you, he can't do anything to me." He squeezed her hand gently.

"You're not invincible, Dylan." She turned back to Chase. "What do we do now?"

"I stay."

"How much room do you think I have here?" She looked back toward the house.

"Send Bailey and Justin home. Neither of them can help, and they aren't deterring him. They are more of a liability now than an asset." He looked at Gage and Dylan. Dylan recognized the steady, warning look in Chase's eyes. This could get dangerous quickly. He nodded his understanding. "The three of us will be with you at all times."

"And how am I going to explain you being here?"

Chase reached over and petted Tango's head. "You're helping me find a dog for the department, of course. We've been tossing around the idea of starting some sort of search and rescue for years." She shot him a dubious glance. "Okay, maybe not, but no one else will know that. I'll let Dad know what we're planning, but, if we get lucky, my being here might be enough to lure Evan out in the open again."

Dylan jumped up again. "You can't use her as a pawn."

"You have a better plan?" Roscoe whined, but Chase didn't break Dylan's stare. "As long as you're okay with this, Julia, I think we should do it."

"Julia, this is stupid and dangerous."

"I don't really see that there's any other option, Dylan. If this means he can be put away for good, if this will end it sooner and still keep everyone safe, I'm all for it. I'm tired of being afraid." She looked at Chase.

Dylan rubbed a hand over his head. Gage met his eyes, and he could see the concern there. He clearly didn't like this idea either. But Dylan didn't have a clue how to convince Julia different. She didn't realize how much danger she was putting herself into, trying to keep everyone else safe.

"I'll get my stuff and be back in about an hour. Right now, let's plan on a week."

"That long?"

"Hopefully not, but it's really going to depend on how much patience Evan has."

Dylan clenched his jaw. Evan had already proved his patience, and a week wouldn't be long enough. The man had held a grudge in prison for the past four years. He'd waited months after getting out, watching Julia, until he was ready to contact her again. He'd been hiding, in town, right under the noses of people actively searching for him before following her into the store. They weren't going to be able to fool him with this harebrained scheme. It might protect Julia in the short term, but Evan was going to find a way to get to her—and Dylan had to stop it.

Chapter Fourteen

JULIA SAT IN the corner of the couch with Tango curled up beside her. Justin had left, hesitantly, but trusting in Chase's plan to keep her safe. She wasn't as convinced this plan would work, but she was willing to give it a shot. Dylan, on the other hand, was downright peevish. He didn't like the idea of her being a live pawn to lure Evan into the open. Even Gage had voiced his concerns. In the end, it came down to wanting her freedom back. She was tired of living in fear and was willing to try just about anything. Until she did, she'd be a prisoner to her past.

She'd had a measure of that freedom after Evan went to prison and she adopted Tango. Since his release, Evan had haunted her every thought again. She was plagued with thoughts of being watched or attacked. If this plan freed her, she could take steps toward her future.

The more time she spent with Dylan, the more she realized she wanted that future. The one from her girlish fantasies. The one that had a happily ever after with a husband and kids. She'd thought that future had died after Evan's attack and the resulting trauma she dealt with on a daily basis. She'd given up hope of finding someone she could trust, who could help her trust herself again. But Dylan was different.

She looked up as he entered the room and leaned against the door frame. "Gage is going to get some work done. He wants to know if he can use your office."

"Of course." She tucked her feet under her, making more room for him on the couch, but Tango saw it as an opportunity to spread out farther. Instead of sitting on the couch, Dylan sat on the edge of the coffee table in front of her and reached for a hand.

"You know I don't like this so-called plan of Chase's, right? I don't like you being right in the sights of that maniac."

Julia sighed. She didn't want to have this argument again. She'd already had it with Justin. No one else would understand unless they'd been in her shoes. Dylan should understand the dream to go back to what she'd been before. "I know, I don't either. But I want my life back, at least what's left of it. I thought you'd get that."

"Julia."

"Dylan, if you were able to go back, to change what happened to you, wouldn't you? If you could fix it?"

"Honey, you're not going back. You're being reckless. You're risking yourself to catch a stalker."

She slid her hand away from his. "I'm trying to set things right. I was helpless the last time. He took me by surprise. He used my trust and my faith in him against me. This time, he's not catching me unaware. I'm waiting for him, and I'm turning the tables."

She felt fire burning in her chest, the desire to grasp her destiny with her hands instead of letting someone else shape it. "I'm setting up the attack on him and luring him into it."

"You want to be in a position of control."

"Yes." She was relieved he'd understood.

"No."

Her face fell as disappointment filled her. Why couldn't he see this wasn't as dangerous as he was making it sound? She pulled her knees up and hugged them to her chest, creating a barrier between them. She laid her cheek against them, refusing to look at him. It really didn't matter if he agreed. This was her choice. But she wanted him to be on board with the decision.

"This is just the illusion of control, Julia." She turned her head away, not wanting him to see her tears of frustration. "I told you I was a medic, but did I ever tell you that in my seven years, I never lost a man? I was great at my job because I knew exactly what to do and when."

She turned back to face him, but he wasn't looking at her. Dylan was staring down at his hands, rubbing his thumb over the back of the other in agitation before running one hand over the top of his head. Then he met her gaze. She could see agony in the deep mahogany depths, but there was more, a need to purge the demon inside. She recognized it because she'd felt the same way when she told him about what Evan had done. It had hurt to open the wound, but it also led to healing. Since that night, since sharing the painful memory, it had held less power over her.

"But that last day was different. We'd been ordered to scout out an abandoned base to see if it would be possible to retake it. It was supposed give us a foothold in enemy territory. We should have known something wasn't right. It was too easy to slip in. Once we were all inside, they came at us. Sprang it like a mousetrap. We tried to pull out. We managed to get everyone back, but then one of our guys took a bullet. It was bad."

She saw his eyes glaze over as his voice fell silent for a moment. He was reliving the scene in his head and experiencing the horror again. Roscoe jumped into his lap and bumped his chin with his nose. Dylan's eyes cleared quickly.

"I lied to him and told him I could save him." He went on as if he hadn't paused. Julia wondered if he even realized he had, or that Roscoe had almost instantly drawn him from the flashback. "He had a family. A wife and kids. It was my job, but I couldn't do anything."

Dylan shook his head and buried his forehead into his hands. "I refused to leave him there. I knew what would happen if they got a hold of him. We were trying to get him out when they hit us again. They were both killed, Julia."

"They?"

"Jefferies and Michaels." He rubbed a hand over his face.

"That's when you were shot?"

He shook his head. "I heard the bullet ricochet off the wall just before the grenade hit behind me. It knocked me off my feet again. I have no idea how I lived. I have no idea *why* I lived." His voice caught, choked with emotion. "They both had families, kids who will never see their dads again. I was supposed to save them."

Roscoe nudged his elbow, and Julia moved to be closer to him, dropping to her knees in front of him, forcing him to look at her. She could see the tears in his eyes, see that retelling this story was ripping his heart out. But Dylan was here, in the present, and she knew how hard that was for him. According to what Gage told her, to remain focused in the face of the terror he was reliving was an accomplishment he couldn't have achieved a week ago.

Dylan's hands curved around the back of her head, curling into her hair. "I thought I had everything under control. I was wrong. You can't control this, Julia, and I won't lose you."

Before she could respond, to tell him again how this was different, he bent forward, his mouth seeking hers. This wasn't the tenderness she'd come to expect from him, and the intensity frightened her even as it excited her. His tongue swept into her mouth—searing, branding, mating with her, and shivers of anticipation danced over her. Dylan slid his hands over her hips, dragging her against his body before easing onto the couch with her, shoving Tango aside.

Tango voiced his disapproval but jumped down. Dylan never tore his mouth from hers as he leaned over her. She wound her hands around the back of his head, his short hair tickling her palms. She was just as desperate for his touch. The thought that this man trusted her enough to open up, to be vulnerable and tell her what happened to him, filled her eyes with tears of her own.

"Oh, sorry. I didn't realize." Gage stopped in the doorway.

Dylan pressed his forehead against hers, barely tearing himself away from her mouth. He growled deep in his throat, but she slid her hand over his cheek and pressed a quick, embarrassed kiss to his chin and squirmed from under him.

"It's fine, Gage." She saw the muscle working in Dylan's cheek. "We were talking about Evan."

A grin slid to Gage's face. "That didn't look like talking." Julia felt the heat rise in her cheeks, burning her face.

Dylan, ever her hero, rose and moved to stand beside her. "Stop, Gage. Don't embarrass her." He frowned at his brother. "We were talking about why I think this plan of Chase's is too dangerous to try. I ended up telling her what happened."

"Oh? Oh!" Surprise arched Gage's brows high on his forehead. "Just for the record, I know you didn't ask me, but I think Dylan is right. This is a dangerous plan with a lot that can go wrong. All it takes is one wrong move and someone could get hurt."

Julia sighed again. How was she supposed to trust herself when no one else seemed to trust her judgment? "So, I'm intelligent enough to help your brother overcome his PTSD, to train service dogs, and run this ranch, but I'm not smart enough to make this decision on my own?"

She felt her temper flare up. She was trying to stand on her own feet again, and everyone seemed determined to remind her she was too weak. She was tired of being viewed as weak. Evan saw her as weak. She refused to be powerless any longer.

"I don't remember asking for input on this decision. I'm staying." She looked up at Dylan. "I was hoping for your support in this, but if you can't do it, you and Gage are welcome to take Roscoe and leave. I can give you the name of another great trainer, and you can finish with him. But I'm seeing this through until Evan is back behind bars. I won't be a victim anymore."

She stormed out of the room, leaving Gage staring openmouthed and Dylan rubbing his forehead in frustration.

"Julia, open the door."

"Go away Dylan."

It broke her heart to turn him away, especially after what he'd just shared with her, but she couldn't back down from this decision. They both had a choice to make. He could either stay and they could see this through together, or he could turn his back on her, and the danger Evan posed. He could take Roscoe and she would help him find someone else to finish their training. The thought of him leaving made her chest ache, and she couldn't breathe. She wanted to believe she cared about Roscoe and Dylan's training, the progress they were making, more than she did her relationship with him, but the truth was that the man had her twisting in the wind. She was head over heels and couldn't do a damn thing to stop it. The worst part was that she had to keep it to herself.

Her siblings already second-guessed her decisions after what had happened with Evan. If she told Justin she'd fallen for a client again, he'd read her the riot act. It was clear he already suspected she was starting to, which explained his attitude toward Dylan, but if she confessed that she was in love with him, Justin would go nuts.

"Julia, let me in." His voice was quietly insistent and she caved, unable to find it within her to deny him. She opened the door a crack but didn't say anything. "I don't agree with this choice, but you know I won't leave. You're safer with me here than with me gone."

"That's why you're staying?" She felt her chest constrict painfully. She wanted to be more than an obligation to him. She didn't want him to see her as another job responsibility. "I have enough people trying to rescue me, Dylan." She started to close the door.

Dylan held his hand against it and pushed it open, stepping inside the room. "Not the way I can." He let the dog in and shut the door behind him. His hands found her waist. "I didn't come here looking to be your savior, Julia." He ran his thumb over her lower lip, his eyes focused on hers. "And I didn't come here looking for this. But, I'm not willing to throw it away now that I've found it."

"I don't want you to go," she whispered, wanting nothing more than to go back to the simplicity they'd had this morning.

"Good, because I'm not leaving until you ask me to." A cocky grin lifted the corner of his mouth. "Maybe not even then."

Julia frowned, trying not to let his words remind her of the last time a man had refused to leave.

He must have seen it and realized what she was thinking. "That's not what I meant."

"I know. It's just..." She wasn't sure how to explain it to him.

"It's just that your mind feels like it's operating on two different systems. One is just like everyone else and, at times, convinces you everything is completely normal. The other chooses moments, little things that flip a switch like a trigger on a gun, and take you back to that point in time when it all went wrong."

"Exactly." She looked up at him, surprised he put her feelings into words. "I think that's why I love you so much. Because you get it."

His brows lifted in shock he tried to hide. She grasped what she'd accidentally revealed, and her face paled. "I mean...I..."

Dylan bent his head and brushed his lips against hers, sliding his hand into her hair. She sighed, unable to stop the pleasure from enveloping her. His kiss was new and exciting, but it was also comfortable and safe. The flutters in her belly were overwhelmed by the warmth that spread through her veins. His lips moved over her jaw, pressing against the racing pulse at her throat as his hands circled her waist.

"Dylan, I..." Her brain continued to betray her as his hand slid over the curve of her breast, his thumb toying with the beaded peak through her bra and shirt.

"Shh," he whispered against her skin. "I *do* get it." He met her eyes and brushed her bangs back with his fingertips. "I love you, too. It's too soon and it doesn't make sense to me either, but it doesn't change how I feel, Julia."

She felt as if he'd just opened the floodgates of her soul. Tears filled her eyes, and he brushed them away and smiled tenderly. "That wasn't supposed to make you cry, you know."

"I know." She swiped at her cheeks, looking up at him through her lashes. "Dylan, what are we going to do?" The single question encompassed so many others she didn't dare ask. Where did they go from here? Would he stay or leave eventually? What would everyone think when they found out? What would happen with Evan?

His lips were a mere breath from hers. "We'll figure everything out. Right now, I'm going to show you how much I love you."

Dylan lay on his back with Julia curled in his arms, asleep. He trailed his fingers over her skin, feeling the goosebumps breaking out over her smooth flesh, and she sighed against him. Her warm breath heated his skin, making desire seep into parts he thought were satiated. Apparently his body couldn't get enough of Julia any more than his heart could. He took a deep breath, wondering what in the world he thought he was doing. It wasn't fair to tie her down to the likes of him.

He'd been here less than a week and, while it had been extremely positive for his treatment so far, he wasn't anywhere near where he needed to be to live a productive life again. He might never be there. He couldn't burden Julia with half a man, half a life.

It would make him no better than his father, who'd been so drunk most nights he couldn't even function. When he wasn't passed out, he was yelling at them, striking out at them for the misery within him. Dylan couldn't be sure he wouldn't turn out the same way. He might not be taking his sleeping pills any longer, but there were still the anxiety medications, and he hadn't completely stopped the painkillers yet. Too many medications he was still taking just to function, and he might never be off of them. He could end up hating his life like his father. He might abandon what he thought he'd once wanted the way his father had. He didn't want to hurt Julia, and he was nothing more than a walking grenade, just as destructive as the one that ended his career.

Roscoe moved to the side of the bed and stealthily jumped up to lie stretched out alongside Dylan, nudging his elbow. "Hey, boy, you're going to wake Julia." He reached over and rubbed the dog's head. "You know exactly what I'm thinking, don't you?"

Roscoe lifted one eyebrow and looked at him, compassion easily visible in his golden brown eyes.

"I'm okay," Dylan reassured the dog, wondering if he'd lost his mind completely to have a conversation with an animal.

His therapist would probably tell him it was a good thing, that he was starting to reach out again and make connections. Relationships had been strained if not nonexistent since his return. The only person he was still connected to was his brother, and even that bond had been labored. Once outgoing and gregarious, Dylan had become withdrawn since his discharge. He found himself caring less about others, even his brother, while he retreated further into his own shell. But that had changed since arriving here.

Roscoe and Julia had given him a purpose to his life again. He found it less desirable to hide behind a barrier than the joy he found in Julia's smile, or working Roscoe on the obstacle course. He wanted to take the dog out, to put their bond to the test. The fact that he'd barely suffered from any flashbacks and that the sleeping pills sat unused in the guest room floored him. Any attempt doctors had made to lower them had resulted in the opposite—more flashbacks, violent outbursts, and excruciating pain from the headaches that plagued him. But here, he'd been able to forgo the pain medication, since he hadn't had a headache yet. He hadn't touched his sleeping pills, yet he was sleeping better than he had in years, even before the attack. There was only one explanation.

And Dylan refused to ruin her life. He cared about her too much for that.

He needed answers, but he wasn't going to get them tonight. That didn't stop his mind from spinning, playing out every scenario in his head, keeping him from sleep. Not wanting to disturb Julia, Dylan motioned to Roscoe to get off the bed and followed the dog, pulling on his sweats as he rose. The pair made their way down the hall to the kitchen in the early dawn, where Dylan found Chase seated at the table, a cup of coffee in hand while he stared out the window intently.

Chase didn't even bother to look his way. "Have a seat, Dylan. There's fresh coffee in the pot if you are staying up."

"What are you doing up?"

"Someone has to keep an eye out, so I planned on watching the place during the night since you and Gage will be with her most of the day anyway."

"What makes you think I'd be any good at protecting her?" Dylan poured himself a cup. "I'm here for a reason, you know."

"I'm betting you're ex-military, PTSD." Dylan had either misjudged Chase's astuteness, or his ability to hide his issues.

"Good guess," Dylan confirmed as he took a sip of the bitter brew. Chase's gut must be lined with cast iron to stomach this coffee. "You were military, too, right?"

Chase raised a brow. "How'd you guess?"

Dylan shrugged. "Certain tells…the haircut, but mostly the lock in your eyes. We all have a hardness, like we've seen too much of the wrong things." He grimaced as he took another sip of the coffee. "Not to mention only a soldier would suggest using a woman as bait for a madman. She's not collateral damage."

Dylan had already made his position on this plan clear to Julia, but he wasn't about to let this man risk her life, even if she was willing.

"That's not what I'm doing, Dylan."

"You know damn well he is going to come for her eventually, and you're using her to make your job easier. You couldn't find him. This way, your presence will piss him off and draw him out sooner. Do I have it about right?"

"We both know he's coming for her whether I'm here or not." Chase shook his head. "At least this way, she has some protection. I like Julia. We grew up together. Unless you're from a small town, you don't understand. Everyone is part of a big extended family, sort of like in the military."

"Then why are you doing this?"

"Why are you staying?" Chase confronted him with the same question he'd been asking himself for days. "Your presence here is likely what drew him out in the first place. To see her with another man must be making him crazy, well, crazier. He's been quiet for the past two months, and he suddenly comes out of the woodwork when you show up. You know as well as I do, it's not a coincidence."

Dylan didn't need Chase to point it out. He was well aware that he'd likely been the cause, considering the timing and the fact that he was now Evan's main target. Guilt washed over him, and he clenched his jaw, trying to stem the flow as it made his chest constrict. If anything happened to Julia, it was his fault.

"He's already on the warpath, Dylan. He's out to prove to Julia she's his, and he's not going to stop now. Even if we leave. Leaving would only make her more vulnerable to another attack. By staying, we have a chance at catching him." Chase spun his cup slowly between his hands. "As much as I hate this, it's the best plan we've got. Because, if he gets his hands on her again, I don't think he'll let her live long enough to make it to the hospital again."

Chapter Fifteen

JULIA WOKE THE next morning, reaching across the bed, her fingers caressing Tango's head, sprawled out where Dylan had been lying when she fell asleep. She sat up and looked around the room, but there was no sign of him having been there other than his musky scent that still clung to her pillow. She inhaled it, feeling her insides throb heavily as her pulse immediately sped up at the thought of their lovemaking. She smiled. At least this time they'd been prepared.

She rose and dug through her dresser for a tank top and pair of lounge pants before running her fingers through her hair and brushing her teeth quickly. She looked at her reflection. She could see the toll Evan's reappearance had taken on her in the dark circles that framed her eyes. Had it not been for Dylan's presence, she would look far worse since she'd be unable to sleep at all.

She heard Tango jump off the bed and saw him plop his big butt in front of the door.

"Ready for breakfast?" He let out a quick bark. "Okay, come on. Let's go find Roscoe and Dylan."

Tango led the way into the kitchen, where Dylan sat, staring out the window with Roscoe sleeping at his feet. Had the dog been in any other position, she'd have worried at Dylan's hyperfocused state.

"Good morning," she greeted him as she walked into the room.

"Morning. Coffee is hot and I made it." Her brows creased in confusion, and he gave her a lopsided grin. "Wait until you taste Chase's coffee, you'll be more grateful for mine."

"Great." She rolled her eyes. "You were up early. It's barely seven now."

Dylan rubbed his eyes and raised his mug to his lips. "Never went to sleep."

She turned to him, surprised by his admission. "Are you okay?"

"Yeah. Just tired now." He rose from his seat and walked toward her, his hands falling at her waist and pulling her toward him. Heat curled along her spine at his touch. "Want some help feeding the dogs this morning?"

"I wouldn't turn it down." She slid her hands around his neck, loving the way her entire body seemed to warm at his nearness. Like a hot toddy on a cold night, it spread through her slowly and relaxed her.

Dylan tipped his head toward her, his mouth brushing against hers.

"Crap, again?" Gage threw his hands up as he walked into the kitchen. "Either you two need to take a break for a while, or I have the world's worst timing."

Dylan looked back over his shoulder at his brother but refused to let her go. "Would you ever stop kissing her?"

Julia felt the heat flood into her cheeks as Dylan and Gage laughed. "No, I don't think I would," Gage admitted as Dylan dropped a quick kiss on the tip of her nose.

"Have your coffee and I'll go start cleaning the kennels for you."

"I'll come out, just let me change."

"Relax, Roscoe and I have this. Enjoy your coffee." The dog looked up at him and cocked his head to the side. Dylan loaded his cup into the dishwasher and slipped out the back door with Roscoe.

"I don't know what you've done with him, but I have to thank you Julia."

She watched Dylan walk toward the kennel. "I haven't done anything, I swear."

"My brother would never *offer* to clean dog crap unless you'd done something." Gage grinned and shook his head in disbelief. "You have no idea how much he's already changed since being here. He's like the older brother I remember when I was growing up. He used to joke around and enjoy just being with people. He loved people. It didn't matter who. Since he came home, he never leaves his room."

She took the seat across from him as Dylan disappeared inside the building. It was interesting to see Dylan through Gage's eyes. "I think he would have made a great doctor, but he went into the military instead."

"Why?" Dylan was such a magnetic person; she'd wondered, in spite of what he said, how he'd ended up in the military instead of college.

"Mr. Responsible?" He tipped his chin down to give her a teasing look. "He saw it as his job to take Dad's place as man of the house. Even when he was young. He worked several jobs in high school just to help Mom make ends meet. He made sure I went to college, but he'd always assumed the military was the only place where he could still take care of his family. It's just who he was."

"You don't agree with his choice?"

Gage shrugged. "I think he had a choice, even if he didn't think so." He sipped his own coffee. "But he's always taken his role as the family provider seriously. That meant sacrificing his own future for mine. Although, he excelled in the military. It actually suited him since it gave him the opportunity to protect and help others." He took another drink, pausing as if he was thinking about what he'd told her. "I don't know, maybe it *was* the only choice for him. He's always done exactly what he loved to do. Who am I to judge?"

"You know him better than most. Was he happy?"

"I think he was." Gage shrugged, and his eyes grew distant and sad. "Until he came home. He was a different person once he was discharged. Remember how he was that first day? Bitter, angry? Distant?" She nodded. "Well, that was a huge improvement. I can't tell you how many nights I've been woken by his nightmares, or how many holes I've had to repair in my walls when he gets frustrated."

"PTSD isn't something you can rush your way through. I should know." She twisted her mouth to the side, biting the inside of her cheek. "It never really goes away, you know. It can get better, but you just learn to live around it and minimize the symptoms as much as possible. From what I've seen, he's come farther than most in a short time."

"Have you told him that?" Gage looked at her pointedly. "My brother doesn't see himself ever having a 'normal' life again." He held up his fingers for air quotes. "He might be a great medic, but he's a horrible patient. Except where you're concerned. You seem to have broken through that barrier for him. I've heard him laugh more since we got here than since he enlisted. You're giving him a reason to engage in life again." Gage swigged the last of his coffee as Chase shuffled into the kitchen, looking exhausted.

"Coffee?" Chase grunted.

Julia wasn't sure what to think of this many visitors in her house at once. It was usually her and Tango in the big house alone, and now the kitchen was filled with the bustle of constant motion. She rose and grabbed a mug for Chase. "You want anything in it?"

He waved her off and took the mug from her hands, taking a big gulp. Her eyes grew wide. Gage laughed out loud. "Dude, if you ask Dylan, he might be able to put that into an IV for you."

Chase scratched his head and slid into the chair, flipping his middle finger at Gage, burying his chin into his palm and fighting to keep his eyes open. Julia watched him sympathetically. "Are you sure you really want to work one of the dogs today?"

Chase yawned and nodded. "If nothing else, we need to make it look legit. But after talking with Dad last night, he really does want a search and rescue dog the station can call on. You wouldn't be willing to keep it here, would you?"

"Honestly, search and rescue dogs need to be with their handlers all the time. I can help you train one, but since I'm not the one who'd be going out with the team, it wouldn't do much good to keep it here."

Chase took a deep breath and downed the entire mug of coffee. "Then, let's head out and find me a dog."

DYLAN SAT ON the stoop with Roscoe as Julia and Chase worked the dogs. It didn't take long before Chase had chosen a beautiful black German shepherd. Rather, she had chosen him. As soon as Julia turned the four dogs she thought were best suited to the job into the yard, Gracie ignored the other dogs and lay down at Chase's feet. When he moved, she went with him, and when he squatted down to watch the dogs work, she sat down.

"Do you really think we need to keep going, Chase? I don't think Gracie is going to give you any option but her," Julia pointed out.

"You think she'll work?"

"Let's experiment with them." Julia called all the dogs to her and found a rope toy, letting all the animals play with it for a moment. Gracie obeyed begrudgingly, casting a baleful glance back at Chase. Julia turned all the dogs to face Dylan and told Chase to hide the toy. He finished and returned to her.

"Okay, now what?"

She smiled. "Tell them to find it."

She showed him the command, which he repeated. All four dogs took off, noses to the ground, searching the yard for the missing toy. Dylan watched in awe as they circled the areas he'd watched Chase drag it through, but Gracie ignored the many twists and turns he'd made, lifting her face to the sky and moving straight for the hedge along the fence where he'd hidden the rope. Gracie began barking a full minute before any of the other dogs even moved toward her. Within a few minutes, all four dogs ended up at the same location.

"Give it to her and praise her," Julia said as he pulled the toy from deep within the recesses of the shrub. "You saw how she picked up the trail right away? Let's put the others away and see if she will do it without your scent on the object." Julia turned to Dylan. "Can you hide this while we are inside?"

She handed him the baseball cap she wore, letting her hair fall around her shoulders. He could smell her shampoo and her unique scent, like sunshine and hope. He felt the desire for her rear its head again, and his hands itched to move through her hair, to pull her into another kiss, to forget about training the dogs and take her back into the house. He let his hand move over the back of hers, and saw her eyes darken. She held Gracie by the collar and held the hat to her nose to sniff.

"Any specific place?"

"Wherever you want." Her voice was slightly breathless, and he wondered if they were still talking about hiding the hat. Dylan watched her walk inside with Chase, and then he walked the perimeter of the yard.

He needed to get control of himself. He was acting like a horny teenager. If he was going to keep her safe, he needed to keep focused on their surroundings. With several hundred acres to the ranch, anyone could be hiding out in the woods and creep up on them at any time. He and Chase needed to constantly be on guard. He'd already learned the hard way that one mistake could cost him dearly. Julia wasn't someone he was willing to risk. Chase was right, his mere presence had put her in the sights of this madman again, and he was going to get her out unharmed.

He tossed the hat on the edge of the gutter at the corner of the kennel roof and walked back to the stoop with Roscoe beside him. He'd quickly come to rely on the dog's constant presence. When Dylan began to drift into his head, usually leading into dangerous territory of flashbacks and living nightmares, Roscoe was right there to paw at him, grounding him in reality. He hadn't thought it possible, but he already couldn't imagine a life outside this property. And staying was something he had no right to think about.

Chase and Julia came back out with Gracie, dragging him back from his wild thoughts of a future with Julia. "Are you ready?" she asked, a wide smile breaking over her lips at the sight of him.

Damn but this woman had him twisted in knots. Just seeing her reaction was enough to fuel his desire. "Yep, let her do her best."

Chase sent Gracie on her way, and she paused for a moment to look at Julia before hurrying into the middle of the yard. She stopped and turned back to them, cocking her head and looking skyward before running toward the side of the yard and tracing Dylan's steps. Chase followed behind her until she sat in the corner and barked as she looked up. Chase backed up a step and looked on the roof.

"I'll be damned."

"Grab it and show it to her. Don't forget to praise her." Chase did as she said, rubbing the dog vigorously. "Who's a good girl?" He dropped to one knee as Gracie began to yip excitedly and jump around him, licking his face.

"That's kinda gross." Bailey stepped into the yard and laughed at Chase. "And you wonder why you don't have a woman in your life? You keep that up and she's the only girl who's going to kiss you."

He blushed slightly and stood up, dusting off his pants, giving Bailey a sly grin. "You offering to take her place, Bailey?"

"You wish." She rolled her eyes and held Julia's cell phone out to her. "I found it on the kitchen table. Justin couldn't get a hold of you, so he wanted me to come check and make sure everything was okay."

Julia shook her head, taking the phone. "So you got nominated to do his dirty work and spy?"

"Something like that."

Chase walked toward them and gave Gracie the command to sit.

"If someone would just convince Justin that you guys had this under control"—Bailey looked pointedly at

Chase—"I could concentrate on one job today instead of running between here and the clinic several times."

"Several?" Julia looked at her, confused.

"You think he's not going to send me back this afternoon? You know how overprotective he gets. He's like a dog with a bone."

"Let him know he can calm down," Dylan said as Julia scrolled through her missed calls and texts. "The two of us have this under control." He saw her face go white, her hand moving to her throat. She looked as if she'd just seen a ghost. "Julia?"

Chase and Bailey looked at her.

"No, no." She backed up a step and almost fell from the stoop. She handed her phone to Dylan, and he looked at the screen.

"I said no cops. You should have listened," he read aloud, and showed Chase the picture that accompanied the text. It showed Dylan hiding the hat through what appeared to be a gun sight.

Chapter Sixteen

EVERYONE TURNED TO look into the trees opposite the corner of the building where the picture would have been taken from. Julia didn't bother to look. She knew Evan would be gone already. He wasn't there. He wouldn't stay around. He was simply reminding her of what he could have easily done. Dylan was still standing because Evan had been merciful, for now. He wanted her to know the time would come when he chose to kill Dylan, but until it did, he was just watching, toying with them.

Julia's knees buckled and she slid toward the ground. Gracie shoved her nose into Julia's waist as Tango whimpered from her other side.

"Whoa." Dylan reached out and grasped her, holding her up. "Come on, let's get inside." He guided her into the kitchen in the kennel while Bailey and Chase followed. He slid Julia into a chair and searched the cupboards for a cup.

He finally set a disposable cup of water in front of her on the table as she rested her forehead in the heel of her palm. "This isn't going to work. You have to leave, Dylan."

"I already told you, I'm not going anywhere." Reaching out, he caressed the inside of her arm. "I'm fine. It was nothing more than a scare tactic."

"Well, it worked, because I'm scared." She shook her head. "Dylan, that is a picture of you through the sight of a gun. He could have shot you, and we had no idea he was here."

"It's not a gun sight," Chase spoke up. "It's through a monocular, probably military surplus."

Julia looked up at him. "That looks like a gun sight to me."

"He's right," Dylan said. "See the crosshairs, here? A sniper rifle would be far more precise and have more defined crosshairs."

"He knew you wouldn't know that and wanted you to think he could kill Dylan anytime he wanted. He's trying to get you to react in fear. He probably wants to get you to chase Dylan off so he can do whatever he wants." Chase sounded more excited than she'd like him to.

"You do realize this isn't a game, right Chase? This is my life."

He frowned. "I know that."

"I don't think that's what Chase meant, Julia." Bailey jumped in while Dylan shot Chase a warning glance, silencing him.

"I think this just means he was right about the way Evan would react," Dylan supplied. "Our being here is flushing him out, forcing him to do things without thinking them through." He tapped the phone. "This was a stupid mistake on his part and means he's shooting from the hip and not making careful plans any longer."

Dylan reached for her hand, wrapping it in both of his. "Chase and I are taking shifts staying up. Evan's going to make a move, and when he does, we're going to be there to stop him. He's not going to hurt you."

She looked at him, unable to stop the tears from filling her eyes. "It's not me I'm worried about."

He smiled at her. "He's not going to hurt me either." His eyes took on a ferocity she hadn't seen before. "He's not getting any closer to you or this ranch than that picture unless he wants to die. If he so much as lays a hand on you, I will kill him."

"I'm going to pretend I didn't hear that," Chase said. "Remember? Deputy sheriff right here."

"Yeah?" Dylan didn't flinch. "Well, special ops trumps deputy on this ranch."

"So, Bailey tells me things are looking serious with you and Mr. Military Man?" Jessie winked at Julia as she slid a coffee mug onto her kitchen table. Dylan, Nathan, Justin, Chase, and Gage had all headed into Nathan's newly christened home theater to watch a preseason football game. Julia had missed visiting her sister, but Jessie had been swamped with a weeklong camp of troubled teens and their family members. It was a magical combination that paired previously abused horses with the teens and worked wonders for the hardened kids to soften their hearts and open them up.

Julia felt the blush creep over her neck and knew Jessie would pick up on it if she didn't change the subject quickly. "How did camp go?"

"Great!" Jessie's face lit up. "But don't try to change the subject on me."

Damn, she thought. "I don't know that it's serious."

"Julia, you haven't dated a man in almost four years. For you to be interested at all, he must be pretty special." She tucked a dark curl behind her ear and reached for Julia's hand. "I know how hard it must be for you to even trust someone again."

Julia looked at their hands. "Not as hard as it is to trust myself again."

"Why? You didn't do anything wrong."

"I should've seen through Evan. He didn't change overnight, I just didn't see it. I let myself get so blinded by what I hoped was there that I didn't listen to my gut. Misty knew. I should have trusted her instincts."

"Julia," Jessie began softly.

"I fell for a stranger, and look what happened." Tears blurred her vision and she swiped at her eyes. She hadn't cried this much in years. "I can't let myself do that again. I don't even want to think about what could happen this time."

"Julia, Evan is sick. He's just damn good at pretending he isn't. You're not the first person he's fooled, or the last. Otherwise, they never would have allowed him out on parole." She squeezed her sister's hand. "Dylan isn't Evan. Roscoe wouldn't have accepted him the way he has. If you can't trust yourself, trust Roscoe and Tango. They both adore him."

Tango looked up from his place at her side at the mention of his name. She wanted to believe Jessie, but as much as she wanted to, there was a part of her holding back. Not from Dylan. Her heart was completely his. It was her mind that still needed to be convinced. It wasn't fair to him.

As if conjured by their discussion, Dylan appeared in the doorway with Roscoe at his side. "I'm supposed to bring beer back for everyone."

"You guys have already gone through the stock in the refrigerator?" Jessie rose and grabbed a new case in the pantry. "We don't usually keep it here when we have kids around, so they aren't cold," she warned as she passed it to him.

Dylan set the case on the floor and moved toward Julia, stepping around Tango and leaning close for a kiss. Her heartbeat immediately sped up, and Julia wondered which fluttered faster, the butterflies in her stomach or her heart. She'd expected a quick brush of his lips before he headed back with the other guys, but his fingers brushed behind her ear, touching the shell softly before he took possession of her lips. It was hardly the chaste kiss she expected, and once his mouth connected with hers, she almost forgot her sister was in the room.

"You need some help, Dylan? They just went to halftime and...Again?" Gage complained as he walked into the kitchen. "This is getting old," he muttered to Jessie.

Dylan pulled away from Julia, his eyes heated with desire. "We'll finish this when we don't have so many eyes on us," he whispered quietly.

Julia felt her blood turn into lava in her veins. "Don't make promises you can't keep." She smiled against his lips. "We always have eyes at the house."

"Hmm, I accept your challenge." He winked at her as he stood and reached for the case of beer. "And you, little brother, need to find a woman of your own and shut up."

Jessie laughed as the pair walked out. "I think I like him. A lot."

Julia nodded. "Me, too. That's the problem."

AS MUCH AS Julia loved visiting with her sister, she couldn't help but think about Dylan and his promise as they drove back to her house. They were like two teenagers, unable to keep their hands off of one another as soon as the others left the room. As amazing as the physical side of their relationship was, and it was nothing less than earth-shattering, it was the emotional connection she valued most. Dylan reached over Roscoe, curled up between them, and took her hand in his, letting his thumb brush over the pulse racing at her wrist. Tango stuck his head through the open back window of the truck and rested it on Julia's left shoulder.

Dylan shook his head. "He is a whole different level of jealous."

She reached up with her right hand to pat Tango's head. "He just knows my moods."

"And he interprets me holding your hand as fear?"

She arched her brow playfully. "I'm sure he can tell when I'm anxious, or angry," she suggested. "Or excited."

"Ah." She could see the grin spread over his lips in the fading sunset. "And I suppose he must be picking up on some *anxiety* now?"

"Not exactly."

"Anger?"

"Keep trying." This playful mood was a side of him she'd barely glimpsed, and she found it irresistible.

"That only leaves me one other option," he pointed out.

"Um, maybe. I think there's an entire gambit of emotions I could be having," she teased.

Dylan pulled to a stop in front of the house, and she let Tango out of the back of the truck. "Wait here," he instructed as he opened the front door and disappeared inside.

Julia watched him go into her house, tired of the added precautions, and just plain sick of the extra watchfulness. She wanted to be able to walk into the house with Dylan, to make love whenever and wherever they wanted to. To fall asleep with him and not wonder what time he was getting up for his watch. When he appeared in the doorway and crooked a finger at her, giving her that cocky grin, she returned it with one of her own and jutted her hip to one side.

"You think that's all it takes? I've got news for you."

She never finished what she'd been about to say because he jogged down the steps and scooped her into his arms. "I texted Chase and Gage and told them to find somewhere else to go for a while. I want you all to myself."

"You did not!" She widened her eyes. "Dylan, they'll know—"

"You think they didn't already?" He laughed. "I hate to tell you, but it's pretty obvious by the way you look at me with those big brown eyes."

She knew she couldn't deny it, but she wasn't about to let him off that easily. "Yeah, well, those hungry eyes you shoot my way tell quite a story, too."

"Speaking of being hungry," Dylan began, setting her feet on the floor and winding his arms around her waist, letting her back curve against the front of him as he walked her down the hall toward her room. "I'm feeling pretty famished right now."

She ran a hand over his forearm and smiled innocently as he brushed her hair from her shoulder. "You are? Maybe we should take this to the kitchen and I could fix you something to eat."

Dylan dipped his head, pressing his lips to the side of her neck, making her shiver as desire heated her body. His hands slid over stomach, slipping below the hem of her shirt, and she wondered if he could feel the butterflies inside. They'd barely reached the room and kicked off their shoes when he lifted the shirt over her head, tossing it aside as his lips pressed soft kisses over her shoulder. Her fingers dug into his arms as she tried to hold herself up when her legs wanted to give way. Dylan moved his hand to cup her breast, his thumb brushing over the exposed curve of flesh at the top of her bra.

She spun in his arms, unable to keep from touching him, and stood on her toes, pulling his head toward her.

Dylan was more than willing to comply, taking her lips hostage, his tongue sweeping into her mouth. Julia unbuttoned his shirt, desperate to feel his flesh under her hands, and inhaled the scent of him as they shared a breath.

"Dylan," she whispered as his lips trailed over her collarbone. Her hands fell to the waistband of his pants and fumbled with the button. He unbuttoned them for her, letting them fall to the ground, and stood shamelessly before her in nothing but his boxer briefs.

Julia was sure she would never tire of looking at him. Every part of him was hard muscle, ridges and valleys, hollows and crevices beckoning her eyes. And her hands. Dylan closed his eyes as her fingers traced the lines of his tattoo over his chest. "Did you have this before?"

"The part over my chest. The rest was added after I got back." She looked at the extension of the tattoo over his neck and arm and saw the scars beneath the colored ink. "I couldn't stand to look at the scars. They were just a reminder of how I failed."

Julia wondered how she hadn't noticed the scars before. Her eyes misted as she realized the agony he'd endured with his injuries. Her fingers ran over the marred flesh, and she pressed her lips against the scar on his arm. Dylan winced, tensing, but didn't move away from her. "Dylan, you didn't fail. What you went through was horrible, but every bit of it was what brought you here."

He buried his hands into her hair, tipping her chin up so she was looking at him. "If you would have asked me a month ago, I would have changed it all. Now?" He shook his head.

Julia knew the bittersweet pain he was going through. A part of her was dying to go back and change what happened with Evan. In hindsight, she would never have allowed him on the ranch, would have kept more distance between them. She would have watched Misty's reactions to him closer. But her past had brought her to this point in her life, where she was able to train service dogs with more depth than she'd ever thought possible. Her own battle with PTSD helped her understand and help others, and that was an experience that had given her far more than it had ever taken. Without it, she never would have met Dylan, never have learned to trust again, or to love again. The cost to reach this place was steep and painful.

"I know." She held a hand to his cheek, looking into his eyes, seeing the grief he still felt for his friends. "I know." Her voice caught. There was nothing else to say.

Julia unbuttoned her jeans and pushed them over her hips before stepping back into Dylan's arms. There were no words that would take away the sting of what they had lost. But she could show him there was a reason they were spared, a future that could be had, if they were brave enough to grasp it. What had only moments before been teasing kisses with smiles and laughter turned into something far more sacred, their heated mouths pressed together and reminding one another of the frailty of life.

Dylan's hands slid over her back to pull her against his chest, her breasts pressed against him. He slid one strap of her bra off her shoulder, and his teeth grazed over her flesh. She whimpered in thrilling agony. As he unclasped the wisp of material, her hands slid down his back to lightly drag her nails over his rounded buttocks, and he growled against her neck. The vibration of his breath against her skin paired with the shadow of beard growth on his jaw made her shake with need, and she pulled him backward toward the bed, dropping the rest of her clothing along the way.

Laying her on the mattress, Dylan stretched out beside her, his finger trailing between her breasts to her stomach. "You are so beautiful. So much more than I deserve."

His words broke her heart. Didn't he understand how amazing he was? How honorable? He saw failures where she only saw strength. He saw himself as lacking where she saw him as overflowing with goodness.

And she had no idea how to prove to him that he was more than an injured soldier. He was a loyal friend, a devoted brother, a tender lover, a hero. He was the most amazing man she had ever known, and he didn't see it. Telling him proved nothing. She could only show him how she felt.

Julia pushed Dylan so he lay flat on the bed, and straddled his hips. "Why can't you see what I see?" Her hair fell around their faces like a curtain, forcing him to focus on her eyes. "Why can't you believe me when I tell you how incredible you are?"

She leaned closer, her lips brushing against his. "Why won't you quit fighting against the truth and accept what everyone else sees in you?"

Julia rose over him and slid down his length. A hiss of pleasure slipped past his lips, and he arched beneath her. Pure pleasure, white hot and electrifying, shot through her, and she bit her lip to contain it. Dylan's fingers dug into the curve of her hips as he tried to hold her still. Ignoring him, she slowly moved against him again.

He lifted her slightly and thrust into her. It was too much. She wanted to hold back, to let him find ecstasy with her, but her body wouldn't wait. Her release came with the force of an explosion, shattering her as she clung to him.

She opened her eyes and found him staring at her. "I love you, Dylan."

He slowed himself, drawing out her release as she trembled. When she could take no more, he held her against him, with her head tucked in his neck. His hand trailed over her back, making her shiver. He groaned, his body reacting within her, still connected.

"Don't move yet," he warned.

"But—"

His fingertips brushed over the curve of her breast against his chest. "We've only begun," he promised. "Unless you move again." A smile lifted the corner of his lips as he ducked his chin to look at her. The smile on his lips made her heart soar. "I love you, Julia Hart." He brushed her hair back from her face and cupped his fingers around the back of her head, his tongue sneaking between her lips to warm every limb again.

The simple touch was enough to ignite her body again. He groaned against her mouth and rolled so she lay beneath him, and he moved deeper into her. Julia clutched his back, the muscles beneath her fingers rippling.

"Dylan," she whispered against his lips. "Please."

She felt the change in him as he plunged into her. Whatever self-control he'd possessed disappeared as she rocked with him, his hands caressing her body into a frenzy of hunger. She felt her body shatter again as he captured her mouth, her name a prayer on his lips and a lifeline to her soul.

Chapter Seventeen

DYLAN WOKE BEFORE light broke into the bedroom and snuck out of the bed, barely jostling Tango, who was sprawled upside down over Julia's feet.

How in the world does that dog protect her against anything?

As if reading his mind, Tango opened an eye and winked at him. Dylan shook his head at the animal, wondering if he wasn't a police officer reincarnated. He slipped on a pair of sweats and snuck out of the room, shutting the door behind Roscoe. He rubbed a hand over his head and made his way to the kitchen, praying Chase had a fresh pot of coffee on. How in the world had his life become this chaotic twist of abnormal routine? When he'd come out here, it had been to gain a service dog and eventually his freedom. Instead, he'd found friends, a purpose, and a passion he hadn't ever expected in his future. The problem now was that he wasn't sure it would last.

"Hey," Chase greeted him as he walked into the kitchen. Gracie looked up at Roscoe before laying her muzzle back onto her paws. "Just started a fresh pot."

"Thanks." Dylan grabbed a clean mug from the cupboard and yawned.

"You know, you don't have to do this."

Dylan turned slowly. If Chase was suggesting he leave Julia to deal with Evan alone, he might put his fist into Chase's face now.

"Get up early each morning," he clarified. "I can handle it. You can stay with her."

Dylan felt ashamed for assuming the worst about the man. "I'm not going to leave you to handle it alone."

"You're a better man than I am. I wouldn't want to leave her."

Dylan arched his brows skyward in surprise as jealousy twisted in his gut. "Is there something you want to tell me? Do you have a thing for Julia?"

"What?" Chase frowned for a moment before he chuckled. "No. That's not what I meant. Well, at least, not about Julia. I just meant I wouldn't want to leave a woman I was in love with to sit in here and sip coffee with a grouchy cop."

Dylan clenched his jaw, unconvinced. "Sure."

"Chill out, Dylan. You haven't been around long enough to know Chase here is head over heels for Bailey, but she won't give him the time of day." Justin came through the back door and let it slam shut behind him. "No breakfast?" He looked around the kitchen.

"Your sister is still sleeping."

Justin sighed loudly and glared at Dylan. "Between you and Nathan, I'm losing my sisters. They used to cook me breakfast every day."

"Aw, you poor thing, you might have to learn to cook for yourself like the rest of us bachelors who don't have sisters," Chase teased.

Dylan watched the pair razz each other as only old friends could. He missed the camaraderie of friendships like these, like the ones he'd had in the military.

"So, what are your plans once this is all over, Dylan? You going to look for a place here? Because I don't see Julia moving anywhere." Justin sipped his coffee before opening the refrigerator and grabbing eggs, sliding the container onto the sink.

"I think the fire department is looking for some guys who have their EMT certification. I could put you in touch with Craig," Chase offered.

Justin reached for the bacon, pausing when Dylan still didn't answer. "You are planning on staying, aren't you?"

Dylan felt as if he'd just been led in front of the firing squad. He and Julia hadn't even talked about what would come next. He had no idea what the future held for either of them. Both men stared at him, expecting him to agree that he would just find a job here and stay with Julia; but he couldn't promise that yet. He hadn't held a job since he'd left the military. Sure, he'd been medically retired, but he'd never thought of that as permanent. He couldn't work until he was off of his medications completely. He couldn't live off Julia's charity. He needed to feel he was contributing, and until he did, he couldn't make a commitment to anyone. Until he brought something worthwhile to the table for Julia, his was a solitary future.

The vision of Julia hovering over him last night filled his mind. She offered him all of her; she believed in him and their future together. But it wasn't enough. He had to believe it, too.

Roscoe sat at his feet and pawed at his leg. Dylan knew the dog was sensing his anxiety over a simple question. "Excuse me," he muttered and hurried out the back door with the dog at his side.

He knew Justin and Chase must be wondering what sort of freak he was, but Justin dredged up too many questions he didn't have answers to. Questions he needed to answer.

Dylan sat on the back stoop and slipped his cell phone from his pocket, scrolling through his contacts until he saw his therapist's office number. His finger hovered over the call button. If he called him, he was going to have to tell him everything that had happened since getting on the plane. He set the phone down as Roscoe laid his head on Dylan's thigh. He ran a hand over the dog's head.

"You don't want to go, do you, boy?" Roscoe simply lifted one brow and blinked. "Me neither."

"Then don't." Gage sat down on the stoop beside his brother. "I don't think Julia would ask you to."

"I can't be what she needs." He shook his head and looked down at the dog, avoiding his brother's piercing gaze. "I can't do this."

"Which is what, Dylan?"

"Be a husband, a father, the house with the white picket fence. You know, the fantasy every woman has."

Gage chuckled and shook his head. "Have you met Julia?" Dylan glared at him. "Take a look around. I'm pretty sure she already has the house. As far as the rest, isn't that exactly what you want someday? Have you even asked her what she wants?"

"I can't even get through a day without medication. What kind of husband and father would that make me? When I get stressed out, I don't want anything to do with people."

"Not since you got here," Gage pointed out. "And you are not Dad," he said quietly. "Is that what you're afraid of? Turning into Dad?"

"I'm already turning into him." Dylan couldn't hide the defeat in his voice.

"Dylan, the issue with the pills wasn't entirely your fault, and you're past that. You are *the* most responsible man I've ever known. You took care of me and Mom, even when you should have been taking care of yourself. You took care of every man in your unit for years. You're taking care of a woman you barely know."

Dylan looked at his brother. "I know her."

"You know what I mean," Gage clarified. "You take care of everyone."

"I got two men killed." His guilt surrounded him, choking him.

"No, you didn't. Those two men were killed during a mission." Dylan looked at him. Gage had a way of getting straight to the point. He was almost painfully blunt. "You did everything you could to save them. That wasn't your fault. You aren't a superhero, Dylan."

He looked down at Roscoe. His brother wasn't saying anything he hadn't already heard from his therapist for the past year. He wasn't to blame for the raid, the mistakes his unit made, trying to carry his fallen brother back. Had he made it where the rest of his unit had hunkered to wait, all three of them would have been killed when the missile hit. It didn't change the guilt he shouldered that a husband and father was dead, another medic who'd stayed behind to help him—both gone forever because he hadn't been able to save either of them. Two families were without men they needed because of Dylan. What right did he have to a future when they were without? He gripped his knees, his hands wanting to clench into fists, even as he fought the urge to allow the rage to flow through him, to put his fist through a wall.

"I need to be alone."

"This is where this conversation always ends up, Dylan." Gage shook his head. "Why can't you stop fighting the truth and accept it?"

Dylan heard Julia's words from the night before echo in his brother's comment. How could they both be so mistaken?

Were they mistaken?

"Do you want me to get your medication?" Gage stood up as Roscoe nudged Dylan's hands insistently.

"No." He was tired of relying on the drugs to help him function. It was just one more sign that he wasn't whole. He took a deep breath, but the rage wouldn't quite loosen its hold on him. Roscoe shoved his nose under Dylan's arms and pressed his snout under his chin, bumping him harder, knocking his head backward slightly. It was enough to force him to focus on the dog. He opened his hand and Roscoe slid his head under Dylan's palm. He made up his mind that he was going to call his doctor and get off of them. It was going to take time, but it was a step toward becoming the man Julia believed him to be.

"No, I'm okay." He took another deep breath and looked up at Gage as Roscoe lolled his tongue out, appearing to smile. "I'm good."

Gage stared at him for a moment, still unsure, before a smile widened over his face. "Yeah, you are. At least, you will be."

EVAN HAD DISAPPEARED from the face of the earth. At least, that was the way it seemed. For the past two days, Julia had ventured outside only to help Chase and Dylan train the dogs. She was able to bring a few of the other dogs out for a little training in a group, but nothing like she usually would, and it was wearing on her nerves. It wasn't fair to her dogs to be cooped up so long, but she just couldn't bring herself to take the risk. She knew Evan wanted her in this position: fearful, confined to a single area under his watch. Several times during the day she felt as if there were unseen eyes watching her, but Chase and Dylan had both assured her that they'd gone over the property with a fine-tooth comb and found no signs of Evan.

She knew they needed to leave the property again in order to properly train the dogs, but after the incident in the grocery store, she was sure Evan would be waiting for her somewhere else. Being cooped up was starting to make her irritable, and she'd snapped at her brother again this morning when he showed up for breakfast. Paranoia was beginning to set in, and she wondered if she shouldn't just call an end to this madness.

Dylan seemed to understand her fear and would hold her through it when she would break down in tears in the middle of the night. He was there when she woke from multiple nightmares, something she hadn't experienced for years, until Evan's return. Dylan seemed to know she didn't need him to psychoanalyze her or try to convince her that there was nothing to be afraid of. He simply held her, letting her release the tears and terror against his broad chest.

The only time she was able to forget the insanity that had become her daily life was when Dylan touched her, as they made love. In his arms, she lived in the present. His hands made her soar, away from deranged ex-boyfriends, beyond overprotective siblings, hidden from self-doubt, if only for a short time. But each morning, reality came crashing in just before sunrise when Dylan rose to relieve Chase. It had to stop. It was a dangerous version of *Groundhog Day*, and she was finished with her role in it.

"We're taking the dogs into town today," she announced as she walked into the kitchen.

All four men seated around her kitchen table looked up at her in surprise. Justin was the first to speak. "I'm not sure that's a good—"

"I don't care." She crossed her arms and raised a brow, daring anyone else to argue. "I'm done hiding in this house. We're making ourselves sitting ducks here. I'm not a victim any longer, and I'm tired of acting like one."

Dylan's mouth lifted at one corner. "You sure?"

She returned the smile. "Being stuck with you four is making me crazy. I'm sick of the testosterone overload in this house. Right, Gracie?" The shepherd lifted her head and cocked it sideways.

"Road trip," Gage yelled. "Dibs on the guest shower." He pointed at Chase. "You used all the hot water last time."

He raised his hands. "That wasn't me." He shifted his eyes to Dylan before glancing at Julia. A blush flooded her cheeks as she recalled the shower the two of them had taken together the morning before.

"Ew!" Justin dropped his fork onto his empty plate. "I'm glad I ate before you decided to ruin my appetite, Chase. Thanks." He glared at Dylan. "That's the last thing I want to think about over my breakfast. Or ever."

"Maybe you should eat breakfast at home then," Julia offered.

"Look who's feeling feisty this morning." Chase laughed, smacking Justin's arm, and put his own dishes into the sink. "Little sister just told you."

Julia cleared her throat. "Do I look like your maid? Dishwasher," she warned, pointing at the sink before walking out the back door to feed the dogs in the kennel. Dylan followed her with Roscoe and Tango running ahead.

"You okay?"

"Fine, why?"

"You seem a little on edge." He moved behind her and wound his arms around her waist, walking in step behind her. His lips moved against the shell of her ear, sending a warm shiver of desire between her thighs. What was it about this man that turned her into a puddle of quivering Jell-O when he was near?

She tipped her head to one side, giving him access to her neck and sighing as his lips caressed her. "I'm tired of running and hiding."

His hand slid under the hem of her shirtfront, his fingers teasing her bared flesh. "Okay."

"I'm tired of being afraid. I want to control my own life again." Dylan turned her to face him at the door of the kennel and held her against it, looking into her eyes, searching them for something. "I guess I just have a touch of cabin fever."

"You know what they say about fevers, right?" He dipped his head and nipped at the corner of her mouth.

"That you're supposed to starve a fever?"

He lifted his head and looked confused. "I thought you were supposed to sweat with a fever."

She knew she must have a stupid grin on her face, but his attempt at dirty talk was so funny and illogical that she couldn't help herself. "Um, no. But did you have something in mind?"

Dylan opened the door to the kennel amid several barks, yips, and calls of delight from the dogs. "I did, but I don't think these guys are going to wait for breakfast," he yelled over the din.

"Probably not," she agreed but turned and pulled him toward her, raising on her toes and giving him a kiss that he wouldn't forget. Her hands wrapped around his neck, her fingers massaging the back of his head as her mouth teased him.

Dylan growled, sliding his hands over her rear and pulling her against him. She could feel his arousal and wished they had time and the privacy to give in to their passion now. "Come on, these dogs will just get louder if we don't get them fed," he complained as he walked toward the kennels to gather the food bowls.

"I promise to make it up to you later."

Dylan stopped and looked back at her over his shoulder. "You better believe it."

"Why are we going to the park when Julia has several hundred acres?" Gage parked the Camaro next to Julia's truck in the field turned into a parking lot.

"Why not?" Dylan glared at his brother as they locked the cars.

"Because there are people and distractions here that we can't replicate at my place," Julia pointed out. "Like the kids swimming in the community pool over there, or those kids on the playground there. Those things are all noises and smells the dogs don't have at home, and Roscoe and Gracie need to learn to ignore them and focus on their handlers."

"Wow, she is feeling feisty today." Dylan laughed at his brother as he reached for Julia's left hand, moving Roscoe to his left side.

"Yeah, well, if you two don't keep your hands off each other while we're here, I'm going home."

Julia laughed as she looked down at Dylan's hand. "Can't do it. You need to keep him on your right. Today we're going to teach him how to move between you and other people."

He frowned before pursing his lips. "How do we do that?"

She gave Tango the command to sit and stay and moved toward Dylan. "Tell him to stand, and step behind him." When he did as she said, Roscoe looked back at him. "Now tell him to stay close."

He did as she said while Gage and Chase watched. Tango laid his head on his paws, appearing to go to sleep, and Gracie cocked her head to the side, her ears alert.

"Chase, tell Gracie to stay and approach Dylan." Chase followed her orders and walked toward Dylan. Roscoe remained firmly rooted in position, facing Chase but not allowing him to move any closer than his body length toward Dylan. Chase took a step to the side, but Roscoe shifted to block him without hesitation.

"Praise him and release him from position," Julia said.

"Good boy, Roscoe." Dylan squatted down and rubbed the dog's neck. "Okay, you're a good boy, aren't you?" The dog's mouth opened and his chin lifted.

"That was exactly what he should do. Did you see how he blocked Chase from moving toward you? Let's try it again, but this time watching behind you. Then we'll try a down-stay with him lying down in front of you so no one can come close."

Julia helped Dylan teach Roscoe the new commands and was surprised by his patience with the dog. When they began working with Chase and Gracie, she had Gage hide a toy in the middle of the playground as they walked

Gracie away from it. Teaching dogs to scent train was one of her favorite tasks, and the dogs actually loved the work. It was a skill that only a few breeds were able to master, and Gracie was one of the best she'd ever worked with. She turned to see where Gage hid the toy, at the top of the tallest twisting slide, and smiled. He wasn't about to make it easy on Chase or the dog.

A crying child running to her mother near the fence caught Julia's attention. The noise was new to the dogs, and she could see Gracie was trying to focus in spite of the distractions. "Okay, are you—"

Her heart raced, even as it dropped into her toes. Evan stood just outside the fence, watching their group. She opened her mouth to tell Chase, but before she could say anything, Evan dipped his head toward her and disappeared. There was no vehicle, no witnesses. He simply disappeared without a trace, almost as if she'd imagined his presence entirely.

"Julia, are you ready?" Chase asked.

She tore her eyes from the fence line. "I...yes."

Julia looked at Chase and wondered if she shouldn't tell him what she thought she'd seen. She glanced back to where Evan had stood. Maybe it hadn't been him. But, then why would a stranger be watching them? Why would he nod in her direction and vanish? In the end, she decided not to say anything, not yet, because if she was wrong, they would think she was losing her marbles. Maybe she was.

"Let her go," she told him.

"Find it, Gracie," he instructed. The dog took off like a shot toward the playground and began sniffing under the swings, quickly moving on to the jungle gym and navigating the plastic stairs with reckless disregard for her own safety. She picked her way to the top of the slide and sat outside the entrance, looked back at Chase following her, and began barking excitedly. "Well, that didn't take long."

He led the dog back to where Julia, Dylan, and Gage waited. "Too easy." He tossed the toy to Gage. "Try harder, unless she's just smarter than you," he teased.

Julia loved hearing the men joke with each other, and watching how relaxed Dylan was becoming around them. Normally, she would be the first to jump in and tease, but her gaze kept straying back to the fence, keeping an eye out for the man she'd seen. The more time that passed, the more she wondered if it had really been Evan. It was very possible she was so paranoid that he would find her that she was imagining anyone might look like him.

"Julia, are you listening?" Dylan's brow was etched with concern when she finally responded. She could see the anxiety rise in him as he looked off in the distance, following her gaze.

"I'm fine," she said, shaking her head. "I was just lost in my thoughts for a second." She looked down at Gracie, who sat at Chase's feet, a happy dog grin on her face as she beamed up at him. "Let's try something harder. I'll hold her and I want you to go hide, Chase."

Dylan scanned the area again. "Are you sure about that?"

"It's fine, Dylan," Chase said. "Dad's already patrolled the area twice just since we've arrived."

Julia looked at him, surprised.

"What? I let him know we'd be here. Didn't you see the patrol car drive by a few minutes ago?"

She hadn't, but if the sheriff was in the area, Evan certainly wouldn't have risked being seen.

Unless that was what made him run.

She didn't know what to think at this point.

"I want to see what she can do." Chase sounded like a little boy with a new toy he loved. "Admit it, she's doing even better than you'd thought she would."

She arched a brow at him. "I'm encouraged by how well she's doing."

"Psh, don't listen to her, Gracie." The shepherd cocked her head to the side and lifted her ears high, listening to him. "She likes that slobbery Great Dane. She can't appreciate a smart girl like you."

"It's official." Gage threw his hands into the air and slapped his thighs. "Chase has crossed over into insanity and is flirting with a dog. Dude, you *really* need to find a girlfriend."

Chapter Eighteen

DYLAN AND GAGE had been at the ranch for a little over a week, and things seemed perfect. Too perfect. If Dylan had been anyone else, Julia would have let him know that he would be ready to leave after another week of training. He and Roscoe had bonded better than she'd hoped, and with only a week under their belt, the dog was as devoted to him as he would have been if Dylan had raised him from a puppy. She couldn't ask for more. Except she wanted to.

She and Dylan spent every moment together, and like him and his bonding with Roscoe, their relationship had progressed faster than most would. She sat on the couch with him, tucked into his side, watching a movie with him, both dogs on the floor. Gage had gone to get some work finished in her office. Chase glanced their way and twisted his mouth to the side thoughtfully. She caught his gaze and reached for the remote to pause the movie.

"What's that look for?"

"I'm just thinking." He waved his hand, but his thoughtful expression remained.

"About?" Dylan jumped in.

"How much longer do you think Gracie will need?"

Julia laughed. "Chase, it's only been three days. Search and rescue dogs train for years before they are tested, and you have to pass several certifications. We're just laying the groundwork."

"Seriously? I thought we just taught her to sniff out things and that was it." He looked at the dog lying at his feet. She looked up at him adoringly.

"Would you hand any Joe Blow a gun and call him a deputy?"

"I see your point." He shrugged. "She needs to be doing this, even if I did just start this as an excuse to be out here to protect you." He looked back at Julia and Dylan, his expression growing somber. "This isn't working. Either Evan is gone or he's not falling for the ruse."

"He's not gone." Dylan sounded so certain, Julia's heart began to beat quickly, and she wondered if he'd seen him at the park as well. "He wouldn't go through all of this trouble just to disappear at the first sign of resistance." Dylan reached out and took her hand in his, as if he knew the mere mention of Evan had sent her stomach plummeting to her toes. "Are you thinking of leaving?"

"I'm debating it. This isn't doing anyone any good."

"It's protecting Julia. What do you think he's going to do when you leave?" Dylan looked down at her as she sat up, feeling more uncomfortable with this discussion with each passing moment. "If you leave, Julia will be a sitting target."

"She'll have you." Chase looked at Dylan pointedly.

Dylan looked away and Julia looked from one to the other, knowing she was missing something. Some sort of communication was passing unspoken between them, and they were leaving her in the dark. Dylan went from being completely relaxed to pissed in a matter of seconds. Roscoe sensed it as well and was already nudging Dylan's arm, trying to get his attention.

"What's going on, Chase?"

"He wants to leave in order to lure Evan into the open. He was hoping him being here at all might do that, but Evan is smarter than he gave him credit for." He scowled at Chase. "Now he wants to be more aggressive. You think if you leave Julia unprotected, he'll come out of the woodwork."

"If you didn't agree with me, you wouldn't be this pissed off, would you?"

"I'm not leaving her here to get hurt. You're an ass for even suggesting it." She felt Dylan's hand tighten over hers, almost painfully. Roscoe tried to climb into Dylan's lap. "She's not a puppet to lure him out. You've already put her in enough danger."

"I'm trying to keep her safe. That's why I'm here." Chase leaned forward in the chair, and Gracie immediately sat up, watching the two men intently. "The sooner we put Evan away, the sooner she's safe and the two of you can have a real life."

She felt the shock radiate through Dylan, like a current from one man to the other, and it immediately diffused his temper. They had yet to talk about the future, and the fact that Chase had just confronted him with the idea was enough to bring him back from the rage he'd been heading toward.

Julia rose quickly and pulled Dylan to his feet. "We can talk about this tomorrow, Chase," she said quietly. "Enough for tonight, okay?"

She pleaded with her eyes for him to understand that this wasn't something they could talk about now. She made her way toward the hallway. Chase clenched his jaw as they walked past him, and she felt the tension flow through Dylan. Roscoe whined and continued to nose his hand as Julia pushed him through the door to her room and closed it behind them.

Dylan paced the room, running his hands over his head, unable to calm the storm she could see raging in his eyes. "Dylan?" Roscoe jumped up in front of him and knocked him off balance. When Dylan ignored him, Roscoe jumped onto the bed and put his front paws on his shoulders. "Talk to me."

"It was bad enough that he insisted on staying here in the first place, knowing that might put you in jeopardy, but to deliberately try to put you in harm's way. I'm going to kill him."

"Dylan, stop," She moved in front of him, much the way Roscoe did, and put her hands on his chest. "He's not suggesting anything I haven't already thought of. What has you so pissed about this?"

"Because I can't protect you alone."

His voice broke at his confession, and Julia realized the crux of his anger. He wanted to be her hero, he was using her to redeem himself of what had happened in the past. Dylan hadn't been able to save his brothers during the attack on their base, and he wanted to assuage his guilt by protecting her. In his eyes, if he couldn't do that, he was a failure. Again. She took a step back from him.

"I didn't ask you to protect me." She only wanted his heart, for him to love her. Was he still just doing his duty and fulfilling his overburdened sense of honor? Was she nothing more than another responsibility he'd taken on?

"I know you didn't ask. But it's what I do. The only thing I *can* do." His voice trailed off, and she felt her heart crumble in her chest, like wasted ash after a blazing fire had consumed all it needed. He met her gaze and she saw the dejection there, and she realized the truth. He thought she was weak, a victim. He didn't have faith in her to take care of herself.

"I don't need your pity, Dylan." Tango moved to her side and buried his head against her hip. "You came to me for help, remember? I was doing just fine."

"Julia, that's not what I—"

"Yes, you did." She held up a hand, not letting him speak. "I'm not your penance, or your second chance. I don't want to be where you find your worth. That's too much weight for any person to bear. What happened to you, to the other men in your unit—it was horrible, but don't make me your project."

Dylan's eyes flashed with anger and frustration.

The way she felt about him was real. She loved him, but she wouldn't be a pawn to help him feel better about himself any more than she would be a plaything for Evan's sick game. "You don't even see it, do you?" She shook her head, her heart aching as she bared it to him. "Protecting me from Evan is just a way for you to feel like the man you used to be. You're not the same man, Dylan. Life has changed you."

"I liked the man I was," he snapped, his voice quiet but dangerous. "I worked hard to become that man. I was strong, and capable, and someone people could rely on. They trusted me."

Her body reacted to his words without permission from her brain, and she moved toward him, her hand cupping his jaw. "You are still that man, Dylan." Her eyes misted with unshed tears. She was unable to hold them back when she could see the agony in his tense stance. "You may not see it, but I can. What you've been through has made you even more than you were. You're stronger now."

Dylan clasped his fingers around her wrist and pulled her toward him. One arm wound around her waist while his other hand moved to her face. He put his forehead against hers and closed his eyes. "You don't know, Julia. You didn't know me before." His breath came in ragged gasps, as if he was trying to gain control of emotions that had long since gone wild. "This is not who I was."

"Maybe not," she agreed. "But this is who you are *now*, and until you learn to accept that, with all the strengths and flaws you bring to the table, there can't be an us. Not now or in the future."

She moved away from his touch and felt as if she was ripping her heart from her chest with a dull blade. The physical ache was unbearable as she forced herself to take a step back. Then another.

"You aren't afraid you can't protect me, Dylan. You're afraid of what happens after this is over. There is a future after this, and it scares you so you'd rather run from it than face it. You wanted to run from it when you first arrived, and apparently you still want to."

Julia walked to her door and opened it. "I've always had people who wanted to protect me, Dylan, but sometimes things happen and you can't be sheltered from them, ever. ugly things. What I wanted was someone who understood what I'd been through. You still want to live in the past, to make up for what is already gone. I can't live there any longer."

Dylan stared at Roscoe, unable to watch Julia walk out of the room. He could feel the rage scratching inside him, clawing its way to the surface, dying to be released, to get out and ruin whatever he might salvage of this relationship. He left her room, unable to see the reminders of her around him. The anger, the rage, was choking him, hot and cloying, enveloping him like thick smoke from the ruins of his life. He slammed the door to the room she'd given him and ran his hands over his head, fighting to keep the beast at bay.

His eyes scanned the room for something to hit, or throw, some way to release this animal inside, ripping at his chest. He didn't want to feel. This is what he'd tried to hide from, was still trying to hide from. This was what he'd avoided by withdrawing from everyone over the past year. No amount of special ops, macho bullshit was going to make this ache disappear. His skin was hot, his scars throbbing with pain he hadn't felt since he'd arrived here. All of him felt raw, like an open wound that couldn't heal.

His eyes fell on the pill bottles, most unused since his arrival, sitting like sentinels on the top of the dresser. Those were one answer. He heard Roscoe scratching at the door, trying to find a way in, but ignored him and picked up one of the bottles for sleeping pills. What he wanted was to disappear, to find that dark oblivion he'd had before.

Before Evan, Roscoe, or Julia. Before he did the one thing he swore he'd never do again—hope for more. Hope for a real life again. He flipped the lid from the pills and dumped several into his hand. Just for tonight, just to help him sleep.

Julia was right; he was running away, escaping into the painful nothingness that his doctors had so willingly offered because they didn't know a better way. And it had worked. Before. But now, the thought of sleeping, of lying down without Julia's soft curves tucked against him, held no appeal. There was no going back, no escaping. She'd shown him he wanted more, and no pill was going to take that desire away. He hurled the pills at the wall, watching them scatter to the floor.

The anger in him snuffed out, like a candle in a hurricane.

Roscoe's insistent scratching had quieted, and Dylan felt as if the entire house had gone suddenly silent. He opened the door, feeling physically exhausted from the mental battle he'd just waged. It wasn't over, but in not shutting down, in forcing his demon to retreat, he'd won a small victory.

Roscoe looked up at him, and Dylan could see the accusation in his eyes. How could a dog make him feel so guilty? He patted his hands against his stomach and Roscoe jumped up. Dylan rubbed his ears and over his head.

"I'm sorry, boy, but this was something I had to do alone."

He realized the truth of the words as they fell from his lips. As much as he needed Roscoe and Julia, she'd forced him to face his reality—there was a future, whether he wanted to accept it or not. Leaning over to pick up the pills, his eyes fell on Julia's door, praying that he hadn't waited too long or cut her too deeply.

JULIA SAT UP in bed, staring into the darkness of her room, unsure of what woke her. A low growl came from Tango, lying at the foot of her bed. His ears were perked and alert, eyes focused on her closed door. She heard a muffled sound, like someone talking, and slipped from the bed, pressing her ear against the door. Tango whimpered quietly as he jumped down and padded to her side. This soft growl wasn't his normal warning, so she didn't think there was an intruder, but something had stirred both of them.

She cracked her door open, rubbing at her eyes, still sore from crying herself to sleep, and heard the voice again down the hall. Tango looked up at her before slowly creeping down the hall ahead of her, stopping at Dylan's door. She hadn't seen him since she walked out of her room earlier that night. It had nearly killed her to stand her ground, knowing she was doing what was best for both of them, and walk away when what she really wanted was to fall into his arms and make love to him until he forgot about the future and the past.

But that's what they had already been doing. Pretending the future didn't exist, that there wouldn't come a time when one of them had to make a decision to move forward or die of suffocation. Since the attack that left her in the hospital, trying to recover from the head trauma Evan inflicted, Julia had quickly learned if you weren't moving forward you were falling backward. She couldn't go back. She'd worked too hard to put the past, and the worst of her PTSD symptoms, behind her.

She knocked quietly on Dylan's door, but when she heard the quiet whimper from Roscoe, she opened it a crack. She felt her heart sink when she saw Roscoe standing over Dylan, nudging him with his muzzle insistently with no response. Dylan struggled in his sleep, thrashing against the sheets wound tightly around his legs, hitting Roscoe in the ribcage. The dog whimpered again but ignored the pain, trying to wake Dylan, shoving his nose into Dylan's ear and pawing at his sweat-soaked chest.

"Tango, stay," she commanded. Julia flipped on the light while Tango whimpered in the doorway. She hurried to the side of the bed, calling to Dylan quietly, trying to rouse him from his nightmare. "Dylan, wake up." She saw his eyes fly open, but they were glazed over, as if he couldn't really see her. "Dylan?"

Julia reached for his arm, her fingers sliding over his slick skin as he jerked away from her. His other arm swung around as he sat up and grabbed her before she could react. Tango and Roscoe began barking immediately, and she saw Tango lean toward the bed. Dylan ripped the sheets loose and flipped her onto her back on the bed, straddling her, holding her down with one hand against her chest. Seeing him pull his fist back, she screamed his name. His eyes cleared, finally focusing as Roscoe jumped against him, knocking him off balance and to the floor.

Julia gasped for breath as Tango stood in the doorway, barking frantically but not breaking his command to stay in place. She scrambled from the bed to Dylan's side as he sat up and touched his fingers to the side of his head. He looked at the blood on his hands dumbly. Julia reached for the sheet on the bed to stem the blood flow.

"You're going to need stitches."

Roscoe jumped to the floor and began licking Dylan's face, but he pushed the dog away.

"God, Julia." He reached out to her and she flinched, instinctively jerking backward. "What did I do?"

"I'm fine." She helped him stand, leaning his weight against the dresser, but she took a step back once he had his balance.

"I hurt you." He didn't have to ask. She'd seen the redness where a bruise would form below her throat, and her sternum ached from where he'd held her down. She doubted he'd miss it. His eyes fell to the top of her chest. "I did that, didn't I?"

She could read the agony in his eyes, but she couldn't speak. She couldn't deny what he'd done, even in the midst of a flashback, any more than she could reassure him that it wouldn't happen again. His eyes lifted to the door, where Gage and Chase stood, looking inside. The men were silent, but both seemed to realize what had happened.

Gage looked at Julia compassionately before moving forward and looping Dylan's arm over his shoulder. "You're going to need stitches. Chase can take you to the ER."

Julia glanced at Chase as she followed the pair into the hallway to the bathroom. Dylan looked at the wound in the mirror, ignoring his brother's attempt to talk him into going to the hospital.

"Get me a Steri-Strip and the glue from the kit. I'll be fine." He watched Gage walk out of the bathroom, and then his gaze met Julia's. She could feel him silently pleading with her.

She wanted to go to him, to tell him they could work through this, but she was afraid. Afraid he wouldn't believe her, afraid she would be lying, but more than anything, afraid that she'd made the same mistake again. She ducked her head and walked back into her room with Tango at her side, shutting the door behind her. If only she could suture her bleeding heart as quickly as Dylan could his head.

Chapter Nineteen

"Julia?" The quiet rap on the office door wasn't unexpected, but she was surprised to see Gage enter. "Hey, can we talk for a second?"

She bit her lip. "I really need to return these calls." She pointed to a stack of old messages she'd never thrown away, hating that she was lying to him to avoid talking about Dylan.

Gage picked one off the top of the pile and scanned it. "From three months ago?" He arched a brow at her. "Hiding, huh?"

"No," she denied, ashamed to admit the truth out loud. "Selectively avoiding reality."

Gage dropped into the worn couch opposite her desk. "I see. Because of this morning?"

"Why else would I be?" She didn't bother to hide the sarcasm in her voice. Tango opened one eye and raised his brow before returning to his nap. Julia sighed. "I know nightmares are all part of PTSD. Trust me, I've had more than my fair share. I still do."

"But it isn't the nightmare that's keeping you in here, is it?"

Julia covered her face with both of her hands and rubbed her eyes, taking a deep breath. How could she explain it to Gage, or Dylan? How could she confess that the anger she'd seen him fighting, his violent rage during his flashback this morning, was reminiscent of Evan's attack, and she couldn't willingly put herself in that position again?

Gage leaned forward on his elbows. "Julia, that was a flashback. His body was here, but his mind was there. Dylan would never deliberately hurt you."

"Not deliberately," she agreed, her hands moving to her arms, avoiding the bruise that was just starting to turn an ugly shade of blue against her sternum.

"He's done so well since we got here."

She nodded. "And it was likely brought on by stress and the argument we'd just had."

"Argument?" He raised his brows in surprise. "Anything I should know about?"

Julia shrugged. "The subject of the future came up, and you know how he is. He's afraid to look ahead."

"You have to know he loves you."

"I know he does." She fought back the grief that threatened to overtake her again. This was what she'd been trying to avoid. "And I love him. But he's not willing to move forward. He's letting guilt and sorrow and regrets chain him to the past. As long as he remains drowning in them, he'll keep having flashbacks and nightmares. Roscoe can help, but he can't cure what is eating Dylan alive."

"Roscoe is helping him control his triggers, and the anger, Julia. I've seen that." Gage rose from the couch and leaned forward with his hands on the desk, closing the gap between them. "But you've been able to reach him when no one else could." He turned and walked to the door, pausing to turn back. "He trusts you. We both do."

Gage disappeared down the hall, and the tears began to fall down her cheeks, unbidden and unchecked. "That was Dylan's first mistake."

As much as falling in love with him was hers.

DYLAN AVOIDED JULIA. What could he possibly say to make this right? *Sorry I nearly punched you this morning.*

What did it matter if he was in the middle of a flashback? That he had no idea what he'd been doing? That all he heard and saw were the bullets whizzing past? He'd felt the heat of the desert, and thought she'd been an enemy from the village sneaking up on him. He shoved his clothing into his duffel bag and looked over at Roscoe, lying on the bed watching him. When he noticed Dylan's attention, he tipped his head to one side curiously.

He knew they were going to have to talk about Roscoe. He couldn't imagine not having him at his side now. Other than this morning, the dog had been able to control each and every trigger as it presented. And, it wasn't a lack of trying on Roscoe's part this morning. Dylan absently rubbed at the scratches where Roscoe dug into his chest, hard enough to break the surface of the skin because of his lack of response. He could only imagine the pain he'd inflicted on Julia, but it had almost been far worse. If it hadn't been for Roscoe…

The dog's actions had left him with a cut on his head and a woman hiding scared in her office, but it could have been far worse. He didn't blame Julia for hiding, for being afraid of him. Especially after what she'd already gone through with Evan. She deserved far better than what he could offer. He'd known it all along. This was just the proof he'd wanted to avoid facing the truth.

"What are you doing?" Julia's voice was soft but hesitant from the doorway. He could hear the unease in the slight tremor, and when he turned to look at her, he could see the doubt in her eyes.

In one night, he'd gone from being her hero, a man she looked at with love and adoration, to seeing him with apprehension and fear. He'd done the one thing he promised not to do—hurt her—and in more ways than he wanted to count. He turned his back to her, unable to bear the agony her hesitation was causing within him.

"Packing. Gage and I are going to stay in town. I can come back every day to finish working with Roscoe until you think I'm ready for him to come with me."

"You're leaving?"

"I think it's for the best." He felt the lump in his throat choke him on the half-truth. Only a part of him believed it. Dylan wanted her to disagree, to argue, to reach out and give him hope again.

"I think you should take Roscoe with you now."

He looked at her over his shoulder, surprised that she would agree to his leaving so readily, but trying not to show that it felt as if she'd just ripped him open with a dull knife. "Are you sure?"

His voice was raspy, raw from the pain, and he cleared his throat, wanting nothing more than to walk across the room and pull her into his arms. To tip her face up to his and take her mouth in a kiss, to hear her sigh of surrender and to make love to her, to show her how he wanted to worship her. His eyes fell to the bruise he could barely make out along the collar of her T-shirt.

Dylan crossed the room, without thinking, and moved her shirt down so he could fully see what he'd done. She gasped in surprise, or fear, but continued to look up at him with her beautiful innocent eyes. An ugly purple bruise was just beginning to mar her skin. It would turn purple and black later but, for now, the mark taunted him, reminding him of how he'd hurt her, of how much worse it would have been if not for Roscoe knocking him from the bed. He couldn't even keep her safe from himself, let alone someone else. He had no idea how dangerous he was, what sort of monster lurked within him, that he could hurt her this way.

He moved his hand away from the material as if it burned. Julia's chest heaved, as if she'd just finished running. She shuddered and Dylan fell to his knees in front of her, his hands holding her hips, and pressed his face to her stomach.

"I'm so sorry, Julia. I never meant to—"

"Shh," she whispered, her hands moving to hold his face. Dylan refused to look up at her, until he felt her tears hit the top of his head. "I know."

He'd failed again, but this time, the agony, the guilt, was far worse. Julia had trusted him, had placed her heart in his hands, and he'd betrayed that trust. As surely as if he'd pulled the trigger, he'd killed her love for him. He had to leave her, for her own safety. He was no better than Evan, even if it had been an accident.

"Dylan?"

She looked down at him, and in the depths of her eyes he saw that she wanted him to tell her it would be okay, that it had been a misunderstanding, or a nightmare. She needed to hear him tell her how much he loved her, that he wouldn't ever let it happen again. He'd already broken so many promises to her, to himself; he couldn't make one he knew he could never keep. Breaking her heart once was bad enough, doing it twice would be unforgivable.

He rose, his hands finding the curve of her jaw, and he buried his fingers into her long hair. He gave himself permission, just this last time, to kiss her. He had to feel her lips against his one final time, to inhale the sweet scent of her shampoo and the coconut lotion she put on her hands each night. He had to taste her, to have a glimpse of heaven one more time before he raised the wall between them, separating himself from her. His lips plucked at hers, at the corners of her mouth, his tongue finding hers to dance.

Julia clung to his arms, trembling against his chest. He wanted to wrap his arms around her and carry her to the bed, to bury himself within her and lose himself to the passion that ran between them like a river—strong and sure, enough to drown them both. He fought for control, not allowing his hands to move from her face. He felt his own hot tears scalding his cheeks, mingling with hers, at the sacrifice he knew he had to make.

"Julia, I can't do this to you. I won't condemn you to living a life like this. I love you too much for that." He took a step back and grabbed his duffel from the bed. Brushing past her, he hurried for the front door with Roscoe on his heels. He had to get away before he began to second-guess his decision.

"Dylan." He heard her footsteps behind him.

He knew he couldn't turn around. The minute he did, he would return and hurt her again. Until he could erect a solid wall around his heart again, to force himself to ignore the pull between them and shut out his feelings, he couldn't look back. Tomorrow. Tomorrow he would come back and get the rest of his things. Tomorrow he could return and train Roscoe with her as if there had never been an explosive connection between them. Tomorrow, he could go back to the cold, unfeeling shell of a man he'd been when he first arrived. That man could protect Julia without hurting her.

JULIA RUBBED THE dark circles under her eyes and prayed it was just a trick of the light. Nope, and no amount of makeup would cover them, even if she knew what she was doing, which she didn't. She dragged her fingers through her hair and pulled it back into a messy ponytail. What did it matter? There was no one she was trying to impress.

The one person she wanted to look pretty for had up and walked away last night without even talking to her. She pulled a clean T-shirt from her drawer and pulled it over her head and slid on a worn pair of jeans before slipping on her sneakers.

She found Chase with his chin in his hand and his head dipping toward the cold mug of coffee on the table. "Morning," she muttered, reaching for her own cup.

"You look like crap."

She turned and cast him a baleful glare. "You don't look much better, I assure you."

Chase scrubbed at his face, his day-old stubble rasping against his hands. "Yeah, well, I was up all night. What's your excuse?"

"Same."

Her frank answer was enough to make him take pause. "Julia, I'm really sorry about what happened yesterday. I never meant to cause any trouble."

She shook her head and poured the coffee. "You didn't. It was a storm already on the horizon."

"You're going to call him today, right?"

She picked up the mug and blew on the coffee, giving herself time to think of how best to answer his question. She'd been asking herself the same thing all night and had yet to come up with a concrete solution. "We need to continue training Roscoe for a little longer."

Chase gave her his most parentally disapproving frown. "I have never, in my life, seen two people more head over heels. It was almost disgusting. You can't just throw it away."

"I'm not throwing anything away."

His brow furrowed. "It *was* an accident, right?"

"What was an accident?" Justin came strolling into the kitchen as if he owned the place. Technically, he was a partial owner in the training facility, but it irritated her when he acted as though he was entitled to her home as well.

"Nothing." She sipped the coffee and prayed Chase would follow her lead. The last thing she needed was for Justin to get all protective over an accident.

Justin looked around, bending to pet Tango and Gracie before grabbing his own mug. "Where are Gage and Dylan?"

"They're staying in town."

He spun slowly on his heel, as if unsure whether he heard her correctly. "Why? What happened?"

She shrugged. "He thought it was a better idea."

"Does that mean no more Dyl-ia?" She caught Chase's glare as he shook his head at Justin. "That's what we've been calling you guys." He chuckled at his own joke.

"No."

Justin paused at her clipped tone and walked over to her. "What's goin' on, sis? The truth."

"I told you, nothing." She sipped her coffee. Julia knew the instant he saw the bruise at her collarbone, because his eyes grew huge and blind rage set in.

"What the hell is that?"

She forced herself not to react. Justin was like a toddler at times, and she just needed to remain calm and he would match her mood. "That was an accident."

"An accident?" He looked to Chase for confirmation, his voice now booming in the kitchen. "An accident? How the hell did this happen? Who did this? Evan?"

"Relax, Justin."

"My sister is sporting a bruise that looks like one of Jessie's horses kicked her square in the chest, and you don't want to tell me what happened. Somebody better be under arrest, and one of you better start talking." Justin began pacing the kitchen.

"Justin, sit down," Julia begged, rubbing her temples. "You're giving me a headache."

"Julia," he warned.

"Oh, for crying out loud, Dylan had a flashback and Julia tried to bring him out of it. She got too close, and that's what happened."

"Chase!" she warned, trying to stop the drama her brother was sure to start.

"I'm going to kill him. Is that why he left?" He moved toward her, trying to grab the edge of her collar and look at the bruise.

Julia slapped at his hands. "Get away. Yes, Justin, the special ops soldier was so afraid of what you're capable of, he ran away to hide."

Justin grasped the edge of the table, his knuckles turning white from the strain of trying to control his temper. "The sarcasm is a beautiful change of pace, Julia, very mature." He spoke through gritted teeth.

She wasn't in a frame of mind to have this discussion with him, not now and not later.

She stood up and dumped her coffee in the sink. "Since Chase is so talkative and knows all the details, he can fill you in on this one. I'm too tired and, honestly, I just don't want to think about it anymore. I have dogs to feed and take care of. Chase, you and Gracie can join me out there in about an hour and we can get started."

She snatched her cell phone and slipped it into her back pocket. "Tango, come." Her voice was sharper than usual, and the dog jumped up to do her bidding. But he didn't give her his usual tail thump, and she felt guilty for yelling at him. Between Justin, Chase, and Dylan, Tango was the only man in her life she wanted to spend any time with right now.

She'd no more walked into the kennel amid the din of barks and wild yips from the dogs when the phone rang. Julia looked down at the screen to see Gage's number. She hated herself for wishing it was Dylan as she answered the call and shut the door. "Hey, Gage." Julia ran her fingers over her forehead, brushing her bangs back as she shifted the phone to her shoulder and plugged her ear to hear him better. "What's up?"

"Hi, Julia." Her heart came to a complete stop in her throat as soon as she heard Dylan's voice. "Sorry, I think I left my phone at your place. Would you be willing to come into town to work Roscoe today?"

"I suppose." He sounded tired and there was a cold edge to his voice. Nothing seemed warm or familiar, or apologetic. This wasn't a friendly call. He was all business. She took a deep breath, steeling her will to remain professional, to hide the pain she felt at his abandonment. "Is everything...okay?"

"Yeah, I'm just tired. It was a long night," he confessed, and she could imagine that he would be rubbing his hand over his head, the way he always did when he was frustrated. She didn't want to acknowledge the flip her heart did against her ribs while wondering if he'd spent his night missing her as much as she had him.

"What did you have in mind?" Just the thought of seeing him later warmed her, and she had difficulty catching her breath. He'd been gone only twelve hours, and yet it felt like days. "Did you want to do the park again? I could bring Chase and Gracie."

"Okay." The icy tone had returned, and she wondered what she'd said to cause the change.

"Dylan, I miss you." She heard his breath catch in the phone before he sighed into the receiver.

"I'll see you at the park at one." He disconnected the call before she could say anything else. A painful lump lodged in her throat, and her eyes blurred with tears. She leaned back against the kennel door and slid down the wood, burying her face in her hands. She'd used what little strength she had this morning to deal with Justin, and Dylan's phone call had sapped whatever was left.

Her phone rang in her hand again. She sniffed and looked at it dumbly. Her heart skipped, nearly skidding to a stop in her throat as she saw Dylan's number on the screen. She cleared her throat, not wanting him to know she'd been crying.

"Dylan, you found it?"

"Guess again, sweetheart."

The hair rose on Tango's neck, and he let out a low growl, his lips curling back over his teeth.

Chapter Twenty

EVAN'S VOICE ECHOED in the receiver. Her mind raced, trying to figure out how he got his hands on Dylan's phone and why the connection sounded so clear. She heard the click of footfalls and looked up in time to see Evan walk out of her office into the hall of the kennel.

"*On guard!*" Tango jumped up at her command, staring at Evan.

She knew it was a bluff command she'd taught him. She'd never trained Tango to attack, but she'd never trained Misty to attack either, and her protective instinct had gotten her killed. She wouldn't let that happen to another one of her dogs, ever.

"You don't want to do that," he warned, disconnecting the call. "Remember the last dog you put between us?"

Julia worked her way up the wall, watching him, still at the other end of the aisle, looking like a snake ready to strike. It was shocking to see how much he'd aged over the past four years. She hadn't noticed the sallow, wrinkled tone of his skin in the store. She'd been too afraid. But he looked sick, and she wondered if his illness had gained the upper hand on him. If so, she might be able to use the knowledge to her benefit.

"What are you doing here, Evan? How did you get Dylan's phone?"

"You know, it's a funny thing. You and lover boy started having trouble in paradise right when I was making my way through the backyard again, so I hopped into his room and grabbed it. Deputy Dawg had no idea I was even there." He smiled, pleased with himself. "And I got to hear the entire conversation." He stuck out his lower lip, mocking her. "It was so sweet."

She reached down and grasped Tango's collar. She wasn't about to take a chance that he might lunge forward. Every movement that came from Evan sent him into a new frenzy of snarls and deep barks of warning.

Evan suddenly raised his hands to his head and cringed. "Can't you shut these animals up?" He eyed the dogs in their runs.

"They want breakfast. You remember how that works." She could practically see the wheels turning in his head. "If I feed them, they'll quiet down."

He glared at her. "We aren't going to be here long enough to worry about it. Come on."

"I'm not going with you." If she left this ranch with Evan, no one would ever find her.

He pulled a gun from the back of his waistband. "You are or I will put a bullet into that dog right now. I have a clip of twenty here. There are plenty to go around." The cruel smile that spread over his face was evil. She could only imagine the horrors he would have waiting for her if she didn't comply. "Oh, look," he offered, reaching into his pocket. "Another clip. Enough for every dog here and your brother and the cop in the kitchen."

She bit her lip, and Evan shook his head at her. "Did you really think I didn't know who was here and where they are? We're going to take a little ride, and you're going to leave that dog here." He waved the gun at Tango.

She couldn't put Tango in danger. "Where are you taking me?"

The gleeful grin that split his face scared her more than anything else he'd done. He gave her a maniacal laugh she'd heard only from villains in movies. Who acted this way?

"You'll see. And it's going to be fun." He waved the gun in the air. He took a step toward her again, and Tango's lip curled back once more, baring his long teeth. "You'd better calm him down, or I'll shoot him right now."

"Tango, down, stay," she commanded. He lay down at the door, but he remained alert, watching her walk toward Evan. She never would have imagined in a million years she would willingly walk away from her ranch with this madman, but she couldn't risk what Evan might do to someone else. She would figure out a way to get away from him, somehow, and complying with him would buy her some time.

Evan reached his hand out when she was within arm's distance and grasped her by the hair, tugging hard enough to bring tears to her eyes. She blinked them away.

She knew he liked her pain. It gave him the power he wanted to feel, and she refused to surrender to him.

He bent his face close to hers and arched a brow. "Oh, sweetheart, you can pretend you're not enjoying this, but I know better. The longer you pretend, the more I'll have to do to get you to crack."

His breath was hot, reeking of stale coffee and hatred. She could almost feel the sting of the blows he'd delivered four years ago and knew she probably wouldn't be so lucky this time. Evan shoved her out the back door, into the yard, pointing at the back gate.

"What are you going to do?"

He tucked the gun into his waistband, and she wondered how quickly she might be able to grab it. Evan squatted down and quickly picked up a roll of duct tape he'd left on the stoop. "Put your hands in front of you."

He ripped off a piece and slapped it over her mouth before she could protest. The sickly sweet scent of the tape filled her nostrils, and her hands automatically drew up to yank it off.

"Oh, no you don't." He shoved her against the door, her back slamming against the hard wood and knocking the breath from her lungs. "You don't want to piss me off, because then I'll have to punish you. Don't make me do that." His voice sounded almost parentally sympathetic. "Remember what happens when I do that?"

How could she forget losing nearly a week of her life in an induced coma, and two more weeks recuperating from the swelling in her skull? She heard the click of Tango's nails on the tile flooring in the hall. He'd heard the commotion and read her emotions, even from this distance. He could smell her fear and would ignore her command in order to help her. His loyalty was going to get him killed. Julia thrust her hands in front of her and gave a muffled grunt from under the tape.

Evan smiled and wrapped tape around her wrists. She winced as he jerked it painfully tight and pushed her toward the back gate.

"See how much easier it is when you cooperate? But if you even think of running or calling for help, I'll shoot you before you can take more than one step." The grin fell from his face and he pushed her into the woods, leading her down an old pathway she used to walk the dogs. "I'm not going to hurt you, Julia." His voice held a sickening-sweet note, and her heart raced. "We are finally going to be together."

DYLAN RAN A hand over his head and rubbed the back of his neck as Roscoe bumped against his leg, looking up at him with his sad brown eyes. "I know, I miss her, too."

The dog sighed and flopped to the dingy carpet at Dylan's feet. The Crazy 8 Motel was nothing more than a place to crash for the night, and he was feeling cooped up. He couldn't wait to head out to the park and work the dogs. Calling Julia this morning had been a mistake, but he was tired from not sleeping the night before and pulled up her number, never intending to call. His fingers dialed and, before he realized what he was doing, she'd answered.

She sounded tired, and hurt. He hated what he'd done to her, both physically and emotionally. There was no way to make an easy transition from lovers back to colleagues.

He needed to get as far from Julia Hart as he could, as soon as possible. His self-control would last only so long.

"Ready for breakfast?" Gage entered carrying two bags of crappy takeout that smelled as if it had been dipped in old grease. "At least the coffee is hot." He set the cup on the nightstand.

Dylan took a tentative sip and grimaced. "How long was this sitting in the pot?" He looked into the bag and quickly decided that the coffee would be more than enough bravery for one day. He debated feeding Roscoe the meal but doubted even he'd eat it and dished him up dry kibble instead. Roscoe looked up at him, pathetically.

"See? Even he wants to know why we are doing this." Gage picked at his food. "We could be drinking a fresh cup of coffee and eating Julia's pancakes in the kitchen while we listen to Justin and Chase talk football."

Dylan didn't bother to look at him. Gage knew exactly why they were doing it. If he didn't, the nightmare Dylan had last night that had brought the manager banging on the door at three in the morning should be enough of a reminder. He was too dangerous and unpredictable to be around Julia.

"Did you take your meds this morning?"

"Do I look like a child? You don't have to remind me," Dylan snapped.

Gage held up his hands. "Whoa, I see the happy pills haven't kicked in yet."

"Shut up, Gage." Dylan rose and headed for the door. Roscoe jumped up from the floor and followed him. "We have to meet Julia at the park in a few hours."

"We're meeting her here in town? Why? How do you even know that?"

"I called her this morning."

Gage's brows jumped toward his hairline. "You what?" He rose from the bed and began pacing the small room. "Do you really think that was fair? You told her last night you were walking away."

"We are still going to see each other while we work Roscoe. I'm not disappearing." He reached down and patted the dog's head as he looked up at his name. "You were right. He's helping, or I wouldn't have been able to come out of the episodes as quickly as I am."

"I just don't see where it's fair—" Gage was cut off as his cell phone rang. He looked at the screen then at Dylan. "It's Chase." Gage answered the phone, and his face fell as he immediately paled.

A shiver ran down Dylan's spine before he could push it aside.

"Okay, we'll be right there," Gage said, hanging up.

Dread took up residence in his chest, turning it cold and hollow. "What's going on?"

"Julia's missing. She went out to feed the dogs, and they found Tango scratching at the back door of the kennel, howling." Gage didn't bother to temper the news.

"She wouldn't leave Tango behind." Dylan reached for his wallet and Gage's keys, opening the door.

"Hey! What do you think you're doing?"

"I'm driving and I'm going to find her. You can either stay here or you can get in the car with me."

Gage ran toward the door, tucking his phone into his pocket. "At least let me lock the door."

Dylan opened the back door of the Camaro and Roscoe jumped inside. He revved the engine as Gage climbed into the passenger seat, barely getting the door shut before Dylan peeled out of the parking lot and headed back to find Julia, trying to remember why he'd ever thought leaving her was a good idea.

"What the hell are you good for, Chase, if you can't manage to keep her safe in her own house?"

Dylan knew he sounded like the world's biggest ass, but he didn't care. Julia was missing and there could be only one reason for that. Evan had her.

He should have been here to protect her instead of trusting her safety to a small-town deputy. "When was the last time you saw her?"

"It was around seven this morning. Justin came over for breakfast, and she got irritated with us and went to feed the dogs."

Justin paced the kennel, aggravating the dogs into a frenzy of barking. "I knew I should have come out here before I left for the clinic. If I'd have checked on her, we'd have known sooner."

"Then what?" Dylan didn't want to hear their excuses. He needed to get the facts straight so that he could begin searching for her. When he found Evan, he was going to murder him where he stood. "What time did you find Tango?"

"When she didn't come back in right away, I assumed she was cleaning out here and wanted to be alone. She was pretty upset this morning." Dylan didn't miss the barb Chase cast his way. "Justin went to work, and I waited another hour or so before I decided to go out and check on her."

Dylan's hands balled into fists at his side. "She was out here over two hours. He could have her clear across the county by now. He could have hit the airport with her and be anywhere."

"I found this on the ground." Chase handed Dylan a cell phone and a roll of duct tape. "Tango was doing everything possible to get into the yard. I'm betting that's where he took her."

"My phone?" Dylan stared at the phone, now in a zipped plastic bag, dumbly. "I left it out here?"

"Maybe." Chase pushed the home button through the plastic and showed him the last text received on the phone.

"That son of a bitch," Dylan muttered as he stared at the phone. Staring up at him was a text from Julia's phone that simply read: *She's mine. Let's play.*

"It was sent thirty minutes ago. He's toying with us."

"He won't take her far," Dylan supplied. "He wants to prove he's smarter than we are." His hand found the back of his neck and rubbed the tight muscles there. "In the meantime, Julia is somewhere with a man who nearly killed her once. Who knows what he'll do this time?"

"I've got an APB out. If he's still in this area, we'll find him."

Dylan's gaze shot to Gage. At this point, he didn't trust these guys to find their way out of a wet paper bag without help. Chase didn't have answers. Justin didn't have a clue. Gage was the only person he trusted right now to help him find Julia. And he was going to find her. "You couldn't find him before, what makes you think you'll find him now? Gage, can you find Julia's cell? Let's put those tech skills of yours to good use."

THEY WALKED FOR several miles through the woods before Evan turned her to head back toward the road. When they reached a beat-up sedan, he shoved her against it, knocking her off balance as she hit the door and stumbled. He reached up and ripped the tape from her mouth, taking skin with it. Her bound hands flew to her lips, and she couldn't stop the yelp of pain as it slipped out.

Evan smiled, his teeth crooked and yellowing. "I'm sorry. I probably should have warned you before I did that." He took a step closer, pressing her body between him and the car. The smell of his sweat, like old clothes and hospitals, made her gag. "I'll make it up to you later."

Evan leaned down and tried to kiss her. She turned her head to the side, trying to keep down the bile that rose in her throat. He grasped her chin roughly and forced her to look at him. "What? Now that you've got a new boyfriend, I'm not good enough for you?" He shoved her away from him, and she lost her balance, falling to her knees on the asphalt. "We'll see about that."

Opening the back door, Evan dragged her up from the ground and shoved her into the backseat of the car before climbing into the front. "We're going to go for a little drive, and you're going to stay nice and quiet."

Julia clenched her jaw and struggled to get into a seated position in the car. Her wrists ached, and she knew if he left the property with her, the chance of her returning in one piece would be slim.

"Where are we going?" she whispered. She wanted to stall him as long as possible, hoping her brother or Chase would realize she hadn't returned to the house, or that one of them might come looking for her in the kennel. Evan had already confiscated her cell phone from her pocket, but if she could get him talking, maybe she could figure out some way to get out of the car.

He looked at her reflection in the rearview mirror. "You'll see. And the best part is that no one will have any clue where to look for you. You'll be right under their noses, and they won't even know it." The corners of his eyes crinkled as if he was smiling, but she couldn't see the lower half of his face in the mirror. Julia looked out the window, trying to gather her wits enough to piece together her whereabouts in case she could get away.

"And, Julia, guess what?" Evan called, his voice singsongy. Her eyes shifted back to the mirror. "Come here," he waved for her to lean forward toward the front seat. When she didn't move, he frowned. "I said, come here." His arm snapped backward and fisted a handful of her long hair, dragging her to the front seat. He looked back over his shoulder as she tried to pull away from him. "Tsk, tsk, fighting is only going to get you hurt."

She saw his right arm swing around just before it connected with her temple.

Chapter Twenty-One

DYLAN COULDN'T SIT still any longer listening to Gage and Chase talk about how they needed to form a plan. He was with Justin this time. Sitting around talking wasn't going to find Julia. They needed to *do* something. He paced her kitchen while Chase called the station in town to see if anything suspicious had been reported. This was ridiculous. They weren't going to just spot Evan waiting for them.

The phone on the table rang, and all of them looked at it in surprise. Julia's number showed as the phone vibrated on the table.

"Don't take it out," Chase ordered.

"Are you kidding? I'm not wasting a chance to find her. You do your job, and I'll do whatever I have to." Dylan left the phone in the baggie but punched the button on the phone and turned the speaker on, holding a finger to his lips.

"Well, hello. Who is this?" Evan's voice held a note of mad humor.

"Who's this?"

"Dylan, I was hoping to talk to you again." Evan chuckled as if they were old friends. "You know, I'm not too fond of sharing, but since you two are no longer an item, I suppose it's all working out the way it should, with the better man getting the girl."

"Where is she? If you've hurt her—"

"She's right here."

"Let me talk to her." Dylan was finding it difficult to control the rage that was rising in him like a destructive tide.

"I don't think so. Soon, but not yet." Dylan could hear the sound of traffic in the background. "Who else is there with you, Dylan? I doubt you'd try to handle this alone. What with all your *issues*."

Dylan clenched his jaw, not willing to admit that Evan was right. He couldn't handle this alone.

"Please tell me that our local deputy is with you."

"I'm right here, Reece. Why don't you just give up while you can? I can recommend leniency if you let Julia go now."

Evan began laughing into the phone. "Oh, Deputy, that's a good one. You have no clue where to even start looking for me." He laughed again before his voice suddenly grew serious. "I took Julia right out from under your incompetent nose, you worthless hound. What do you think you can do to me?"

Dylan glared at Chase as he opened his mouth to speak, cutting him off. "You're right, you win. You are far smarter than any of us." Justin started to blow, and Dylan looked at his brother. Gage quickly took control of Justin, quietly warning him to shut up or leave the room.

"Don't try to patronize me or stroke my ego. I've outwitted all of you." He laughed quietly as Dylan heard a muffled groan of pain in the background. If that was Julia, he was going to kill the man without blinking an eye in remorse. "But, I will give you one chance to save her, if you can."

"What do you want?" Dylan didn't believe the madman for a moment. He had no intention of letting Julia go. This was nothing more than a game to him. He wanted to terrorize her and would do the same with them. But, as long as they were playing his game, he was likely to keep Julia alive.

"You'd like to believe you and Julia are soul mates, right? That what you have is true love? That means the two of you should have some sort of *connection*, right? Let's put that to the test."

"What sort of test?" There was another groan in the background and he cringed. Julia was somewhere nearby, and he had no idea where to start looking for her.

"I want to see if you can sense when she is near. As her *soul mate*, it should be no problem for you."

Dylan could hear the mockery in his voice. Evan didn't bother to hide the venom, and Dylan prayed he wouldn't take it out on Julia. There was no reason for him to stay close, but Dylan's gut told him that Evan was just cocky enough to do it, to prove that Dylan wasn't the man for Julia.

"Why should I believe you?"

"Because you don't have any other option." The phone disconnected and the four men were left staring at the phone on the table.

Chase reached for his cell phone and called the station, glancing at Dylan. "I'm calling to see if they can hook up a trace on Julia's phone. If the GPS is enabled, the cell company should be able to track it."

"Unless he was smart enough to turn it off," Gage pointed out.

"Or ditch the phone now that he's used it," Justin added.

Dylan kept his mouth shut. They were both right. Not to mention that it would make more sense for Evan to keep driving with Julia and get as far from them as possible. It wouldn't take much longer for him to hit the airport a few towns over, and then he could be anywhere. But the arrogance in his voice, the smug disdain he'd had for Chase and Dylan, made Dylan believe Evan would keep Julia close, if only to prove his superiority. For now, they needed to play into Evan's ego. His arrogance would prove his downfall.

Tango whined at the back door, and Dylan rose to go to the dog. "You miss her, too, boy." He rubbed the top of the dog's massive head. "We'll bring her back to you." He opened the door, and Tango immediately bolted for the kennel. He hurried after him with Roscoe on his heels.

"Where are you going?" Chase yelled after him. Dylan looked back but before he could answer, Gracie ran to the door and barked at Chase.

"She wants to follow, so get out here." Maybe the dogs knew something they didn't.

JULIA CAME TO and stared up at the dingy, water-stained ceiling. She had no idea where she was, and how she'd gotten there was a blur. She slowly turned toward the only light she could see, coming from a partially opened orange-and-brown curtain in the room's only window. She tried to piece together anything that might make sense. The door was only a few feet from where she lay, prone, on a lumpy mattress that smelled like a musty basement.

"Good morning, darling."

Evan's voice was piercing in the darkness, making her heart race as memories flooded back with blinding intensity. She tried to scramble away from him but found her arms tied to each corner of the top of the bed.

He laughed quietly and rose from his chair in the corner, standing over her and looking down at her immobile frame. "You were always my beautiful Julia when you were sleeping. Do you know how many times I watched you sleep?"

Anger and disgust welled up in her chest as her memory cleared.

"Ah, so you remember?" He brushed his knuckles over her cheek in an awkward tenderness. She cried out in pain when he touched the area near her eye, and she recalled that he'd hit her. "There it is." He grinned. "Your eyes turn yellow when you're angry. It's like watching fire ignite."

She could see the lust in his eyes and fought the urge to vomit. "Where are we?"

She cleared her hoarse voice, wanting to scream until someone heard her but not trusting the calm he was exuding. He could snap again at any moment, and it wasn't a risk she could take, at least not yet. Her best plan would be to convince him to release her hands.

Evan turned his back to her and walked toward what she assumed was the bathroom. "Oh, Julia, why would I tell you that? I can't have you feeling too comfortable."

Son of a bitch.

Panic tried to well up in her chest, choking her, blurring her vision as she wanted to lose herself in the haze. She knew this was when Tango would normally stick his nose in her face, trying to break her from the need to withdraw, to hide, to retreat into the past and her weakness. She clawed at the fear, forcing it to retreat into her psyche, clinging to the anger burning in her belly. She was *not* his victim any longer.

"Can you at least untie me? This hurts my wrists." She was surprised at the calm in her voice when she felt such a storm of emotion swirling within her.

He stopped walking away and looked back at her, cocking his head to one side, as if he was trying to judge her sincerity. His eyes softened for a moment. "I don't mean to hurt you, sweetheart." He walked back to the bed, and she used every ounce of self-control to not cringe from his touch as his fingers found the rope at her wrist. "I don't know why you continue to make me do it." Evan moved to the other side of the bed and untied her other wrist, his eyes turning suddenly frigid. "I only do it when I have to."

Ice water filled her veins at his words. The void in his eyes made one thing clear to her. If she wouldn't love him, Evan would kill her to keep someone else from having her. She had to escape somehow, and quickly.

THE TRAIL WAS cold. Dylan had no idea where to even begin looking for Julia. He'd followed Tango out to the yard of the kennel while he sniffed around and ran to the back gate. After letting the dogs search where their noses led, Dylan had been crushed to find that even Gracie hadn't led them any farther than to a road where fresh tire tracks suggested Evan's car had been waiting. Chase had already called someone to take a cast of the tire mark, but the likelihood of figuring out the make and model was slim at best. They were still waiting for a call from the cell phone company.

Pacing the kitchen wasn't getting him anywhere. He ran a hand over his head. "I'm leaving. I can't just sit here."

"Dylan, you can't go running around. Chase will be back in a few minutes. Just wait for him and we'll decide what to do. If Evan calls again, he's going to want to talk to you. You know that." Gage shook his head. "I've got my guys ready to trace it if he does."

Dylan stared at the cell phone, still bagged on the table. "Fine," he agreed, snatching the bag in his hand. "Now let's go find her."

He didn't wait for Gage to follow. He scooped the Camaro keys from the counter and headed out the door, letting Roscoe jump into the back. Tango bolted through the door and jumped into the backseat as well. Dylan wasn't sure how he'd control both dogs, but he wasn't about to stop and think it through right now. Julia needed him and he wasn't going to rest until he found her.

"Wait up!" Gage jogged to the car and climbed into the passenger seat. "I'm not letting you head out alone, but I still think this is a mistake."

"Noted." Dylan pulled down the driveway and began thinking aloud. "I know Chase thinks Evan's heading toward the airport, but my gut says different. I think she's close."

"Like in-town close?" Dylan could see the confusion in his brother's eyes. "Why would he do that? Why wouldn't he take her as far away as fast as he could?"

"This isn't just about having Julia for him. He wants to play with us. He's not going to think logically. Nothing about any of this is logical. He could have taken her from the grocery store that day. Why wait?"

Gage threw up his hands. "I have no clue. He's insane?"

Dylan shook his head. "No, he's an egomaniac," he muttered. "He's thriving on her fear."

"And surprising her in the store, threatening you, sending the picture of you in the sight…all of those things are just making her more afraid."

"He thinks he really does love her, in his sick, twisted way." Dylan felt the rage rising up again. "We have to find her."

EVAN HAD BEEN staring at her for what seemed like hours. He didn't approach her, didn't even try to talk to her. He just stared with his glassy, dark eyes as she sat with her knees to her chest on the bed. It had been hours since he'd released her hands, and she hadn't seen him eat anything. With his blood-sugar issues, it had to be dropping, which explained the glazed look in his eyes. It would also weaken and confuse him. If she could knock him off balance enough to get out the door, she could try to outrun him in his weakened state.

She had no idea where they were, but it could be almost anywhere. It was obviously some sort of motel room, but she had no idea how long she'd been knocked out, how far he'd driven her, or what else he might have done. Anxiety began to churn in her belly, twisting evilly and conjuring visions of the way he'd touched her cheek and the hunger she'd seen in his eyes. Julia took a deep breath and tried to calm herself. She couldn't lose control now. Unlike the last time she'd faced him, she was stronger and knew better what to expect from him.

She shifted on the bed and moved to stand. His eyes instantly cleared and he jumped up. "Where do you think you're going?"

"I'm just stretching, Evan." Julia forced sweetness into her voice, praying he would believe her act. She saw him relax slightly, although he remained standing and watchful. "I don't suppose I could get a glass of water or something?"

Evan narrowed his eyes. He didn't trust her, and it was going to take more than a few moments of niceties to gain any headway. He pointed at the bathroom sink. "There's a cup in there."

Under normal circumstances, Julia might have thought twice, but she needed something to drink, and if she didn't get some water, he'd think it was nothing more than a ploy. She walked past him to the bathroom sink and filled the spotted glass from the tap. The metallic taste of chlorinated water had never been so refreshing as it slid down her throat. She refilled the glass and closed her eyes as she swallowed more.

"Easy." He moved behind her, and her body reacted, jumping away from his touch and bumping against the sink. She cursed her own response as Evan frowned down at her and plucked the glass from her fingers. "You'll make yourself sick."

She faced him, her hands gripping the curve of the counter to keep from slapping the smug confidence she could see in his eyes. They stood for moments in the silence with only the traffic outside the window and occasional voice marring the stillness. She could hear her heart, pounding in her ears, the blood rushing through her veins, as she stared into his cold brown eyes. His lips spread in a smile.

"I should probably get us some food." His breath was foul, sickeningly sweet, and she fought the urge to gag. "Why don't you stay here and I'll bring us back something?"

He didn't give her the opportunity to argue as he grabbed her by her bruised wrists and shoved her back toward the bed, reaching for the narrow rope and looping it over her hand.

"No," she cried out. If she let him tie her again, escape was impossible unless someone heard her. "I'll stay, I swear," she lied, trying to pry his fingers from her wrist with her free hand.

"I'm not a fool, Julia," he scolded. "But I promise, I won't be gone long." He tightened the knot, and she felt the tears well in her eyes. She didn't want to cry in front of him, but when the first tear slipped down her cheek as he cinched the second rope, he paused to watch. She could see his confidence waver as he reached out a single finger to touch the wetness before he reined in his compassion. "I'll be back soon, so stop it."

She tried to open her mouth to protest when she felt tape being slapped over her lips again. She yelled against it but it only muffled, and he smiled at her sadistically before he clicked on the television, turned up the sound, disappeared out the door, and left her alone in the room with her panic again.

Chapter Twenty-Two

Julia stared up at the ceiling, unblinking. She'd clawed her way through a panic attack once he left and now lay on the bed, still drenched in sweat, chilled, with her throat raw. It had taken a while to come out of it, but she had no real sense of time. She knew she'd been lying there, staring at the ceiling long enough to count the water spots six times, and there were over thirty of them over the bed alone.

Once the suffocating fear had taken hold, she'd grasped at any reality she could find, fighting and scraping her way through the fog of terror. She tried to think about her sister and brother, of Bailey, her dogs. Tango must be frantic. But each thought would disappear like the sun behind a thunder cloud under the pressure of her fear. The one thought that remained constant was Dylan. The deep, raspy quality of his voice, the way he would look at her with his eyes dark and liquid, the feel of his hands on her skin. She wondered if he realized she was missing. It had to be past time for them to have met to work the dogs.

She heard the scrape of a key working in the door, filing the information into the back of her mind that this wasn't a modern motel with key cards. She let her body go still, trying to appear as if her mind had slipped into the depths of fear.

"Dinner is here," Evan called cheerfully. "I—"

He paused as he neared the bed, dropping the food on the desk near the door. "Julia?"

She remained still, her eyes trying to focus as she willed herself to remain in her catatonic ruse. Evan hurried to one side and untied her wrist. *Wait.* She willed herself to remain patient. She didn't want to waste this one chance at escape. It had to be the perfect opportunity, one where she could hit him hard and run. Evan finished untying her left wrist, but she remained lifeless, her eyes fixed on the ceiling.

"Julia, sweetheart, I brought dinner."

He bent over and put his face just above hers, close enough that she could feel his breath on her cheek, and pulled the tape from her mouth. Her eyes flicked to meet his. Evan sucked in a breath of surprise as her arms came down over the back of his neck, making him fall against her. She brought up her knees, quick and hard, connecting with the side of his head before kicking him as hard as she could away from him. Julia leapt up from the bed and ran for the door, stumbling over him as he reached out for her ankle.

She barely managed to kick her foot free when her hands landed against the door. She fumbled for the knob, twisting and jerking at it, but the door would open only a few inches. Julia looked back over her shoulder to see him rising with a hand at the side of his head, over his ear. When he pulled it back, it came away with blood on his palm. Murderous rage lit his eyes. She finally realized that he'd locked the chain, and she flipped it, releasing the door.

Just as she jerked the door open, could feel the cool evening air as it rushed into the dank room, her face was pressed against the metal door as it slammed shut again. Dizzy stars spun behind her eyes, and she could barely remain standing as he raised a hand, laying it against the door. His body pressed up against the back of her, her cheek cold against the metal.

"That was stupid." Bits of spit landed on her cheek as he moved his face only inches from hers. "I thought you learned the last time."

Evan released her and she slid to the floor with a cry of pain. He jerked her up from the carpet by her hair and threw her at the bed. "Face it, Julia, you are never leaving me. You have always been mine and you will always be mine. Nothing is going to change that." He stormed toward her and grasped her wrist, hauling her toward the corner of the bed so he could tie her again.

"No!" She thrashed on the mattress, striking out wherever she could in order to stop him. She couldn't lose this one chance, because once he tied her back up, she knew he wasn't letting her loose again and she'd be helpless to stop whatever he had planned. And she had no doubt he would inflict as much pain as possible.

Julia managed to hit his injured temple, and fresh blood ran down his face, falling on her shirt. She was able to raise her knee between them as he struggled to hold her down. Her heel came in contact with his sternum, and she kicked with every bit of strength she could muster. Evan stumbled backward, falling to the floor. He lay still. She didn't wait to see if he was conscious as she spun to her side and began untying her wrist. He could be dead for all she cared. She had to get out of this room and find a phone.

DYLAN PULLED INTO the parking lot of the Sak 'N Save as his phone vibrated on the seat. Gage shot him a worried glance. "It's a text."

"Well?" Dylan didn't have time to waste on small talk. His mind was racing with possible places Evan might have taken Julia. But he didn't know the town well enough to locate the local dives, and Gage had only spent his time in town working.

"It's a picture." Gage turned the phone for Dylan to see. Evan stood in front of an old-fashioned, drive-up burger joint holding a bag of food. It could have been taken anytime, but Dylan knew better. Evan was giving him the first clue as to his whereabouts. Or at least where he'd been.

Dylan spun the tires as he backed out of the parking spot and pulled back onto the highway, heading straight for the fast-food restaurant in the picture. If Evan had been there in the past twenty-four hours, he would find him.

"Dylan, what are you planning on doing? This isn't the military. You can't just pull out a gun and shoot your way out of this."

"I don't need a gun," he reminded his brother. "Right now, my only concern is to find Julia, make sure she's okay, and get her the hell away from that madman. What happens after that…"

Gage shot him a wary glance from the corner of his eye. "Have you thought about the fact that—"

"Don't even say it." Dylan clenched his teeth. He wouldn't even consider any alternative to him finding Julia unharmed.

"But—"

Dylan slammed on the brakes, making the car skid on the gravel shoulder, and glared at his brother. "Don't! I *will* find her and she *will* be okay."

"And then what?"

Dylan knew what his brother was getting at. Leaving Julia had been the stupidest mistake he'd ever made, and now she was missing. It was his fault. His useless sense of chivalry and honor hadn't protected her. He may have hurt her far worse by leaving her than he ever would have if he'd just stayed. She'd never asked him to be perfect. She'd accepted him, scarred and broken, and knew better than anyone else the struggles his PTSD would offer in the future. But he'd been so certain he knew better than she did.

Gage pulled his phone out of his pocket. "Chase, we have a lead. I know we should have told you we were leaving, but you need to meet us at the Fre-Z-Burger. Bring Gracie."

Dylan shot an inquiring look at his brother.

"Gracie found Julia's hat, and this is what they've been training her for. She led us to where the car was parked. Why not put her to the test? It's better than nothing."

Pressing the gas pedal to the floor, Dylan gunned the Camaro down the highway. He would find Julia, and when he did, nothing was ever going to convince him to leave her side again.

JULIA SAW EVAN moving as she unlatched the door and ran out. She wasn't wasting any time to look back. She ran as fast as she could down the row of motel rooms, past the cars sleeping in the parking lot toward the front office, where a vacancy sign blazed. If she could just get inside and find a phone, she could call Dylan, or Chase.

"Get back here!"

Julia looked back over her shoulder and saw Evan in the doorway of the room he'd rented, five doors away from her. There wasn't enough space between them. She could see a burly man through the front window of the office as she bolted for his door. She waved as she got closer, trying to attract his attention, even though he was looking right at her.

"Help! Hey!" She saw the man walk toward the door and thought he'd open it, rescue her from Evan, who was now limping toward the office as quickly as his injury would allow. Suddenly, the lights in the office were turned off and the man flipped the Open sign, locking the door behind him. "Hey! Wait!"

Julia reached the door as the man turned his back on her. "Help."

She pounded her fists on the door. It rattled, shaking from the force, but he ignored her and walked into a back room, as if she was nothing more than a ghost. Julia looked at Evan.

His lips pulled back into a grimace as he continued to limp toward her. "I plan ahead, sweetheart. And I pay well."

Julia wasn't going to give up now, not when she'd tasted freedom. There was a road that ran in front of the motel. Someone was bound to drive by at some point. She hurried toward it, but both directions were deserted, with nothing more than woods on each side. It looked familiar, but she doubted her intuition. As she waffled on a decision, Evan was quickly closing the distance between them.

She had no other choice. She would rather chance the woods in the dusk with places to hide than be in the open, in plain sight of the man lumbering down the road with murder in his eyes. She dashed through the trees, tripping over roots and barely righting herself. Julia looked around her, trying to get her bearings. She could hear water rushing through Hangtown Creek nearby, but Evan would expect her to move toward it since it led directly into town and the park. Julia didn't think she could outrun him the entire way. She looked up at the pines surrounding her. Most of them were stripped clean of low branches by the power company to avoid downed power lines during the coming storms. She spotted a fallen log, half-rotted and split over a stump. Across from it, she could make out a stream that must run toward the American River.

Quickly, she turned her back on the water and ran toward the log. If she could just get under it, she'd be completely hidden from his view.

Within moments, she heard Evan as he snapped branches underfoot, not even bothering to sneak up on her. "Oh, Julia, I know you're still here."

She felt a chill skitter up her spine, goosebumps breaking out of her skin. A field mouse moved in the log next to her, shuffling through the empty hole and spider webs that decorated the innards of the decaying tree. She tried to calm her breathing, to slow her racing heart, even as panic threatened.

Cowgirl up, Julia. Don't lose your wits. You need them more than ever right now.

"Sweetheart, if you come out now, I'll let you live. You can watch me tear your boyfriend limb from limb."

Julia wondered how insane Evan must be to think he was offering her any sort of incentive. Did he think she would come out to defend Dylan, or believe his lies and think he wouldn't kill them both if he had the opportunity?

"Julia?" His voice held a singsongy quality as it rose and fell, just above her hiding spot. She froze, a spider crawling over her hand in an effort to get away. Julia bit her lower lip to keep from yelping as dirt and pine needles rained into her hair from above. She held her breath as he stopped moving.

"I see you over there." Her heart stopped beating in her chest until she heard him move away from where she cowered in the tree trunk. "You know you can't hide from me."

She inhaled the wet scent of the earth as Evan's voice grew farther away. He was just talking. He hadn't seen where she went, hadn't found her hiding place. He had no clue where she was and was just trying to scare her into giving up. He was doing what he did best—playing games with her mind. But she wasn't about to move until she knew he was gone.

"Have you seen a dark-haired guy with a pretty blonde here today?" Dylan asked the kid at the register.

The scrabble of nails on concrete drew Dylan's attention back to Gage, who was trying to control Tango while Roscoe danced around them, off leash. Dylan hand-signaled Roscoe to sit, allowing Gage to better control Tango as he pulled and tugged against the leash.

The kid barely looked at Dylan. "Dude, I get a lot of dark-haired guys. You expect me to remember someone specific?" He blew air through his lips. Dylan wanted to reach through the window and knock him into the glass. He didn't have time for teenage attitude.

"You'd remember this woman. Really pretty, hair to here." He held his hand at the middle of his chest. "Dark eyes."

"Nope." The kid shook his head. "Haven't seen her."

Dylan yanked the phone from his pocket, the plastic bag catching on his jeans. "What about this guy?" He opened the text message and showed the kid the picture.

"Oh, yeah, he came by. I wondered why he was taking a selfie. It was weird, but…" The kid paused and shrugged. "Lots of people do strange things."

"How long ago?"

"Hmm."

Dylan though he might choke this kid if he didn't hurry up and give him the information. He didn't want to hear this kid hum a tune, he wanted answers. "It's pretty important. I need to know."

"Hour ago? Maybe an hour and a half?" The kid's eyes widened. "Hey, are you guys, like, cops or something?" He leaned closer to the window. "FBI?"

"Did you see which way he left?"

"I think he went that way." The kid pointed down the road.

"Thanks for your help." Dylan led Roscoe back to the car, but the dog pulled up short, trying to drag Dylan back toward the road. "Come on, Roscoe." The dog barked one last time before jumping into the backseat of the Camaro with Tango.

"Hey, aren't you going to compensate me or something?" Dylan heard the kid yell as he shut the car door and sped up the road, praying he would be able to find Julia in time. She'd been gone too long without any word from her. He knew Evan was playing a game of cat and mouse that Dylan couldn't afford to lose. Losing meant that everything that meant anything to him would be gone forever.

"Now what?" Gage asked, eyeing him warily. "I told Chase we'd wait for him there."

"If there's a chance in hell that Julia is up the road, there's no way I'm waiting around for Chase to take his sweet-ass time getting there."

"He's got Gracie. We have no idea where to start looking. For all you know, we could be walking into a trap. What makes you think this guy would make it easy for you to find him? Pull over and wait for Chase," Gage said.

"She's not far. I can feel it."

"Our room is just up the road. Go there and we'll wait for Chase and Justin."

Dylan took a deep breath, trying to control his frustration. Gage was right. They had no idea where to begin looking, and going on his gut instinct wasn't exactly trustworthy any longer. Gracie might be able to at least find a starting point for them. "Fine, call them."

Chapter Twenty-Three

Julia curled her knees to her chest, trying to stay as warm as possible, but the chill of the evening was creeping into her bones. She shivered and rubbed her arms. With nothing but a T-shirt, the goosebumps stood out on her skin. She knew it would have been far worse at any other time of the year. At least it wasn't winter. The summer nights might be chilly, but she had been through far worse. Her mind wanted to trace her steps back to the nightmare with Evan, but she refused to let it. She needed to stay alert, stay focused.

Her stomach growled loudly, and she wished she'd thought to grab the bag of food, but survival had been far more seductive than burgers at that moment. The sun was beginning to set, sending shadows curling through the trees. She had no idea how long she'd been hiding, but she hadn't heard Evan come back this way, and she prayed he'd moved farther downstream looking for her. As much as she wanted to come out of her hidden retreat, she knew it was safer to wait until darkness completely fell. There was no telling where Evan was, and the cover of darkness might be her only ally in this fight for her life.

She wondered if Justin or Chase had told Dylan she was missing. Or what they were doing right now. Justin would be tearing her house apart trying to figure out how to find her, and her sister and Bailey would be frantic. Chase would have sent word to his father and the local deputies. She wondered how long she'd been gone, how far Evan had taken her, and how wide a circle they might have made to find her.

Julia hugged her knees tighter. Her legs were beginning to cramp from the confined space. The wet, earthy scent of decay began to remind her of a grave, as if she was being buried alive. Another tremor worked down her spine, but this one had less to do with being cold than the unexplainable terror that was beginning to hover at the edges of her sanity, trying to gain a foothold in her mind. No one knew where she was, and as far as she knew, no one was even searching for her.

Unable to stand the choking darkness any longer, Julia edged out from where she'd taken refuge. A doe was creeping through the woods with her nose bent to the ground, and the deer raised her head in alarm. Julia stared at the beautiful animal, feeling slightly guilty at being the cause of her fear.

"I wondered when you were finally going to give up and come out of there."

Dread coiled around her heart like a python at the twisted humor she heard in Evan's voice. "You're not nearly as tricky as you'd like to believe."

Julia's eyes scanned the woods around her for an escape route. She heard only a few cars moving down the highway, so there would be no help there. Running back to the motel wasn't an option. She would have to take her chances by going deeper into the woods.

"Don't even think about it." Evan slid the gun from the back of his waistband. "We're going back to the room and waiting for the fun to begin. Your boyfriend should be here soon. I can't wait to see the look on his face when he sees you." He smiled, his teeth looking more like fangs. "We need to clean you up before he gets here. We can't have you looking like you've been rolling around in the dirt."

"You're insane."

Evan shrugged and grinned. "Maybe a little. You wouldn't be the first to say so." He waved the gun back toward the road. "Let's go."

DYLAN PACED IN front of their motel room while Chase let Gracie out of the car and clipped her leash on. "It's about damn time you got here," Dylan growled while Roscoe tugged at his leash, looking across the road. "Julia is somewhere out there with that maniac, and you're having a tea party with your boss."

"Look, I want to find her as badly as you do, but running off half-cocked isn't going to help anyone, including Julia. Evan is being methodical, patient. You need to do the same."

"Evan nearly killed her once."

"He's not trying to kill her this time. He wants her. It's *you* he wants to kill. As long as you're alive, she will be, too."

Dylan's control snapped and he grabbed Chase by the collar with his free hand, dragging him toward his face, his nose nearly touching. "If you keep underestimating him, you're going to get someone killed. If he so much as lays a hand on her, I will rip him apart. Understand?"

Roscoe began barking, pawing at Dylan's leg. It was enough to get his attention. Dylan released his grip on Chase and ran a hand over his head. "I...I'm sorry. I just—"

"I know." Chase laid a hand on his shoulder. "We'll find her."

Dylan was jerked sideways as Roscoe yipped and tugged him into the parking lot. Tango was sniffing the ground, whining and dragging Gage behind him while he tried to keep him under control. "What is with these dogs?" Gage muttered.

Gracie lifted her head, looking at the sky and sniffing the air, before giving a short whimper and nudging Chase with her nose. "I don't know. It's like they miss her, too." Chase squatted down beside Gracie. "What's up, girl?"

Dylan narrowed his eyes as Gracie sniffed the air. "She's trying to find her, Chase. Let her follow her nose." Chase looked at him as if he'd lost his mind. "What's it going to hurt?"

Chase shook his head. "She's not trained yet, Dylan." Dylan wasn't going to let that dissuade him, and Chase must have seen the determination in his face. "Fine. Gracie, find her."

Gracie immediately put her nose to the ground and walked to Dylan and Gage's motel room door, sniffing the area around it before moving down several doors. Stopping at the end of the walkway, she scratched at the door and whined.

"See, I told you," Chase complained. He moved to retrieve the shepherd.

"Knock on the door."

Chase shot Dylan a frustrated look and rolled his eyes at Gage. Gracie continued to scratch at the door, whining. When there was no answer, Dylan moved to the window and tried to see inside. The curtains were drawn, and he couldn't see anything inside other than that there weren't any lights on. Gracie eyed Chase pitifully, as if begging him to let her in, and gave a quick bark.

"This is ridiculous. The two of you are staying at this motel. She probably smells you, or Julia on something of yours."

"That's not our room," Gage pointed out.

Dylan slid the phone from his pocket and hurried for the front desk. The balding man behind the counter barely glanced up from his magazine when he walked inside. "Yeah?"

"Have you seen this man?" Dylan loaded the picture of Evan at the fast-food restaurant. "He might be staying here."

The man shrugged, his gaze sliding over Dylan and Gage behind him before returning to his magazine. "Maybe. How much is it worth to know?"

Dylan clenched his fists at his sides as Chase strolled up to the counter and flipped his badge out. The man laughed. "Don't make no difference to me who you are. This ain't the Ritz. You wanna know something, you're going to have to make it worth my while."

Dylan lunged across the counter and grabbed the front of the man's shirt. All three dogs went crazy barking. Tango jumped up with his massive paws on the counter, and the man's eyes nearly bulged from his meaty face.

"Is my leaving your face intact worth it? I could feed you to this dog." The man's eyes flicked to Tango and back to Dylan, as if unsure who was more dangerous.

"Yeah, okay! He was staying here. Came in yesterday." He pawed at Dylan's shirt until he let him go, and stumbled back a few steps into his chair, knocking the magazine to the floor.

"Was there a woman with him?" Chase asked.

The clerk shot him a dubious look. "Do I seem like the sort of guy who's going to ask questions?"

"Unlock room six," Chase ordered.

"You got a warrant?"

"Do I need one?" Dylan crossed his arms over his massive chest.

"I ain't unlocking anything."

Dylan glared at the clerk, and the man became suddenly helpful.

"Hold on, now." He slid a set of keys onto the counter with one singled out. "I suppose I can't help it if someone was to steal my keys and get into the room while I was on my break." His brows arched high on his wrinkled forehead before he turned and disappeared into a room behind the office.

Dylan snatched the keys. "Let's go."

Chase put a hand on his chest, halting him. "This could be a trap, and Evan wants you dead. *You* wait here."

"Bullshit!" Dylan pushed past Chase and headed for the door. He slid along the wall as he approached and motioned Chase to move forward.

Chase knocked on the door. "Police, open up!" Nothing but silence greeted them. "Okay, give them to me. Let's open it up."

JULIA HEARD DOGS barking in the distance. It sounded so much like Tango, deep and echoing, and she wondered if she'd finally snapped and had some sort of psychological break. At least she knew Tango was safe. No matter what Evan chose to do to her, she'd been able to keep the dogs and her brother safe. She hoped Evan would give up on finding Dylan as well, now that his fury was directed at her for trying to escape.

Evan reached for her upper arm and shoved her forward. Her mind reeled with possibilities, ways that she might get away from him again since she wasn't restrained. He might not have the tape over her wrists and mouth, but that gun was enough to deter her from yelling for help. At least for now. She wondered how she might be able to knock it away from him without getting herself shot.

"You almost had me fooled. I even headed down the riverbank looking for you." Evan chatted as if they were old friends, but she knew he only wanted to hear himself talk. If she spoke up, he'd make her sorry. "Then I realized you hadn't left any footprints, and I backtracked to where I'd last seen you."

Evan jerked her arm, pulling her back into him and pressing his lips close to her ear. "I told you, you're mine and you always will be. I will find you anywhere." He shoved her forward again, and she tripped over a branch on the ground, falling to her knees and tearing through her jeans. "Although, I must say I'm pretty disappointed with your boyfriend. He's no closer to finding you than when I took you from the kennel."

"Dylan?" She knew she shouldn't have spoken, but it fell from her lips, a prayer spoken in a moment of weakness.

Hateful eyes fell on her as she rose from the ground. "When he finally gets here, I'm going to kill him. And I think, because you decided to play your own game with me, I'll make you watch. Now get up and keep walking."

"Walking where? Where are we going?" Julia's legs felt like rubber and barely held her up as she continued to put one foot in front of the other. Thinking about Dylan coming for her was the only thing keeping her moving. "What makes you think Dylan even knows I'm gone?"

"Because I told him, sweetheart," Evan explained. He spoke as if she was an ignorant child and couldn't understand "But even if he didn't know, he'd have come back here. He's staying at this motel. Why do you think I chose it?"

Her heart leapt in her chest, pounding against her ribs. Dylan? Here? Before she could even open her mouth to voice the questions racing through her mind, Evan laughed.

"You look surprised. I took you from right under his nose. What better place to keep you in order to prove he isn't the man for you? I love you. If he can't find you a few doors down, he's worthless."

"You *want* him to find me? To prove he loves me as much as you do?"

Without warning, Evan pulled her against him, pinning her arms to her sides as he wrapped his around her. She felt his body against hers, his arousal pressing against her stomach, and wanted to gag. The man was vile.

"I want to prove to *you* that he doesn't love you like I do. We belong together." A confused frown furrowed his brow as he looked into the distance, toward the road. It cleared and he looked down at her, his eyes hungry. "You're mine."

Tango dragged Gage toward the road, completely disregarding every command to stay. Gracie had done nothing but whine since they'd managed to open the motel room. It had been nearly empty other than a bag of food from the restaurant Evan had taken a picture in front of. Gracie pressed her nose against the corner of the dresser, where Chase was the first to see the blood.

"It's not necessarily Julia's."

Dylan couldn't say anything. There was just as much of a chance that it *was*. He couldn't let himself consider that she might not be alive. He followed his brother out the door as Gage tried to control Tango. Luckily Roscoe was behaving, but Dylan didn't care. It was looking less and less as if they were going to find Julia safe, and his lungs didn't want to cooperate. The air was too thin, and he was struggling to breathe, to remain calm, and think about their next move.

"Okay, I've called in another deputy to get the forensics evidence." Gracie whimpered, tugging at her leash. "What is wrong with them?"

Dylan looked down at her as she tipped her nose to the air, snuffling before turning to look back at Chase. "She smells something."

"Yeah," Chase agreed. "Julia, in the room."

Dylan narrowed his eyes and watched her drag Chase behind her, taking a few steps toward the parking lot before looking back at them expectantly, as if she wanted to follow Tango. Gage was struggling to pull the huge dog back into the parking lot.

"Wait, bring them over here," he instructed both of them, walking across the highway, at the edge of the woods. Gracie barked at Chase as they moved closer to the woods, tipping her nose up again. Dylan's heart picked up its pace. This was exactly how Gracie acted when they'd been training. "She smells her. Let her go."

"Are you nuts?" Chase shook his head. "I'm waiting for a deputy, and you want me to go trekking through the woods in the dark on a wild-goose chase now?"

Dylan took a step closer, looking down at the shorter man. "It's not a wild-goose chase if we find her, and I am going to find her. With or without your help." Dylan reached for Tango's leash. "Let's go find her, boy."

Chase ran after him. "Not without Gracie. You'll just get yourself lost."

"What the hell was that?"

Evan jumped backward. Julia heard the barking that seemed to come closer with every second. It was Tango. She'd recognize his bark anywhere. Her heart soared in her chest and plummeted just as quickly. Evan was too deranged, too dangerous, and likely to shoot anyone who came through the trees if he thought it was a threat.

"There is no way he found us that fast," Even muttered, shoving Julia behind a tree and pressing his hand against her throat. She clawed at his hand, gasping, fighting to keep the panic at bay. "You want me to fire this? Keep making noise."

She immediately quieted. The dogs would find her, especially if Gracie was with them. If they came running toward her without realizing Evan was armed, someone was bound to get hurt. It was something she couldn't allow to happen. She stilled against the tree and felt his grip loosen.

Gracie's bark echoed off the trees as the sun dropped behind the horizon, casting the woods into shadowy darkness. They were close enough that she could hear their feet tearing up the branches and pine needles that made up the undergrowth. There was no hesitation in the steps. Gracie was leading them right to her.

"Stay!" she yelled.

The command had no more left her lips when Evan backhanded her, splitting the corner of her lip. She could taste blood in her mouth as stars blossomed behind her eyes. It didn't matter. She couldn't let them come through the trees. "Stay!" she yelled again.

"Julia!" It was Dylan's voice.

"Stay!" she yelled again just before Evan reached for her throat, cutting off her voice. The footsteps stopped. The night erupted in barks, yips, and a deep growl from Tango. Out of the corner of her eye, she saw Dylan straining to pull her dog back as he spotted her. She saw his mouth form her name, but she couldn't hear him. In fact, she couldn't hear anything any longer as her vision started to blur and bright stars danced at the outer edges of her vision.

She saw the leash snap as Tango launched himself across the distance separating him from her. Evan let her go as he turned toward the animal, leveling his weapon. "No!" She lunged at Evan, hitting him in the stomach and knocking him to the side. But she didn't have the strength left to push him to the ground. An explosion sounded in the darkness, reverberating off the trees in the thin night air. Julia felt the solid form of the dog hit her shoulder as he crashed into Evan, throwing all three of them to the ground.

Dylan and Chase ran toward them. Evan struggled under Tango's weight as Chase retrieved the gun and pointed it at him. Dylan reached for Julia, pulling her from the fray, but she reached for Tango. His yelp of pain had cut through her, chilling her heart.

She ran her hands over the dog in the darkness, barely able to see him in the shadows of the night. Only a sliver of a moon hung above them, not enough to give any light to help her examine Tango. Her fingers slid over his side as he panted, whining and trying to reach her. She felt the sticky warmth that could only be blood as her fingers trailed over his ribs.

She didn't care that Evan was mere feet from her with Chase pointing a gun at his chest. She didn't even watch as Chase handcuffed the furious maniac as he screamed profanities. She didn't care that Roscoe and Gracie were howling and barking nearby, confused by the drama unfolding. She only cared that Tango didn't suffer the same fate Misty had. Nothing could happen to him.

"Dylan." She turned to the man who'd broken her heart. "I need something for his side. Help me," she pleaded.

"We need light." He searched his pockets. "Gage, toss me your phone." Dylan caught the phone as Gage held the other dogs, watching them helplessly. Dylan tapped the button to turn the screen on. Blood covered Tango's side, soaking the short fur. Dylan didn't hesitate, pulling his shirt over his head, ripping a strip from the bottom. "Here, call Justin." He handed her the phone as he examined the dog's wound. "I've got to stop this bleeding."

She heard the sirens in the distance and knew Chase must have called for backup, but she couldn't tear her eyes from Dylan, putting pressure on Tango's side even as he bandaged the wound. Dylan looked up at her. "We need to get him to a vet as soon as possible, Julia. I can't see if the bullet grazed him or if it's still lodged inside. I'm going to have to carry him back to the car."

"How far?"

"It doesn't matter. Hold his head up and stay where he can see you."

He bent down and lifted the dog into his arms as Julia steadied him. She felt the tears burning against her skin but ignored them as they coursed down her cheeks. "Dylan." She could barely speak as her breath caught in her throat unable to voice her fear. "Is he—?"

"I don't know, but I'm going to do everything I can. Don't give up on either of us yet."

Chapter Twenty-Four

Dylan watched Julia sleeping on the hard plastic bench at Justin's clinic. Her face was still smudged with dirt and scrapes, and dried blood caked in the swollen corner of her split lip. Dark circles settled below her eyes. Justin had assured her the bullet had been removed and that Tango was stable, but she refused to leave until he woke from the anesthesia and saw him for herself. She needed to get some real sleep, in her bed. Dylan brushed her bangs back away from her eyes and saw her lashes flutter. She choked off a scream and bolted upright, scooting away from him on the bench until she realized where she was.

"Sorry." She grimaced as she caught her breath. "I didn't realize...I thought..."

"I know," he whispered. "It's okay."

He wanted to touch her, to pull her into his arms, to rid her of any memories of the past twenty-four hours. He wanted to reassure her that he wasn't going anywhere again. He wanted to drive over to the police station and beat the crap out of Evan Reece, until the man was nothing more than a broken mess that barely resembled a human being. The maelstrom of emotions that were coursing through him frustrated him. He'd thought he was doing the right thing leaving her. All he'd done was cause more trouble and nearly get her killed. And Tango wasn't out of the woods yet.

Dylan reached for her hand but sighed as Julia pulled hers away. "Julia, I know I don't deserve it, but I was hoping you'd be willing to give me another chance."

She wouldn't meet his gaze, but he could see the tears in her eyes. "Why, Dylan? I thought you said you couldn't stay."

"I thought if I left, you'd be safer." He ran his hand over his head, unable to bear the pain in her eyes.

"Safer? Does this look safer to you?"

Dylan rose and paced the waiting room, grateful for how empty it was at the early morning hour. "I nearly hit you. If it hadn't been for Roscoe, Julia, there is no telling what I could have done."

"Which is why you came to the ranch in the first place." He turned and found her standing behind him. "I knew the risk when I invited you and Gage to stay at the house. There were never any guarantees that nothing would happen, Dylan. I knew about the flashbacks and the episodes before you came. Gage explained the situation to me. I went into this relationship with my eyes wide open. *You* were the one with blinders on, who wouldn't see the truth."

She ran her hand over his waist and up to his shoulders. "I love you, broken pieces and all. I saw the scars." Her fingers slid over the tattoo on his neck. "And I don't mean just the ones that are visible to everyone. I love every one of them."

"Why?" How could she see how dangerous he was to her, how destructive he could be, and still care about him?

She gave him a soft smile, her lips curving, lighting up her face in spite of the dirt and tear stains. "Do you care about me less because of what I've been through?"

Dylan brushed her hair back behind her ear with his fingers. "I love you more. I see your strength, your determination, and your faith. They make you even more beautiful."

"So, why would you think that I'd love you any less?" She looked at Roscoe, lying on the floor, watching them intently. "You can accept his love, but not mine?" Roscoe shifted his gaze to Dylan, as if he was wondering the same thing. "What happened was just as much my fault, Dylan. I knew better than to approach you, to touch you, in the middle of a flashback. You didn't know it was me. I know you'd never hurt me."

She cupped his jaw with her palm. "You risked your life to save me. Evan wanted to kill you, and you knew it, but you came for me anyway."

"Don't we even get any credit?" Dylan spun to see Chase and Gage enter the office with Gracie. "It was Gracie here who tracked you down." The shepherd barked happily at her name. Chase grew somber and his gaze flicked to Dylan before jumping to Julia.

"Julia, I'm going to need you to come down to the station and give a statement. I've got Evan there now, but I want as much evidence as we can get, which means we need you to have a medical exam."

Dylan tried to hide his rage. They wanted to perform a series of tests on Julia, even in her troubled state, in order to build a solid case against Evan. The longer they waited, the more evidence they might lose, but it infuriated him that she would be subjected to this kind of humiliation when he knew what it meant to her to be with Tango.

"Not until he wakes up."

"We need to do swabs. You could be shedding evidence all over this room," Chase argued.

"Julia, I'll stay with him," Gage said. "It's the least I can do. I'll call you as soon as Justin tells me he's waking. I promise."

She looked to Dylan for a moment. "I can't leave him. What if..."

"Julia," Chase interrupted, "if you don't, there's a chance Evan could get out again. I don't want to risk that ever happening."

Dylan could see the conflict in her eyes. She knew she needed to go, but she wanted to stay for Tango just as desperately. He didn't want to leave her side, but he knew how much Tango meant to her. "I'll stay with him. Go with Chase and I'll be here when you get back."

"Dylan, what if he doesn't—"

"He will." He looked at Gage. "Give her your phone since hers is now evidence." Dylan brushed a finger over the tear slipping down her cheek. "And he's going to be fine. I'll call you when Justin takes me back there with him, and I'll text you a picture as soon as I see him. Now, go so you can hurry back."

JULIA WAITED FOR the doctor to release her so Chase could take her back to Tango. Dylan had sent her a picture, but he still hadn't awakened and she wanted to be there when he did. She hopped off the table where the doctor had already done his myriad of testing, including a rape kit. She'd tried to assure them it wasn't needed, but there had been too many gaps in her memories after he'd knocked her unconscious in the car. She'd been shocked when Chase explained to her how Dylan had pieced together the clues Gracie had provided him.

"I guess she's going to make a good search and rescue dog after all, huh?" He laughed and patted Gracie's head. He looked at the notebook he held and clicked off the recorder. "Off the record, Julia. Why'd you go with him? If you would have yelled, we might have heard you from in the house."

Her tongue found the spot on her lower lip where Evan had hit her and split the skin. The doctor had treated her outer wounds and abrasions, but every part of her felt overly sensitive and raw. It wasn't just the physical injuries, her emotions were shot. Tears welled in her eyes, blurring her vision again when she recalled Evan threatening to shoot Tango and the rest of the dogs in the kennel. How could she ever explain to Chase in a way he'd understand she'd been protecting them all by sacrificing herself? Even if it was only for the moment.

"He had a gun." She shook her head and wiped at her eyes. "I couldn't take a chance that you or Justin might come out. Evan was bound to make some kind of mistake eventually. I just had to be ready when he did."

"It was pretty smart to hide in the woods."

Her gaze met his, and she couldn't hide her frustration. She shouldn't have tried to escape. It had only made things worse. "For all the good that did. He found me anyway. Tango is in the hospital because of it."

"Julia, you bought us time. Who knows what he would have done in the time you were hiding. You gave Gracie a trail to follow."

The doctor entered the room and gave Julia a smile. "All of your tests look good. Other than a few bumps and bruises, you have a clean bill of health." He looked pointedly at Chase and jerked his chin toward the door.

"What?"

"Ms. Hart, I'd like to speak with you privately, if that is all right with you."

"I'll wait just outside the door," Chase offered.

Once he'd exited, the doctor moved to stand in front of her. "There was one thing that came up on your blood work that you should know."

"I thought you said everything was fine?"

"It is," he assured her. "You're pregnant."

"I'm what? I can't be pregnant. How? Wait, no." She shook her head, trying to wrap her mind around what this doctor was telling her. She couldn't possibly be pregnant. She'd only been with Dylan, and they hadn't been together long enough for her to be pregnant. "It would be too soon to tell, even if I were."

"With your counts, it's fairly unlikely I'm wrong. You're only about a week to ten days." He pressed the paper of test results into her hand. "A blood test can tell far sooner than a urine test. Congratulations, Ms. Hart. I'll have the nurse bring in your discharge papers, and you'll be ready to head home."

"Come on." Dylan met her at the door when she entered the vet's office after leaving the hospital. "He's just starting to wake up."

She stared at the man holding the door open for her. A baby? She and Dylan were going to have a baby? She wanted to tell him, but she wasn't sure how he was going to react to this kind of news. And right now, Tango needed her.

She followed him into Justin's back office, where Tango lay stretched out in a kennel on a blanket. She could feel the warmth of his body as she knelt down beside his massive head, stroking her hand over his ears as he snuffled. "Hey, Tango," she murmured.

The dog whined and tried to raise his head. "Easy, boy." She stretched out on the floor beside him, with her nose to his. "I'm right here, and I'm not going anywhere." Tango's tongue snuck out slowly and licked her chin. She looked up at her brother. "He's going to be okay?"

"He is. The bullet grazed his side and ripped some of the muscle, but I've got him all stitched up and heavily sedated. He's on antibiotics as a precaution, but he should be as good as new in a few weeks." He patted Dylan on the shoulder. "I'll let you guys have some privacy. Stay as long as you want."

She heard the soft click of the door as Justin left them alone. "Where's Roscoe?" She slid her fingers over Tango's velvety muzzle as he slept, his whiskers tickling her palm.

"I had Gage take him back to the ranch. He's been through enough for tonight. They both need a night off."

Her gaze flicked up to meet his. "What about you?"

Dylan sank down to sit with his back against the wall of the kennel. "I'm okay, just tired. What about you? What did the doctor say?"

She sat up and moved closer to him. Without waiting for an invitation, she eased herself between his strong thighs and laid her ear against his chest, letting the steady beat of his heart reassure her. She heard him sigh as his arms encircled her. It felt good, like sinking under her down comforter on a cold winter's evening. It felt like home. It felt right.

"He said I'm fine. All of my tests were...normal."

"Good." She could feel his breath against her head, his hand stroking the back of her hair as his other hand toyed along her spine. "Julia?"

"Dylan, don't, please."

They needed to talk, to confront the elephant in the room and decide which difficulties they could face and which they needed to turn their backs on. But not yet.

For now, she only wanted to feel his arms around her, the serenity that seemed to envelop her when she was with him. They were two broken people who came together perfectly. Their pieces fit and made a whole.

"Tomorrow," she whispered. "We'll talk tomorrow. For tonight, just hold me and pretend like none of this happened. Tonight, let's just be two people who love each other."

Dylan tipped her chin up and looked into her eyes. She could see the turmoil in the deep brown depths. He bent his head, and his lips brushed hers in a too-brief touch. "I thought I'd lost you. I refused to rest until I had you right here again."

"You were all I could think about while Evan had me." She wound her arms around his waist, curling into his warmth, letting the nightmare of the past twenty-four hours melt away. "I was so afraid he would hurt you. But I knew you'd come for me."

Dylan's hands played along her back, relaxing her. She fell quiet as her mind fought to stay awake, but her body began to feel lighter, losing the battle with sleep as her eyes closed and exhaustion overcame her desire to simply be with Dylan. Her breathing deepened as she tried to remain conscious.

"You are going to make a great father."

FATHER? WHERE HAD that come from? It was a ridiculous thing to say, but it didn't stop the throbbing ache from pounding within his chest. Dylan wanted a family and kids, someday. At least, he had before his last tour. Now it was a pipe dream. He couldn't subject a wife and children to the nightmare he lived, even in his waking hours.

But Julia and Roscoe were changing that. They had given him back independence and helped him focus on reality instead of the agonies of the past. If there was ever a woman he wanted to share his life with, it was Julia. She'd opened his eyes to an entirely new world than the one he'd confined himself in after returning home. He ran a hand over his head, his fingers moving over the puckered edges of the scars on his neck. She deserved so much more than he could offer her, yet she wanted him. He'd never understand why.

Dylan let his fingers run through the waves of her messy hair. She'd washed her face while at the hospital, but she still had dirt and pine needles in her hair. She smelled like a mixture of earth and pine and the sweet scent that was unique to Julia. He inhaled and felt his heart jump even as desire twisted his gut. He wanted to protect her, but more than that, he wanted to be with her, now and every day of their futures. It just wasn't fair for him to ask of her.

"I love you, Julia. I shouldn't. You deserve far better, but I don't think I can let you go." His lips moved against her hair.

A quiet rumble of a whine sounded in the stillness. Dylan's eyes lit on Tango, who stared back at him, more alert now and watchful. Julia's hand clenched against his side, and she jerked in her sleep. Running his hand over her arm, he wondered how she was strong enough to not only fight off Evan but to withstand the mental torture of his madness yet again. It was sure to take its toll on her psyche. He heard a whimper, but this time it came from the woman in his arms, not the dog struggling to rise and move to her side. Even sedated and in pain, Tango was trying to do his job and help Julia with her own nightmares.

"Tango, down. It's okay, I have her." Tango laid his head over Dylan's foot in an effort to be closer to Julia. "You don't trust me to take care of her either, huh?"

Tango raised his head and cocked it, as if questioning Dylan's assumption. He barked sharply once, and Julia stirred against him. "Is he okay?" she murmured against Dylan's chest.

"He's fine. Just disagreeing with me, I think."

She glanced up at him, and he could see the devotion in her eyes. "When did you start having conversations with dogs?"

He returned her smile, remembering his attitude when he'd first arrived. "He's winning me over," he confessed. Tango gave a throaty, playful bark. Dylan looked down at her, growing serious. "Nightmare?"

He saw the light snuff out in her eyes. "Something like that. I'm sure they'll be back for a while now."

"Tango knew. How bad?"

She shrugged and reached over to pet the dog's head. "Bad enough. Would have gotten worse if he hadn't barked and woken me up."

"He really helps control it, doesn't he?"

She met his questioning gaze, and Dylan could see her searching his eyes. He needed to hear her say yes, that the dog had given her back a normal life, that he could have one, too.

"You've seen the difference since you and Roscoe have been working together. Dylan, the two of you have made enormous strides, faster than most. This is always going to be something you struggle with, it won't just disappear, but it gets better." She knelt between his thighs so that she was eye level with him and cupped his jaw with her fingers. "You won't be the same, but people never are. Life changes everyone—good and bad. If you leave again, I won't be the same."

Chapter Twenty-Five

JULIA WATCHED AS Dylan carried Tango into the house. The dog was out of the woods, and Justin had assured her he was going to make a full recovery in the coming weeks and be back to his goofy self within a matter of days. Chase had already called and alerted her that Evan had been denied bail and was being transferred for a medical evaluation. She shivered at the thought of the man. How could someone be so intent on causing so much pain?

Dylan held open the door with his heel and eyed her cautiously. "You coming?"

She shook her head to dispel the dark thoughts and followed Dylan inside, where he helped Tango get settled on a blanket at the foot of the couch. "Is this where you want him?"

"Sure, at least he won't feel like he's isolated here." She squatted down and petted him. "You stay, and I'll get your food."

She still hadn't told Dylan about the baby. She couldn't let him make the decision to stay because of his sense of honor. She had no doubt he'd stay when he found out, but what kind of life was that for either of them? Once he made his decision, she would tell him. Until then, she could only let him come to recognize the truth on his own.

"Now what?"

She looked up at him. There were so many things he could be asking with that simple question, and her mind raced, unsure of how to answer him. He reached out a hand and pulled her up from beside Tango on the floor. "You should probably get some sleep."

"It's noon. I have dogs to take care of."

"The kennel wasn't the most comfortable bed last night, and I know you didn't sleep well."

He was right. She'd barely slept last night, choosing instead to remain curled in his embrace. She'd been content to stay, with his arms around her, keeping the nightmares at bay. If she tried to sleep now, she'd probably collapse and not wake until the nightmares forced it. "Why don't we do lunch instead?" she offered, deciding quickly that she'd faced enough horror for one night.

Dylan pulled her into his arms, and she had to pinch her lips together to keep from sighing with pleasure. This was exactly what she wanted, what she needed. Now, if only he could see it. He ran his fingertips over her cheekbone. "Should we call someone? A therapist?"

She looked at his throat. His concern wasn't what she wanted to see in his eyes. She wanted to see his hunger again, the desire for her, his love. She didn't want someone to take care of her. She wanted him to love her and be loved in return. "I'll call and set up an appointment for later this week."

She slipped from his arms and walked across the hall into the kitchen, where she saw Justin at the counter, making sandwiches. "Oh!" She jumped backward. "What are you doing?"

Justin glanced back at her over his shoulder. "Well, since I was out making rounds I decided to have lunch with you. So I'm making sandwiches, what's it look like?"

"But you don't cook."

"This is hardly what I'd call cooking," he pointed out. "And I figured it was time I start helping you, Jessie, and Bailey, and stop letting you three mother me."

Julia arched a brow at Justin, planting her fists as she grinned at his playful tone. "*Letting* us? Because, of course, our only desire in life is to take care of you."

He turned and walked toward her. "I know how much you three need to boss someone around, so I just let you do it." He pulled her into a bear hug against his massive chest. "I'm so glad you're okay."

She heard the hitch in his voice and felt the tremor in his chest. Was he *crying*? His arms tightened around her before he let her go and quickly turned away, raising a hand to his face. "So, what's it going to be? Turkey or ham?"

She was surprised by Justin's sudden rush of sentimentality. It wasn't like him. He was the rough and tumble, gruff, stereotypical cowboy, and it was completely out of character for him. That, in itself, spoke volumes about how worried he'd been.

"I'll have turkey," Dylan said from the doorway. She could read the concern in his eyes. He knew better than anyone the strain of hiding her emotions, of trying to maintain a brave facade. Why could he see her so clearly at times, know her so well, but not understand how she felt about him?

Justin looked from Dylan back to Julia. "You know what? On second thought, I'm going to head to the clinic and see how Bailey is doing." He moved forward and hugged her quickly. "I think the two of you need some time to talk."

Her stomach did a nervous flip at the thought of being alone with Dylan. Part of her wanted nothing more, but there was a small, guilty part that jabbed her conscience, pointing out the truth she was hiding from Dylan. He deserved to know, deserved the opportunity to make a fully informed decision. She was hiding as much as he was.

DYLAN WANTED TO move to her, to pull her into his arms, to take her into the bedroom and make love to her. But he could read the uncertainty in her eyes, and he jammed his fists into the pockets of his jeans instead. "Why don't you sit and I'll finish fixing this."

He moved to the counter. This awkwardness was his own doing, but he couldn't seem to break through it and start the conversation he knew they needed to have. How was he supposed to explain his fears to her? How did he confess to her that he'd never felt this way about anyone before? That leaving her had practically ripped his heart from his chest, and he couldn't do it again, in spite of the danger he might put her in?

He slid two slices of bread from the package and laid them on a plate. "Julia, I can't do this." One hand slid over the back of his head and rubbed his neck.

"Okay," she said, pausing midstep. "I'll fix it."

"No," he corrected. "This, us, this...I don't know."

"Don't go," she whispered.

He heard her drop into one of the kitchen chairs and spun to see her bury her face in her hands. Realizing how it sounded, he hurried to her side and dropped in front of her, reaching for her hands. "Shit, I'm already messing this up. I mean that I can't leave again."

Her eyes met his, and he could see the shock in them. "Julia, I love you. I can't help it. But I never want to hurt you. When I had that flashback and almost..." Dylan looked away, too ashamed to even meet her eyes. "I thought if I left, you'd be safer. I hurt you and put your life in jeopardy. I don't deserve it but—"

"Stay." Julia cupped his face in her hands. "I love you, Dylan. When are you going to see yourself through my eyes? When are you going to see how good you are? How deserving you are?"

He buried his hands into her hair. "I could hurt you, physically."

She laughed at him. Dylan frowned. "You won't hurt me. First of all, I told you. I know better than to try to bring you out of a flashback again. Even if I didn't, Roscoe took care of both of us. It was an accident, Dylan." She leaned forward and kissed him, stealing his protest from his lips.

Winding her arms around his neck, Julia pressed her body against him, and he lost all semblance of restraint.

He pulled her against him, dragging her into his arms as he stood. Her tongue swept into his mouth, meeting his in matching need. He ached to touch her, to feel her skin against his, but this was a torture like no other. She was his and he was going to be the man she believed him to be. Even if it meant spending the rest of his life trying to become that man.

Dylan groaned as Julia wrapped her legs around his waist, and he started for the hall, his hands gripping her rear. He was going to spend the rest of his days chasing away the nightmares of her past, starting now.

"Really?" The screen door slammed, and they froze as Gage entered the house. "You two are like a couple of rabbits. Get a room!"

Dylan set Julia on her feet as a blush colored her cheeks. "We were just about to do that until we were interrupted."

Gage glanced at Julia. "Okay, I'm out. And I'm taking this with me." He held up a pizza box.

Dylan shoved his brother out the door. "I love you, but go."

Gage grinned and turned back toward his brother. "I take it this means we're staying a while longer?"

There were so many factors for them to figure out. New therapists, his treatments, a job. But he wasn't going to let the unknown deter him from finding his future with Julia. And Gage could find his again. "It's up to you whether or not you want to stay, but I think it's safe to say Roscoe and I will be here for a long time." Dylan glanced at Julia. "At least as long as Julia will put up with me."

"Good." Gage slapped Dylan's arm and drew him into a one-armed hug. "You deserve this," he whispered into Dylan's ear. "This is what you wanted."

He trotted down the steps to the car and stuck his head out the window as he dropped it into Reverse. "I'll be at Justin's if you need me."

As Dylan watched Gage leave, Julia gave him a half smile and stood on tiptoe to kiss his cheek, her hand against his chest creating a tingle of pleasure that shot straight to his core. "I think I can manage to put up with you for the next eighteen years."

Dylan frowned down at her. It was such a random remark. He shifted his eyes, confused and trying to figure her out. "Only eighteen?"

"That's usually how long it takes to raise a child to adulthood."

Nothing more than confusion registered, and his mind flew back to the comment she'd made as she fell asleep the night before.

You're going to make a great father.

He narrowed his eyes at her and realization hit him. Hard. Pleasure radiated in her smile. "Are you serious? Are you...I mean...Julia?" He met her eyes and saw her searching them for delight, but he wasn't sure he could muster it through the fear coursing through his veins.

A baby? *His* baby? He was going to be a father?

"It's really early to tell, but I'm pregnant, Dylan. They ran a test when I was at the hospital." He saw her frown as she watched him for some indication of his reaction to the news.

Emotions raced through him. He questioned his ability to be the man Julia deserved, but to be a father…he didn't even know where to dig into his past for that kind of knowledge. He ran a hand over his head, trying to comprehend the depth of his fear and doubts even as his heart overflowed with love for Julia.

Gage hadn't realized it, but he was right. This was *exactly* what Dylan wanted, what he'd always hoped was in his future. Before the grenade, before the nightmares and the PTSD. Then he'd given up hoping for it—until Julia.

She had changed everything, turned his life upside down, reminding him that his scars couldn't destroy him. She proved to him that he wasn't defined by his past. There was so much more to come.

Dylan stared at Julia. He didn't miss the concern in her eyes, and he was going to make sure to wipe it away, once and for all. Hope flared brightly in his chest.

A baby…with Julia's sweet smile, her expressive eyes. Something must have changed in his face, because the crease over her brow disappeared and her smile lit up the room.

"Aren't you going to say something?"

Dylan cupped her face with his fingers and brushed his lips against hers, feeling his body instantly respond, even as his heart felt as if it would explode from the exhilaration. Julia sighed against him and melted into his embrace.

"Damn it, I owe Gage now," Dylan whispered against her lips.

"You do?" Dylan didn't miss the sigh of contentment in her voice, or the way her heartbeat raced beneath his thumb on her neck.

"I came here because Gage guilted me into it. To get a dog I didn't want to help me through a life I'd come to hate and thought about ending. You've given me back my hope that this is just one more stepping-stone on the way to my future. But it's a future I don't want without you."

Roscoe barked once from beside them. They both laughed as Dylan looked down at the retriever seated at his feet, his tongue lolling out the side of his mouth with a happy dog grin on his face.

"Or Roscoe," he clarified.

"Dylan," she began, but he silenced her with a kiss this time, pulling her close enough to feel every response he had to her.

Heat surged through him, desire swirling and dancing as their mouths met. He dragged himself away, unwilling to be so selfish after the ordeal she'd just been through, but only enough to lean his forehead against hers as he gasped for breath. His hand found the flat abdomen his child was nestled within.

"A baby." She nodded, a smile pulling at the corner over her lips, her eyes brimming with hope and desire and love. "Everything I've ever wanted is right here. You are the reason I'm still breathing, and I'm not leaving unless you ask me to."

A smile slowly spread over her lips. "Then you might as well unpack your bags for good."

"I don't have a ring to give you, but marry me, Julia." He brushed kisses over her eyes, her cheeks, and, finally, her parted lips. "It's the only way you could make this moment any more perfect."

Before she answered, two giant paws landed on his shoulder, knocking Dylan off balance, and he stepped backward. Stumbling under the weight, he didn't see the huge tongue coming as Tango licked his face, from his chin to his forehead.

Julia's laughter echoed in the kitchen as she tried, unsuccessfully, to stop long enough to command Tango to get down. Finally, on his own accord, the monstrous dog settled back on all fours and sat next to Roscoe.

Dylan swiped a hand over his face, wiping away the dog slobber. "You see how much I love you?"

"Since Tango has given you his seal of approval, my answer is yes." She passed him a towel from the sink. "Now, what do you say we go clean up in my room? We only have this house to ourselves for another nine months."

Dylan felt the heat spread from his chest throughout the rest of his body. "Then we better make the most of every second."

Growing up with two highly independent and determined sisters has turned veterinarian Justin Hart into a sworn bachelor.
But when a pregnant woman crashes her car outside his clinic, claiming to have hit a dog and with nowhere to go,
he can't fight his instinct to help her.

Cast out by her emotionally abusive soon-to-be ex-husband, A-list actress Alyssa Cole has learned the hard way not to trust first impressions, especially not in Hollywood. Yet, four hundred miles from her former life, the kindness of this small-town vet makes her willing to try again. But when the truth catches up to Alyssa, will Justin be willing to stand by her? Or will lies and deception tear them apart forever?

Keep reading for a sneak peek at the sweet and sexy next installment in T. J. Kline's Healing Harts series,

CLOSE TO HEART

An Excerpt from

CLOSE TO HEART

JUSTIN HART ROLLED his neck from side to side, working out the stiffness as he stared at the computer screen in front of him. He wished this new accounting program his cousin, Bailey, had insisted he try was easier to learn. He knew she was right and it would make everything easier, eventually. Right now, it was just one more thing he didn't have time to deal with on his already full plate. With a niece on the way and a holiday double wedding next month, he was trying to get as many items as possible eliminated from his to-do list before the end of the month. And since their accountant had been imprisoned for embezzling from his sister Jessie, that now included doing his own books until he found someone else. Just one more thing on his ever-lengthening to-do list.

Justin rubbed his eyes and leaned back in the chair, flexing his hands before folding them behind his head. He should have let Nathan, his financial guru future brother-in-law, handle it. Nathan had offered to handle Justin's finances until they found another accountant, but that would mean spending even more time on his sister's part of the ranch than he already did. Not that he didn't love Jessie and Julia, but they were both so busy finding a rhythm in their new relationships that, most of the time, he felt like a third wheel. It was frustrating trying to talk to either of them while they made lovey faces at Nathan and Dylan. Making it even harder to keep from punching either man, no matter how much he liked them, considering they were sleeping with his little sisters. In his eyes, it was still his job to protect both of them, the same way he always had.

It would piss both of his sisters off if they heard him say that out loud. He couldn't begin to count how many times they'd both told him to quit acting like their parent over the past year. But, now that Mom and Dad were gone, God rest their souls, he was the only one left to take care of the girls. That included Bailey, the youngest of their clan and, right now, the one frustrating him the most.

She needed to grow up and settle down, but she'd always been the family "wild child." It was obvious from their argument after he closed his veterinary clinic this evening and the way she'd spun her tires as she pulled out that she was getting more irritated with him. He should probably call and check that she got home okay.

Justin rose from behind his desk and made his way to the front windows of the clinic, lifting the blinds to watch the snow that was now coming down heavily. If Bailey hadn't headed straight home, or went to one of the local bars as she'd been doing more often lately...

Hopefully she'd missed driving in this mess. The early snowstorm was unexpected and wet, quickly turning into sludge all over the roads. He was glad he didn't have to walk more than a few feet out the back of the clinic to his house. It might not be ideal for some, but it sure made late-night emergencies convenient for him. Or nights, like tonight, when he just couldn't shut his brain off enough to sleep, he could get his paperwork done.

The wide swing of headlights coming around the bend toward his clinic caught his eye. It was late and, with weather like this, most locals would know to stay inside. Suddenly, the lights spun. He could see the taillights and flashing brake lights moving forward. It had to be someone traveling too fast on the icy stretch of highway. He hung up his call to Bailey and ran back to his desk to grab his jacket when he heard the screech of metal.

Justin ran through the front door, barely noticing the dark shadow that ducked into the bushes by the driveway. He was too focused on the car pressed against the brick wall that lined the entrance to the clinic. He could vaguely make out that the driver was a woman as he ran to the side door. Somehow she had managed to do a complete spin, stopping with the headlights facing the correct direction again, but the front bumper of her very expensive luxury car was firmly planted into his brick wall.

Banging on the driver's side window, he saw a woman look his way. With eyes wide, looking scared and surprised in the light from his phone, she opened the car door.

"No, I'm fine, thank you. I don't need anything but the tow," he heard her say just before she pressed a button to disconnect a call over the speakers in the car. She hurried to the front of the car, looking past the bright lights into the bushes before turning back toward him. "Did you see it?"

"See what? Are you okay? Do I need to call an ambulance?" The airbags in her car hadn't even deployed, so she couldn't have been going too fast, and she didn't appear to be injured, although she seemed frantic as she searched the darkness.

"I'm fine. I wasn't going fast because of the snow, but there was a dog. Where is it? I know I hit it. We have to find it."

The soft *thump* of the windshield wipers was the only sound in the darkness as she moved toward the driveway. Had this woman lost her mind? She was out in the middle of a snowstorm, in a car that cost a small fortune, without chains on her tires, at night with nothing more than a sweater on, looking for a dog that may or may not exist.

"Ma'am, let's get you inside. We can wait inside for the tow truck to come get your car, and you can get warm."

"No, I *know* I hit a dog. I felt it when the car spun."

"Are you sure it wasn't just you hitting the wall?" She turned back toward him, her body silhouetted by the headlights.

Holy crap, she's pregnant!

He ran to her side, yanking his jacket down his arms and wrapping it around her shoulders. "Okay, let's just get you inside, and then I'll come back out and look for the dog."

She narrowed her gaze at him warily. Even in the limited amount of light they had, he could easily read the distrust in them. Or maybe it was the jaunty lift to her chin and stiff shoulders. Either way, she didn't believe him for a second.

He sighed loudly. "Fine, you go inside and sit down. I'll stay and find the dog."

She looked as if she was about to refuse again, but she nodded once, turning off the car and grabbing her purse from the passenger seat before hurrying into the warmth of his clinic. Justin let out a low growl, wishing he could ignore his father's voice in his head reminding him he had to keep his word. He wanted nothing more than to follow her back inside, where he could change into dry clothes. He went back to her car and, moving to the other side of the vehicle, inspected the damage. It wasn't as bad as it could have been, but the bumper was bent forward to the point of scraping against the tire. She wasn't going to be able to drive it until it was fixed.

"That's a damn shame," he muttered. That BMW cost twice what he'd paid for his 4x4 pickup. And her car was brand-new. It was going to cost a small fortune to fix it, if they could even get the parts all the way out here. The headlights turned off automatically, and Justin looked back toward the clinic. He could see her silhouette against the window, watching to see if he really searched for the dog. "Seriously?" he muttered to himself.

Wandering slowly up the driveway, Justin let his eyes scan over the wet shrubs, looking for the mysterious stray dog that, if it existed, was likely long gone. He tried not to think about any worse scenarios. The snow had turned to icy rain, pelting him mercilessly as he tried to use the light from his cell phone to look for the animal. After several minutes of freezing torment, he concluded there was nothing to see. If she had even hit a dog, it had probably crawled off to die. It wasn't pretty but it was common, and there was little he was going to be able to do to save it. He was a veterinarian, not a miracle worker. There was no point in staying out here, freezing, any longer while snow and icy rain slid down the collar of his flannel shirt. He almost regretted giving up his jacket.

Justin turned off his phone and tucked it into his pocket, turning back toward the clinic to see her still watching through the window. He remembered her desperate eyes and how she'd been ready to search for the dog herself. He hated the disappointment he imagined he would see in her face and felt guilty for not finding the dog.

What the hell?

He turned back toward the shrubs and pulled out his phone again. This time, as the light swept over the base of a large pine, he saw the unmistakable glow of eyes. He slowly crept toward the tree, cautious of making any sudden moves that might frighten what could be a dangerous animal.

"Come here, buddy. Are you hurt?" Justin held his hand out slightly, praying that it wasn't a coyote. "It's okay," he said, using a falsetto tone.

He heard the soft whine of an injured dog and saw the wet paws move toward him from under the shrub just before the unmistakable blocky head of a black Lab followed. "Damn it," he muttered.

The dog crawled toward him, low to the ground, and nudged his outstretched hand. "Are you going to let me carry you inside?" he asked the dog.

He was rewarded with a warm lick on his fingers, as if the dog understood and was happy to comply. He moved toward the animal and circled his arms around its soaked body. Justin could feel the poor thing shivering against him, though he was unsure whether from fear, injury, or the cold, and he hurried toward the clinic.

The woman opened the door as he reached it. "You found it!" She rubbed the dog's face. "I'm so sorry, baby." She followed closely as he took the dog into one of the exam rooms.

Justin immediately palpated the animal, looking for blood and broken bones. He immediately noticed a scrape on her hip, and his fingers trailed over the animal's rounded belly. He snatched a stethoscope from one of the drawers and pressed it against the wet dog, under its ribs.

Crap!

"She's pregnant." He should have realized as soon as he picked the dog up, but he'd been too busy trying to get inside that he hadn't paid attention.

"Wha-?" The woman's hands instinctively touched her own rounded abdomen before covering her mouth. "Oh my goodness, is she okay?"

He took the dog's temperature and glanced at the thermometer. It was only slightly lower than normal, but her gums were too red for his liking and she was panting faster than he would like to see. The dog rolled her chocolate brown eyes up at him. There was a good chance she was going into either labor or shock. Maybe both.

He met the woman's gaze and could see the worry in her green eyes, tears forming in the corners. Most of the women around here didn't cry after hitting a stray dog in a snowstorm. They were far too worried about their own well-being or what happened to the car. She moved toward the dog's head, stroking the animal's silky wet ears, apologizing as if the dog could understand her words.

"I'm going to take her to the back. My guess is that she's far enough along to deliver these pups, but I want to see what I'm dealing with. You can't go back there." She remained silent but her eyes flicked up to meet his, and he could read the distrust again.

"I can't have you exposed to the X-rays in your condition. I'm going to do everything I can to keep this dog and her babies safe." He reached for her hand. It was meant to be reassuring, something he'd done with dozens of patients, but the jolt of desire that shot through him took him by surprise. "I...I promise," he stammered, trying to ignore the foreign emotion.

Justin shoved the feeling aside. Sure the woman was beautiful, but it wasn't as if he was lacking beautiful women right now. He knew there were plenty of them in town who'd been trying to nab his attention for more than one or two dates. He didn't need romantic complications now, so he'd made sure to stick with women who wanted the same thing he did—no stress, no ties, friendships with benefits. He scooped the dog in his arms before carrying her into the back room to take the X-rays, wondering if the stress of having too much to plan and his late nights were responsible for his momentary lapse of logic and oversensitized response to the woman in his lobby. As Justin prepped the dog for sedation, he pulled his phone from his pocket and dialed Bailey's number again. He needed her here to help him with this.

No answer and his call went directly to voice mail.

"Bailey, I need you to come back. I have an emergency. A pregnant Lab came in and I need to deliver these puppies by C-section. She's going into shock." He took a deep breath, wondering how he was going to manage this alone. "Get your ass back here now."

Justin disconnected the call and shoved his phone into his pocket. Was she really so pissed at him that she wouldn't answer the phone? Or was it just his shitty luck? Either way, he was screwed.

He looked down at the now-sedated dog lying on the table. He couldn't waste any time if he was going to try to save her and the puppies. He'd seen the proof on the X-rays. The puppies were viable, but she had a small internal hemorrhage he had to control. He was going to have to recruit the only hands he had available.

"I NEED YOU to help me deliver these puppies."

Alyssa stared at him and wondered if he'd lost his mind. She couldn't deliver puppies. She didn't know anything about animals. She hadn't even been around any since she'd moved away from home and her mother's yapping shih tzu. "I thought you said I couldn't come back here," she pointed out.

"That was while I doing the X-rays." He pointed to a door off to one side of the room. "I need another set of hands, and we can't waste a lot of time talking about this. I'm going to open her up. When I get the puppies out, I'll hand them to you, and I need you to wipe them down with those towels. You just need to make sure they're all breathing, then put them over there, so that the mask blows oxygen on them."

She looked where he pointed at what looked like a small nest of bedding with an oxygen mask to one side of it. She looked back at the man in front of her. He was doing everything he could to help this dog, and he could have just walked away. She had been the one who caused the damage, after all.

The dog lay on the table, completely covered with sterile blue paper, except for the exposed section the vet had wiped down with what looked like iodine. Alyssa ran her hand through her loose hair and twisted it into a makeshift knot at the back of her head and squared her shoulders, resolving herself to do this. "Okay, just tell me what you need me to do."

"Take these," he said, surprised by her quick acquiescence, and handed her a pair of latex gloves. He glanced up at her as he set the scalpel against the shaved belly of the Lab. "I'm Justin Hart, by the way." His blue eyes searched hers intensely, making her insides flutter oddly.

"Alyssa."

She heard the breathless quality of her voice and cleared her throat. The corner of his lips curved up on one side as a dimple sunk deep in one cheek. Attraction slammed into her, jolting her more than when her car hit the wall outside.

"Well, Alyssa, hold up that towel in both hands and we'll get started. You're about to have a litter of puppies."

She tried not to study him, from the rugged squared jaw to the too-broad shoulders that looked massive in the gray Henley he wore and his penetrating blue eyes. But it was his voice that drew her attention. It was deep and smooth, reminding her of rich wine and dark chocolate, and, just like those things, it was a luxury she couldn't allow herself to enjoy too much. Not with everything that had just happened in the past twenty-four hours. She needed to keep her focus on her future, and this side trip in the middle of nowhere had already delayed her.

As he made the first incision, her blood went cold and her stomach rolled. She didn't think she'd made any noise, but Justin looked up at her, his eyes searching her face.

"You okay?"

Hold it together, Alyssa. This is no different from biology class.

The scent of antiseptic was all around her, and she felt suddenly queasy. Unable to speak, she nodded. He dabbed at the blood that oozed with gauze, quickly but carefully working his way through the layers of skin before pulling some unrecognizable part of the dog's insides to the outside of her body. Alyssa was surprised to find that instead of being repulsed, her curiosity got the better of her, and she watched him make another incision, revealing the first puppy. Reaching for the tray of equipment beside him, he plucked another piece of gauze from a pile and pulled open the amniotic sac encasing a small black puppy. He pulled the membrane from the puppy's face before clamping, then clipping the umbilical cord and tipping the puppy upside down.

"Okay, we're going to move quickly. Here's the first one. Just rub him really good and make sure he's breathing." He watched her for a moment as she ran the towel over the sides of the puppy. "Don't forget to move over his face and neck, too. That will help work the fluid out."

She tried to follow his instructions, but the puppy gave a gurgled yip. Alyssa froze midstep, her gaze shooting toward his in fear. "What did I do?"

He glanced up and chuckled at her discomfort. "Nothing. That just means he's alive and ready to meet his mom. Get ready, I've got another for you."

She set the puppy on the towels of the makeshift bed, surprised to find them warm. Hurrying back to the operating table, she reached for a clean towel to receive the next puppy. He laid another puppy into her hands, and she began rubbing him as she walked toward the bedding

"Why is the bed warm?"

"It's enough of a shock being born without worrying about getting them sick," he replied as he continued to work, barely glancing her way. "This way, it's a gradual adjustment and it helps regulate their body temperature until they can do it themselves."

They repeated the process in silence while the squirming pile of puppies grew. Some black, some almost white-blond, but all of them grunting now, nudging one another in the pile.

"Last one," he announced, laying it into her hands.

She could feel the difference in this one immediately. He was smaller than the others, and where the others had been plump with round bellies, she could feel the ribs on this one. Alyssa rubbed at the puppy's side, but there was no quiet whine this time. She opened the towel and didn't see the telltale rise and fall of his chest.

"He's too still." She hurried back to Justin at the table.

"Set him down," he ordered. "Grab that stethoscope." She held it out to him, and he arched his brows, nodding at his hands, buried inside the anesthetized dog on the table. "You need to see if he has a heartbeat. I need to stop her bleeding."

"I don't know what I'm listening for," she argued.

"Just put that on." She slipped the earpieces in. "Good, now lay the end on his chest and tell me what you hear."

"Nothing... wait, I hear something but it's quiet."

Justin reached for a piece of gauze and rubbed it over the puppy's face a few times before it gasped, opening its mouth wide. "Okay, take him and put him right in front of the mask. I'll come check on him as soon as I finish with the mom. Just stay with them."

Alyssa laid her head in the crook of her elbow, trying to stay awake. Justin was finishing with the female Lab as she watched the puppies. She was keeping a close eye on the littlest one, the one that had trouble breathing. They were all so small and weak, but he was even more so. Her hand instinctively curled around the side of her pregnant belly, where her child lay, nestled under her ribs. In less than six weeks, she'd be watching her own child sleep. Rather than comforting her, the thought sent vibrations of panic echoing through her.

She had no idea what to do next. The last thing she'd expected when she went out to lunch with Lillian yesterday was to find out her best friend had been sleeping with her husband for the past three years. The confrontation with Elijah that followed had been bad enough, but his apathetic response, coupled with his demand for a divorce, had shattered the last remnants of the illusion she'd clung to that their Hollywood marriage wasn't as fake as everything else in the industry. When he ordered her to leave the house before his return, she'd packed the car up with clothing and her jewelry, assuming she would find a way to sell what she didn't need.

But that would only last so long. She needed to find a way to support her and her child. Her mother had insisted she return home, which would at least give her a roof over her head and buy a little time before the baby was born, but what then? Elijah had already informed her that she wouldn't get anything from him. She didn't even have a way to pay for doctor's visits or the delivery now, she reminded herself. Even worse, she didn't even *have* a doctor any longer. Worries beat against her brain, like the staccato beat of a drum, making her heart race in her chest as her child moved within her.

Two strong hands settled on her shoulders gently. "You did a good job."

"Oh!" Alyssa jerked upright and slid the rolling chair to the side.

Justin's lips curved into an apologetic smile. "Sorry, I didn't mean to scare you. I thought you were awake."

He cocked his head to one side, and his dimple sank into his cheek, giving him a boyish charm. He had full lips, the kind that made you want to bite them gently before kissing them. She brushed back the bangs that had fallen from her bun and tucked them behind her ear. "I was. I just thought you were still with the mom." She realized she was staring at his perfect mouth and quickly looked back at the puppies, which were grunting softly and wiggling against one another. "I was just sort of lost in my own head, I guess."

He nodded as he turned to a cupboard nearby and withdrew two needleless syringes. "What are those for?"

"We need to give them colostrum so they have the antibodies they need and don't get sick." He walked back and handed her the syringe. "Just a little on the back of their tongues, and we'll do it again in an hour. Like this." He reached for the first puppy and put a few drops of the liquid into its mouth.

Justin glanced up at her through thick, dark lashes. Lashes most of the women in her career field would kill for. "This is a nice litter. What do you think you're going to do with them?"

"Me?" she squeaked, pausing as she reached for a puppy. "Doctor, I can't take them with me."

"I think we're beyond the 'doctor' business." He arched a brow and smiled at her, the dimple creasing his cheek before his brows dropped forward between his eyes, thoughtfully, and he set the puppy down, reaching for the next one. "You won't be going anywhere for a while, at least not until your car gets fixed. But I guess you probably wouldn't be able to keep them in a hotel. They could stay here until you head out." His brows lifted again, as if he was certain his explanation was sufficient.

Crap, how am I going to pay for a hotel or to fix the car? Does he really expect me to pay to keep these puppies, or for the surgery?

"Um.. I can't pay for any of this." She tucked the strand of hair behind her ear again and saw his eyes flick to the massive diamond solitaire settled on her left hand under the latex glove. She arched a brow, daring him to comment. She didn't owe him anything. She wondered where her sudden backbone had come from. Where had it been for the last six years of her marriage, when Elijah pressured her to spend less time on set and more time helping him build his agency? Where had it been when she'd allowed him to take control of her already successful career, allowing him to make higher demands in her contracts until producers could no longer meet them and she'd decided to "retire" at the height of her career to focus on her husband and starting a family? Her hand trailed over the baby quiet within her. Now that fantasy lay in rubble at her feet. Her husband had kicked her out, said he didn't love her, and left her pregnant and alone.

Her eyes slid over the man in front of her, his still-wet hair standing at odd angles at the top of his head, and guilt swept in. The least she could do was give him some sort of explanation. He had come to her rescue and stayed in the freezing sleet to find the dog she hit.

Alyssa cleared her throat. "The truth is that expensive things are all I have right now. I don't have any money or any way to get any until I can sell a few things. I'm not even sure I still have insurance on the car to fix it." She looked down at the puppies, praying he wouldn't force her to admit anything more.

She couldn't give him any answers. She didn't have them to give.

Acknowledgments

THIS HAS BEEN such an amazing two years. Looking back I can't believe how far I've come on this journey, but I certainly haven't done it alone.

Rebecca, thank you so much for jumping in and taking my hand. You have pushed and prodded and poked me more than I've ever admitted to you, but I am so much better for it. You have been patient and kind when I needed it most and given me an insistent shove when I tried to slack off. You've made me grow, and I'm so grateful for it.

Suzie, who has taken a chance and has become my cheerleader. You have been a blessing I didn't even realize I needed. I wasn't sure how I was going to reach for the stars, but you have not only given me a road map, you are guiding the way for me.

For the ladies who remind me to enjoy this roller-coaster ride of life—Codi, Jen, Shelly, Kristin, Jodi, Alexis,

Leanne, Tracie, Lashell, and Mary Chris—I can't wait to share more moments with you guys, making memories that we'd probably rather everyone forget, celebrating every success and letting someone else clean up the mess from the party. You guys are the best!

For my readers who continue to walk this path with me, gobbling up each and every story and then asking for more. I love your insatiable appetite and will always do my best to give you what you ask for. You are what drives my coffee-induced rear end to the computer every single day. I love what I do almost as much as I love you. Trust me, that's saying a lot.

For my parents, who keep me grounded, reminding me that there are other things in life besides writing and to spend time doing the things I love with family and my horses. Without the two of you, I'd become a hermit and the "kids" would starve. Never doubt how grateful I am for the two of you, even if I forget to tell you sometimes.

I want to thank my very sweet, dear children—Kassie, Austin, and Aidan—who remind me that life is short and goes by far too quickly. You three have amazed me with how fast you can grow while I don't get any older at all. Your mother orders you to slow down so that I can relish every moment more, spend one more night tucking you in and reading a story, or playing guitar as you fall asleep. As much as I miss the days you were little, I'm so excited to see the adults you are becoming and watching you achieve greatness. I love you three to the moon and back again!

My amazing husband, the first person to tell me to "go for it" in the face of rejection. Without you, I'd be lost.

There really aren't enough words in my writer brain to explain how much you mean to me. When we were dating, my mother told me you made me better. I don't think she understood then how right she was. But I know. I love you with every breath.

To the One who gives it all...I love every minute of this life.

About the Author

T. J. KLINE was raised competing in rodeos and rodeo queen competitions from the age of fourteen and has thorough knowledge of the sport as well as the culture involved. She has written several articles about rodeo for small periodicals, as well as a more recent how-to article for *RevWriter*, and she has written a nonfiction health book and two inspirational fiction titles under the name Tina Klinesmith. She is also an avid reader and book reviewer for both Tyndale and Multnomah. In her spare time, she can be found laughing hysterically with her husband, children, and their menagerie of pets in Northern California.

Discover great authors, exclusive offers, and more at hc.com.

DISCARD
CADL

Made in the USA
Middletown, DE
28 March 2024

One last thing: If this book has helped or inspired you in any way, would you please consider leaving a review wherever you purchased this book? Reviews help spread the word and also help me improve as a writer. I love to hear from my readers!

Thank you, and we wish you the very best in all of your traveling adventures!

—Jolene and Fred

RV with your family and experiencing the road is what makes you happy, don't wait another day. Go for it!

Money can't buy happiness, but it can buy an RV, and that's pretty close! There are few wrong ways to travel and experience the RV life. Keep up with your maintenance, treat your rig well, and it will last you a long time.

The road is calling. And remember, "Home is where you park it!"

insurance will refund me with my receipt. That's *awesome*. This sort of peace of mind is completely worth the cost of insurance, to me at least.

You Don't Need an RV Membership (But It's Nice)

There are a lot of RV clubs out there, with varying levels of offerings. Passport America, Good Sam, and Harvest Hosts are probably the most popular out there. These generally cost, but offer bonuses like money off campgrounds, apps, referral programs, reviews, and more.

How often you travel, where you're going, and what you're looking for is going to determine whether or not it will be worth it for you. I have Passport America, and have had generally good experiences, including half of a great RV park *with a hot tub*. It pays for itself in 2-3 nights, and after that it's pure savings.

Enjoy Your Trip!

The most important tip we can leave you with is to *enjoy your trip*! We only get one life, and one chance to really live the way we truly want. If driving around in an

It's Better to Be Over-Insured

I cannot overstate this enough. *Insurance is important,* and you should have excellent coverage at all times. Talk to your insurance agent, and shop around to find a good price. Your insurance shouldn't be outrageous, but you should be covered in case someone hits you, you hit someone, or something awful happens that is out of your control. (Nationwide, Geico, Progressive, Good Sam, and many others offer RV insurance. Shop around!)

Use Your Insurance Benefits, Too

Insurance is more than just securing you when you get into an accident or have an issue. Some insurances offer huge benefits, like discounts at hotels, campgrounds, and more. My own RV insurance offers to refund a set amount of money each year spend on lodging when your RV is undergoing maintenance.

This means if my RV is in the shop because something mechanical breaks, and I cannot stay in my RV or the mechanic cannot offer me a camping spot there to stay in, I can book a hotel for a night or two *at no cost to me.* My

Know Your Cancellation Policy

Some campsites won't refund you once you've booked. Others, you'll be eating a $10-$25 cancellation fee. I recommend reserving ahead of time *if you have a good cancelation policy*. I don't mind making a $20 mistake for the gamble, but if I'm paying for several nights if I cancel, it's a whole other conversation. Knowing ahead of time will help you in the long run.

Your Booking Must-Haves

Know ahead of time what you really need. Think about what is most important to you when you're looking at a campsite. Do you need WiFi? Prioritize that. What about water hookups, is that a non-negotiable to you? Amenities, like pools, a clubhouse, and more?

It's okay that something like a pool in the summer or WiFi is important to you! Make sure you prioritize finding somewhere for the long haul that has the things you're looking for. Don't feel bad for prioritizing your needs – not everyone wants to boondock every night, after all.

I like starting outside and working my way in, back to front, before I ever leave the campground. Find a system that works for you.

Book Early & Often

More and more people are hitting campsites nowadays, so booking ahead of time is a must. Do your research and make sure you're planning ahead properly. Some campgrounds open all their spots 3 months in advance, some 9 months, some a full year or two.

If you want to secure a spot somewhere specific, make sure you're planning ahead. Some of the freedom or fun might be taken out of the trip, but if there is a campsite or park you have your heart set on, make sure you plan ahead and get your spot early. Weekends fill up faster, as a heads up! We like using goodsam.com and rvparkfinder.com.

Since RVing has become so popular, some of our friends have even purchased their own land or a deeded spot for their RV sites. But make sure you visit it first. You can find them on websites like rvproperty.com.

season, not stuffy, moldy, or otherwise gross.

I also use drops of peppermint essential oil on cotton balls, and let several of those hang out on surfaces, in cabinets, etc. I've heard that they help keep spiders away, and honestly? I'm down with anything that *might* keep a spider from jumping on my face in the spring.

Everything warm or 'nestable' needs to be removed, including bedding, sleeping bags, sheets, and towels. You don't want to give mice or rodents any chance at finding a new home in your RV! Most people I know pack these in big plastic totes and store them in a basement or attic during the winter.

Have a Before-You-Leave Checklist

Before you leave home, or your campground, have a checklist that you go through to make sure you've got everything together you need. Are your steps up? Awning up? Doors are locked? An open door going 60 miles per hour on the highway is true disaster, let me tell you. Are your windows closed? Roof vent closed? Everything secure?

If you're still struggling with storage, talk a walk around your RV and try to find underutilized places, or things you're not using that you can get rid of. Shelves that are only half full or poorly organized, spaces where you can hang extra things, or items or bins you can consolidate to make more space.

Don't Overlook Winterizing

So many people put off winterizing their RV until it's become too late, and do serious damage. If you're storing your RV for the end of the season, you need to properly winterize it so that your pipes stay solid and nothing breaks or cracks.

RV antifreeze is *different* from vehicle antifreeze, and you should only use the antifreeze made for your RV. Don't think you can top off with stuff for your car, because I promise you, you're asking for trouble!

Other winterizing steps I personally take is to stuff dryer sheets into nooks and crannies throughout the RV. This helps keeps mice and rodents away (so important!), and honestly? The RV still smells fresh at the end of the

Keeping Organized Counts

It's really easy to get in a bad habit of throwing things everywhere in your RV and losing things. Shirts, keys, sunscreen, etc. Being organized, and making a commitment to yourself to continue to maintain that organization, is so important! I find the better organized I am in my RV, and the easier I can find the things I need, the happier I am overall.

For me, this means lots of bins on shelves, labels, and knowing everything has a place and a 'home'. For you, it could look totally different! Find an organizational system that works for *your* space and *your* RV.

Vertical Storage

Storage in an RV is a huge struggle; we all know that. Make sure you're maximizing your small space as best as you can – for me, this means vertical storage. I love Command Hooks that stick right on the wall and let me hang jackets, bags, or even things like a produce bag of fruit or vegetables in the kitchen.

just *call* the other person on your cell phone. The driver can have their phone on speakerphone in their lap, and the director won't kill their voice trying to explain just how close they are. It's a simple solution that almost no one does, but it can save a ton of headache and frustration.

Speaking of Directing

If you're the one behind the wheel and someone else is going to be helping you back it in, I recommend you take the extra minute and physically get out of your RV to survey. Look at any obstructions, like trees, rocks, or posts. See where any hookups are, and get a feel for the spot. This takes almost no time, but it makes a big difference.

Google Street View Is Your Best Friend

If you're not sure about the road's condition, how steep it is, or how windy the road will be, check Google Street View! You'll be able to get a great idea of just where you're going, and how the drive will be.

in the morning and practice turning, backing up, handling your rig with the trailer, etc. You cannot be *too* prepared in this situation, and you really want to avoid causing yourself an accident your first time out!

Be Wary of Dips

I can't tell you how many times I've scraped the back of my RV, even now. A dip or a bump seems totally innocent when you're so high looking down on it. Take all dips or bumps nice and slow, and use common sense. It will take time and experience, but you'll learn. Not all parking lots, turns, or roads are going to be RV friendly.

If You're Directing Someone Else

I can't tell you how often one person hops out of their vehicle to direct another into a campsite or a parking space, and how often it is a struggle. It's hard to hear over the sound of the RV motor, and those are *big* vehicles. The person directing would have to really scream in order to be heard.

Pro-tip: Instead of yelling, waving, and being frantic,

Simple Trailer Driving Tips

I used to *hate* towing my car on trips because I could never figure out how to drive our RV to move the trailer properly. However, my husband Fred gave me this tip, and it's helped a *lot*.

Sit in your RV driver's seat and take your hands off the wheel. Start by placing one hand at the bottom of the wheel, or the 6 o'clock position. If you want the back end of your trailer to move left, move your hand on the wheel left, towards the 9 o'clock position. If you want the back end of your trailer to move right, move your *hand* right, towards the 3 o'clock position.

Slow, steady, easy turns – you don't want to jackknife it and have to start over. Watch all around you to ensure you've got clearance in the front and the back.

Practice Driving, Turning, and Moving

Speaking of driving, I *highly recommend* you practice ahead of your first trip! Drive around the block, the neighborhood, or your town. Go into an empty parking lot

Note: This also applies to your driving. Slow down! You're bigger and slower than most things on the road, and you're not going to be breaking any speed records when you're driving your RV. That is a good thing. Let that 18-wheeler pass you; it's not the end of the world. Instead of focusing on how fast you can go, focus on the journey, and getting there safely.

If your GPS says you'll get there in 2 hours, you can expect at least 2 ½ hours of travel time. You're going to be driving slower, not keeping up with traffic quite as well, and probably having to make more stops, too. It's just a fact of RV life, so be prepared.

Listen to Your Gut

As with all traveling, you meet a huge variety of people. This can be one of the wonderful benefits of RV travel. However, it can also be a downside. If you encounter someone and get an uncomfortable feeling, listen to your gut. Don't force yourself to stay in an uncomfortable situation or around people that make you uncomfortable. You never know what's going on, and you don't owe anyone anything.

Remember: As long as you're having a good time, you're not doing much wrong. The whole goal of traveling this way and exploring the world is to live your life, enjoy your freedom, and have a fun time. If you ever feel dread, panic, or anxiety about going out, perhaps it is time to rethink your vacation plans or your lifestyle. If you ever come back home after a long trip and think about how awful your trip was, how unrewarding – think about what went wrong and how to fix it.

Take It Slow

This applies to those in it for the long haul. This could be folks that travel for several weeks or a month at a time, or even full timers just starting out. It's so tempting to bounce from place to place, because you want to see it all immediately. Instead, I encourage you to *slow down.*

There's no rush, no pressure. It will all be there. Take your time in each area, city, and campground. Try the local food, get used to the area, settle in, and feel good. You'll know when you're ready to move on. If you're only staying a night or two in every destination, you could be missing out. Enjoy the journey, too.

The Best Tips We've Picked Up Along the Way

I'm going to leave you with this section, a collection of the best tips we've picked up over our years of traveling in our RV. As I've mentioned before, we've been RVing for a while now, and we've seen and done it all.

This list isn't in any particular order. The tips that are important to me when I'm traveling might not apply to you. We all have a different travel style, and it's possible that you're simply going to find things less important, or more important, than I do.

site has access. Take your time and make sure you make secure connections.

9. Pull out your slides.

If you've got slides/slide outs on your camper, this is the time to pull them out and get everyone comfortable and ready to relax. It's best to do it when you first set up so that you don't have to worry with it when it gets dark.

10. Unpack!

Unpack your campsite, bring out your grill or anything you need, set your awning up, and get your chairs out.

Here's the fun part – you're done!

4. Chock your tires.

You're parked, you're level, and you've got plenty of space? Well, now it's time to put your chocks on so you know you're not going anywhere.

5. Disconnect.

If you've got a trailer, now is the time to disconnect your trailer from the truck, including the hitch, stabilizers, and any chains. Placing a piece of wood or an unused leveling block under the tongue jack so it doesn't dig into the dirt (this is recommended, but not technically needed).

6. Change the height.

Change the height of your tongue jack, if applicable, so that it is level to both the front and the back.

7. Lower any stabilizers.

You're almost to the finish line! Lower any stabilizers you've got.

8. Get yourself camp ready.

Now is the time to hook up the power and water, if your

I encourage you to use this as a *guide*. If your rig has different needs, change it up! Just make sure you take your time and check everything before you get unpacked and settled in. There's no rush, no prize for the fastest setup or takedown of camp, I promise.

1. Are you close enough?

Check the distance of your RV and the electric and water hookups, if they exist. Are they close enough? Is it in an awkward position where you are going to be a bit cramped for space, or you could trip over things? If so, can you reasonably fix it?

2. Do you have enough space?

If your RV has a slideout, did you leave enough space to comfortably expand in your current setup? If you're going to run into a tree, now is the time to move.

3. Are you level?

Take a walk around and look at where you're parked. Is your RV level, or do you need to put leveling blocks under tires to make it level? Get them set up and get your RV comfortably level before you move forward.

Perfect-10 Checklist: Setting Up Camp

Hooray, you finally make it to the ideal campsite! You've parked, and you're ready to relax or even start exploring on your bikes. Before you unpack, let's go over a quick, simple checklist to ensure that you have everything covered, and you're not going to forget or miss anything. Sticking to a routine or a checklist is the best way to ensure you don't miss or forget something, and that you are always set up for success. We have found check lists to be pretty important when we're on the road.

for the road. An e-reader or a Kindle, however, saves space, and offers a thousand books at the tip of my fingers. In addition, if I want a new read or the next in the series, all I need is an internet connection – or a place to quickly download my next read. Or use an app like Libby or Overdrive on your smartphone to borrow ebooks from your library!

bedtime and get a good night's rest! We have found they are worth it for us. You usually need something called an RV size or a Short Queen size, depending on your mattress. Getting the right size is also a must.

Clothes Washing Bag

If you're not going to be somewhere close to a washing machine, a washing *bag* is a pretty great thing to have. It makes it a lot easier to get your clothes cleaned, which for me is essential – but I'll admit, not for everyone. These bags aren't big, but you can easily wash a day or two's worth of clothes.

Pro Tip: We learned a great laundry trick from a friend at a KOA campground. Use a plastic bucket or tub with a tight fitting lid, fill it with water, dirty clothes, and detergent in the morning. As you drive through the day, the motion of the RV will "wash" your clothes for you. When you stop to set up camp, you can simply rinse them out and hang them up on a clothesline to dry!

Kindle or E-Reader

Are you a reader? While I personally prefer a physical book that I can hold in my hand, they're not convenient

Portable Dehumidifier

A mini dehumidifier can really make the difference in a hot, humid climate. While it's not necessary, it can improve your afternoons in the summer, leading to more enjoyment.

Memory Foam Bed Topper

Do you sleep well in your RV? A memory foam topper is a great and relatively inexpensive way to make it feel more like home. Sleep is the most important thing, and getting a good amount of sleep on vacation will help you enjoy your whole trip more.

Comforter/Duvet

A nice, big, fluffy comforter can bring your bedtime experience to a 10. Not necessary at all, but I always look forward to crawling under ours. A duvet is a great option because you can buy washable covers for them, and there are even hypoallergenic options nowadays if you can't sleep with feathers.

Nice Sheets

What's your "dream" bed sheet? Egyptian cotton, flannel, or satin? Cozy sheets means you're more likely to enjoy

DISH or DIRECTV RV Satellite. Or, if you would just like to tune in to local TV stations without paying for any kind of subscription, you can get something like the Antop AT-414B Outdoor Amplified Antenna.

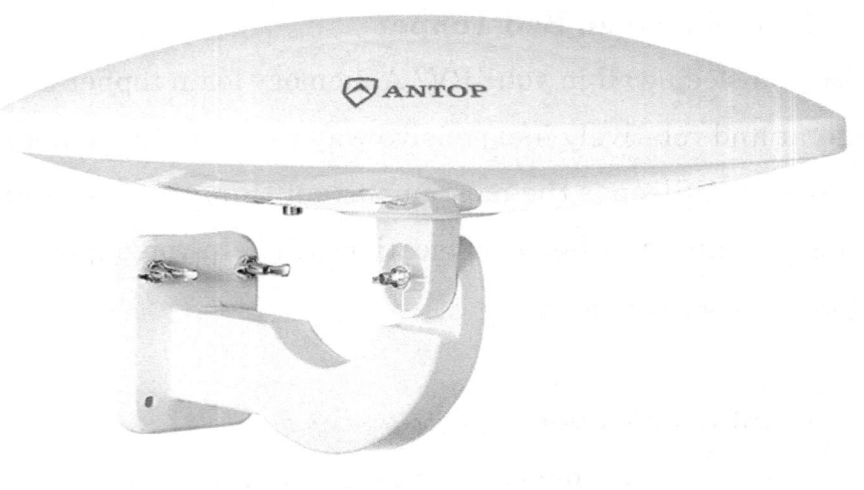

Outdoor Coaxial Cable

If you're looking to get cable, some campgrounds have cable hookups, but you'll need to supply your own coaxial cable to access it. Make sure that you find a cable which is sealed for all weather, and won't degrade in the sun or rain. Look for one that has weatherproof connectors. You may only need 25 feet, but it never hurts to have 50 feet or more. You can order several types on Amazon.

Mobile Hotspot

Need wifi? So many of us do nowadays. Whether you need to check your email during your weekends away, you're RVing full-time, or you just really want to stream your favorite movies at night, a mobile hotspot is a great comfort item that will improve your quality of life. Nowadays you can spend anywhere from $50 to $200 for a prepaid hotspot device (Amazon, Walmart, or Best Buy).

Cell Phone Booster

These are not magic, but they do feel like it. A cell phone booster is something that plugs into the wall, and can give you access to a better cell signal when you're in a normally spotty area. This isn't just important for the vital things, like making emergency calls, but it can be great if you're somewhere remote and really want to stream Netflix or Prime.

Portable Satellite TV Antenna/Receiver

A satellite TV antenna will let you watch your favorite channels or catch the Sunday game. There are several antenna options for your RV that are waterproof and mount to your camper. If you have a subscription to cable, you can get an antenna or a booster like a Winegard

Comfort Items

Listen, your RV is your home away from home. You should be comfortable. Are all of the items in this section strictly necessary? No, not really – but you also deserve some ease and relaxation. I find that a few quality of life items go a long way. Are you really 'roughing it' if you've got a TV or cable? Well, *no*. But that's why you bought an RV, so you don't have to rough it! Enjoy your space; make it your home. Don't feel bad if you choose to have some of these creature comforts in your RV. If they make you happy, you deserve them!

Nail Clippers

You probably don't need a whole manicure set, but nail clippers and a nail file will save you when you're struggling with a hangnail after a long day out.

Deodorant

No one wants to smell you without it. Trust me.

Toothbrush + Toothpaste

Dental hygiene is not a joke. Take care of your teeth, even on the road!

Toilet Cleaner + Toilet Brush

Keep your RV toilet clean. When you're living in such small quarters, a clean and fresh-smelling bathroom is essential.

Shower Shoes

Do you need shower shoes in your *own* RV shower? Nope, but you're going to want them if you shower in the campground facilities. You can use crocs, a cheap pair of flip-flops... whatever works for you!

Shower Caddy

I really like having a portable shower caddy for convenience when getting to the campground shower, or keep it neat and tidy in my own bathroom. This also helps with things flying everywhere while I'm driving around – it's all nice and secure in the caddy.

Note: You may want to have more than one caddy (or stackable caddies) so that each of you can visit the camp showers at the same time. Everyone having their own set saves time.

Lotion

I like doing an all-in-one lotion, but you may need something for your face and your body. Lotion is one of those luxury items that really makes a difference! Some lotions (like Avon's Skin So Soft or Trader Joe's Lemongrass Coconut oil) even act as mosquito repellants!

Hairbrush

This isn't a luxury item, just a must. If you've got enough hair to comb, make sure you bring one! Like many items, I have a dedicated hairbrush that never leaves the RV; that way, I'll never accidentally forget it.

Electric Water Heater

Some people don't realize it, but you don't have to rely on propane to heat your water for things like baths, showers, or even dishes and cooking. It's sometimes called a lightning rod connector, and it screws into your hot water heater. This is often a lot cheaper than using propane, and it's great if you have a touchy pilot light or you camp for long periods of time. Nowadays, there are also tankless electric water heaters which might be worth looking into.

Shampoo + Conditioner

Even if you're not going to be showering inside your RV, but instead using campground facilities, you're going to want to have your own supplies.

Soap

Bar or liquid, whatever your preference is, make sure you've got enough to last you the trip – or you'll end up washing with your shampoo by the end of it! We like biodegradable soap so that it makes less of an impact on the environment. Plus, as mentioned before, you can use it in a basin to wash your hands and then pitch it in the woods (cutting down on your gray water).

For the Bathroom

No one likes to talk about the bathroom (I hope!), but there are some common-sense supplies that will make your life easier when it comes to your RV privy.

RV-Friendly Toilet Paper

Forget about squeezing the Charmin, folks! Your favorite brand is probably not safe for your RV septic system. Find a toilet paper that will break down well in your system, and you'll never have problems. There are actually a lot of options nowadays. Scott makes a rapid-dissolving RV paper, Camco sells a RV and Marine Toilet paper, and more. You can even buy it in bulk and store it in your garage at home to save space.

Bathroom Chemicals

Speaking of the toilet paper situation, be sure to read up on your bathroom's septic needs thoroughly, and always have plenty of chemicals to break everything down. It can get very expensive to fix the mistakes caused by not using these chemicals, and each system is a little different, so make sure you do your research on your own specific needs. I can't tell you what is right, or wrong!

on an open fire for dinner! Plastic wrap is great for keeping things covered and fresh, and parchment paper is great if you're doing any sort of baking at all.

S'mores Supplies

Like Leslie Knope on TV, I always carry emergency s'mores supplies at all times. It's a great, quick desert, and a fun activity to do around an open campfire—not just for little visitors, but for anyone who may drop by.

a bottle opener, you've got two issues covered in one.

Dish Soap

Don't be like me, and forget that you need soap to wash dishes in your sink.

Scrub Brush

I like having something small with a suction cup on the one end, so it sticks to the sink by itself and doesn't have to be put away anywhere.

Trash Bags

An easily forgettable item, trash bags are a must! You can't rely on your campground's facilities.

Food Storage Options

Don't forget about leftovers! I like having a small selection of Tupperware containers that stack neatly together, so they take up minimal room when I'm not using them. Ziploc bags are also a great choice.

Aluminum Foil, Plastic Wrap, Etc

I love using aluminum fool for easy clean up. I also regularly make foil packs of vegetables and meat to throw

Wine Key/Corkscrew

You can get a waiter's wine key, or a corkscrew wine opener, for a few dollars online or at almost any liquor store. Even if you don't drink a ton of wine out of a bottle with a cork, your neighbors might, and you'll be the hero.

Unbreakable Beer Mugs

I don't think I need to explain this one. Pouring your bottled beer out into a cold mug from the fridge really enhances your experience, and again – betting something that is shatterproof means you don't have to worry about it rolling around anywhere.

Collapsible Dish Strainer

I found an incredible over-the-sink dish drier that folds up tight for easy storage. It's *awesome*, and I encourage you to seriously consider getting one. After all these years, I still hate doing dishes, and I hate drying dishes. Being able to let them hang out and drain over the sink is very appealing, and it folds up pretty small. Or, you can store it in your cabinet as an organizer.

Can Opener

Have one to go in your RV specifically. If you get one with

Ice Cream Scoop

You should always be prepared for emergency ice cream situations. A solid, sturdy ice cream scoop always has a place in my RV kitchen.

Unbreakable Tableware

Plastic or enamel camping plates, bowls, and cups are *pretty much* essential. Would I like to pretend I enjoyed these more than, say, a "real" bowl or plate? Sure, but that would be a lie, and I'm not here to lie to you. I started my RV journey carrying traditional plate ware I loved. And then, when I broke all of that, I replaced pieces with thrifted items. Finally, I cracked, and "invested" in relatively high-quality unbreakable plates.

I've never have to replace them because we took a turn too fast, or had to break, and they hold up well under any kind of abuse. Plus, they're usually a lot easier to clean.

Unbreakable Wine Glasses

In the same vein, get yourself 2-4 unbreakable wine glasses without the stem. Can I drink out of my camp mugs? Sure, but the wine glasses make me feel a little more human.

whole RV. You can make full roasts in under an hour, make beans from dry to done without overnight soaking, and so much more. An Instant Pot takes up a small amount of space, and you can do a *lot* with it. If you haven't tried one, it's really worth it – and now they have a smaller, 3-quart size.

French Press Coffee

Coffee is not a negotiable situation for us, no matter where we are. Our RV is no exception. A traditional coffee pot takes up way too much space. Instead, we opt for a French press coffee maker. We discovered these while on a trip to Europe before they were very well known in the US. They are great for RVing! Heat water on the stove, outdoor grill, or even an open fire, and you can get a good, reliable cup of coffee quickly (no filter needed!).

AeroPress Coffee Maker

If you don't like the French press, check out an AeroPress machine. These are even smaller and make a really excellent cup of coffee (or espresso!). You can't make it while in motion, though. But if you don't want to rely on gas station coffee or instant, gritty coffee, either of these coffee choices are great.

If your skillet is properly seasoned and cared for, nothing will stick, and it will heat consistently. They aren't hard to care for. Don't soak it for too long, and rub it down with oil periodically to keep it from rusting.

Cast Iron Dutch Oven

Okay, okay, so maybe you want two pieces of cast iron in your kitchen. A dutch oven will let you bake, cook, and more. I love making bread in my dutch oven, but you can stews, roasts, and more. If you get one with a lid that doubles as a skillet, you're ahead of the game – and *most* real cast iron products will have this.

Serving Spoons

Easily overlooked, several serving spoons will make serving and eating with friends and family a lot easier. It's also more sanitary than everyone shoving their own forks into the serving bowls.

Instant Pot or Electric Pressure Cooker

This is pretty new to the RV scene, and I almost didn't include it – but using a pressure cooker in your RV is actually really pleasant. Just like the bonus to your stove top oven set up, a pressure cooker won't heat up your

Wall Mounted Paper Towel Holder

Wall-mounted paper towel holders save precious space on the countertops and are very convenient.

Dish Towels

Keep a good stock of sturdy dish towels. Need to dry something? Use a towel. Need to clean something – like, really clean it? Use a towel. Need to grab something hot and I can't find my gloves? I've got a towel for that!

Chip Clips

Keep a handful of chip clips available at all times. A good, sturdy clip will prevent bugs from getting into your things and help keep food fresher, longer. My husband likes the super sturdy black and metal ones you can get at Staples (I guess they are called document clips), but use what you like. And they actually come in handy for other things too, like keeping cords out of the way.

Cast Iron Skillet

You need to purchase at least one of these. If you take care of it, it will probably outlast your RV. I can cook on the open fire, over a grill, on my propane camping stove, or inside my RV. It can go in an oven; it can go anywhere.

Immersion Blender

We're big fans of smoothies now. These little immersion blenders (aka stick blenders) work great and take up less space. They are also super for making blended soups!

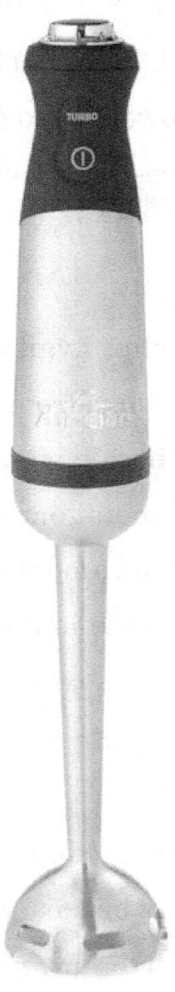

Cupboard Bars

These little tension rods look just like regular tension rods for curtains, but they are only about a foot long and stretch up to about 20 inches. Just like the fridge bars, these extendable tension rods fit within your RV cabinets and help keep everything in place. You don't want to take a long trip without them; otherwise, you could be resetting your cabinet every night. They are a real timesaver.

Mini Stacking Ice Cube Trays

There's a good chance that a traditional ice cube tray isn't going to fit into your freezer. Even if it does, a lot isn't going to fit in addition to it. Instead, invest in a set of mini ice cube trays that stack. Your drinks will stay cold (extra nice when you're sitting outside!), and you'll have more freezer space.

Gripping, Hanging Spice Racks

Once again, another tool to keep everything in place. You can purchase a spice rack that mounts to the *inside* of a cabinet, and uses little grippers to hold your spices in place. This is essential if you cook a lot, and saves space *inside* the cabinet too.

RV Refrigerator Fan

Speaking of your fridge, consider investing in a camping and RV refrigerator fan if you're going to be camping during the summer. These fans help circulate air evenly, which means your RV is ultimately using less power to cool it. It also works great in your freezer if you have to defrost it!

Dishwashing Basin

If you're not interested in doing dishes inside, well, I can't blame you. The small sink is frustrating at best, and if you don't have a large grey water tank, it can be an annoying process to keep emptying it out every few days.

Having a heavy-duty washing basin is great. You can wash all your dirty dishes outside, store food in the heavy-duty plastic while they're empty, or to shuttle ingredients inside and out if you're cooking outdoors. Because you can store things in it, it doesn't take up useless space. Plus, you can spend more time outdoors (washing dishes, prepping food, etc). Dump the dirty water down a campground sink or use biodegradable soap so you can dump in the woods, and you'll also reduce your grey water output.

Knives with Guards

If you're going to be cooking in your RV, you're going to need a good set of knives. I recommend investing in a handful with full cover **guards** because you're in an RV. Knives and tools shift and move as you drive around, and having those covers is so important!

Lightweight Cutting Boards

The less space your cutting boards take up, the better. I have a handful of lightweight, super flexible plastic cutting boards that live in my RV kitchen. I can cut different things without risking cross-contamination, and they take up almost no room. I started with a beautiful, but very heavy and bulky, wooden cutting board. It was replaced quickly.

Refrigerator Bar

RV fridge bars are essential in your fridge. These extendable, adjustable bars help keep everything from rolling around unnecessarily. There's nothing like stopping for the night and realizing your pickle jar shattered, and you have to spend 20 minutes picking glass shards out of your fridge before you can make dinner.

Baking Soda

Even if you're not baking, baking soda can be used to deodorize your fridge or rooms, clean, fix a clogged pipe with some vinegar, and more. It's an all-purpose item that must have a place in your kitchen!

Grilling Gloves

These seem a little silly, but if you cook on a grill or on an open fire, these are so vital. Get gloves that go fairly high up – at least cover your wrists – and ones that are rated to a high heat. Being able to reach out and grab a hot handle without worry makes cooking so much more pleasant. It's easy to underestimate just how hot a campfire can be.

Nesting Bowls

To economize your storage space in your RV kitchen, nesting dishes are great. Nesting bowls for food prep, serving, and eating are a must for your kitchen space. Look for a set of *unbreakable* mixing bowls in a variety of sizes that nest, plus measuring cups and spoons that fit right on top. Also look for cups and plates that nest. This reduces space so that instead of a series of shelves, you can make due with one or two.

Stove Top Oven Kit

If you don't use your oven a lot in your everyday life, you might not find this helpful. But I love baking, and it was one thing I struggled with a lot when traveling in our RV. A stove top oven kit lets you use *less* fuel and make thing faster and better than using your RV's oven, if it even has one. (Some don't!) If used outside, you don't heat up the entire RV in the summer when you want to bake. This Coleman Camp oven is about a foot square, for $40.

For Your Kitchen

RV kitchens can be an adjustment, especially if you're coming from a fully stocked kitchen with all the bells and whistles. Don't fret — these items are going to make cooking in your new RV kitchen a lot easier. Don't tear your hair out about space or size; just get the right tools so you *enjoy* cooking in your kitchen.

Headlamp Flashlight

Are you going to feel a little silly at first? Maybe. But having a headlamp is really great for crawling around under your RV, hunting for firewood, or even walking to the showers at night or in the early morning.

Outdoor Shower

This one isn't for everyone, but if you want to avoid dumping your gray water in the middle of a camping trip, or minimize trips to do so, an outdoor shower can help.

Clothesline

Even if you *don't* want to do your laundry in your RV, a clothesline is great for drying swimsuits and towels between uses. Bring clips for your things, and store it all together for easy setup.

have several tablecloth holders so you can continue to enjoy the outdoors *without* having to chase it down in the middle of the day when it blows away, taking whatever was on the table with it.

Fishing Gear

If you're a fisherman, there is always room for fishing gear in your rig. Don't forget extras, like fishing line, extra hooks, and more. I recommend a small, well-stocked tackle box for any occasion.

Solar Battery

If you're in your RV and you don't have access to a hookup, a solar battery pack is great! It's going to depend heavily on *where* you camp and *how* you camp, whether you need one or not.

Outdoor Motion Sensing Lights

This can give you an added sense of security when you're out camping, and it can also be a fun way to spot wildlife if you're still awake when the lights go on. You can even pick up a set of solar-powered ones, so you're not draining your batteries and they're super easy to install.

Collapsible Garbage Can

It's so nice to have a trash can outside if you're going to hang out in one place for more than a day or two! It's super convenient, and it stores flat and small, so it won't take up a ton of space when you don't need it.

Reflective Window Coverings

You can buy pre-made ones, or buy a roll of Reflectix and cut them to size. It will help keep your RV cool in the sun, which is a big deal in the summer! It also provides a level of privacy if you're concerned about that.

Big Beach Towels

There's nothing better than laying out on a towel in the sun! Even if you're not planning on hitting the coast, plenty of large lakes have beach areas, and a beach towel really is multi-functional.

Mouse Traps

You never want to have to use them... but they're nice to have when you do need to.

Tablecloth Holder

A windy day can bring any tablecloth down. Be sure to

Portable Propane Fire Pit

We've been disappointed too many times by campgrounds without a fire ring. Now, we bring our own. It runs from the propane we already have, and it's great for a cozy night under the stars. You can pick one up at Lowe's for about $130.

Bike Racks

For many of us, the point of RVing is to spend more time doing the things we love. We absolutely love going for bike rides at our destinations. If you have bikes, bring them with you. You'll enjoy exploring your new destination at your own pace and getting the exercise. I encourage you to invest in a bike hitch rack for your RV. An outside rack keeps the bikes out of your way, makes them easy to get to, and doesn't take up a lot of space inside the camper. A sturdy two-bike rack should meet all your needs, and nowadays you can find them for as little as $50. And they make a nice towel rack at camp!

Proper BBQ Tools

Even if you don't spring for a camping grill, you're going to want proper tools for cooking outdoors. A nice, heavy duty BBQ set is going to last you for a long time if you take care of it, and will make cooking a joy.

Marshmallow Roasting Sticks

Is it fun to dig around in the woods for the perfect marshmallow stick? Maybe the first time. But when you've been on the road for a while, sometimes you just want to kick back. Picking up a pack of marshmallow roasting sticks means you never have to search – especially helpful if you're in the desert! – and s'mores are never far away. I like the ones with extendable handles, so even the smokey fire won't deter you.

Camping hammock

If you find yourself camping in an area with lots of trees, there is almost nothing more satisfying than laying in a hammock and having a nap, or reading a book (or both!). A typical camping hammock doesn't take up a lot of space to store, and there are many inexpensive options nowadays, which are both a big plus.

Inline Water Filter

You don't strictly need this, but I've found that some campground water sources taste – well, not amazing. Which is fine to cook with, but actually drinking the water is another story. An inline water filter attaches directly to your water hose, and filter the water. A single filter can last upwards of a full season.

Camping Grill

"But I'll be at a campground! I'll have a fire ring! Why would I ever want to use anything else?"

Look, you're not wrong – it's so satisfying to grill a hot dog or a burger over an open flame. But sometimes it's just not convenient. If you're cooking for a lot of people, too, you're going to run into a space problem. I recommend a 2 burner camping grill for ease of use, plenty of space, and speed. Using a propane grill, you can also control the heat better, so you have a more accurate final product.

Of course you can still roast marshmallows or make s'mores after dinner!

dining room table, and dozens of other things. I prefer a larger folding table versus a smaller camping one because they're sturdier and have more space. I've never been upset about having extra space.

Playing Cards

There's no way to make faster friends with other RVers than to pull out a deck of cards and see who wants to play! A little deck of cards takes up almost no space, and it's a great way to bond and pass the time while keeping the mood light and fun.

Patio Mat

If you're going to be moving your RV every single day, you may not find use for a patio mat — but if you're full timing, or spend a few days at each campground, this is a really excellent addition. A patio mat helps people not track dirt, grass, and grossness inside your RV every time they enter, and it's a lot more comfortable to walk on, especially when you're camping somewhere with lots of gravel, rocks, or even on pavement.

Portable Chairs

What are you going to sit on in your awning? A couple portable camping chairs are comfortable, easy to store, easy to move, and they come with a built-in cup holder! Is a wooden rocker more comfortable? Probably, but you can't beat the convenience of a chair that folds up. I always keep at least 4 on hand, in case I have visitors, but if you want to discourage other people... well, not having enough chairs is a good reason to turn them away!

Folding Tables

I love cooking outside, and a large folding utility table has been invaluable to me during my time outdoors. It can be used as a prep area, a buffet, a study area for kids, a

RV Awning

The best quality of life upgrade we did was getting an awning. Hanging out in its shade on a summer's day with a cold beverage is just a great experience. It also blocks out rain, which means that even if you're stuck in a downpour, you're not stuck inside.

The Sunshade Upgrade

If you love your awning, consider upgrading to a sunshade as well. It's like a lightweight tarp designed specifically to give you more shade. While these aren't necessary, it's great if you spend a lot of time in the *summer* in your RV. Most sunshades can attach to your existing awning, and provide additional sun coverage for you.

These also lend more privacy if you tend to park in smaller RV parks or value your outdoor privacy. Some are opaque; others are a semi-transparent mesh.

Awning Lights

I very much enjoy sitting outside at night, and my awning provides a porch-like experience. But in a more secluded campsite, it can get dark *fast*.

Bug Spray

Similar to sunscreen but arguably slightly less important, I always have at least 2 bottles of insect repellant. One to use, and one as a backup. There's no easier way to ruin an evening than battling with mosquitoes or other bugs.

Insect Candles

If you're like me and spend a lot of time outdoors, consider getting a few of those citronella bug candles. They're easy to carry and make life much more enjoyable.

Bear Spray

In some places this is a requirement, but I recommend it no matter where you go. Your own safety is so important. The spray will not permanently hurt the bear, but the bear could very well hurt you if you don't scare it off. And a bear that attacks you or your campsite will have to be put down. Bear spray is the best solution for everyone.

Cooler

Fridge space is at a premium in the RV. We keep a cooler that all our drinks go into and refresh it with ice now and again. It's great to have cold drinks on hand, and that extra fridge space makes a huge difference.

Sunscreen

I'm not sure this one needs much explanation. Seriously, invest in a good, high SPF sunscreen, and reapply often. You're going to be outside in the sun a lot, and your skin doesn't need that kind of abuse.

Sun Hats

Years ago, we invested in some fun sun hats. We have learned to wear ours whenever we're outside. It's amazing how just a few hours of sun every day can add up to a lot of UV exposure for your skin. Plus, we look really good in hats, don't you think?

Things for the KOA

When you're at the campgrounds or the KOA, you might think you don't need anything extra. After all, your RV is already a step above the normal tent-and-stake setup, right? Well, sure – but there are some items that, for one reason or another, will make your life more enjoyable.

Some of these are absolute necessities; some will make you enjoy your outdoor experience so much more that you'll *deem* them necessary after your first trip.

last you years, properly cared for. They fold up small, and you'll be thankful you have one (or two!).

Deadbolt Locks

Take a hard look at the door to your RV. Is it *really* secure? Most aren't. They're just not made to withstand pressure, attacks, or anything like that. Even if you think about an angry, hungry bear, your door isn't going to withstand that. Upgrading the lock on your door is a great idea for added protection.

Broom

To clean your outdoor mat, your floors, and even knock cobwebs from hard-to-reach places, a good, sturdy broom is essential to your outdoor adventure.

Extra Rope

You never know when you're going to need rope, for a variety of purposes. Keep extra rope for tying things down, securing things, and more.

Tarp(s)

We like having at least two tarps on hand at all times. It helps extend the outdoor area if we want to go further than the awning; it can cover things outside during a rainfall; provide a dry, clean place to sit in nature; and many more uses. A sturdy tarp is easy to clean and will

just going to make it worse, and lower the value of your RV. Wire brushes can also be used to clean a variety of other things, including grill grates.

Bottle Brush Set

These are great for cleaning hard-to-reach places on your RV, like water heaters or plumbing places. They're also good for water bottles and other camping supplies, but having a set handy can make your cleaning a lot easier.

RV Wash Brush

This is important for everyone, but *especially* important if you choose to go the solar panel route, as dust, dirt, and debris can seriously hurt your output. Get one with an extendable brush and an adjustable handle, and you'll have the cleanest RV in the park with minimal effort.

Gutter Extenders

If you've had your RV for a while, you've seen those unsightly streaks that come down the side of the RV after a rainstorm. Gutter extenders basically move that dripping water, preventing those streaks and keeping your RV looking better, longer.

X-Chock acts as an additional safety feature, as they lock in place between tandem tires. They fold up and are easy to store. In addition, the X-Chocks provide a little bit better stability, which is important if you're camping somewhere that experiences high winds.

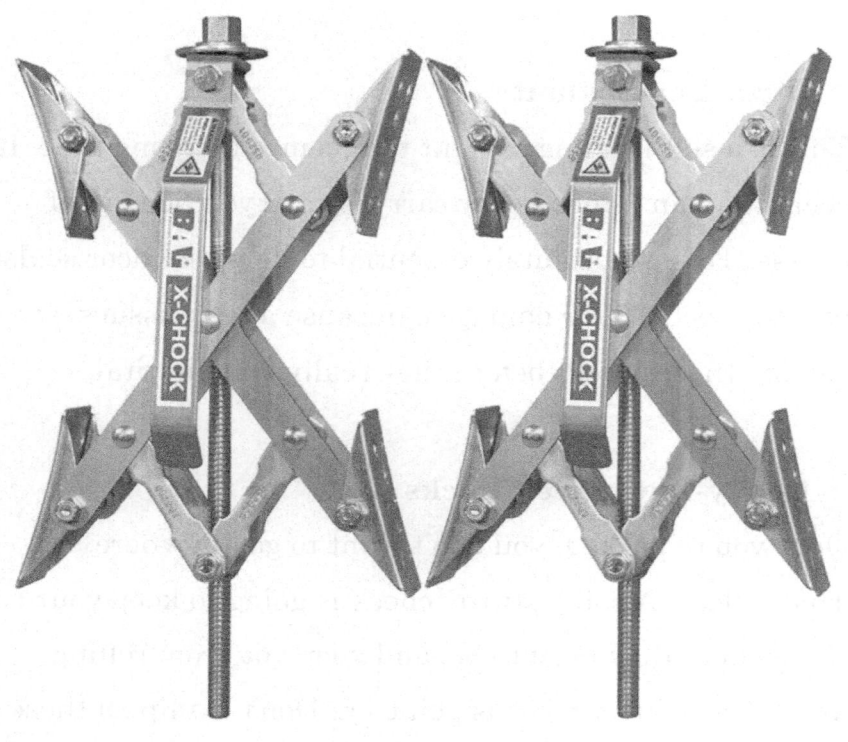

Wire Brush Set

You should walk your RV at least once every few months, if not once a month, to keep an eye on corrosion or rust, and take care of it immediately. Letting it sit and fester is

gas stations you pass? Sure, but that's a gamble. You may not notice that you need one until you're miles from any station. Having a small, portable air compressor in your rig means you never get stranded in a bad situation. Plus, you could potentially help someone else out. Nowadays, you can get a small hand-held one for about $30.

Dicor Lap Sealant

This is a self-leveling sealant that comes in a long tube. It seems like an unnecessary carry – until you need it, of course. This is absolutely essential to help seal door seals and the roof. Water damage can cause a *lot* of issues, so sealing these cracks before they really start is vital.

Heavy-Duty Tire Chocks

Once you're parked, you don't want to go anywhere. That's clear! A solid, sturdy chock is going to keep your tires where they need to be, and keep you from rolling around no matter what is going on. Don't skimp on these – you really don't want to end up somewhere surprising!

X-Chocks

Okay, this is optional, but an X-chock (or tandem chock) is a nice upgrade to the traditional chock. Made of steel, an

Lithium Jump Starter

You're ready to get on the road, and oh no! You can't start your engine for whatever reason. Instead of calling AAA or searching around for someone to give you a jump, you can use this to jump your RV and get on the road. Some new ones will even let you charge your phone or device if you need to. These are really great things to have.

Tow Kit

If you want to tow your car behind you for better, easier traveling – like visiting a nearby town in a sedan, instead of a giant RV – get a tow kit so you can easily hook it up.

Roof Vent Cover

This is truly genius, in my opinion. A vent cover for your roof lets you keep the roof vent open even when it rains, so that you get that extra airflow. This is important during the summer, when it takes almost nothing to overheat your RV. It also has the added benefit of keeping the gunk out!

Portable Air Compressor

You'll be on your tires a lot, so what happens when they get low? Couldn't you just use the air compressors at the

cabinet, and you'll be thankful you have it.

Laundry Soap

While you're probably not doing your laundry in your RV, being prepared to wash your clothes, linens, and more while you're in town or around is important. Keep a few extras for those emergency situations, or to help out neighbors who forgot theirs.

If you want to use appliances without having shore power, an inverter generator is essential. If you only want to run a handful of things, like appliances on your RV and a few personal electronics, a 2000-to-3000-watt generator should be more than enough.

RV Surge Protector

Just like you would plug your computer at home into a surge protector, you should have an RV-rated surge electrical protector for your rig. There are a *lot* of electronics in RVs anymore, and if you plug into an improperly wired or damaged outlet, or get hit by a lightning strike, you're going to fry your electronics. That's a *big* bill. Investing in a proper protector will save you a ton of headaches down the line.

Small, Foldable Shovel

Need to dig a hole? Bury something? Dig something up, in your way? A small, folding shovel will take up little space, but you'll find yourself reaching for it a lot.

J-B Weld

Even better than superglue, J-B Weld will hold together almost anything. It takes almost no space up in the

important!

Lightweight Propane Tank

While not strictly necessary, a *composite* propane tank is significantly lighter, especially when full. These are easier to carry around and make the process more enjoyable in general.

Rubber Lubricant

A good quality rubber lubricant is super important to maintain your slideouts. Even if you don't have slideouts, window seals – and really, all seals in the RV – can use a good cleaning and lubrication now and again. These rubbers are exposed to a lot of sun, heat, and potential damage, so it's important (and easy) to keep them properly maintained.

Propane Regulator

If your RV already has one of these, awesome! You don't need it. But if it *doesn't*, I highly recommend picking up a propane regulator to keep track of your propane levels. You'll never get caught off guard.

RV Inverter Generator

different from your drinking hose, in size, style, and color. Making that mistake will **ruin** your week.

Sewer Hose Kit

I recommend having a shorter hose and a longer hose – 10 and 20 feet are standard – so you don't have to struggle when you need to use it. Look for a hose that is sturdy, with thick walls and a good connection. I cannot stress enough how much you *absolutely, positively do not* want to deal with a leak or a broken hose. For storage, screw the ends together. This helps prevent a mess.

Water Level Monitoring System

You probably have a built-in system for monitoring the water levels in your RV, but these are generally *not great*. The newest ones are a little better, but they're still sometimes unreliable. It's easy to install a new one, and the ones with foil strips (for plastic tanks) are generally very reliable.

Carbon Monoxide Detector and Smoke Detector

These are seriously non-negotiables. Get good ones and check your batteries often. Be sure to check before each trip, and after winterizing your RV. Safety is so

reduce the pressure from the water source to the RV, saving your plumbing.

Water Bandit

Though this is *optional*, I've used it so many times I can't imagine traveling without it. A water bandit helps you connect to a strangely sized spigot, so you never run into water connection problems. One end is basically stretchy rubber, and will connect over anything.

Water Tank Clean Out Hose

You're not going to ever want to use your potable water hose for anything other than drinking water, but you're going to need a hose for cleaning out your grey/black water tanks. You should choose a hose *completely*

Drinking Water Hose

We recommend *at least* a 25-foot hose since you never know how far you'll be from a hookup. RV potable water hoses should be BPA and lead-free, so buy from a reputable company. You'll want to connect the ends together while storing to keep out any ants or other critters!

Water Pressure Regulator

This might first seem like an unnecessary item, but you can damage your plumbing. Most RVs can only handle pressure up to 60 PSI. However, city water is usually *highly* pressurized. A water pressure regulator is going to

A Funnel

It's great for putting *any* fluids into your RV, and it doesn't take up much space. I keep a few funnels of varying sizes on hand.

Electrical Hookup Cords

Electrics are kind of complicated in an RV, but there are two main types – the 12 volt you're getting from the batteries, and the 120 volt you'll be drawing from a camping spot. You're going to need a specific extension cord to pull power from your campsites. Make sure it's weatherproof! You can buy RV-specific extension cords, which I highly recommend doing. Messing around with a power source is not fun. We use the 25-foot Camco PowerGrip 30 Amp:

Bungee Cords with Hooks

This sounds unnecessary until you come across a cute antique shop with something you can't live without. Or until something breaks and it's all going flying. Having backup bungee cords just makes sense.

Leveling Blocks

You might be thinking, "I don't need leveling blocks! I can just use the rocks/sticks/stuff at the campsite!" Sure, you *can*. Until you can't, and you're stuck trying to function on a slope. A set of good, sturdy leveling blocks is the difference between an annoying trip and a fun one, so invest in a decent set. It's important that your RV is level not just for comfort, but for function – some appliances, like your fridge for instance, won't function as well if they're not kept level.

Extra Motor Oil

You shouldn't ever *need* it, but keeping some on hand can save your expensive parts from major damage.

Extra Transmission Fluid

Again, you hope you never need it, but having some extra on hand can really help in a pinch.

to get in somewhere close and tight.

Zip ties are those additions to my tool kit I never thought I would use, but always reach for them. I have a few sizes on hand, and they're great for holding things in place, tying up loose cords, or making temporary fixes until you can get a permanent solution in place.

Tire Pressure Gauge

You should always be able to identify if your tires are low or not. Always have a reliable tire pressure gauge.

GPS

While not strictly essential anymore, with smartphones, an actual GPS is a really helpful addition. Be sure to purchase a well-reviewed one that you can update regularly for map data, and one that is specifically made for RVs. Yes, they make a GPS for RVs!

While Google Maps or Apple Maps work great with a car, an RV GPS will take you a route that your RV will be able to handle – no super narrow roads, low bridges, or sketchy corners.

You don't really *think* about needing this until something breaks, but having a basic tool kit is pretty essential. You can buy one in pieces and put it all together in a small **tool box**, but you can also buy a tool box already assembled.

The basics you should have include a **wrench**, to smack things around or bend them back in place, **duct tape** to fix any leaks, and yes, *another* battery-powered **flashlight**. It never hurts to have a back up.

A **multi-bit screwdriver** is the best bang for your buck, overall. Look for something sturdy with variety, like Phillips's head, flat head, and even a square bit or two. This saves you from carrying 7 or 10 different screwdrivers around!

A **pocket knife** is a pretty great tool to have in your arsenal. From cutting open packages to taking out twigs and branches, slicing an apple, and more, it's a must.

1-3 adjustable **wrenches** are a great addition when you consider how much space is at a premium. A strong pair of **needle nose pliers** are great for when you need

If you get a flat tire on the side of the road, you're going to need to do something about it! Be sure you have the proper jack for your RV, it's a lot different from the standard car jack.

Tow Strap

Obviously, no one wants to be towed. But it's better to be prepared and never need it, than need it and not have it. Invest in a tow strap that is especially made for the weight of an RV in case you ever need a tow to the shop.

Tire Chains

If you only go out in warm climates, you probably don't need these. But if you plan on doing any winter travel or camping, tire chains are a great purchase.

Window Breaker & Seatbelt Cutter

Again, these are items you hope you don't have to use – but you should really, really have them. In case of an emergency, these could make the difference. Keep them close at hand at all times; they'll do you no good all the way in the back.

Basic Tool Kit

Jumper Cables

Really, this is a must-have for any vehicle with a motor, not just an RV. Be sure you always have an extra set on hand, and you'll be able to jump your own vehicles, or someone else's.

Spare Tire

You would think it would be common sense to have a spare tire in your RV, but you'd be surprised. Having a spare tire is going to save you from a costly call to a tow truck when you (not if, but when) pop a tire on the side of the road, or run over a stray nail. I cannot stress enough as to how important this is.

We have suffered a great deal once on a Sunday afternoon while we were driving through South Carolina on interstate 85. Most roadside assistance will help you to change a tire but if you don't have one, they won't help you to repair one. Therefore, you are stuck and have to wait for a tow truck to tow you to a repair shop, but remember most tire repair shops are closed in the evening.

Proper Jack

A small kitchen **fire extinguisher** is essential. You're going to be *cooking*, after all, and you're sitting on a lot of very flammable things.

A **battery-powered radio** with extra batteries sounds silly until you're in a tornado or storm area and the sky is looking questionable. Having this extra level of protection to listen to reports is really a necessity.

Battery-operated **flashlights**, with extra batteries, are also super important! Also please do have **matches** and a few **candles** in your RV, just in case.

Water purification tablets might seem a bit overkill, but they last forever and they're a great backup safety measure if you're stranded somewhere. An **emergency blanket,** at least 1 for every person you reasonably expect to be driving around, is also a must.

An **analog compass** is also a nice addition. The compass on your phone or a GPS system is great, don't get me wrong – but if something happens to one or both of those things, knowing where North and South are can be a big help.

supplies. It's best to be prepared!

Road flares for emergencies in the middle of the night are so vital! Keep at least twice what you'll need in an emergency on hand, so you're always prepared. A high-visibility vest is also good to have. We like these LED emergency flares that you can turn on and off:

In addition, I recommend tweezers to remove any splinters or other annoyances. Emergency sunscreen, pain relievers, and eye drops are also good. You may consider stocking anti-nausea medication, chewable indigestion pills, butterfly sutures, liquid skin, and QuikClot. Latex gloves are also nice to have on hand.

Think about the items you reach for most often in your medicine cabinet at home, and make sure you bring those things with you. All of this should be well labeled, easy to find, and together in one place, so that in an emergency, you can grab your kit for everything you need.

Eyeglass Repair Kit

If you have glasses, this is absolutely essential. Being able to see is essential, and these little kits don't cost very much. The small screwdrivers and tools in a repair kit work for a variety of things, and you'll never know when you'll need a teeny, tiny screwdriver.

Emergency Supplies

You never know what you're going to encounter on the road, so you should have a good stock of emergency

Waterproof, Windproof Lighter

This is less of a 'nice to have' item and more of an 'absolutely essential' item. A windproof and waterproof lighter is important when you're going out in the wilderness. You can light a fire, a lantern, start your cooking method, and so many more things. Know that you can't always rely on other methods, and fire can sometimes be essential.

First-Aid Kit

While every vehicle should have a first-aid kit of some kind, having one in your RV is even more important. This is essentially your mini-home, so be sure to keep your first aid kit well stocked. You never know when burns or scrapes or accidents will happen while you're out far from civilization, and you want to be prepared.

First-Aid Kit must-haves: Band-Aids, antiseptic wipes, antibiotic ointment, burn cream, calamine lotion, and (if you need it) poison ivy cream/soap. Gauze pads of varying sizes and medical tape. Instant cold packs, alcohol, and hydrogen peroxide. I keep several packs of aloe not only for kitchen burns, but sun disasters. Who hasn't fallen asleep in the sun reading?

your registration on hand, even if you have an insurance app that covers you. You're just asking for trouble when you're traveling if you forget these essential items.

RV Tire Covers

We ask a lot of our tires, but they are just rubber. When you're parked for any period of time especially an *extended* period of time (like you will be in your RV), that rubber can break down from the sun and general use. One thing you should be doing if you have your own RV is covering your tires with tire covers. You do *not* want to have a blowout on the highway.

Using and caring for your tire covers greatly reduces the damage your tires take to the sun and the elements, and keeps everything in tip-top shape. Some people say tire covers are only needed if you park for more than a week at a time, but I would argue if your RV is staying put for at least 2 days, you should put your covers on. RV tires are *expensive,* and I encourage you to keep the ones you have in good condition so you con't have to replace them as frequently. Spend $25 on a pair of covers instead of $500 on a pair of tires.

In fact, I recommend having a front *and* rear camera. That way, if someone rear-ends you and tries to flee the scene, you've got the whole thing recorded. Heaven forbid it should happen; but if it does, you're covered.

Registration + Insurance

Having your vital paperwork is absolutely essential. You should always have copies of both your insurance and

Practical Things Everyone Should Have

These are the practical, everyday items that you should always have. Whether you're going for a short trip, a long weekend, or months at a time, these items won't just make your life easier – they serve important purposes!

Dashcam

These are just what they sound like a little camera that attaches to your dash, or your windshield (see next page).

Before you roll your eyes at me and tell me they are too expensive, you should know that there are some very reasonably priced ones on the market – ranging from $15 to $99 at Walmart or Target. Or, if you're a handy type, you can follow a few simple tutorials online and turn an old cell phone into a dashcam.

I cannot overstate the importance of having a dashcam! It's like a security system for your home away from home. Also, it's going to keep you safe on the road, and document any accidents or incidents, including someone poking around your RV or breaking in.

A regular car needs its oil changed every 5,000 miles or so, right? Some of the newer vehicles can go even longer, up to 10,000 miles or more. However, RVs *sit* for a long time, so the mileage you're putting on your RV is not indicative of the amount you need to change your oil.

Schedule an oil change *at least* every year, or every 3,000 miles – whatever comes first. If your oil is not changed properly and regularly, you could be causing a whole host of issues within your RV engine. This can lead to damage and costly repairs.

Don't Forget Your Filters

When you change your oil, check your coolant, fuel, air, and hydraulic filters, too. These should be changed each season, or as you change your oil. Just like ignoring old oil, ignoring damaged filters can put undue strain on your engine or internal parts of the RV, leading to an early death – or a big nasty bill.

sap, and junk in the slideout can cause major issues. We check ours monthly.

To clean your slideouts, lubricate your slider and make sure that they are properly sliding in and out without any drag or resistance. If you have too much friction, your seals will tear, and you can be in for a costly replacement. Depending on the type of slideout you have, you may use different types of lubricants. Check your manual.

Window Seals

Window seals should also be cleaned and maintained. Use a good quality rubber lubricant and clean them regularly, at least once a month while you're actively traveling or before going on a trip. Your goal is that everything should open, close, and latch seamlessly – no pulling, tearing, or friction. If you have old, hard rubber or you struggle with it even though you have lubricated the seal, look into getting it replaced *before* it starts to leak, mold, or damage your RV.

Oil Changes, Not Optional

Maintain Your Water and Sewage Systems

It's so important to keep your sewage systems well maintained and working properly. There's nothing worse than being out in the country and realizing your sewage system is having issues.

Your black water tank needs proper cleaning; otherwise, it can hold a ton of bacteria that can infect your whole system. Check your RV guide to find out what chemicals need to go into it in order to keep it well maintained. These chemicals are often added when you're rinsing the tank out after emptying.

You may need to flow a *lot* of water into these tanks to remove the solid waste that collects. Most tanks need at least 2 gallons of liquid inside before you start adding to it.

Keep Your Slideouts Clean

If you've got a slideout in your RV, it's great to have that extra space! It's also extra work. Slideouts need regular cleaning to move properly and seal right. Dirt,

wasps – to build their home there.

Always make sure nothing heavy is resting on your awning or pulling it down, or you could wear out the support poles over time. Don't hang things from the awning for the same reason.

Check Your Batteries

Your RV batteries are like the lifeblood of your system. Without a good, working battery, you're going to have a *very bad time*. Each brand and type of RV is going to have a little bit different battery setup, so be sure to familiarize yourself with your own rig and the ins and outs of it.

Remember that RV batteries are only made to last for 3 to 5 years. Maintain your battery and check it constantly to see if it is holding a charge by using a hydrometer or a digital voltmeter. Keep the discharge level at least 50 percent. If you're buying your RV used, inquire about the last time the battery was replaced, and get it changed immediately if it has lost its capacity. You may want to invest in a trickle charger based on your battery type.

worth the money – especially if the water has gotten into the electrical system or the heating system.

In our section below on must-haves for the road, I've included a common brand of sealant (J-B Weld). Anytime you spot what could be a crack or a leak, fix it up in a jiffy and you'll keep your RV in good condition for longer.

Your Awning Needs Maintenance, Too

We're going to mention awnings below, in the section of things you probably want but don't technically need. However, if you do have an awning, it's important you keep it in good shape so it will last a long time for you.

Keep your awning clean and dry to prevent mold and mildew build-up. When you pull it out, inspect it regularly. Any tears need to be repaired immediately, so they do not spread and get worse.

Be sure that you clean the awning fairly regularly, especially on long trips. Dirt and debris can damage it over time. They can cause it to get stuck and tear apart when moving, and can even encourage bugs – like bees or

before you hit the road again. Learn how to maintain and lubricate the bearings so that you will be able to do basic maintenance yourself – this is especially important in the summer, as they can dry out.

Brake replacements can cost between $200-$600, depending on your RV and model. You can understand why keeping your existing brakes in good condition is best when you're facing that kind of repair bill.

Check Your Roof Seams and Seals

Your roof is *so important*. It's literally keeping the water from destroying your RV's interior. Once a month, you should inspect your roof for any leaks, cracks, or other damage. Usually you are going to find issues within the weak spots, like skylights, vents, or AC units, so be sure to pay close attention to these areas.

Water coming through a small crack might not seem like a big deal, but it can cause mold, rot, and rust. Fixing this damage is a *lot* more expensive and time-consuming than fixing the leak when it first starts. And sometimes, that type of extensive damage can't be fixed at all, or isn't

want is a flat, a blowout on the highway, or general tire failings. Buying new tires can be expensive – but it can also be twice as expensive, and dangerous to have an issue with them.

Before you head out on the road, be sure to check your RV's wheel lug nuts and tighten them as needed. Check the pressure of each tire to know that they are properly inflated, because a flat tire is a big concern. However, over inflation can also be an issue and hurt the control you have while driving.

Maintain Your Brakes

Please don't overlook your brakes. Being able to stop quickly and smoothly in an RV is really important for your safety, and the other people on the road. RVs are very heavy, and they take a lot to come to a complete stop. You never know when you're going to be going through areas with tight turns or quick stops, so there is no 'risking it' when it comes to brakes.

Get to know how your brakes feel. If you notice any damage or they feel off in any way, get them checked

Basic Maintenance and Routine Checks

For your safety and the longevity of your RV, you should be performing regular maintenance and checks on your vehicle. This might sound like a lot of work, especially if you're used to a home or living situation that needs little upkeep. But remember: You're not just maintaining your home or your vehicle, but *both*.

If you ignore minor issues, they will become a big deal. A minor leak and cause rot, mold, or rust. A little dirt or debris in the wrong area, left unchecked, can cause a whole system malfunction.

I'm not saying this to scare you – instead, I'm saying this so you take me seriously, and pay attention to your RV. Consider this your one-and-done basic maintenance guide. Check with your RV's manual as well, and add on what they specifically recommend to do overall.

Maintain Your Tires

Your tires keep you safe on the road. The last thing you

important to know that sometimes *we need* these connections, especially, as I mentioned above, how lacking your community can be.

Some folks work online or remotely, making RV life all the more appealing. Without this constant, reliable connection to the internet, working on the road can be difficult and frustrating.

You Can't Predict the Weather

It's nice to dream about sunny skies and beaches, but you're not always going to get great weather. Sometimes you'll get stuck in an area with storms for weeks. If you travel 12 months of the year, sometimes you may even wind up in the middle of a freak snowstorm.

There's not a lot you can do about this, so it's important to remember that these things *happen*. You need to always be watching the weather and preparing for the worst. When you're stationary in a traditional home situation, you don't have to worry so much about snowstorms, heatwaves, etc. They're a minor annoyance most of the time, but nothing more. In an RV situation, it's a *much* bigger deal.

Spotty Connections

In this day and age, staying connected can be *so important*. We carry our smartphones everywhere we go, keeping in contact with dozens of people. This might be what you're trying to break away from, going full time in your RV, and that's very admirable. However, it's

on routine and structure in your life, this can be a big adjustment.

Travel Fatigue Is Real

Travel fatigue is a very real thing that almost all full timers experience at one point or another. Physically, all the jostling and jarring of the road can leave your body feeling a bit bruised. Driving for hours can cause physical stress. Emotionally, sometimes you may feel tired of living a nomadic lifestyle, of traveling all the time, and never experiencing stability or security. Travel fatigue is not a failure – it's just a part of life on the road.

Keeping all that in mind, let me say this: It's okay if you need a break. If you need to pause, to rest in a single place for a week or even a month. This doesn't mean you're failing as a full timer, just that you need to give yourself a break. After all, it could just be physical exhaustion. So slow down a little.

If these feelings of stress or fatigue continue, however, perhaps you should take a closer look at whether this lifestyle is really right for you.

No Neighbors, No Community

Like many of the cons on this list, this is person-specific. It can be *lonely* on the road all the time, and you can often lack a true sense of community and structure. You don't really have regular neighbors, and you rarely get to truly know the people parked around you before you get up and move again.

Having this lack of community and neighborhood feel can be isolating, especially after a while. Although I will say, we have made friends on the road that we plan to meet up with from time to time. Just know that it doesn't happen every day. That's part of the 'no neighbors' lifestyle. Of course, some people see everyone as their neighbor, so that's up to your personal preference.

Unpredictability

When you live a more traditional lifestyle, you have a set routine, usually – or at least some sort of routine in your life. When you're traveling full time, however, routine and predictability go out the window. For some, this isn't a bad thing. But if you're a person that thrives

This doesn't include the fuel you need to put into your RV to move it, or any fixes you need to make to your home on wheels. These costs add up, so having a good safety net is vitally important!

Minimalism Isn't for Everyone

While a simplified, minimalist lifestyle is a real pro to many people, it can also be a big downside for others. Do we *need* all of the things we surround ourselves with on a daily basis? Not at all. However, many of us *like* these things. We like having our stuff and our possessions, and they bring us comfort. Some of us have spent years collecting memories and mementos. These treasures are important to us. Family heirlooms, important moments from our past, and so much more.

For some, giving up these things can be a very big deal. Think long and hard about if this is what you want out of life, and if you're willing to give up as much as you will need to in order to live full time in such a small space. Of course, you can always rent a storage unit to store your valuable things in, but you can't bring it with you!

longer than a weekend also lets you dig deep into that culture. You can experience things and learn things a visitor for just a few days never will be able to, and that truly is amazing.

The Cons:

It's not always sunshine and roses on the road. You might have an optimistic point of view, and there's nothing wrong with that. But it's important to weigh the good *and* the bad before you hit the open road. Knowing what you're getting into is a huge part of making an informed decision.

It's Not as Cheap as You Think

I'm not going to lie to you – living full time in an RV is often cheaper than a more traditional lifestyle, and that's a big draw for a lot of people. However, it's not as cheap as some would like to believe. Keeping your RV in good shape so that it lasts a long time takes both time *and* money. Also, campgrounds can cost anywhere from $300 a month up to $1500 or more a month.

afternoon, and be on the road by tomorrow. And if you get there and you hate it, well, you can easily pick up and move again.

A Variety of People

Do you love meeting new people? Do you enjoy getting to know a new group of people and learning about them? Well, the RV lifestyle is great for that! You never know who you are going to meet, or where they will be from. And there really is a special sort of camaraderie out in the RV community. People have been so kind to us, and we like to pay that forward to others.

You Can Explore the World

This is truly the biggest draw for most of us who are considering full-time travel. You can explore some of the most amazing parts of the country, all within the confines of what is your home. From amazing food to incredible nature, the ocean, beautiful parks... you think of it, you can visit it.

Being able to immerse yourself in an area or culture for

Minimalist Lifestyle

Many people are looking to simplify their style of living, also called a minimalist lifestyle. Shedding personal belongings can be very freeing for many people. Simplifying their lives helps them enjoy what they really value as important—like seeing the world or spending time outdoors or with family.

Flexibility

Are you dissatisfied with your 9-5? Do you hate the routine, the mundane, the everyday? We have been surprised to meet so many young people who did not wait to retire before they hit the open road. Full-time RV life can offer you the chance to have something new every day, and move when *you* feel like you are ready, not a moment before. For many, this is a huge plus.

With this flexibility is also *freedom*. Want to visit Arizona? Well, get behind the wheel. Want to spend your summers up north? You can do that – and you *don't* need months to plan or prepare, or think too much about where it is you'll end up. You can plan a new trip or route in an

The Pros:

There are a lot of upsides to traveling in your RV full time. These are just a handful, but I'm sure there will be more in your own personal situation.

All the Things You've Always Wanted to Do

The biggest positive for full-time RV living is that you have the freedom to do all the things you've always wanted to do, but never were able to. This could be visiting the US from coast to coast, revisiting all of your old friends across the country no matter where they are, learning how to fish, read all those books you've got in your TBR pile (maybe for decades!).

Perhaps you're just ready for a slower pace, the ability to just sit in nature and drink coffee every single morning. To have the freedom to enjoy life on your terms.

By living the RV lifestyle, you have gained an amount of freedom many people will never truly know or understand, let alone achieve.

The Pros & Cons of Full-Time RV Living

This section might not be for you. If you're only looking to be a weekend warrior and live a vacation lifestyle, feel free to skip this! However, if you are thinking about living the full-time RV lifestyle, either now or in the future, these are some big pros and cons to consider.

If not, feel free to jump to the next section. But if you take your first trip and think, *wow, I think I could never come home,* maybe revisit this.

often stay here months or even a whole season.

Full Hookup Site - A full hookup site, sometimes just referred to as FHU, provides you everything you need, from electricity, water, and even sewage.

Gray Water Tank - A gray water tank is where the used water is stored. All of the runoff from washing dishes to taking a shower is called gray water.

Black Water Tank - This is where your waste is held, all of the water from your toilet system.

Hula Skirt -A lot less fun than the name suggests, a hula skirt is the 'skirt' that goes around the back bumper of your motorhome. This prevents debris and other junk from being kicked up from your back tires, potentially damaging any vehicles behind you.

Slideout - Some RVs expand – their sides *slide out* – in order to accommodate more living space.

Other RV terms

Basement - This is the storage area below your motorhome that is only accessible from the outside.

Batwing - Sort of an old term, a batwing refers to the standard RV TV antenna. If you look at it just right, it looks like a pair of wings.

Chucking – This usually refers to the jarring movement that a fifth-wheel trailer hitch makes when the tow vehicle or the trailer hits uneven ground, causing fore and aft movement between the two vehicles. Some people also use the term to describe the jostling from an RV bumping along uneven ground or hitting potholes.

Dump Station - Aptly named, this is the place where you empty your black and grey tanks.

Sani-Dump - A sani-dump is *only* for depositing black tanks, or your waste. It is not for grey tanks.

Extended Stay Site - This is a campsite that you can stay for a longer period of time. Instead of a week, you can

Mooch Docking

This is when you stay at a friend or family's place, and normally park in their driveway or back yard. You're not paying them to stay there; instead, you're just there to enjoy the company. Mooch docking seems kind of a rude term, but that's all it means.

Workamping

Not a very common term, workamping refers to RVers who exchange a set amount of work for a free campsite and utilities. Sometimes workamping provides a small wage, or meals are included. This is relatively common with full-timers who are looking to reduce their expenses while they are traveling. Some even live in their RVs full time, which they love – although it's not for everyone. (See workampingjobs.com or workamper.com)

Full Timers

Speaking of full timers, these are folks who live the RV lifestyle full time. They don't have a "home" to go back to, and this isn't a vacation for them. This is just their life, living and traveling in their RV.

you just 'wing it' while you're planning on boondocking, because you never really want to risk not finding somewhere to park at.

Wally Docking

A sort of sub-set of boondocking, Wally docking is a term you might hear in conversations with other travelers. Wally docking is specifically staying in a Walmart parking lot overnight. Some Walmarts even offer RV spaces. If you're handy with a smart phone, you can use mobile apps like Allstays (or allstays.com/campgrounds) to see where you can Wally dock.

Other stores that might let you park overnight are Bass Pro Shops, Cabelas, Camping World, Costco, Cracker Barrel, Home Depot, Lowes, Kmart, or Sam's Club. Also some Pilot or Flying J Truck Stops. (Also see Bureau of Land Management on the next page.)

Tips: Always ask permission first; buy something from the store; don't literally set up camp outside your RV; do not ever dump tanks or trash on their grounds. Good etiquette helps all of us RVers in the long run!

and Canada, and they all have a fairly standard set of offerings, and options. Some people exclusively use KOA campsites to park their RV, while others just keep them as an option.

BLM

BLM (the Bureau of Land Management) manages public land in almost every state. There's a good chance you could camp on a BLM property, and many sites are free or low cost for RVs. (See blm.gov)

Boondocking

Unlike camping at a designated park, **boondocking** is when you park and camp for free. This could be in a public park, on state land, in a Walmart parking lot, to even at a beach. This is sometimes also called dry camping.

When you're boondocking, you're not paying for your spot or any perks that come with it. That means that you need to live without additional electricity and conserve your water use because it isn't easy to fill up. Rarely can

Helpful Info & Common Terms

There are some common terms that you might run into while you're reading about the RV lifestyle and looking at tools, kits, and more. This is going to help you figure out what all these terms mean, and if they apply to you at all.

Free or Low-Cost Camping

KOA

KOA stands for Kampgrounds of America, and it's the largest network of privately owned campgrounds in the entire world. There are nearly 500 locations across the US

RV veterans tell you that suffering through a few miserable trips is a rite of passage. *It doesn't have to be.*

At the end, I'll also include vital tips we've picked up over the years that lead to a more enjoyable trip overall. You are going to find a system and a process that works for you, but if you're just starting out – or you're looking to make the whole RV travel experience more enjoyable – these may be helpful to you! Keep them in mind while you're packing up, getting yourself together, and getting on the road.

get around the US, if you've got the time – and the patience to learn how to do it right.

But we also get a lot of questions from newbies. "What is that? Do I really need that? What does that do? Where did you buy it? Why didn't I think of that?" It's easy to overlook the things you need until you're out on the road, and – uh oh! You don't really know you need them until you actually need them, after all.

I've compiled this book for the people at KOAs who ask to borrow something in the middle of the night. For my friends, who call me mid-trip to brainstorm solutions because they forgot something. For the brand-new RVer who just dropped a huge chunk of their savings on the latest and greatest RV to hit the market, and they're ready for freedom.

This is for you.

These are 101+ things you need to have if you're going out in your RV. Whether it's your first trip or your 100th trip, having these tools in your arsenal will help make your trip significantly easier and more enjoyable. Don't let having a traditional brick and motor home to live on the road in an HOW (Houses on Wheels).

Some are retired couples who want to focus on traveling and exploring instead of lawn care or household maintenance. Others are 20-somethings who want to break out of traditional roles and find meaning through travel and exploration. It could even be a new family looking for financial freedom to raise their children.

Not everyone, after all, likes the static life of living in the same place. The freedom of the road is very appealing. Just think, nothing to tie you down, go where you want, when you want. It's quite a draw for some of us.

Whatever your reasons for getting into RVing, I'm here to help. It might seem as simple as buying your first set of wheels, packing a bag, and hitting the open road, but I must tell you: It's more complicated than that.

We've been RVing for *years*. Since we've started, there have been a lot of upgrades, benefits, and changes to the RV world. I've also convinced quite a few friends and family members that traveling in an RV is the best way to

RVs Are Big Business

Did you know that over 9 million households in the US own their very own RV? That's up from 7.9 million in 2005, and the number continues to grow each year. That works out to 11% of all households, and approximately 40 million Americans regularly going RVing. In fact, over 25 million go each year.

Some people even **live** in their RV. Called "full-timers" or "modern nomads," over 1 million Americans exchanged

came with it. On our first couple trips, we were so woefully unprepared that we almost gave up entirely.

Fred is great with numbers, and he wrote a book last year: *Full-Time RV Life for Seniors on a Budget.* People loved it! And that got me to thinking about all of the things we have discovered to make our travels easier and more comfortable. So he encouraged me to write my own book for RVers, and here it is! (I hope I didn't leave out anything important. There are actually over 150 items and accessories mentioned, if you want to know!)

Learn from our mistakes, successes, and experience, so you can have the best time out there possible. And remember: ***Always take the scenic route!***

–Jolene

We liked the flexibility and freedom of camping, but as the years went on, we got tired of tents and air mattresses. We'd wake up feeling battered and bruised. They just weren't working for us any more.

Thankfully, in our late 50s, we met some friends who had an RV. I always thought RVs were big and bulky, hard to drive, and impossible to turn. Turns out, I was right – but what I didn't know was that they were also fun. We could go anywhere in one and have the creature comforts we really required. I was too tired, too old, and deeply uninterested in the idea of backpacking to see the world. But driving my home around? I could get into that.

We soon realized that there was a *lot* to learn. We picked up tips and tricks from new friends we met at KOA campgrounds. Lately, it seems that more and more people are hitting the road to travel, so we thought maybe we could share our hard-earned wisdom with the next generation of RVers!

We made a lot of mistakes starting out. We didn't keep up with maintenance correctly, we didn't understand all that being an RV owner entailed, or the expenses that

What Got Us Into RVing?

My husband Fred and I have been long-time travel enthusiasts. We had a so-called "bucket list" before we ever knew what that was! For many years, we spent our vacations cooped up in hotels or condos, visiting family in their homes, or even going to a few far-flung exotic travel destinations. Yet we usually came home exhausted, not really feeling like we had truly relaxed – or even had time to stop and smell the roses, or enjoy our destination.

The Best Tips We've Picked Up Along the Way...................102

Enjoy Your Trip!...114

Contents

What Got Us Into RVing? 6

RVs Are Big Business 9

Helpful Info & Common Terms 13

    Free or Low-Cost Camping 13

    Boondocking 14

    Wally Docking...15

    Mooch Docking 16

    Other RV terms 17

The Pros & Cons of Full-Time RV Living 19

    The Pros: 20

    The Cons:...23

Basic Maintenance and Routine Checks 29

Practical Things Everyone Should Have 37

    Emergency Supplies 41

Things for the KOA..61

For Your Kitchen 74

For the Bathroom 88

Comfort Items 92

Perfect-10 Checklist: Setting Up Camp 98

4

For my husband Fred, who shares my travel lust and need to wander. There's no one else I'd rather be with on this adventure called life!

Copyright © Autumn Leaf Publishing Press, 2021

Email: Publisher@AutumnLeafPub@gmail.com

All Rights Reserved.

Without limiting the rights under the copyright laws, no part of this publication may be reproduced, stored in or introduced into a retrieval system, or transmitted, in any form or by any means (electronic, mechanical, photocopying, recording or otherwise), without the prior written consent of the publisher of this book.

Autumn Leaf Publishing Press publishes its books and guides in a variety of electronic and print formats, Some content that appears in print may not be available in electronic format, and vice versa.

Design & Illustration by Jordy Roberts

First Edition

101+ Must-Have RV Accessories You NEED for the Road

Your Guide to Comfort & Adventure, from X-Chocks, Cable TV, to Gray Water

For Newbies, Full-Timers, Occasional Campers & Boondockers

By

Jolene Donovan